THE WAR CHAPTERS SERIES™

D1684626

BOOK 2 PART 2

TEANCUM

THE GHOST SOLDIER™

AUTHOR:
JASON MOW

ILLUSTRATOR:
GABE BONILLA

ETHOS™ PRODUCTIONS

Teancum: The Ghost Soldier Part 2
Author: Jason Mow
Illustrator: Gabe Bonilla
Graphic Design: Nicole Bonilla

© 2018 Ethos Productions LLC. All rights reserved.
The Moroni sword icon, The War Chapters Series, Teancum: The Ghost Soldier, and Ethos Productions logos are trademarks of Ethos Productions LLC.
Published by: Ethos Productions LLC

No part of this publication, including all the artwork, may be reproduced, or stored in a retrieval system, or transmitted in any form or by any means, electronic, mechanical, photocopying, recording, or otherwise, without written permission of the publisher.

For information regarding permission, please email info@ethospro.com.

ISBN 978-0-9905953-2-8
First English Edition, June, 2018
Printed in the USA

DEDICATION

This book is dedicated to the brave men and women who took a vow and stand watch against evil. Remember my brothers and sisters, the Sheep Dog answers to the Good Shepherd, not the flock.

Contents

DEDICATION 3

PREFACE 7

ACKNOWLEDGEMENTS 11

CHAPTER ONE
Home 13

CHAPTER TWO
Waking Up the Predator 31

CHAPTER THREE
A Captain of Men 49

CHAPTER FOUR
Teancum Meets Moroni 63

CHAPTER FIVE
Morianton Goes Too Far 95

CHAPTER SIX
A Warrant for His Arrest 129

CHAPTER SEVEN
The Kill, Capture & Rescue 141

CHAPTER EIGHT
Pachus Makes a Deal 161

CHAPTER NINE
Assault From the Sea 185

CHAPTER TEN
The King is Dead 215

CHAPTER ELEVEN
The Last Great War Council 237

CHAPTER TWELVE
The Predator Finds His Prey 257

CHAPTER THIRTEEN
The Hunter is Now Hunted 301

CHAPTER FOURTEEN
No Greater Friend to Liberty 315

CHAPTER FIFTEEN
The Last Full Measure 331

AUTHOR: JASON MOW 379

ILLUSTRATOR: GABE BONILLA 381

PREFACE

The War Chapters Series of books are based on characters appearing in the Book of Mormon—a volume of scripture of The Church of Jesus Christ of Latter-day Saints. In our book, as in the Book of Mormon, the characters frequently affirm their faith and commitment to the Savior, Jesus Christ. We believe the messages of faith, honor, courage and sacrifice in these stories are universal and should appeal to everyone, regardless of religious belief.

While we hope this book contains insights that will help the reader in their effort to better understand the great messages contained in the Book of Mormon, this book is a work of fiction by its author. It is not produced, endorsed or aided by The Church of Jesus Christ of Latter-day Saints, or its leadership, in any way. While the author is a faithful member of the church, this book should not be used in the place of true scripture study, prayer and reflection. These books are meant to serve as catalysts to inspire readers in their efforts to further study the war chapters in the Book of Mormon.

There are plenty of theories as to where the Book of Mormon lands were located. There is not, as of yet, a definitive location acceptable to the majority of historians. We are not endorsing any of these theories. While we are using the actual place names from the Book of Mormon, there are also some fictional places the author has created for the benefit of the story. Any geographical similarity to existing locations is purely coincidental.

The label "War Chapters" is often used to describe the long period of war, civil war and social upheaval that is described in the book of Alma, chapters 43-62, in the Book of Mormon.

ACKNOWLEDGEMENTS

The journey I took while writing book two of the War Chapters series was such an amazing adventure. There were so many people who came into my life along the way. You all inspired and pushed me to tell this story. I know I can not possibly acknowledge everyone who had a hand in this process, but there are a few I would like to give my thanks to.

To Nikki, my beautiful bride. When you found me I was a shell of a man. You gave me the inspiration to heal and push myself towards greatness. I want nothing more than to be the man you deserve. To your children and extended family, I say thank you for making me and my family feel welcome among you.

To Gabe and Nicole Bonilla; thank you for not rolling your eyes in front of me when I would come up with some of my crazy ideas or say, "I am still working on the book." You and the support staff at Ethos Productions are the true heroes of this story. Gabe, your artwork can say more in one page then I can in a hundred pages of written words. Nicole, you are the creative engine that runs this whole operation. Thank you all.

To my editing staff, Amy Faulkinbury, Danielle Bonilla, Sandra Bonilla, Katey Bersch, and Jenna Roundy…You would think that after writing my first book I would have learned to spell, punctuate and form a complete sentence… Your patience with me is the stuff of legends. I am so grateful for your time and talents. This would have been monumentally more difficult without your help.

To Nick and Rachael, my Prince and Princess. You two are my heroes. Daddy loves you both more than you will ever know.

To all of my friends who stood by me during the most difficult time in my life I have ever experienced— I cannot express enough my love and gratitude to you all. I will not forget your loyalty. Mine is a debt of honor.

To my fans, thank you for your continued excitement and enthusiasm for the stories in the War Chapters!

Honor, Courage, Strength, Discipline.

For Liberty!

–Jason

"The two most important days of your life are the day you are born and the day you figure out why...."

– Mark Twain

CHAPTER ONE

Home

It was almost two years to the day, from when his family was slaughtered and his ranch destroyed, that Teancum emerged from the remote woodlands where he had chased those evil men who had taken his little child. He slowly walked from the safety and shadows of the large trees and into the open space and sunlight. Stopping about fifty yards from the trees, he looked back into the darkness of the woodline and the protection it gave him. Out here in the open, he was a target. But in the thickness of the mountain forest he could move with impunity.

Gingerly, he started toward the burned-out shells of his once grand ranch house and barns. He moved with a slight limp as he walked through the unkempt grass and underbrush, helping himself along with the aid of a stout spear he had gathered from one of his victims during the countless engagements and ambushes of his one-man war. His clothing was tattered, stained and clearly showed the signs of the almost constant battle he had waged against the Nehor bandits and their Lamanite cohorts. His thick beard was matted, his face and hands dirty and his long uncut hair was pulled back into a loosely-held ponytail. The scars of combat covered his body, and all his meager possessions were tucked into a large pack resting on his back. During his time fighting the Nehors, Teancum had learned, among many other things, to master the art of field craft and survival. Through trial and error, he had developed the ability to slip unseen in and out of Nehor strongholds and Lamanite camps, taking what he needed to survive and killing bandits and raiders at will. Now it was time for Teancum

CHAPTER ONE

to face his greatest opponent— the demons of his past. It was time for him to reconcile his loss and try to salvage what was left of his life.

As he moved closer and closer to what used to be his well-manicured property, the memories of that fateful day came rushing back. Teancum started to relive every painful, emotional moment as if it had just happened. Climbing over a dilapidated fence, he slowly reached the spot where he had last seen his wife and children lying on the grass and dying before his eyes. He stood frozen in place, hearing the sounds of the past, his children, laughing and dancing around him. Happy memories from an almost-forgotten time. He glanced at the corral where he taught Kaila how to ride her first pony, and across the large yard where he would push Hanni in the big wooden swing under the grand shade tree. All the pain of those memories came back, cushing his body and soul as Teancum stood powerless to stop the tide.

"You there!" A man's voice called out from somewhere off to Teancum's side, but Teancum did not react. As the onslaught of feelings continued to roll over him, Teancum could not discern between memory and reality. For him, the unseen man's voice was just another echo from the past.

"You, brigand! Off with you!" The male voice was more clear now. It was a labored voice, cracked and heavy with age. Teancum blinked and took a quick, startled, breath as he tried to focus on the here and now. "Are you deaf, boy? I said be off! There is nothing here for you." When Teancum realized the voice he was hearing was from the present and not part of his tragic memories, he turned to face the direction from which it was coming. "Your kind has picked the bones of this great house clean ten times over, now leave this land."

It was Tum speaking. He was holding a pitch fork in his hand, and there was a small Lamanite boy with a hatchet standing behind him. Time had not been kind to Tum. He had aged rapidly, and his clothing was a home-spun shirt and stained britches. Clearly, dealing with the aftermath of the tragedy and living among the ruins of the house of Pilio had not been easy. His cheeks were sunken from hard labor and little food, and he had grown a small beard, but Teancum would recognize him anywhere. He was as much a father figure to Teancum as was his grandfather, Lord Pilio. The small boy was scared but standing firm behind Tum, waiting for his instructions. Teancum knew that to avoid conflict, he needed to move slowly and without aggression. In Tum's eyes, he was a trespasser and no better than the bandits who killed his master

and family.

"I mean you no harm." Teancum raised his hands in a symbolic gesture of surrender. "I am going to drop my pack and put my weapons down, okay?" Teancum tried to make eye contact with Tum who was fidgeting and moving back and forth, all the while keeping a good distance from the stranger before him. Teancum could see there was a glimmer of recognition in Tum's mind as he spoke, but he was still being cautious. He was not sure what condition Tum's mind was in and Teancum did not want to hurt his only living friend. "The beard, the grime and torn clothing; my own mother would not recognize me like this." Teancum lowered his spear with one hand while keeping his free hand up for Tum to see. Tum shook the farm tool as a warning for Teancum not to try anything funny. "But there is something familiar about my voice, is that not right old man? You know me." Teancum stood back up and loosened the shoulder straps of his heavy pack.

"The master of this land, his name was Pilio and he died defending his wife and family, right over there." Teancum spoke as he pointed to the charred remains of the great house. Tum loosened his shoulders and blinked several times. "My wife Hanni, and my two older daughters laid here." Teancum pointed to a patch of green grass just behind him. Tum stood up straight and lowered the farm tool. "The last time you saw me, I was heading into the mountains over there, to find my baby girl and avenge what had happened here so long ago." Teancum pointed to the spot in the distance where the thick underbrush and trees met the open meadow.

"Master Teancum?" Tum almost sounded like he was pleading to the stranger. "Is that you?"

"Tum, my dear friend and mentor, I have come home."

"It can't be… It can't be true. We thought you were dead!" Tum carefully moved forward to let his old and tired eyes get a better look at the bearded and tattered man. "Run and fetch your mother," Tum waved his hand behind his body and the small Lamanite boy ran for the other side of the barn.

Teancum moved his hands to unbuckle his weapons belt and Tum jerked the pitch fork back up into the ready position and crouched down, ready to fight. Teancum could see he had startled Tum and he made his next few movements very carefully. "I am just lowering my weapons." Teancum showed Tum his hands and moved slowly as he loosened his

Home

belt and let the weight of the heavy steel and handmade weapons pull his belt to the ground.

"My apologies," Tum hesitantly responded, as he lowered the farm tool and stood up. "These have been difficult times and I reacted out of instinct."

"No need to apologize, my friend," Teancum said quietly. "They have been difficult times for us all."

"The child...?" Tum inquired with reservation. He looked around and could see Carra was not with Teancum. He'd held on to hope for so long, and now Teancum was back, but alone. Was she still alive, too? He could barely whisper it. "Does she yet live?" Tum loved Teancum and his family as if they were his own children. Only Teancum himself bore a heavier sorrow for their murders.

Teancum had been so consumed with revenge and fighting against the Nehors he had pushed the memories of little Carra and the rest of his family to the back of his mind for quite some time. But coming back here, reliving the emotions of it all, and now being quizzed about the welfare of his youngest child was too much for him. He began to weep. Teancum could see the sadness on Tum's face and it only made things worse for him. Tum, with tears in his own eyes, moved toward his young master, taking him by the arm. "It is okay, Master Teancum. They are all together and with God."

It was not so much the words causing the cascading flow of emotions, but the touch of Tum's hand on his bare arm which brought Teancum to his knees. For the first time in more months than he could remember, he was being touched by someone who cared for him. Teancum could feel the love and positive energy transfer from Tum's hand into his arm and across his body. He had been alone for so long and had relied on his own strength for survival. The feeling of warmth from a friend's hand made him too weak to stand and Teancum collapsed. Tum grunted as he tried to hold Teancum up but relinquished his grasp as Teancum fell to his knees and then rolled onto his side in the grass. Sobbing great tears, Teancum wailed as only a wounded father could. It was his final purge of emotions and he held nothing back.

Startled, Tum took two steps back. His young companion had returned with a Lamanite woman and two more male children, both older than the boy. They all looked at Tum for understanding as to why a grown man was crying while lying in the grass. Tum waved them to move back and

CHAPTER ONE

he took three paces to be by the woman's side.

"This is Master Teancum, the one I have told you about. He has returned home." The woman needed no more explanation. She knew what had happened here on the ranch, so long ago. She knew of the slayings and the kidnapping. She knew, as only a mother could perceive, what Teancum needed most— a simple act of compassion. Calling out to her three boys in their native language to follow her, she moved over to Teancum and knelt down. She gently stroked his head while speaking softly in his ear. Teancum calmed a little and she nodded to her boys to help her pick up Teancum. They struggled to get him to his feet and with all of them bracing against him, they walked him back to their sleeping hut, carefully laying him down on one of the boy's beds. Tum covered Teancum with a light blanket, and before he could take three full breaths, Teancum was fast asleep.

"Let him sleep." the kind woman spoke to Tum. She had raised three boys and cared for Tum. She knew exactly what the man needed in this moment. "We must get supper ready. When he awakes, he will be very hungry."

It was supper time when Teancum awoke and he ate as if he had a hole in his stomach. It quickly became a joke among the rest of those gathered around the family table that night as they watched him shovel food into his mouth and consume nearly everything in sight.

When the ranch was attacked, the bandits had taken most of the valuables and killed the owners. Those who had lived and worked on the ranch were left with nothing. Some had moved on, taking what items and property were left to help finance their new life. Others had just walked away, never to be seen or heard from again. Tum and a handful of families stayed and tried to rebuild from the remnants. Over the past two years, most of the livestock had been stolen and the gardens plundered by returning bandits. But then, unexpectedly, the raiding stopped and the ranch had started to prosper. It was as if the criminals had all disappeared. Unbeknownst to them, the man sitting at the table eating like a hungry lion had killed the raiders or run them off the land for good.

Teancum had been raised to be a proper gentleman at the dinner table but, under the circumstances, he had forgone any decorum and was pushing large portions of food into his mouth. The kids and other adults, sitting around the table, laughed as they watched him chewing loudly and gulping the sweet liquid of Tum's homemade fruit juice. Tum was growing ever more concerned with Teancum's behavior. He was trained as a butler; it was his job to ensure his master's home was run properly, including table manners. When the survivors of the bandit raid gathered together, to form a new family, the adults elected Tum to be their leader. He had tried the best he could to teach everyone, including little ones under his care, to be proper ladies and gentlemen. This was an uphill battle, given the situation in which they found themselves. They were left with almost nothing, and simply existing was a daily challenge. Sitting up straight at the table and chewing your food were the last things on the list of daily priorities, but still he tried to raise them right. The other children, sitting around the table, were starting to have fun at Teancum's expense. Tum had finally had enough of this.

Calling out to Teancum, Tum tried to get his attention. When Teancum looked up from his bowl, he had bits and scraps of food hanging from his beard. This sent the others in the room into a fit of laughter. Tum's face turned bright red. Teancum was clueless as to why the others were laughing. He started to look around, and the shadows from the lit candles only accentuated the mess on his face. Not realizing he was the focus of the laughter, Teancum gave Tum a puzzled look. Tum cleared his throat and casually wiped his face with his napkin. He then gave Teancum a stern look, signaling to him, with his facial gestures, for him to do the same. Teancum had been in Tum's presence long enough to instantly know the meaning of Tum's gesture. Teancum sat up and put down his large metal spoon. Grabbing his cloth napkin from the table, he wiped his own face and took extra care to ensure the food was out of his beard. When he was done, he looked back at Tum, who gave him an approving wink and nod.

"I guess this is next," Teancum sheepishly spoke as he tugged at the tip of his beard.

Tum smiled, "And may I also recommend a bath?"

Teancum looked at the small child sitting to his right with a question on his face. "Is it that bad?" The child smiled back and nodded vigorously while pinching her nose. He sniffed his underarms and the dirty shirt he still wore. "Sorry," he quietly mouthed back to her. There was more laughter and the night continued on. After Teancum stuffed himself with fresh bread, thick Lamanite stew and Tum's fruit juice, exhaustion overcame him once again. He barely made it back to his bed before he was again fast asleep.

CHAPTER ONE

A large fire was roaring beneath two big kettles full of water as Teancum stepped out from the humble thatch-roofed nut and into the fresh morning air, his shirtless torso exposing the scars and wounds of his two-year long fight against the Nehors. Now, rested, fed and facing a new day, Teancum greeted the morning sun with squinting eyes and a sore body. Teancum had lost more than twenty pounds while he was in the wilds. His tall frame now carried an impressive display of taut muscle. Physically, he was definitely not the same pampered and soft Nephite statesman who haphazardly took off after the bandits those many months ago.

"Good morning, Master Teancum," Tum called out, from the opposite side of a watering trough set up near the large fire. Tum was pouring a bucket of water into the trough then handing the empty bucket to a tall boy, who held a second bucket, still full of liquid. "Your bath is almost ready."

Teancum stretched his arms over his head and yawned. Twisting to his left and right, then reaching down to his toes, Teancum heard and felt the bones in his body crackle and pop. Standing up straight, his stomach grumbled and complained for food. Rubbing his muscular belly, he smiled back at Tum. "Yeah…" he said with a big breath, "we should get this over with."

The hot water in the kettles was added to the trough and Teancum stepped carefully into the makeshift bathtub. The temperature was a bit warm, but considering it was his first real bath since he left this property, Teancum was not complaining. Sliding down into the water, he let his body relax. The heat and steam from the water instantly started to loosen his stiff joints and sore muscles.

"I almost forgot how good a hot bath feels," Teancum whispered, as he let his body sink down into the trough until only his face remained above the water line.

"Don't get too comfortable, Master Teancum," Tum responded, in the tone of a seasoned butler. "We still have some grooming to do." Tum clapped his hands and the same Lamanite woman appeared, from around the corner of the thatched cottage. She was followed by two of her sons who were carrying soaps, towels and an assortment of small cutting tools and sharp blades.

The first thing to go was Teancum's long hair. The majority of it was unceremoniously hacked off with the swipe of the woman's large trimming scissors, then tossed into the fire. Teancum sat in the tub, submitting to his fate.

Next came the more precise trimming. There was dirt, dried blood and old scabs from head wounds, matted in and around his hair, so the woman used a smaller set of shears, bringing Teancum's hair to almost a stubble. She struggled as she cut, while muttering in her native language, then cleaned Teancum's scalp. Teancum knew enough of the Lamanite language to know she was not happy with the condition he was in. Teancum looked up at Tum as he tried not to struggle against the pulling and scraping, silently asking with his eyes if this was necessary. Tum smiled and nodded back in approval.

When the Lamanite woman was finally finished with Teancum's hair, she pushed his head under the water to rinse the remnants away. He was caught off guard and came out of the water choking and spitting. It was a long-forgotten sensation for Teancum to not have wet, sloppy hair in his eyes and covering his face. He blinked in confusion as he surfaced and instinctively wiped his face. After a moment, he rubbed his stubbly hair, turned and smiled at the Lamanite. She smiled back while holding up the large shears, again.

"The beard," she said, in a thick accent.

"Yeah, the beard," Teancum smiled back, shaking his head. He was not looking forward to more of the rough treatment he already received from the haircut. The lady could see he was slightly distressed, causing her to grin.

The beard came off much easier than the long, dirty hair. Before long, Teancum was admiring his reflection in a small mirror made of polished metal. "Welcome back, Master Teancum," Tum commented as he looked down at the fresh face of the young lord of the land.

"It's good to be back," Teancum responded. He took a few more seconds to inspect the woman's handiwork, then put the mirror down. "I am ready to get out and get dressed. Do you have anything that might fit me?" He asked, looking up at Tum.

"Yes, I think I have just the thing." Tum gestured to one of the boys to come to him. He spoke to him in a low tone, and the boy ran to the other side of the barn, returning in short order with clothing under his arm. "These are the remains of one of the farmhands' belongings. He left them behind when he went away a few months ago. They might be a bit large on you, but they will do for now," Tum spoke as he set the clothing as well as a pair of old, but sturdy leather sandals on a chair next to Teancum. Tum handed Teancum a large towel and continued, "When you are ready, we can meet in the barn to discuss the business of this ranch." Tum turned and walked away, leaving Teancum alone in the trough.

" The business of the ranch." Teancum ran those words over and over again in his mind. *Do I even have any business being here?* He questioned his own feelings and emotions. A part of him wanted to climb out of the tub and go back into the woods to hunt criminals again. It was his new reality. He could hide from the world and his own demons out in the thick underbrush. Another side of him wanted to stay put and try to rebuild his heritage. *This is my land… I can make this work*, he reassured himself, as he looked around at the broken and overgrown ranch. Still another part of him wanted to return to Zarahemla and rekindle his life as an important member of the ruling body. *You are still Doctor Teancum, common judge and counsel to the presiding Chief Judge of the land.* What was most apparent was the fact he could not stay in the murky water any longer. It had grown cold and cloudy with the soap residue and layers of dirt which had been washed off. Grabbing the towel, Teancum stood up and wrapped his body in order to dry off. He carefully slipped on the sandals and took the pile of borrowed clothing. Teancum headed to the cottage to put on his new outfit. He moved slowly with his head down.

The clothing was almost a true fit. Tum was right, they were a bit large on Teancum, but they were clean, sturdy and well made, so they would do. Walking in through the open barn door, Teancum could see Tum had salvaged the structure and turned the barn into a large, open work room and storage house. There was a working blacksmith area in the back, and a pottery wheel with a kiln. Food storage was stacked along the walls, and the smaller stalls had goats and chickens wandering around in them. Everyone inside the big barn looked busy with daily tasks and chores. Tum was inspecting the quality of some seeds which had been stored for the winter when he saw Teancum wandering around the front of the barn.

"Master Teancum, over here," Tum waved and gestured for Teancum to join him over by the stacks of bailed hay. "None the worse for wear," he softly spoke as he surveyed the articles of clothing he had provided to Teancum. "I almost did not recognize you." Tum smiled as Teancum stood still for the sharp-eyed inspection by his old friend. The physical and emotional damage the past two years had taken on Teancum, were even more conspicuous on his sunken and hollow, now clean-shaven face. "Some good, clean country living will put some weight back on you," Tum looked into his young master's eyes and smiled. Teancum could see Tum was hiding a level of sadness deep inside his soul. The only living member of this once great house had been reduced to no more than a battered and nervous scarecrow in someone else's clothing. He was overjoyed at Teancum's return, but he still held the pain of the loss of the rest of the family very close to his heart. "We have work to do, my lord." Tum wanted to quickly address the business of the day, it was his way of hiding the pain.

" Thank you, for the clothing and the bath," Teancum said. "I am not sure what help I could be right now. Everything is still very surreal for me." Teancum took a deep, sorrow-filled breath as he looked around at the remains of the large barn and his once-prosperous horse ranch.

"Well, my lord, I guess we could start with showing you what is working and what remains." Teancum thought for a second then nodded his head in agreement. Tum held out his hand to show Teancum which direction to walk and allowed him to go first.

They moved over to the blacksmith's work area. Tum spent some time describing the ingenious way the smith had set up the forge and billows. "With this new style of billows, the craftsman can do twice the work with half the fuel needed to heat the ore." Tum finished with a smile on his face as he offered his final assessment. He and the smith looked at Teancum who appeared lost in his own thoughts. His eyes were glazed over and he appeared oblivious to what Tum had been saying.

"My lord?" Tum tried to regain Teancum's attention. The smith was offended by the lack of regard given by Teancum to his invention. Returning to his duties, he began to clank away on a piece of forged metal with his hammer.

"What? Oh yes, I agree, well done... Please continue," Teancum responded, when he realized he had lost focus and let his mind wander. The enclosed space of the blacksmith shop, along with the movement around him was starting to affect Teancum. He became anxious as it had been a long time since he had even been indoors. Now he was surrounded by walls with an old, creaking roof with holes for the light to shine through. Teancum felt a flash of panic well up inside him. It reminded him of the feelings he would experience before a possible ambush, around

CHAPTER ONE

the corner of some dark jungle trail. Beads of sweat started to form on his brow and his hands were trembling. He needed to go outside, he needed to feel safe.

They continued speaking and Teancum tried to interrupt Tum. "Perhaps…" Teancum tried to speak but the words got caught so he cleared his throat instead.

"Perhaps, what? You had something you wish to say, Lord Teancum?" Tum questioned as he continued his walking tour of the barn.

Tum could see Teancum was not ready for the grand tour and quickly devised an alternative. "Perhaps a walking tour of the grounds instead? Some fresh air might be just what the doctor ordered for the both of us."

"Yes, it would be nice to be outside." Teancum was relieved as they made their way out the main doors of the barn.

The two men stood in the open air outside the barn for some time not talking or moving. The other members of the small community Tum had established, moved around them as they continued their daily tasks. Teancum still appeared nervous but it was clear he felt better in the sun light. "Shall we start with the stables and inspect the few remaining horses?" Tum asked. There was a pause as he waited for Teancum to respond. When Teancum did not answer, Tum knew he had to do something. "Teancum?" Tum spoke just above a whisper. "Son, if this is too much for you right now, we can stop and continue another day." He put his arm on Teancum's shoulder. There was visible pain in Teancum's eyes. "What you have been through," Tum shook his head, "The physical trauma alone would have killed most men." There was sincerity in his voice as the old gentleman tried to connect with his young master. "We can take this as slow as you need. There is no rush when it comes to healing the soul. A wise young doctor once told me that." Tum made eye contact with Teancum and winked at Teancum's tear-filled eyes. Teancum broke a half smile in return. "Coming back from the dead is not an easy thing to do, but you are not alone anymore." Tum waited a moment for those words to settle into Teancum's mind. "Come." He pulled ever so slightly at Teancum's shoulder. "Let's go inspect the horses, you always had such a good eye for quality. I could really use your opinion on the small herd."

"Maybe I could eat one of those red apples along the way?" Teancum asked in an innocent voice.

"My lord, everything on this ranch belongs to you. You can eat as many apples as you wish," Tum jokingly reacted, then took the three steps needed to reach the large barrel of freshly harvested apples ready for storage. Pulling two large apples from the top, Tum tossed one to Teancum and then bit down hard on his own. Smiling at Teancum, he chewed the fresh fruit with his mouth open in a rare moment of levity.

Seeing his old mentor eating the apple like a hungry mule, Teancum could not help but chuckle. Taking a massive bite of his own apple, Teancum joined Tum in the frivolous apple eating contest.

Slowly making their way along the road leading to what remained of the stables, Teancum and Tum casually spoke about the condition of the ranch and the people who now called this place their home. There was a true mixed bag of residents. Several different Nephite clans were represented as well as a few peaceful Lamanite families who had come, seeking a new life and a place where they could be safe and practice their new Christian religion. Tum knew Teancum had been fighting the Nehor bandits and Lamanite raiders in the mountains and wilds of the wilderness. " Those Lamanites here with us, are truly a peaceful group." Tum was afraid Teancum would not react well when he saw how many of the Lamanite people were living on his land.

Teancum could read Tum's thoughts. "Most of the criminals I killed were Nephite men, my own blood and kin." Teancum turned to look at Tum as they walked. "I don't hold an entire culture accountable for the actions of a few." He looked back down the road and continued, " The Lamanite families are welcome to live here and help restore this ranch to its former greatness, as long as they do so in peace and are respectful of others."

" They are true converts to the gospel of Christ, my lord." Tum reassured Teancum. "A better group of people as a whole, I have not seen, in some time."

"Good." Teancum spoke as they reached the first set of corrals. "Now, tell me about these ponies?"

Days folded into weeks and slowly Teancum began to heal in both mind and body. With access to plenty of food and rest, he started to put on weight. The women of the collective community took turns caring for the wounds covering his body. He was treated with ointments, aloes and fresh bandages daily, as well as warm water baths to help heal and clean the infections away. After a few weeks, Teancum even started to exercise. He would run around the perimeter of the ranch, chop wood and wrestle

CHAPTER ONE

with the younger men and strong boys. Slowly, the man who was once known as the young lord of the ranch started to re-emerge. With time, along with the love and security of this new family surrounding him, Teancum was healing. Tum could see this and was overjoyed at the prospect of Teancum finding love and starting another family to continue the legacy of the house of Pilio. Tum was not surprised when Teancum walked into the barn during the middle of an inventory count and asked,

"Where did you bury them?"

"My lord?" Tum responded. He was not quite sure he understood Teancum's question.

"Hanni, my children, Lord and Lady Pilio— where are they buried?"

Tum's heart sank as he took one step back and looked right at Teancum. He could see Teancum had a small leather pouch in his hand and a hard look on his face. Tum had been dreading this moment. Teancum was making such good progress with the physical healing. Tum was hoping this question, and the answer, would not cause his mental healing to waiver. Putting down his parchment paper and ink quill, Tum gestured for Teancum to walk with him, outside the barn. "Please, my lord, follow me." The others with Tum were all concerned, but remained at their tasks as the two men walked outside.

"I have a promise to keep— the last promise I made to Hanni." Teancum held out the leather bag containing the lock of hair he took from Carra's body on the cliff so long ago. "I was going through my pack and found it at the bottom of the bag." He was almost disgusted with himself as he snorted and shook his head. "I forgot it was there."

"May I ask what it is?" Tum inquired.

"It is a lock of Carra's hair. I kept it with a promise I would bury it where her mother and sisters are resting so they can all be together."

Tum's eyes began tearing up as he reached out and touched the bottom of the bag. " That dear sweet child. She was the light of this ranch, everyone loved her so." Tum sniffed and stood up straight. "I will escort you to the grave site, my lord. May I assist you in helping Carra be with her mother and sisters, once again?"

"Of course." Teancum was grateful for Tum's friendship and he really did not want to do this alone.

Tum turned to a stable boy standing not far off, "Set up the wagon and put two shovels in the bed, then tell your mother Lord Teancum and I will be late for supper, and we will dine alone by the main house."

Home

"Yes, sir." The boy was off like an arrow, and in no time the farm wagon was brought around to the front of the barn.

"Is it far?" Teancum asked, as he climbed into the teamster's seat.

"No, just a short ride down by the river," Tum responded as he looked back to ensure there were shovels ready. Satisfied, Tum slapped down on the reins and the two horses moved off, pulling the large wooden wagon with them.

The route took them out the main gate, toward the large, slow moving river not far from the ranch. This route was well traveled and easy to follow. It was the same one the people from the ranch would take to go refill the large water barrels used for most of their daily water needs.

"Over there, on that rise." Tum pointed off to the distance. "Under that great oak tree. Your mother loved to go there and reflect. Do you remember the spot? Your father, Lieutenant Kail is also there."

Teancum thought for a moment, then the memories came rushing back to him. He smiled and nodded as he remembered the times he would join his mother as she would sit under the expansive tree, looking out over the flowing river and the mountains beyond. "She would talk to my father up there."

"It's a favorite spot, as well as being off the beaten trail. I thought it would be appropriate to lay them to rest up there," Tum continued as he directed the horses to pull the wagon up a slight incline and next to the oak tree. "The markers are on the other side, where they can all enjoy the evening air and shade."

Teancum hesitated for a moment before he jumped down from the wagon seat. "You don't have to do this today, we can come back," Tum said, reassuring Teancum he was not alone and there was no hurry.

"No, I have put this off far too long." He started to slowly walk toward the grave markers, all in a neat row, like soldiers standing guard. "Father," Teancum nodded toward the marker bearing the name Kail. He then moved to the next set of markers and read the inscription chiseled into the stone. "Lord and Lady Pilio… Hanni." The tears of pain and anguish formed in his eyes. His children were next, all except one. He squeezed the little leather bag containing Carra's hair tight in his hand. "I found her and brought her home. Just like you asked, my queen." Teancum spoke to his wife's marker.

His knees suddenly buckled and Teancum dropped to the grass, sobbing great tears. Tum let him be. He could see the poison and hate

CHAPTER ONE

Teancum had been holding onto begin to flow out of his young master with every gulp of air and every tear falling to the earth.

It was not long before Teancum regained his composure and stood up. Reaching out behind him, he silently requested a shovel and Tum handed it to him. "I need to do this myself," Teancum spoke without looking back at Tum.

"As you wish."

Gently, Teancum pulled several large shovelfuls of dirt and grass from the area where Hanni was buried. He dug down about three feet and stopped. *That's far enough*, he thought. *Don't want to disturb her body.* Stepping to one side of the freshly dug hole, Teancum knelt down and gently placed the bag of Carra's hair into the hole. "Rest in peace, my little child," he whispered. Then he closed his eyes and did something he had not done in a very long time. "My Father in Heaven," he started slowly, at first, unsure of his words. "I ask you to watch over and take care of the souls of my family. I don't understand why you took them all from me. I was told to trust you, and believe that all will be made right." He took a deep breath and could sense Tum moving closer to him. "The best I can do right now is to want to believe. Please be patient with me. Please forgive me for finding joy in killing all those evil men." He paused again, searching for the right words to use. It had been a very long time since he had prayed out loud, or even prayed at all. "Tell my family I love and miss them and ask them to forgive me for failing to protect them." He turned to look back at Tum who had gently moved in behind him. "I don't remember how to end a prayer."

"Close it in Christ's name and then say, 'amen'."

Teancum nodded in remembrance and turned back around. He was unsure but cautiously continued "I say this prayer in Christ's name… Amen."

"Well done, Master Teancum." Tum was beaming from ear-to-ear. He knew it took considerable courage for Teancum to pray out loud. Finding peace with God was something Tum had hoped his young lord would be able to do some day. A relationship with Christ was never a priority with Teancum growing up, but it was for Tum and Lord Pilio. They both tried to influence Teancum to seek the face of God, but it never really had any effect. Now, with Teancum at his lowest and reaching out to the God he never knew, Tum felt there was real hope for the future.

The two men stayed under the oak tree and absorbed the remaining day in silent passing. As the sun was setting, Tum made the first overt move to return to the ranch. "Oh, these old bones are not what they used to be," he lamented as he stretched and tried to stand up. "I think that's the longest I have sat still, doing nothing, in quite some time."

Teancum took in a big, cleansing breath of fresh air. "Yes, we should probably start heading back," he grunted as he stood up and shook off the stiffness in his legs from sitting for so long. "Besides, I have kind of grown accustomed to eating a regular hot supper again," he quipped. "I was told it is beef stew, cheese, and fresh bread, tonight."

"Well," Tum responded jokingly while picking up the two shovels, "Let's not keep the cook waiting any longer."

As they climbed into the wagon and took their seats, Teancum reached out with his hand gesturing for the reins. Without hesitation, Tum handed him control of the wagon and they started moving down the small hill toward the worn path. *He is finally coming back to life*, Tum thought as he looked at Teancum out the corner of his eye. *Facing the graves of his family, a prayer in the open, now driving a team of horses. A great day indeed!* Tum was grinning for the rest of the short trip back to the ranch as he bounced in the wagon seat. Teancum could see the grin on Tum's face and knew he was the reason for it. It made him feel good.

CHAPTER TWO

Waking Up the Predator

It was just past sunset when they arrived back in front of the large barn. As they pulled up, Teancum was the first to notice there was no one out and moving around. "Where is everyone?" he questioned. Usually the area around the barn was a buzz of activity. Tum turned around in the seat and looked but didn't see any member of his small communal family, either. "That's interesting, the chickens are not cooped up yet. I wonder where everyone is?" He turned back to face Teancum. Tum could see Teancum was starting to become anxious and he tried to calm him down. "Most likely, they're still enjoying the fine meal they prepared."

Teancum was not so optimistic. His sense for trouble which had served him so well in the wilds was banging away at his emotions. Something felt wrong. Tum could see the hard look forming on Teancum's face and the earlier, cheery disposition, instantly fade away as he tried to put Teancum at ease. Tum was concerned all their progress would be destroyed in one moment. "Not to worry. You will see. All is well, here," he patted Teancum's leg. "This is a safe place. Take the wagon around to the stable. I will have one of the boys come out and secure the horses for you." Tum slid off the seat and onto the hard ground. "Off you go," he smiled up at Teancum and waved his hand toward the stable. "I will meet you right here and we can dine together."

Teancum shook his head and obediently responded, but he still felt things were not right. He moved the wagon to the stable and dismounted from the driver's seat. He walked around the wagon and removed the two

CHAPTER TWO

shovels from the bed then stood next to the horses. Looking out into the night, Teancum could not shake the feeling something was wrong. He trusted Tum and desperately wanted to leave the past behind him. But suddenly he felt the sharp tip of a blade sticking in the small of his back and a hand grab the tuft of hair from the back of his head and jerk him backwards.

"Move, make a noise, or try to fight and you're a dead man. Do you understand?" The voice hissed in his ear.

Everything in Teancum's body and mind went instantly hard and cold.

"Drop those shovels and put your hands up. Do it!" The still unseen voice ordered Teancum to respond. Teancum could feel the hot breath on the back of his neck from the man holding the knife and smell his unmistakable stench of sweat, grime, and too much strong wine. Teancum knew it all too well.

Teancum became the predator again. His senses were alive and he was absorbing everything happening around him. He could hear something moving behind him and off to his right. *More than one bandit, the man with the knife is not alone*, Teancum figured. *At least two, maybe more*, he concluded. This was the reason no one was outside moving around or working. They were all being held, against their will, someplace on the ranch. *That would require more than two, and they will be well armed*, Teancum blinked, as he continued to deduce the situation in his mind.

"Drop the shovels!" The unseen criminal shouted, shaking Teancum's head.

Teancum released his grip and let the two shovels fall to the ground. Then he slowly brought his hands up, in a gesture of surrender. In his mind he was doing everything but giving up. The last two years of fighting had sharpened his mind and body to a razor's edge, and all he was doing was preparing himself to strike.

"Master Teancum?" It was Tum in a loud whisper. He was calling out from around the corner. " Teancum, there are men in the barn with the others. I think they are—" Tum stopped speaking when he came into the corral and saw Teancum with his hands up and two bandits standing behind him. There was a look of embarrassment on Tum's face as the two made eye contact. Teancum raised up his eye brows and gave Tum a look back as if to say, *'Yeah, I know.'*

"Get him!" the bandit holding Teancum by the hair shouted to his partner, gesturing with his head.

Waking Up the Predator

Teancum could tell the bandit giving the orders, sounded a bit annoyed, he had to tell the second man to react. Teancum logged this away in his memory. *That one, he is new to this. Not as experienced as the other one.* Teancum sized up the threats.

The second bandit came out from the shadows and moved quickly to Tum's side. Tum was too old and too tired to put up much of a resistance. He grudgingly put his hands up, also. Teancum was watching the bandit and using his medical mind to analyze the bandit's every action.

Medium build, shorter than the other man. Left handed, malnourished. With his medical training and his tactical experience, Teancum could see things others did not. He continued to watch and analyze the second bandit as the man tried to control Tum. *He can't see well at night, and he has a problem with his left hip.* Teancum had already figured out the most efficient way to kill the second bandit before the bandit had even finished dealing with Tum. Teancum now needed to distract the first bandit and get him off balance. "What do you want?" he asked in a disarming tone. He was trying to get the two criminals to lower their defenses.

"Your valuables, food and horses," the first man responded as he adjusted his stance and grip on Teancum's hair. Teancum's submissive tone made the bandit feel empowered and dominant. Teancum could sense the bandit was dropping his guard and ever so subtly, relaxing.

"Okay… Please don't hurt us," Teancum responded in a submissive tone. He made eye contact with Tum as the second bandit was searching Tum for weapons. Tum looked puzzled as Teancum winked at him, telling Tum he was pretending to give in to the bandits and to stand by for action. Tum knew he was no fighter but he could distract the second bandit long enough to give Teancum a fighting chance with the man holding a knife to his back.

"Oh, my back!" Tum bellowed as he winced in imaginary pain, pulling to his right. The bandit let go of Tum and took two steps back. For a second, the novice criminal forgot he was a kidnapper and was concerned for the general health of the old man.

The leader of the marauders holding Teancum moved his face closer to Teancum's right shoulder and shouted at the second bandit, "Hey, what are you doing?"

The leader's response provided the break Teancum was hoping for and in an instant, he reacted. Sweeping his right arm behind him as he spun to his right, Teancum dipped his head, knocking away the bandit's knife

CHAPTER TWO

in his back, out away from his body. The sudden counter move caught the bandit off balance and his hand was caught up in Teancum's hair. Teancum stood up straight, grabbing the fingers of the man holding his hair. He clamped down hard on the fingers, and felt a few of them pop as he twisted and yanked on them while pulling them out of his hair. Teancum was on him like a ravenous dog catching a rabbit. Striking savagely, Teancum kicked down and to the inside of the bandit's left knee, completely destroying the joints and ligaments. The man screamed and grabbed for kis knee. Then cupping the back of the bandit's head, Teancum jerked the man's neck down as Teancum brought up his own knee into the bandit's face. There was a sickening cruch as the criminal's face exploded apart. Blood went everywhere. It was not a death blow, but the bandit was knocked unconscious and out of the fight for good.

Tum saw Teancum make his move and he was ready. He still had pep in his own steps, and Tum jerked away from the second bandit. The second bandit was completely caught off guard by what was happening, standing motionless and in shock. Teancum kicked his foot under one of the shovels laying on the ground at his feet. The shovel jumped up in a cloud of dust in front of Teancum. As it hung in the air, Teancum reached out and grabbed the wooden handle with both hands. Swinging the shovel across his body like a bat, Teancum connected the flat end of the metal spade with the side of the second bandit's face. There was a loud metal clang as Teancum knocked the second bandit so hard the blow killed him almost instantly. The body of the second bandit dropped with a thud and Teancum put his finger up to his lips to tell Tum to be still and quiet. Teancum lowered the shovel and grabbed the first bandit's long knife off the ground.

"Watch the barn." Teancum whispered to Tum as he pointed toward the structure in the distance. Tum's body was flush with adrenaline and he began to shake.

"O-Okay," he half choked in response. Teancum gave him a quick smile with a thumbs-up, telling Tum he was safe now and he'd done a good job. Tum tried to smile back while stepping over the dead bandit at his feet.

Teancum knew the second bandit would be no more trouble so he turned his attention back to the first one. The damage to leader's face was extensive but not fatal, if he was provided with proper medical treatment. "Sorry." Teancum spoke, as he bound the bandit's hands behind his back and then to his feet. "I need to deal with your friends before I can come back to help you." Teancum made sure the bands were good and set. He didn't want the bandit to escape. Standing up, he looked around for additional weapons the two might have brought with them. "Nothing," he grunted, after checking around the corral. He looked down at the simply-made, long knife in his hand that he took from the first bandit. "You will have to do," he spoke as he checked the edge of the blade for its sharpness. Teancum was pleasantly surprised to find it to be a very sharp edge. He looked up at Tum, who was still standing in the shadows, keeping a vigil at the entrance to the corral while watching the barn.

"Anything?"

"No," Tum responded, taking his eyes off the barn. He was looking back and forth at the mess Teancum made while dealing with the dangerous men. Tum had not seen this side of Teancum before— the power, the focus, and the violence of action. Suddenly, Tum understood the reason Teancum cried out at night, and was slow to assimilate with the rest of the families now living on the ranch. There was an obvious big breath and sigh, then Tum continued, "Is this what it was like out in the wilds? Killing, and all of this madness?" He turned around again and looked at Teancum. "Is this the cause of your nightmares?"

"I made peace with killing the enemies of freedom long ago." Teancum responded to Tum. He bent down, picking up the same shovel he used to kill the second bandit. Checking the weight and balance of the tool in his hands, Teancum continued, "What bothers me now is I have become good at hunting and killing other men." Teancum looked down at the two men lying in the dirt surrounded by spattered blood. "Am I a monster now?" He looked right at Tum earnestly. "I have killed many men— old and young, Nephite and Lamanite alike; it did not matter to me who they were after a while. I killed to survive and to stop the bandits and criminals from hurting anyone else."

It took a moment for Tum to respond. He knew Teancum needed the kind of advice only a father-figure or mentor could give his son, at a time like this. "Is the sheepdog a monster for killing a wolf? What about the mother bear protecting her young? Or a good soldier defending his family and home?" Tum stepped toward his young friend.

"No, Master Teancum, you are *not* a monster. You are a good and decent man who had this thrust upon him. These men," he gestured to the two at their feet. "as well as those in the mountains, were evil, and

CHAPTER TWO

they brought this upon themselves." Tum touched Teancum on the arm exactly where he touched him the first day Teancum returned. The love and kindness Teancum felt on the day he came home was boiling up inside of him again. "God has commanded us to fight and defend our homes and families, but we must never take the offence. Only when we strike to stop the attack or prevent harm from coming to another are we justified in our actions." Tum looked into Teancum's watering eyes. "You are a good man, and you did what you had to do to protect the innocent from harm. No Teancum, you're not a monster… You are a warrior."

Upon hearing these words, Teancum lowered his head as tears streamed down his cheeks. Tum let it go for a moment but in the back of his mind he knew the others in the old barn were still in real danger. He needed Teancum to be the hero again.

" Teancum?" Tum inquired softly. "Son, there are others." That was all he needed to say. Teancum jerked back to life and was moving toward the corral door before Tum could adjust his stance.

"How many did you see?" Teancum asked, while still moving.

"I saw two. They have separated the men from the women and children." Tum was happy his motivational speech had worked. He quickly grabbed the other shovel and moved to Teancum's side. "Both had spears and swords but no armor. Both were Nephites, come to think of it, there might be a third one whom I could not see," Tum pointed to the back door of the barn. " They did not see me when I walked in. It's dark in that corner. I was able to come back out before they knew I was there." Tum was getting excited now and anticipating the coming fight. "What's the plan?"

Teancum looked down at his old mentor and smiled, "I am going to need a distraction."

The blood drained from Tum's face as he realized he was to be the bait in Teancum's trap.

The three bandits were standing together in the center of the barn watching their prisoners and staying alert. They looked like all the rest of the common criminals and Nehors, which Teancum had faced. They were dirty and unkempt, traveling light and existing on what they could steal. Like a pack of wild dogs, living hand-to-mouth and preying on the good and decent. They had moved all the men and strong boys into a stable and had them sitting on the ground, facing away from them. The women and children were clustered into a small group, on the opposite side of the barn. Two of the men were eating and drinking from large goblets while the third man held his spear at the ready.

"What's taking them so long?" The man with the spear spoke.

"Relax…" A second bandit spoke with a mouth full of bread, the crumbs gathered on his beard. Nothing but farm hands and old men around here anyway. He burped, snickered and gestured toward the stable full of men and boys.

" The sooner we get what we need and get out of this land, the better off I will feel. For all we know, *he* is still out there." The bandit with the spear responded. He was nervous and not afraid to express his fear of some unseen, person. "You saw what happened at the Gathering Grove, you know the stories of the attacks on the trails and hideouts."

The third bandit hissed at the both of them, "Quiet, you two. One man could not do all that. I am not going to tell you again, use your brains for once." The bandit took a long drink from his goblet and continued, " Those stories of a lone man— what did you call him, the Ghost Soldier? One man wandering the mountains and killing Nehors at will? Please," he adjusted his sword and continued, " The entire Nephite army tried but could not root us out." He sneered as he spoke. "And you think one lone man can do all of that?"

" They say he does not take prisoners, or show mercy. They say no one is left alive when he attacks," the one with the spear responded.

"If no one is left alive, then who told you the story?" The second bandit chimed in with a sarcastic tone.

The speaking bandit tried to respond, but he could not find a retort. There was an awkward pause as the third bandit smiled and continued drinking from his goblet. The two bandits were snickering at the one who was holding the spear when there was a sudden and loud crashing sound coming from just outside the barn doors. All three men were startled. They nervously readied themselves for action.

"Scared?" The first bandit whispered to the third one in jest.

"Hold your tongue, boy."

As they waited and listened, the sounds of a man singing and metal clanking could be heard coming from outside. The three men were very puzzled as they tried to discern what was happening. The sounds coming from outside were causing the hostages to get excited and the first bandit shouted at them.

"Quiet! Sit back down and be still, or I will run you through with my spear!"

The third bandit looked at the second, gesturing with his head, for him to move to the door and take a look outside. The second bandit eased himself forward and reached for the handle on the barn door. Pushing it aside, he poked his head out to see. After a second, he stepped back inside the door, pushing it the rest of the way open, exposing the other criminals to the night air and the scene before him. "Would you get a look at this?" There was humor and a question in his voice.

There was Tum, dancing around a small fire, his shirt off and singing while banging two frying pans together.

When the people in the barn saw it was Tum outside acting crazy, they all rose to their feet and started shouting and crying out.

"You," the third bandit barked to the first one, "come with me. We need to get them to sit down!" He then pointed at the second man. "You, deal with that crazy old man!" He pointed at Tum. The two bandits moved back toward the hostages and the second criminal moved cautiously toward Tum, he was still banging away on the metal pans and singing at the top of his lungs.

"Hey, old man!" The bandit shouted, as he approached Tum. The criminal was not taking any chances as he stepped out from the protection of the barn, into the night. He moved, carefully, with his spear at the ready. "What are you doing?"

Tum waited until the bandit was close to him before he stopped dancing and singing. He smiled and looked right at the bandit. "What am I doing?" he said, in a high-pitched, crazy voice. "Why, I am distracting you!" Tum smiled and sang even louder and banged harder on the pans.

The bandit blinked several times, then the word 'distracting' raced across his mind. He stiffened and tried to turn around to shout a warning but Teancum had moved in behind him. Teancum, his face covered with axle grease to hide his facial features and help him blend into the shadows, knew exactly where to strike on the human body. He grabbed the forehead of the bandit with his left hand and drove the sharp tip of the long knife up at an angle into the base of the bandit's skull. The bandit's body went rigid, twitched, and then completely limp and flopped to the ground like a rag doll. In an instant, Teancum disappeared into the shadows and darkness, quiet as the night, itself, taking the long knife with him.

Waking Up the Predator

Looking down at the dead body and then back at the other bandits still in the barn, Tum continued to sing and bang away like nothing had happened.

The two other bandits heard the clanking continue and assumed their companion was still dealing with the crazy, old man. Besides, they were too busy trying to maintain control of the people still in the barn. They separated and started to jab with their spears as they drove the trapped ranch hands back into the corners of the barn. "Get back!" they shouted as the hostages became even more aggressive.

Teancum was moving like the wind as he ran around to the back of the barn. Silent and completely focused, Teancum was the predator again. His prey would quickly regret ever stepping foot on his land. He was not going to allow what happened to him all those years ago happen to another father or mother tonight.

Teancum reached the back of the barn, stopping to listen and absorb his surroundings. Everything outside the barn was quiet and still. Only the shouting and commotion coming from inside could be heard. Anyone unfamiliar with the barn layout would have missed the small access door along the far wall, opposite of the big barn doors. Clearly, these bandits did not do a good sweep of the barn when they took the people hostage, or they would have locked the door and posted a guard. This was the same door Tum entered and quickly exited earlier, when he realized what was taking place. Teancum could see inside the barn through the cracks in the wood. He could hear the screams and see the bandits herding the good folks of his ranch against the walls. He saw the look of terror in the eyes of the children, and the helplessness in the faces of the parents as they desperately tried to protect their little ones from the dangerous men before them.

He felt himself reaching for the door latch but stopped just before he pulled it open. *Wait for it.* He commanded his muscles to relax and be patient. *Wait for them to turn around.* Teancum knew they would turn to check on their friend and find him dead. He knew what they would do next— panic. Lying in wait caused a surge of adrenaline, and it was burning up the oxygen in his blood. He took some deep breaths to calm his nerves. If there is one thing he understood better than most, it was human nature under stress. Breathing was the key to staying focused. He had perfected his craft in the forests and now these hapless criminals were going to bear the brunt of his righteous anger. How dare they come

CHAPTER TWO

to this ranch and threaten the lives of these people who had shown him nothing but kindness? How dare they hold women and children as hostages?

Courage.

This one word echoed through his mind again like it had so long ago. It had been some time since Teancum felt the presence and heard the masculine, guiding voice. His wife's voice came next like a calming breeze, blowing in his heart. *Live for justice.*

In those few moments in the dark, crouching like a lion and waiting for the exact moment to strike, Teancum had an epiphany. It hit him like the rush of a thousand ocean waves as the answer to his most burning question came crashing down over him. The one haunting his dreams and consuming his every waking thought— *Why me?* He would ask in painful fits of sleeplessness, or moments of lonely agony. For the first time since the murderous event two years ago, he now understood with complete clarity the answer to the question— why him? While looking at the faces through the slats in the barn wall of the helpless and frightened, images of his past— the training at a young age, the medical education, the politics, the pain and loss of his family and learning through trial and error the art of death— it all came into view. It all made sense. Now he understood his purpose on earth.

You are the watchman on the wall. You are the sentry at the gate. You are the protector of the flock, and the sword of justice. He felt the hands of a long-lost father on his shoulders as those words rang in his ears. *God has forged you in the fire of adversity and turned you into a weapon. An instrument to be used for the protection and welfare of his people. Save these people, as only you can.*

Teancum felt a huge emotional weight lifted from his muscled shoulders. He had been carrying a heavy burden for some time. He knew he had grown into someone who was very good at killing, but he did not understand why until now. *Someone needs to stand up to the thugs and murderers.* Teancum shook his head as these thoughts crossed his mind. He was agreeing with the promptings; *Someone needs to stand between the good and decent people of this world and all the evil.* He looked through the crack in the boards and saw a small child crying in her mother's arms. The mother was clutching the child closely and panic was on her face. *I am a man, I am a well-trained and experienced fighter. I know the inner workings of the Nehors and the Lamanite raiders. I know the inner workings of the dishonest politicians.* He looked again at the face of the mother holding the child. There was blood on her lip and swelling next to her eye. She had been struck by the kidnappers. She and her small child were innocent victims and no one was helping them. *I know how to fix this, and I know how to heal her. Of course it should be me.*

A surge of energy went shooting through his body and Teancum felt stronger than he had ever felt before. The power of his newly-found righteous indignation was fueling his body and readying his mind for the next few moments. Moving to a crouching position, Teancum adjusted the handle of the knife in his hand and waited for the exact moment when the other criminals would be distracted and he could strike. The moment came when Tum stopped banging the pans and stealthily disappeared into the night. Both kidnappers moved to find Tum and instead saw their companion lying in a pool of his own blood.

"Where did he go?" One of the men shouted as they both moved next to their slain friend. They were looking out into the darkness and scanning for a threat, as Teancum quietly opened the back door and signaled for the ranch hands standing next to the door to escape. Teancum stepped through the opening and gestured with his hand for the others to follow the first few out the back door. The people were frightened at first of this man with the camouflaged face who suddenly appeared behind them. After a moment, they recognized Teancum as he held his finger up to his lip telling them to stay quiet as they went.

"Children and women first," he whispered with authority, as the bulk of the ranch folks reached the small door opening. There was a hint of panic as the people crowded the exit and Teancum tried to instruct the men to do the right thing, letting the women and little ones go through first.

"Hey!" One of the bandits shouted when he turned around and saw his hostages escaping. The two of them moved quickly toward the back of the barn with their spears out front. Several of the frightened women and children still in the barn screamed out of fear.

Teancum pushed on the shoulders of a man next to him and shouted, "Keep moving!" He then moved to the gap of space behind the crowd and placed himself between the good people and the evil men moving his way. He readied the knife in his hand and positioned his body for a fight.

The two bandits stopped moving and both of them gave Teancum a long, confused look. "You some kind of hero?" One of the bandits

CHAPTER TWO

snickered in disgust. He thought the odds were in his favor, seeing how they outnumbered the lone man and they were much better armed. If only they knew the truth.

"Keep moving!" Teancum shouted over his shoulder, as he maintained his fighting stance and refused to back down from the threat before him.

"Who do you think you are?" The other bandit responded. "We are the Sons of Nehor!" He puffed out his chest as he continued speaking. "We are here for your valuables, not your lives. But we will take both if you don't back down and drop the knife." There was a hint of hesitation creeping into the bandit's voice but he was doing his best to mask his uneasiness with false bravado. He knew one of his brother criminals was dead and he could not account for the two other bandits who were supposed to be checking the horse corral and surroundings.

"Sons of Nehor?" Teancum very calmly smiled through the grease hiding his face. "I will make a deal with you, scum." Teancum adjusted his stance and focused his dangerous energy toward the last two bandits. "Over the last two years, I have lost count of how many of you Nehor dogs I have sent to hell." Both the bandits adjusted the grip they had on their spears and shuffled their feet. They were not used to someone standing up to them and were not quite sure how to respond to Teancum's insults. Then the thought crept into both of their minds, *Is this man the rumored Ghost Soldier?* This idea made both of them very uneasy.

"There is one thing I do remember about every single Nehor I have killed, including the ones tonight." Teancum pointed with the knife in his hand to the body lying on the ground just outside the barn door. He could see his words were starting to have the intended emotional effect. Teancum knew that when fighting for his life, he must take every advantage to win. If planting a seed of fear in the minds of his enemy was going to give him the tactical advantage, then so be it. He was not bragging, he was beating his opponents at the mental game before he challenged them to the physical one. "You all bleed like a stuck pig."

Teancum's taunting infuriated the two remaining Nehors. If what this mysterious man was saying was true, that he was in fact the Ghost Soldier, then they both had a chance to become legends in the Nehor clan. Killing the one man responsible for more Nehor deaths than the entire Nephite army would elevate them both to the status of hero. They looked at each other and came to the same conclusion— to attack. They both shouted and charged.

Waking Up the Predator

Teancum took half of a breath as the essence of the super predator swelled inside of him. Everything slowed down for Teancum and the fight became almost surreal. Teancum saw the bandits charging at him. The one on his right was moving faster than the one on the left. He took a half-step to his right and readied himself for close fighting. The bandit on the right reached the distance where he could deploy his spear. While running, he thrust it toward Teancum's chest. Teancum saw the bandit's body shift along with the muscles and bones in the bandit's arms. He knew what was coming and was already two moves ahead of the bandits. He knew the thrust was the first move almost before the bandit did and Teancum was ready. Waiting until the last possible moment, Teancum spun his body out of the way of the spear as the long wooden shaft went past him. He reached out and grabbed the wooden shaft with his left hand as he spun his body around. This move pulled the first bandit off balance and exposed his unarmored back to Teancum while blocking the second bandit with his body. Teancum took advantage of the exposed back and quickly stabbed the first bandit twice in the back, once in each lung. The move was so quick and exact the bandit did not even stop moving. His momentum kept him falling forward and he passed by Teancum and crumpled to the ground in blinding pain.

The second bandit tried to readjust his position but Teancum saw the next attack before it happened. He tried to bring his spear around to stab at Teancum, but again, Teancum simply moved effortlessly out of the way of the spear point. The second bandit tried to readjust his feet again, but the body of his fellow Nehor was in the way so he continued to jab off balance at Teancum with the spear. Teancum continued to twist and lean his body out of the way as he countered every move from the bandit.

The second bandit was so focused on trying to kill Teancum, he failed to realize he was completely outmatched. The skill and ability Teancum was demonstrating by avoiding the continued thrusts of the spear tip were far superior to anything the bandit, or for that matter, the crowd of ranch hands who were watching had ever seen. Even Tum, who had moved into the light, stood in awe as he watched his young master move, duck and dodge the repeated attempts to strike him with the spear.

It was time for Teancum to end this dance of death. He waited for the next strong thrust, then reached out and grabbed the spear shaft with his left hand. Holding onto it, with a firm grip, Teancum pulled hard, bringing the bandit off balance. With the long knife in his right hand,

CHAPTER TWO

Teancum passed the sharp blade over the right forearm of the bandit, severing the tendons and nerves in his arm. Bellowing, the bandit let go of the spear and tried to pull his right arm back and away from Teancum's blade. Out of pure instinct, the bandit balled up his left fist and tried to punch Teancum in the head. Teancum was too fast. He ducked under the wild punch and drove the blade of his knife across the belly of the bandit as the momentum of the wild punch twisted the bandit's body around.

Dropping to both knees, the bandit tried to hold in the blood and flesh, gashed open by the blade, but it was no use. The damage was done and the injury too severe. As the life poured out of him, the bandit looked up at Teancum and then fell to his side. He was moments away from joining the rest of his band in the afterlife and the eternal reward set aside for murderers and kidnappers. With his last breath the bandit looked up and gasped. "Who…are you?"

Teancum stood up straight and roared like a lion to its prey, "I am the Ghost Soldier!"

Tum could see the fight was over and moved carefully up to Teancum's side. Tum looked around and saw several sets of eyes looking back at him through the open door and the cracks in the wooden walls. Tum was not a dangerous or violent man; this kind of action and the emotional aftermath was completely alien to him. He did not know what to do or say so he remained motionless. The two men stood together silently.

"Any sign of others still loose on the property?" Teancum broke the awkward stillness with a question. He wiped the blood from the knife, with the shirt of the dead Nehor at his feet and tucked the weapon in his belt.

"No." Tum tried to get the word to sound confident, but at this moment, he was still unsure of his own emotions. Tum was an old man, a trained butler and ranch manager, not a fighter. He was good at his job and had been doing it his whole adult life. Killing was not something he did. He accepted it as part of the rough life of living outside the walls of the great city but still, it was not who he was. His lord Pilio was a soldier before he found his fortune. Pilio understood that life. Tum would defer to Pilio or to some of the bigger and stronger ranch hands, if and when trouble arose it was not in his nature and he was fine with that. Or so he thought. Now he was questioning everything. His thoughts were racing. *What if Teancum had not been here tonight? What would have happened?* He looked back at Teancum with a new respect. *What if I had put up more of a fight with the bandits when they would come in the past to steal our food and livestock?* Tum turned to look at the others who were slowly coming back into the light of the bright candles still burning in the barn. *I am too old to change into a warrior, but what about the others, the young? Could they do such things if they needed to?* His mind flashed to moments ago, when Teancum was killing two men with little effort. *Did I set the right example for the others by cowering and allowing evil to dominate us?* Tum could see the same woman with the bruised eye, bloody lip and the fearful child in her arms. *What about justice?* He looked at the bodies of the two dead criminals. *Was this true justice?* He then remembered the words of a great holy man who gave a speech, when Tum was very young. *'Peace is not found in just the absence of conflict, but true peace can only be found in the presence of justice.* The bearded holy man shouted from the top of a large rock, to a gathered crowd including young Tum and his own family.

Tum reflected and then made up his mind to speak. "Warriors, guardians, protectors— such men are truly needed in society. I know enough to realize I am not the sort." He looked Teancum directly in his eyes and continued, "But you are." Teancum blinked and nodded his head in agreement. This was the same conclusion Teancum had come to just before he faced these last two men in hand-to-hand combat.

Tum was still contemplating when Teancum rushed past him and went to the aid of the woman with the injured face and the others who had been assaulted by the bandits. The fight was over, and now it was time for the physician in him to do his job. With the gentle hands of a true healer, Teancum administered the best he could. He did a quick assessment of the wounds and asked for ointments, rags and clean water. Quickly, those items were found and brought to him. A table was cleared and Teancum moved his patients closer to the candle's light. Tum moved up next to Teancum and watched as he worked his medical magic. Teancum was out of practice, but the basics of first aid are universal and it quickly came back to him. He moved through each injured person with compassion and dignity, doing the best he could to help them recover from the trauma they had all experienced.

"Keep this clean and put more of the aloe ointment on it in the morning." He instructed and smiled at a boy who had been struck in the face with the back of one of the criminal's hands. A small cut had opened on his cheek and Teancum expertly patched him up. "He will be fine," Teancum turned and spoke to the boy's mother. The lady holding the

CHAPTER TWO

hand of the boy was keeping a very close eye on Teancum. She saw what he did to those two men who were trying to kill him with their spears. Anyone who was capable of doing that was suspicious in her eyes. She thanked him quickly and jerked on her son's arm, getting him away from Teancum as fast as she could.

Tum and Teancum shared a look and Teancum spoke, "I don't blame them for their distrust in me. I would be wary too of a strange man who did what I did." He gestured back to the bodies of the criminals who were now being loaded into a wagon to be disposed of in an unmarked grave. He looked back at Tum and continued, "I can see much more clearly now that God has a plan for me, but I do not know what to do or where to start," Teancum said, as he held out his hands, gesturing with a questioning tone and showing Tum his palms and fingers. Tum could see blood on Teancum's hands. It was a mixture of the blood from the bandits and the good people of the ranch. Tum reached for a rag and gave it to Teancum to wipe away the blood.

"Well…" Tum started, "It's clear you are meant for bigger things than life on a struggling ranch." He put his hands on his hips and continued, "You were a man of influence and power once, your name still commands respect in the capital city."

"What good could I possibly do there?" Teancum struggled to follow Tum's path of logic. "I gave up my medical practice, my fortune is gone. The only skill I have left is the ability to kill men."

" That is where you are wrong, my young friend." Like a thunderclap, the answer came to Tum. He held up his finger to tell Teancum to be still and listen. "You are a natural leader of men. You have skills and abilities far beyond anyone else I have known. From what you have told me, these Nehors have infiltrated into every level of the government and prey on the weak." He pointed to the bodies as the men from the ranch tossed the last one into the back of the wagon. "From the way they reacted when you told them who you are, they know and fear this Ghost Soldier you became." He pointed back at Teancum who was listening to Tum's words with real interest. "So *be* the Ghost Soldier."

Teancum sat motionless, lost in his own thoughts. "Be the Ghost Soldier…?" He whispered dubiously. "You mean like a job?"

"Yes!" Tum exclaimed clapping his hands. " Teancum, the Ghost Soldier." Tum put his hand on Teancum shoulder, "Can you show others how to fight like you did here, tonight?"

"Yes, I suppose I could… Why?"

Tum smiled and excitedly patted Teancum's shoulder, like a proud father.

CHAPTER THREE

A Captain of Men

The ride, to the main gates of the grand city of Zarahemla was pleasant and uneventful. Tum did most of the talking as Teancum sat next to him on the old wagon and enjoyed the ride. Both of them were dressed in plain , unassuming clothing. Teancum was still trying to regain some weight and his skin color had improved, but he still had a long road to recovery. His physical scars would heal in time, but the emotional ones—those cuts were very deep. Today, however, he felt good, and closed his eyes as he let the warmth of the mid-day sun bask over his face and arms.

Along the way they stopped at Teancum's favorite rock formation. It had been many years but Teancum found his seat and closed his eyes. He whispered a quick prayer to a God he was still trying to connect with.

"I still don't fully understand the plan you have for me, but I am willing to show faith and trust in you," he mouthed the words as he spoke them in his mind. "Please give me the strength to do what is right."

"Master Teancum?" Tum called out from the wagon. He had given the horses a drink and was ready to keep traveling. "If you still wish to reach your in-laws by night fall, we should get moving."

"Coming," Teancum called out. He had almost fallen asleep as he sat, after saying his prayer and pondering his future. Grunting as he stood up, Teancum could still feel the lingering effects of the hard few years he spent in the bush. A specter of sadness and doubt crossed his mind as he rubbed his legs to get the blood flowing.

Are you really the right man for the job? The shadow voice spoke to him

CHAPTER THREE

from deep inside. *Everyone will know you let your family die, and that you murdered all those men in the forests and on the trails. You know how politicians think— will they believe they can trust you like they did before?*

This was not the first time Teancum had considered the idea, that the Nephite people would reject him outright and accuse him of being no better than the criminals he had hunted down and killed. He and Tum had spoken about this fact just a few days ago, as they were planning their trip to the capital.

"Yes, you scare people." Tum was firm in his tone. "Honestly, when I saw what you were capable of, it scared me too." Tum made sure Teancum was looking at him as he continued to speak. "Consider this— your grandfather taught me this important lesson about warriors living among society. You had a large flock of sheep here at the ranch, yes?" Teancum nodded his head in agreement. "Does the shepherd who tends to your flock use a dog to help keep the sheep safe and chase off the wolves?" Teancum shook his head again and was a bit curious as to where this conversation was going. "Think of the Nephite people as the flock and you are the sheepdog; the criminals and enemies of freedom, they are the wolves." Teancum blinked as the analogy sank in. "You, as the sheepdog, have claws and fur and teeth just like the wolf. You can kill anyone of the sheep at will, and the sheep can see this. The sheep can tell you are not like them. As a matter of fact, you are much more like the wolf than the sheep." Teancum shook his head in agreement. "So, what is it that makes you different than the wolf?" There was a pause as Tum let Teancum think on that question. "It is your *intent*." Tum continued. "You are not there to harm the sheep. You are there to protect them and kill the wolves. The sheep know that fact. They know you are not the enemy, but you still scare them. There will always be distance between you and them." There was a questioning look on Teancum's face. He was quietly asking how the sheep would know this. "Because your only job is to get between them and the evil of this world. Show them you are worthy of the shepherd's trust and never attack the sheep. The people will come to respect and love their sheepdog."

In Teancum's mind, Tum's words were interrupted by the dark voice challenging his confidence. Teancum sharply responded. *Yes... I am the right man for the job. God has forged me in the fires of adversity and I am his sharp sword.*

We will see if the people agree with you, the faceless voice tried to counter

Teancum's boldness, but it did not work. Teancum was already walking back to the wagon and getting ready for the final leg of his journey to Zarahemla.

The two men reached the main gates of the city as the sun was starting to set behind the distant rain clouds. It was going to be a warm night, but the color in the dark clouds gave a different, rainy forecast.

"State your business!" One of the gate guards called out to Tum and Teancum as the guard grabbed the horse's reins.

"Remember, I don't want anyone to know I am here." Teancum whispered under his hooded cloak to Tum as the guards closed in on them.

Tum cleared his throat and tried to address the guards. "Gentlemen, my name is Tum and I am the steward of my lord Pilio's horse and cattle ranch. My traveling companion and I have come to purchase dry goods in the market tomorrow and to sample some of your city's fine libations before we travel back to our humble home in the wilds, at the foot of those mountains, over there." Tum pointed toward the distant ridge line.

"A drink, is it?" The squad leader piped up as he took a slow stroll around the wagon, looking inside for anything resembling contraband. "We have enough drunks here already. And what of your friend. Does he have a name?"

"Oh, I assure you good gentlemen, we are not the drunken sort. Just weary merchants doing our duty, in need of a soft, dry bed and some good ale," Tum smiled. He was hoping to connect in some way with the lowly guards by appealing to their commonality all the while trying to deflect attention away from Teancum.

As Teancum sat quietly next to Tum and listened to the goings on, he took some interest in the guard who was still holding the bridle of one of the horses to keep them from moving. As Teancum continued to watch the guard, he could see the dark-colored ends of a tattoo on the man's right arm, just above the sleeve-line of his tunic. As the guard turned and twisted, the tattoo was partially exposed and Teancum could make out lines and details. The horse the guard was standing next to was not happy at having this odorous stranger close to him and holding his bridle. The horse started to complain by stomping its feet and jerking its head up and down. The guard holding the horse was not familiar with horses, and did not know what to do, so he acted out of ignorance and rage.

"Calm down!" He shouted as he pulled down hard on the bit in the horse's mouth. This caused pain to the horse, which only made the animal more agitated.

"Good sir, please!" Tum tried to shout a warning, but it was too late. The scared horse tried rearing up to kick at the man, but the wagon tongue was keeping it from getting all the way up. The power of the horse trying to buck knocked the guard off balance, causing him to fall to the ground. As he was trying to stand back up, his right upper arm was exposed. Teancum's body locked in rage as he saw the sign of the Nehor tattooed on the man's upper arm. Without thinking, Teancum was on his feet. He jumped from the wagon seat, leaving his heavy cloak behind. He had seen the symbol so many times while fighting for his life that he had an ingrained emotional response to it. For the next few moments, Teancum was acting purely on muscle memory.

Teancum landed on his feet and was moving toward the guard before Tum could even shout out or any of the other guards could react. The guard with the tattoo was on one knee, trying to rise as Teancum grabbed him by the neck bringing him to his feet. Teancum pushed the man up against the stone wall surrounding the city, squeezing down on his wind pipe, choking the guard. The other guards saw Teancum grab their squad mate and moved to intervene. Teancum had pulled out the small knife he was carrying on his belt, and drew it back to thrust it into the belly of the man with the Nehor tattoo. At the last possible second, Teancum's arm was stopped from pushing the knife forward by one of the other guards. As Teancum's hand was stopped, the guard he attacked recovered from the surprise and shock of Teancum's attack. He started to fight against the grip on his neck. He reached up, grabbing hold of Teancum's arm while the second guard, who stopped the knife thrust, had hold of Teancum's left arm.

Teancum felt the two men playing a sort of tug of war against him as they both pulled his arms in different directions. Teancum was able to calculate the distance between him and the man who was pulling his left arm and knew exactly where to strike to get him to let go. Teancum readjusted his stance, turned his hips away from the first guard so he could extend his right leg out toward the man who had stopped his knife thrust. In a fraction of a second, Teancum located his target on the man's body. He did a snap-kick to the man's upper chest, hitting him with the heel of his foot. Teancum could see and hear the air escaping as the man he just kicked crumpled to the ground in pain. He then turned back to the other guard he was still holding against the wall. Bringing his knee up in a violent strike, Teancum hit the man with the Nehor tattoo right in the nerve complex located on the outside of his upper thigh. The pain from Teancum's knee strike was so overwhelming, the guard released his grip on Teancum's arm and collapsed onto his knee. The sergeant of the guard and the last soldier were still at the back of the wagon when Teancum made his move.

When they saw Teancum attack their fellow guards, they pulled out their swords and started to move around the wagon to confront Teancum. The other Nephites standing around the massive gate tried to move back and not get involved in the struggle unfolding before them. The civilians, rushing to get out of the way, caused a delay in the other two guards getting to Teancum.

Teancum was in full combat mode now. He did not know if he was only dealing with one Nehor or if the entire guard force had been infiltrated by the bandit clan. Since he had killed most of the high leaders of the Nehor, he suspected someone else had taken over and they were continuing to be a scourge to the land. He could see the sergeant was on one side of the wagon, fighting the crush from the panicked crowd as they attempted to flee. The second soldier appeared to be smaller and younger than the seasoned leader. Teancum made a quick decision to face the younger man first. He would deal with him before he turned his attention on the older and more experienced sergeant.

"Master Teancum, no!" Tum called out. He watched helplessly as Teancum attacked the first guard. He could see Teancum was now completely focused on facing the advancing soldiers, but he did not understand why. If he had seen the Nehor symbol tattooed on the man's arm and experienced all Teancum had at the hands of those murdering thugs, things would be much clearer for the old man. Unable to see the tattoo, Tum tried in vain to get Teancum to stop his attack.

Teancum moved to the right side of the wagon, reaching the younger guard first. The guard swung his one-handed sword in a wild attempt to deliver a killer blow to the side of Teancum's head. Like a dancer, Teancum ducked under the sword and spun to his left. As he came around, Teancum punched the guard right in the side of his body, just below the breast plate. Wincing in pain from the punch, the young guard bent to his left, trying to swing his sword in a back stroke to cut Teancum. Teancum caught the guard's arm in midair and twisted

CHAPTER THREE

it, locking the shoulder joint. He used the stiff arm as a bar, pushing the guard forward and to the ground. Knowing the older and more experienced soldier was still advancing, Teancum struck the guard he had pinned to the ground in the back of the head with a hard hammer-fist and knocked him unconscious.

"Please! Teancum, stop!" Tum was beside himself. No one had been killed yet. He had seen what Teancum was capable of doing in a hand-to-hand fight, and these second-rate guards had no chance. If he could get Teancum to stop now, he might be able to talk to the city fathers and keep Teancum out of prison. Tum tried to get off the wagon but his old and frail body was not moving as fast as he wanted it to.

Teancum felt the body of the pinned soldier go limp. He did a forward roll and came up to his feet, ready to face the last opponent. Teancum had his knife in his hand and was positioned like a cat, ready to pounce as the sergeant squared up to him with his own sword drawn. The two men paused for a second as they made eye contact, measuring each other's resolve. "Before this day is over your friend, the Nehor, will face justice," Teancum spat while pointing to the younger man with the tattoo, as he bellowed in pain from the damage to his leg.

The sergeant looked a bit confused when Teancum spoke. "What are you talking about?" He shook his head while refocusing on the threat before him. This stranger had just assaulted his men and, for all he knew, at least one of them had been killed. He needed to stop this assailant before anyone else got hurt. He was not going to let Teancum confuse and distract him. The sergeant readjusted his stance and flexed his arms. "Drop the knife and get on your knees, this is your only warning!" He pointed right at Teancum with the tip of his sword.

"Anyone who defends or supports the Nehor are just as guilty!" Teancum shouted back, gesturing with his arms for the soldier to advance toward him.

"Master Teancum!" Tum jumped between the two fighters, grabbing Teancum by the arms. "You must stop this, now!" he shouted, right into Teancum's face. "This man— he is not your enemy!" Tum could feel Teancum's body relax and saw a spark of clarity gleam in his eyes. For a moment, Tum had hope of diffusing the situation, but a shout came from behind him and across the way.

"What is all this?"

Tum could hear the horses trotting closer and felt Teancum's body tighten. He saw Teancum look in the direction of the shout and could feel the reemergence of the predator inside him. Everything about Teancum suddenly changed. Tum watched helplessly as Teancum's eyes went dark and every muscle in his body contracted as if he was shocked with electricity. The full measure of Teancum's fighting readiness was on display as he set his feet and squared his body, ready for the coming conflict. Tum closed his eyes and said a quick prayer for God's mercy, then turned to face Teancum's new threat.

"Mister Tum? Is that you?"

The lead horseman was a Nephite army officer in full battle armor. He was followed by a squad of heavily armed cavalry moving toward the main gates of the city. The face and voice were familiar to Tum but he was having a hard time remembering where he had met this man before.

"Yes! Yes, it is," Tum replied, in an attempt to sound cherry while he waved. But anyone could clearly see he was nervous and trying to keep Teancum out of trouble.

As the mounted soldiers approached the wagon, they could see their fellow soldiers on the ground and the sergeant in a fighting stance, with his weapon out facing Teancum. Recognizing trouble, they instantly reacted and fanned out, pointing their heavy spears at Teancum. Teancum, who was still holding his small knife, pushed Tum out of his way and readjusted his fighting posture to better address the cavalrymen.

"Teancum, please!" Tum shouted in one final attempt, to get his friend to stop fighting.

"Teancum? Doctor Teancum?" The army officer questioned. The officer looked at Teancum and then at Tum. "Is that *Doctor* Teancum?" He quizzed Tum as he pointed.

"Yes!" Tum pleaded with the officer. "Please, tell your men to stand down. This was a horrible misunderstanding— this can all be explained."

The officer took off his helmet and ordered his men to raise up their spears and take a few paces back.

"Doctor Teancum." The officer called out as he slid off his horse. "I don't know if you remember me, my name is Gid." He slowly walked toward Teancum, with his hands out and open to show he was not armed. He could see the rage in Teancum's eyes and wanted to try to calm the situation. "My friend, Teomner and I were your armed escort back to your ranch when your family was murdered. I was there. Do you remember me?" Teancum blinked several times, then stood up, relaxing his posture.

CHAPTER THREE

"I was with Tum and watched as you went after the kidnappers. I helped to bury your family." Gid knew the face. The body was thinner and hard, but it was Doctor Teancum.

Teancum put his knife down to his side as Gid continued to speak. "Teomner and I pulled you and your children from the fire. Do you remember?" Several of the Nephites who had fled the area around the fight were slowly moving back so they could hear what Gid was saying. The story of the death of Lord Pilio and the disappearance of Doctor Teancum, common judge of Zarahemla, was all the gossip for quite some time after it all happened. Most of the people standing around knew the story and wanted to see firsthand if this really was Teancum.

Teancum tried to focus on Gid's face and recall those memories. He remembered the ride in the carriage as well as the dead ranch hands at the side of the burning house, then the surreal and blurred faces of Gid and Teomner standing over him after they pulled him from the burning home. "Yes… Yes, I do remember you." Teancum turned, pointing his knife at the Nehor still on the ground and in pain. "This man bears the symbol, on his arm, of the criminals responsible for that day."

Gid turned to two of his cavalrymen, gesturing with his head for them to investigate. The two soldiers dismounted then walked over to the guard with the tattoo. They stood him up as the injured man shouted in pain. They pulled up the sleeves of his tunic. There, for the entire world to see, was the markings of the Nehor imprinted in the man's arm.

"It does not mean anything! I am innocent of his claim," the tattooed soldier lamented.

"I have seen that marking all over the city. How do you know it is the mark of the Nehor clan?" Gid asked.

Teancum squared his shoulders and spoke with the authority of thunder. "I am the Ghost Soldier. I have been hunting the Nehor for two years."

When the injured soldier with the tattoo heard those words, he tried to jerk away from the armored men holding him, then hissed at Teancum. "Murderer!" He shouted. "You killed my friends and left their bodies to rot in the forest!"

"You are the Ghost Soldier?" Gid was surprised and taken aback. The legend of a Ghost Soldier single-handedly dismantling the entire Nehor criminal syndicate was almost as interesting to tell as the murder of Lord Pilio. Some people thought it might have been Teancum who was doing all the killing, but those who knew him best disagreed. They remembered the doctor and politician and could not imagine him doing all those things. He then looked around and saw Teancum had disarmed and taken down three soldiers and was ready to fight a squad of cavalry with just a knife, providing all the convincing Gid needed. He turned to the sergeant, who was still holding his sword out, ready to fight. "Stand down, sergeant. See to your men." Gid then looked at the tattooed solder and the two men still holding him as he squirmed. " Take him to the stockade."

"On what charges? You have no proof!" The soldier shouted back as he fought against the grips of the two men holding him. "I see— this is because you are a racist!" It had nothing to do with his skin color, status, or religion. The Nehor sympathizer was trying to misdirect and change the facts. It was an old and well-used tactic in the criminal underworld to make false and outrageous allegations toward the officials charged with keeping the peace and enforcing the laws. It worked with the common folk, in the past, the lies and false statements. They were all too good-natured to truly understand the evil behind the race-baiting; but not anymore. Most had seen and experienced the aftermath of a society where the people entrusted with the protection of lives and property were discouraged from doing their jobs. Things were different now, and Gid was having none of it.

"Take him away!" He shouted at his men. They understood the forcefulness behind Gid's words and dragged the tattooed man away.

"Sir, he assaulted my men." the sergeant spoke, in a low but hard tone as he pointed to Teancum. "What about him?"

"I will take him before the Chief Judge myself. All will be made right. Get your men the medical attention they need, then meet me at the justice building."

"Yes, sir," the tired sergeant lamented. He knew it was a losing battle to complain anymore so he turned to tend to his men. "One man disarmed the lot of you!" He bellowed as he tried to help his stunned and aching soldiers to their feet. "Pride of the Zarahemla legion, my eye."

Gid responded as he turned and winked at Tum. "You men!" Gid spoke to the rest of his squad still mounted on their horses. "Escort this wagon to the justice building."

Tum reached out his hand to Gid in thanks. "Lieutenant Gid, so good to see you again. I don't think it was a coincidence you were here today."

CHAPTER THREE

Gid extended his hand back, shaking Tum's. "Perhaps not."

They both turned to look at Teancum. "A fine mess you made," Tum scolded him. Teancum lowered his head and climbed into the wagon.

The news that Teancum was alive spread through the entire city in a wave of gossip. The fact he also claimed to be the Ghost Soldier, the man who was killing the Nehor and Lamanite bandits in the wilds of the mountains, spread through the city like a wildfire. Not long after the wagon and armed escorts arrived at the justice building, a large group of citizens started to gather to see if the story was true. There were many in the city who owed their lives to the miracles Doctor Teancum performed with his healing herbs. Others realized his influence in the creation of the new form of government they were now enjoying, while still others were now feeling the results of the almost complete disappearance of the criminals who roamed the country side. They had the mysterious Ghost Soldier to thank. Teancum was a leader, a man of influence, and wealth. His disappearance had a great effect on the city and the Nephite people as a whole. So, the people came to see for themselves if Teancum was back and if the stories were true.

Teancum sat in a lone chair with his back against the far wall in a small, almost empty room. The only other items in the room, on a small table, were a large candle holder with a lit candle and a washbasin with a clean towel near it. Several people stood in the doorway or just outside the room, looking at him from a distance. Teancum could hear the whispers between the people looking at him. He did not know why, but he felt very alone and very vulnerable at this moment. He had been in this building several times during his short career as a judge, but he did not remember this room. Looking around, he noticed the walls were made completely of stone and there was a high ceiling, much too high for a man to reach. "One door in and out, no windows or vents," he smirked and whispered. "A prison cell... or a tomb." Teancum lowered his head. "So, I am to be a prisoner." He said to himself. "What has happened to this world? A Nehor guards the main gate of the city and I am caged like an animal."

He lifted his head and could see Tum standing outside the doorway. Tum was arguing with someone who was wearing a bright colored cloak and fancy soft leather shoes. As he sat, Teancum noticed the type of footwear the people had on. He was judging them based on the practicality of their shoes and dress. He remembered his ordeal with not having the right clothing or proper shoes when he chased after the kidnappers. He was holding the strangers before him to that standard.

Weak and soft, he thought of one man, as he looked him over. *Useless*, he judged another. *Dead in a day, tops*, he thought of a fat man whose face was flush red while sweating from standing. Teancum smirked as he continued to look them over. Then he saw the guards at the door. They were standing outside the door and facing out not in toward him. *Funny*, he thought to himself. *If I am such a dangerous prisoner to be kept in isolation, why are the guards not watching me? Why do they guard the door and not the prisoner?* He was feeling very confused and frustrated when suddenly, the sounds of a man shouting came echoing through the room.

"Out of my way!" The boisterous and familiar command rang out. There was a crash of sounds—metal clanking off stone and heavy footsteps in the hall. Everyone who was standing outside the door quickly moved out of the way, making room for someone or something coming in this direction. "Where? Where is he?" The man's voice rang out again. The voice was much closer now. Teancum was searching his memory to place the voice with a face. He knew the voice, but his mind was too clouded to recognize it. Teancum looked at the doorway when the two guards moved from their positions, and saluted. "In there?" The unseen voice asked as both guards shook their heads in positive response to the question. One of the guards then gestured, with his free hand, into the room, telling the unseen man exactly where he could find Teancum.

"I know that voice." Teancum whispered. Something inside of him sparked to life as Teancum suddenly realized who was speaking. Before he could get out of his seat, Teancum came face-to-face with his father-in-law, the garrison commander. He entered the room like a half-crazed father searching for a lost child. He was fully armed; his metal breastplate glinted in the candlelight. Taking two steps into the room, the commander made eye contact with Teancum. The two men stood frozen, neither one knowing what to do. Hanni's regal mother stepped out from behind the commander's imposing frame, and entered the room. She had been crying but was trying to hold back her tears with a white handkerchief.

"Oh my dear, sweet boy!" She cried out with arms wide open, moving to embrace Teancum. Teancum took her completely in his arms, holding tightly as she sobbed, then kissed him on the cheek.

"It is him." The commander barked over his shoulder to the others

CHAPTER THREE

waiting in the doorway. He then moved to join the family reunion in the center of the room. The guards were dismissed. Most of the gathered onlookers slowly moved away. The drama was over and the truth had been revealed— Doctor Teancum had been found and returned home.

The three of them stood in the middle of the small room holding each other, examining faces, looking into each other's eyes, hugging and crying.

"Where have you been?" Hanni's mother spoke between sobs, as she softly pounded on Teancum's chest.

"Are you well? Do you need medical attention?" The commander, ever the good soldier, spoke next as he inspected Teancum's physique, seeing the wounds from his life in the wilds.

"Sir." Teancum called out in gentle protest to the commanders probing, "I am fine. A little underweight, but I will be okay." He then turned to the lady. "I was in the mountains, seeking revenge for what happened to them... To us." Teancum could see the level of sadness in Hanni's parents' eyes as he spoke these words. The only people in the entire world to suffer as much as he had over the criminal acts of those barbarians were the people in the room with him. This moment of raw emotion overwhelmed Teancum and he also began to cry. They all remained in the room holding each other and feeling the love and support they had all been missing since that tragic day.

Tum had made his way back into the room but stood a few paces off. When the emotions had begun to subside, he cleared his throat to let the commander know he was present. The old soldier turned to face Tum.

" Tum, it is good to see you again." The commander held out his hand to greet the butler and ranch master of his old and dear martyred friend Lord Pilio.

"And you commander, it is good to see you and your wife again, as well." Tum responded in his best and most proper manner as he took the soldier's hand and shook it. "My lord commander, there are several people outside who would like a word with Master Teancum."

"Nonsense!" The old soldier bellowed loudly enough for everyone in the area to hear. "He is coming home with us. When he is good and ready to entertain guests, I will let them know." The commander looked back at his wife, who was still clutching Teancum's waist. She nodded her head in approval. She would have been more diplomatic in her response, but she wanted out of the dank and dark room as badly as Teancum did. The commander wrapped his beefy arm around Teancum's shoulder, with his wife between them. Looking at the crowd in the doorway the commander shouted, "Make a hole!" He moved what remained of his family out through the door and down the long hallway. No one was going to attempt to stop the garrison commander of all the Nephite military forces in the capital city of Zarahemla, from walking out the justice building with his family. When he gave the word, the people who were standing in the hallway and door moved to make way for him. Like Moses cutting a path through the Red Sea, the way down the hall was opened as the fellow Nephites parted, then closed behind them. Teancum and his in-laws walked toward the evening sunlight coming in from the exit.

CHAPTER FOUR

Teancum Meets Moroni

Tum spent the rest of the night and some of the next morning making sure Teancum was settled in at his in-laws' cottage on the military base. The sleeping arrangements at the ranch were not ideal, but they were much better than the ground Teancum had called a bed when was in the wilds. So when he awoke the next morning after a restless night sleeping in his first real bed in over two years, Teancum felt sore and awkward. He walked barefoot, into the dining area, still half-asleep and rubbing his back. "Good morning, dear." Hanni's mother called out as she sat at the grand table, eating her breakfast. "The commander will be in shortly. He and Tum are speaking on the porch." She flicked her hand in the general direction of the front porch, giving the impression she did not know, or even care, what the two men were speaking about— but everyone knew the truth. Nothing happening in the house, or on the military base, without her knowing. Teancum grinned when she spoke as he quickly remembered her mannerisms.

"Thank you, ma'am," he spoke, then nodded, and moved to the doorway to walk outside. He knew what she was really saying: "I know exactly what they are talking about and you, young man, need to go outside to join them."

Teancum reached the front door of the large cottage, then stopped just before walking out. He could hear Tum speaking. "If you had *seen* what I saw. If you had only seen what he is capable of!"

"I am not turning the only remaining member of my family into a weapon!" The commander barked back.

"Not a weapon." Tum moved in his seat to look the old soldier in the

CHAPTER FOUR

eyes. "Make him a leader."

Teancum did not like the fact the two of them were talking about him so he walked out onto the porch. "Make who a leader?" he interrupted. He startled them both with his sudden appearance. They turned in their seats to face him.

"Good morning, Master Teancum." Tum spoke as he rose from his seat to greet Teancum.

"Is this about me?" He could see his sudden appearance had made the two older gentlemen uneasy. "What are the two of you plotting?"

"Son, please sit down." The commander gently spoke as he handed Teancum a cup of juice and pointed to the empty chair next to him. Teancum took the cup and sat down facing Tum and his father-in-law.

"What of the guards from yesterday? Are they hurt badly?" Teancum inquired remorsefully.

"None the worse for wear." The old soldier moved in his seat. "I was informed by the sheriff your actions at the gate yesterday actually helped to uncover a Nehor plot. After he was taken for questioning, the boy with the tattoo suddenly became more than helpful in letting us know about plans to rob a large caravan set to arrive in a few days."

Teancum sneered as he drank for the cup. " Typical— my experience with the Nehor showed me who they really are. Most of them are nothing more than cowards who use the mystique of the Nehor name to get respect. They would mostly run and cower, begging for mercy when confronted."

"And the others? You said *most* of them?" The commander asked. Like any good military leader, he was pressing for better intelligence on his enemies.

"Well, there is a reason they are feared and respected. A few of them are very dangerous." Teancum stopped speaking and his expression went blank. He was remembering the hard times and it showed on his face.

"But you survived." Tum reassured him. "Not only the wilds, but the criminal hordes who roam the mountains and trade routes." Tum's voice was like an anchor for Teancum's thoughts. Tum reached out as he spoke and put his hand on Teancum's forearm for support.

"Yes." Teancum smiled and took another drink, finishing the glass and holding it out for a refill. "Yes I did." The juice was cool and sweet. It helped to calm his mind.

"Can you explain to me, son, how you managed to survive?" The commander asked as he poured more of the sweet, amber-colored liquid into Teancum's cup.

Teancum lowered his head. "I figured you would have asked me about the babies, or Hanni." It was clear Teancum was uncomfortable but determined to continue the conversation.

"I know something of the wounds of battle." The old soldier took control of the conversation but kept his demeanor calm. He was a good man and had experienced the emotions Teancum was dealing with himself. "When you are ready, we can talk about my grandchildren. But for now there is a pressing need to confront the Nehor and the Lamanite raiders threatening our city, and I need your help."

Teancum nodded his head up and down to let the two other men know he was still in the conversation. " The Nehor are set up like a military unit. They have commanders, lieutenants and soldiers. Each man has a job: common soldiers, scouts, enforcers, logistics…assassins." He made eye contact with the commander as spoke the last word. " They are even involved in politics." Tum and the old man looked at each other when Teancum spoke of the political arena, suggesting they knew something Teancum did not know and were afraid to tell him.

"I thought I would have made a difference with my actions these last two years. But clearly, if they are still planning and committing crimes, then my efforts have had little effect."

"On the contrary." The commander interrupted. "Your actions in the forest pushed them out into the open and exposed them to us as never before."

Tum continued the conversation. "In the past six months, local officials have made several high-profile arrests of ranking members of Zarahemla society with ties to the Nehor." He raised his own cup up in a small toast to Teancum. "All because of the fear they had for the Ghost Soldier. They were forced out of the shadows of the trees and rocks and into the city where we could see them better."

"Like a pebble dropped into a pond, the ripple effect of your brave actions have helped all of the Nephites be more secure." The wise old commander spread his hands out away from his body to demonstrate how vast Teancum's effects could be. There was a long pause as Teancum absorbed his words. He was gaining courage from the knowledge his actions had a greater affect on the Nehors than only fulfilling his desire for vengeance.

CHAPTER FOUR

Moving his head as if he agreed with the two older men, Teancum turned to look at Tum as he asked a question. "You spoke of making me a leader, what did you mean?"

Tum pointed to the commander sitting next to him and responded. "I was explaining to your father-in-law that we have a unique opportunity now that you have returned to us." Teancum furrowed his brow in a questioning gesture. "Allow me to explain." Tum adjusted in his seat to face Teancum as he continued. "As you know, the Sons of Nehor started out as a religious cult following the teachings of a man named Nehor. After Nehor was put to death for killing the hero Gideon," Tum paused and looked at Teancum to ensure he knew the story and was following along. "His followers went underground and began their crime spree. But now, not only are they a criminal syndicate, they have infiltrated every facet of Nephite life. Politics, education, commerce, the military, they are everywhere and people are afraid to even speak up."

Teancum slowly sat back in his chair as he soaked in the information. All this time he only thought they were a loosely organized band of criminal thugs. He had no idea how deep the evil infection had spread. Tum continued, "We have lost more than one leader who dared to stand up to them. The ones they could not buy off were found dead." Tum made a quick glance toward the commander.

Teancum caught the glance. "What?" He asked.

"There was an attempt on my life a while back." The old soldier spoke matter-of-factly. "Fools, the lot of them!" He snorted. "Clearly they underestimated me."

'What? What happened!?" Teancum was outraged.

"A story for another day." The commander retorted. "Let Tum finish."

"Thank you, my lord commander." Tum quickly spoke to direct the focus back on the events at hand. "What is needed now is a strong charismatic leader who is fearless and well respected." Tum gestured with his hand toward Teancum.

"Wait—" Teancum tried to interject but he was stopped by Tum.

"Please, let me finish before you respond. A great many of the people of Zarahemla know who you are Teancum, but outside those high walls you are another face in the crowd. On the other hand, everyone from the lowest stable boy living in a village far from here, to the Chief Judge of the land, and the High Priest himself sitting in the temple knows the story of the Ghost Soldier. Your alter ego has become larger than life; you are a legend now. We can use your reputation as a warrior and your skill as a politician and doctor to unravel the Sons of Nehor and root out the evil once and for all."

"But…" Teancum again tried to stop this conversation but Tum was having none of it. He was on a roll now and there was no way he was going to let Teancum interrupt him until he had said his piece.

"No one knows the Nehor like you do. No one is feared by the Nehor like the Ghost Soldier. You are loved and respected by the Nephite people, and hated and feared by your enemies. That puts you in a perfect position to assume command and take the fight to the bandits on a much larger scale than you had ever dreamed." Tum smiled as he finished those words. He had hoped he would say the right things to inspire his young friend into action.

Teancum was expressionless, his eyes darted back and forth in his head as he pondered what Tum had said. "Command? You said take command— command of what?"

Tum nodded at the old soldier to answer Teancum's question. Teancum turned to face his father-in-law and waited for the answer. Slowly the words came out of the tired warrior. "They killed most of my family, they almost killed me and my wife." He took a big breath as he tried to calmly speak the next few words. Clearly this part of the conversation was upsetting to the commander but he held his emotions in check and continued. "I cannot ask my only living relative to risk his life once again…" This was becoming too much for him.

He lowered his head as he spoke the next few words. He was in pain, but he understood doing one's duty comes with a price. It was a price only people of honor paid, and exactly what made people honorable— persevering through the sting of the refiner's fire. "But the need is too great and justice must be done if we are to all live in true peace." The old soldier looked back up at Teancum. "If you accept, you will have the pick of the litter. The finest men under my command will be at your disposal. Train them as you see fit, lead them against the Nehor where ever they may be, and exterminate them from the Nephite lands. You will be free to use whatever means necessary to fight them, staying within the bounds of the laws of God and of this land." He leaned in close to Teancum. "You must remain confined by the law. If you do not follow the law, then you will be no better than the criminals you hunt."

Something stirred inside of Teancum as he sat there and listened to the words of his father-in-law. Something deep within him— a spark of fervent truth was igniting a flame he had tried to extinguish and move away from.

But he knew.

Deep down in the dark recesses of his soul, Teancum knew who he was. He knew he was very good at what he did. He knew he was good at hunting and killing the scum who murdered and robbed innocent folk. As he listened, it became clear that whatever it was— fate, divine intervention, the luck of the stars, whatever was controlling his destiny— he knew his life's circumstances had brought him to this point in time and he knew he was the best man for the job. The problem now was convincing himself he wanted the job.

Tum and the old commander finished pleading their case before Teancum and they left him to consider their offer. "Command of a fighting force, charged with ridding the land of the accursed Nehor, how did I end up here?" Teancum shook his head and laughed quietly to himself as he contemplated his future. He was leaning over the rail of the porch and watching as the military recruits marched past the cottage on their way to the morning formations when he sensed someone standing close to him. He turned and found his ever-cheerful mother-in-law standing next to him. She was slowing sipping from a large cup of herbal tea. She was still in her morning robe and her hair was loosely bound.

"All done with your morning conversation?" She spoke sweetly with a gleam in her eye as she took another sip.

"Yes ma' am." Teancum replied as he stood up straight. He had not forgotten his manners. *In the presence of a lady, you will always stand up tall and proud and speak with kindness*, the voice of his grandfather echoed in his mind.

"Good. So when do you start?"

Teancum blinked several times. He was not surprised she knew of the content of their conversation. She had her finger on everything happening in her world. He was taken back by her forward question. She may outwardly appear to be a kind, high-born lady, but Teancum knew she could scheme with the best of them.

"Uh, I have not really—" He tried to stammer out some type of response but she was well ahead of him.

"Of course you have, dear." She smiled and patted his arm. "You go and give those cursed barbarians a dose of their own medicine." She continued in her best 'regal grandmother' facade. " Trust in the Lord God and all will be well, you will see." Simple and to the point, her pep talk was over and she sipped again at her tea and hummed as she turned and walked to the other side of the porch and sat in her favorite sunchair. "Good morning ladies!" She called out to two other women walking past her home. They both acknowledged her and waved back.

Teancum smiled and shook his head. He knew there was no sense in trying to argue or state his point of view. She was right and she knew it. "Like mother, like daughter," he whispered, and reflected on happier times when he was the husband to his dear departed Hanni. As if she had heard him say those words, his mother-in-law looked back at him and winked. *Justice*, rang out in his inner ear. He knew in that moment what he had to do. Teancum looked back out at the coming day and the people moving around the camp. "Well…" He murmured to himself after drinking the remains of the juice in his cup. "That's that."

The garrison commander used his political influence and arranged to speak during the next meeting of the grand council of judges. A few days later, the meeting hall was filled to capacity. Tum and the commander felt that if the people knew about the topic of the meeting and the idea they were proposing, and showed their support, the idea would be accepted.

The word was carefully leaked out the Ghost Soldier would be at the meeting, and he would be speaking about fighting the Nehor. That alone drew the interest of many who came to see firsthand if the stories were true about Teancum not only being alive, but also the Ghost Soldier. After the invocation and introductions were made, the meeting was called to order and the weekly business of governing the land was quickly dispensed with. Even the judges wanted to hear from the guest speaker and, considering the audience chamber was standing-room only, they kept their comments brief and to the point. This was a pleasant surprise for those who know how politicians think. Many sitting in the chamber wondered why all business of the government couldn't be handled like this all the time— quick, efficient and to the point.

"Quiet in the chamber!" A very serious-looking man with a trimmed beard and large wooden staff in his hand barked several times. The people in the chamber were growing restless and loud. He pounded on the wooden floor with his staff and continued to shout, "Quiet in the

CHAPTER FOUR

chamber!"

Most of the gathered were there to see and hear from the Ghost Soldier. But there were others in the crowd who supported the Nehor; they had ulterior motives. The Nehor clan feared only one man—Teancum. He had done more damage and killed more members of the brotherhood then the entire Nephite army. Teancum had found a way to defeat them by using their tactics against them. If the rumors were true, and Teancum was going to ask permission from the people to build a fighting force with the one goal of eliminating the Nehor, they needed to find a way to stop him. So they were first going to try to use their community organizers to gain support for the Nehor among the commoners and plant the seeds of distrust for Teancum and his planned efforts to enforce the laws of the land.

"I heard he went mad in the forest." One man would whisper loud enough for those gathered around him to hear as he spoke to his friend. He was hoping to cast a shadow of doubt over those Nephites standing nearby, while another man at the opposite side of the chamber was doing the exact same thing. "My brother said he saw this Teancum murder innocent people on the road, and claim they were Nehor criminals…" They were all lies, but the Nehor did not care. They wanted power and wealth and they were willing to do anything to stop Teancum from interfering with their plans.

Other Nehor supporters were tasked with open defiance. Those men would shout out and try to disrupt the proceedings by pushing people in the crowd or challenging the soldiers who were guarding the building and keeping order. When some of the dissenters became too unruly, the guards would grab hold of them and forcefully remove them from the chamber. As they were being removed, the Nehor infiltrators would shout out for the crowd to hear. "Do you see how they treat someone who does not think like them and agree with them? My rights are being trampled, I am not resisting!"

The man with the wooden staff was finally able to get the crowd to settle down, so he proceeded to announce the speaker. "Ladies and gentlemen, The Council of Judges has decided the remainder of the time this evening will be allotted to a guest speaker." The crowd cheered, but there were a few boos as well. The crowd settled and Teancum moved forward toward the podium from a side room flanked by the commander and several of his personal guards. The word was out, and the Nehor were not happy about the government's move to create an armed force with the task of dealing with them. The commander was taking no chances. Ironically, some of the armored soldiers walking with Teancum had been the commander's guards when Teancum was courting Hanni. Those soldiers who knew him as a boy were beaming with pride and being especially careful now.

Teancum looked out from his place at the podium. "My fellow judges, honored guests, and ladies and gentlemen of the Nephite nation." Teancum began, "My name is Doctor Teancum of the house of Pilio, common judge of Zarahemla… And I am the Ghost Soldier."

The crowd erupted.

"Silence!" The man with the wooden staff shouted as he pounded on the floor. Teancum stood still as the people cheered him and the proclamation he was truly the face behind the mysterious stories and plague to the Nehors. As Teancum waited for the gathered to settle, he detected some movement out of the corner of his eye. Before he even realized he was reacting, his left hand came up and he caught a large apple in flight headed right for his face. Instantly the audience gasped and then became quiet. Teancum, holding the apple out for all to see turned to face the man who threw the fruit at him. The man was stunned Teancum foiled his plan and was counting on the confusion his stunt would have caused to cover his escape. Now he stood alone with Teancum, and all the other Nephites staring at him.

"Seize him." Teancum spoke in an emotionless monotone. Fifty hands shot out of the crowd and before the man could react he was hoisted up off his feet and being carried forward by several others toward where the guards were waiting.

"I did nothing wrong! Release me, you are being judgmental toward me because of my beliefs!" The man was twisting and shouting as the crowd took control of him. It was the standard Nehor response to the crowd's negative reactions. The good people where having none of it. They were tired of the cursed Nehor and their wave of illegal activities. With Teancum's return, they now had a leader who would stand up to the Nehors, thus restoring power back to the people. The man was bound and led away from the great hall to the cheers of the vast majority.

Others in the crowd were not so happy at the outcome. They made eye contact with each other and the signal was given for them to withdraw and reconsider their approach to dealing with Teancum. From his vantage

CHAPTER FOUR

point, Teancum could see the Nehor supporters moving toward the exits, and he made a mental note of their faces and dress.

The man who appeared to be directing the Nehor movements stopped before he walked out of the great hall and turned to look back at Teancum. He was a large man with dark hair and eyes. His beard was trimmed to a point at the base of his chin and there was a scar across his cheek. Teancum and the bearded man locked eyes and volumes were spoken in silence. Teancum knew he had the upper hand and he wanted to make a point to the Nehor leader. He smiled, took a large bite out of the apple and chewed it with his mouth open. 'I am the Ghost Soldier,' Teancum's gesture of biting the apple told the Nehor. 'and I am coming for you.' The Nehor smirked and spun on his heels, moving out the exit before the guards realized he was also involved in the disruption.

Order was quickly restored and Teancum raised up his hands for the crowd to listen. "My story is simple. Two years ago I was living among you, working and raising my family the best way I could. But that was all taken from me by the Nehor." The great hall was filled to capacity and everyone in attendance nodded their heads as Teancum spoke. He was one of them, he was a much respected doctor and politician. Most had heard the story of the raid and tragedy at the ranch of Lord and Lady Pilio. "I went into the woods to try to save my only remaining daughter, but… I failed. She too was murdered right before my eyes, by a man whose final words were his pledge of allegiance to that barbarous clan."

This was part of the story no one knew. There were gasps and cries as Teancum continued to speak. A few even dabbed away the tears in their eyes. They could all see the pain on his face and hear the sincerity in Teancum's voice as he spoke. "I was all alone and ready to die because of what they had done to me." He paused to draw strength from the air he breathed deeply. "But I was inspired by a higher power to live and fight on; some may call it God, or the powers of the universe, or the fates. Regardless, I spent the next two years learning their ways, and then exacting true justice on those who would murder and rob the innocent and helpless." The crowd clapped and cheered. They all knew he had driven the Nehor out of the hills and exposed them for who they were. "I came home to find some measure of peace and try to move on with my life. But the Nehor had other plans and they attacked me and those I love and care for." He turned and made eye contact with his in-laws who were sitting behind him near the judge's bench, and they smiled back. "They brought the fight to me and my kin, and now I am ready to answer the challenge." He paused and looked down at some notes he had written on a scrap of papyrus.

Taking a deep breath, Teancum looked back up at the adoring crowd and continued. They all knew what was going to happen. They were just waiting to hear it from Teancum himself. "After careful consideration and prayer, I have decided to volunteer for the army. I am here to ask the council of judges and the people of Zarahemla for a commission into the military and to be granted the rank of captain." More gasps of joy come from the crowd and a few shouts of encouragement.

Some of the judges moved nervously in their seats at Teancum's words. More than one of them had been bribed by the Nehor to render judgement in the clan's favor. The last thing they wanted was to be exposed by the Ghost Soldier, and they did not like where this was going. "I am volunteering to train and lead a new elite unit of soldiers. I will teach them in the new ways of fighting that I have discovered and perfected during my time in the wilds. This new unit will have one goal in mind— to take the fight to the enemy of freedom and root them out of every dark corner of this land." His voice raised as he spoke with more passion now, using his hands to help emphasize his words. "Justice; this word has been ringing in my ears from the very start of my path down this road." He scanned the crowd and continued. "I have learned true peace is not the absence of conflict, but the presence of justice, and justice is the first duty of a government. Without true justice none of this is possible." He held out both hands to gesture to the gathered that they are all involved. "I am a man of action, not words. I offer my services to the Nephite people and ask only one thing in return— your trust and support." He took two steps back from the podium as the audience went wild.

The word went out for any able-bodied man who wanted to volunteer for Captain Teancum's new unit to gather one week later. As promised, Teancum, the commander and his two trusted lieutenants were standing inside the closed gate to the garrison camp. It was moments before dawn, and they wanted a look at the volunteers who had answered the call. To Teancum's surprise, when he looked out past the iron bars of the locked gate he could not see the end of the line which had formed. It looked like

CHAPTER FOUR

some of the men had been there all night and slept outside the gate just for a chance at joining up with the Ghost Soldier.

"Gracious," the old commander spoke, "I have never seen a group this large for a military recruitment." As the commander continued to look over the line of waiting hopefuls, one of his own men from his personal security detail approached.

"Sir!" The armored guard called out.

"Yes, what is it?" The commander replied without taking his eyes off the spectacle in the street.

"The invitation to join up with Captain Teancum, does it extend to all current members of the army?"

"Yes…?" The commander almost sounded annoyed with his answer.

The guard smiled and put his thumb and finger in his mouth and whistled and waved to some unseen men near the main barracks. At his signal, a flood of soldiers came out and walked toward the gate.

"Sir." Gid nudged his leader and gestured with his head for the older man to look behind him. The commander spun around and his eyes grew wide as he watched many of his own soldiers walking toward the gate to take their place in the tryout process.

"It's not personal, sir." The original guard spoke. He could see the look in the old man's eyes as soldier after soldier moved past him and out the gate. "The boys and I are grateful for your leadership and guidance, we just…" he lowered his head as he tried to say the next few words. "We just wanted to fight for our freedom, and it sounds like this new unit is going to be in the thick of things."

"I understand." The commander put his hand on the young warrior's shoulder. "If I was thirty years younger I would be out there in line with you." He winked and smiled. "Now, off with you. Go before your place in line is taken." The young soldier smiled back and after saluting his leader, he raced to join his comrades.

"You are creating something special here, Teancum." The old soldier declared after a few moments of awkward silence.

"Thank you sir, although I do not know quite where to start."

"I will be here to assist you, and you have the use of two of my best lieutenants." The commander gestured toward Gid and Teomner, "But most importantly, you must trust in God."

Teancum was caught off guard by his last statement. Religion was rarely discussed in the open around his in-laws. To hear this man speak of relying on the grace of God was very unusual.

"I will," Teancum responded with some hesitancy.

The commander smiled and turned to walk away. "Oh, one last thing." He stopped and spoke. "I have informed Chief Captain Joshua of your plans, and he will be coming by to check on your progress. His son Lieutenant Moroni would be a fine candidate for your new unit. The boy is a bit young, but he is big and strong and has a commanding presence."

"Yes, sir." Teancum responded as his mind flashed back to his first meeting with Chief Captain Joshua when Teancum was a young medical intern and helping those wounded soldiers on the grassy area outside the hospital.

The moment had come for Teancum to begin the grandest adventure of his life. The rest of the first day was spent conducting individual interviews with the volunteers. Teancum, Gid and Teomner sat together behind a small desk in a brightly lit room and personally interviewed each man.

As the morning progressed, Teancum was not sure what he was looking for, but he knew that when he recognized that intangible warrior spirit, he would add the respective man's name to his list. "Keep your list to yourself," he told his two assistants prior to starting the day. "Don't show me your names. If you like someone, write them down and make a note explaining why you like him. At the end of the interview process, we will compare our notes and start our unit with the men all three of us independently agree upon."

Teancum kept good notes, and was surprised at the quality and diversity of candidates parading before him. Old and young, from experienced fighters to artisans, farmers and shop owners. Men who were in peak physical shape, to some who had no business on the battlefield. So many different sizes and shapes, with such varied levels of experience not just in combat, but life itself. The only commonality was a desire to serve their country and fight the Nehor scum. After several hours of asking questions and listening to each man explain why he was there to volunteer for this dangerous assignment, Teancum called for a break so he and his two assistants could enjoy a quick lunch and discuss how the day had progressed.

"Thoughts, gentlemen?" The three men were sitting in the afternoon sun on a bench behind the main building on the army post with stacks of parchment papers and plates of food before them.

CHAPTER FOUR

Gid was drinking when Teancum asked the question so Teomner spoke first. "Well sir, there are some very good candidates, and some who I am still scratching my head as to why they even showed up."

"Agreed." Gid spoke after swallowing the liquid and gesturing with the cup still in his hand. "Some of them are nothing more than soft and pampered children, while others have seen too many winters and are past their prime."

"Gentlemen," Teancum gently reminded them of some facts. "I was soft and pampered when the Nehor attacked my home, remember?" They both reflected on the past and collectively nodded their heads. Of course they remembered— they were assigned to protect him and were both at the ranch during the raid. "Your garrison commander is more than twice your age, and do either of you doubt his fighting abilities?" He was trying to make a point and gave them a questioning look. "It's not how you start the race that matters, as much as how you finish. Some of these men are looking for inspiration and a reason to change their lives for the better. First, we need to find the ones with the warrior spirit and then help them bring it out." Teancum took a bite of the roasted meat before him and chewed quickly. "We can teach them to think like soldiers." He continued as he swallowed the food in his mouth. "We can train them to be stronger and faster, we can show them how to use their weapons and work like a team… But what we cannot do is change their hearts."

Teancum paused as he cut more meat into bite-size pieces. "That is what I am looking for." He tapped his list with his knife. "The men who have the heart of a warrior. The rest will come with time and training." He took another bite and stopped talking as he chewed. While we was chewing, he looked at both of his lieutenants for some sign of understanding.

"I did see a few I thought had something extra, something special about them." Gid spoke. "Like the blacksmith from the south end of the city, do you remember him? The big guy with the arms of iron." Gid looked at Teomner.

"I do, he is on my list too."

"As well as mine." Teancum added. He got a little excited and wanted to see if they saw the same thing he did. "So tell me, what about the smith did you like?"

The conversation went on for about an hour. They spoke about those who impressed them. From the morning's interviews, the names of twenty strong and capable men made it on the final list. Men of conviction and personal courage, men who had overcome hardships and proven their worth to society. Most had skills and abilities outside of the military which Teancum found very useful. If he was truly going to take the fight to the Nehor, he would need men who understood commerce, the trades, craftsmanship and such.

The day progressed, and by sundown they had finished meeting with the first batch of volunteers. Teancum was a politician in his past life and had forgotten how exhausting sitting and talking all day could be. The three of them met back at the bench behind the main building with their supper to discuss their findings. When they were done, they had a list of thirty more men who they all agreed would move to the next phase of training. Teancum wanted to establish a small cohort of men to act as junior officers and sergeants for his unit. His hope was to personally train this first batch of fifty men and stand up the unit, then have those he trained continue the training and recruit more men to fill the ranks until he had a force of three hundred warriors.

The next morning a large formation was called and the names of the first fifty were read off. Those who did not hear their names were told to not be discouraged and to look for additional chances to join in the near future. They were thanked for their time and dismissed. When the rest had cleared off the grass-covered parade grounds, the remaining men whose names were called were assembled into two platoons of twenty five. Gid and Teomner stood at the head of each platoon and Teancum addressed them all.

"Gentlemen, thank you for answering the call for volunteers to join with me in fighting the Nehor." Teancum was standing on a raised wooden platform. As he spoke he cast his eyes over the gathered men. He observed they were all fit and physically capable men. Some were tall and others were short. Some were large and robust men, bristling with muscles, while others were thin and lean like distance runners. Regardless of size or age, every man had a fire in his eyes and a desire to see justice done. Teancum liked what he saw.

"I am not going to be easy on you as we train together. My officers and I will bear every burden with you, hike every mountain, run over every obstacle, climb every rope and tree, swim every river and learn every task. We will bond like a family and think and move like one man. I will only promise you two things if you make it through the training and become a member of my team." He held up his first finger. "One—you will become a honed weapon, forged in the fire of adversity and ready at a moment's notice to strike anywhere, under any condition, with any weapon at your disposal." The men looking up at Teancum were exhilarated at his words. "And two—" He held up his second finger. "You will face the enemy in mortal combat." Teancum's words ignited a thunderous response from the men; they all wanted to prove to Teancum they deserved a spot in his elite group of warriors. Teancum let them cheer and congratulate each other for a few moments then he held up his hands to tell the men to quiet down. "Training starts in five minutes. Secure your gear in the bunk house behind you and report back here ready to exercise. Officers, take control of your men and get them ready to run."

"Sir, yes sir!" Both Gid and Teomner shouted back in unison. They both gave a hand salute and Teancum returned it and then moved off the podium.

The men were dismissed and there was a moment of clustering and confusion as the men all tried to enter the bunk house at the same time with their meager belongings. Gid and Teomner were shouting and pushing them as the men quickly found beds and stored their gear. Some men had different footwear they wanted to put on to exercise in, while others were changing clothing or trying to stow their gear.

As Teancum stood at the bottom of the podium waiting for his men to return he was met by the garrison commander who had walked up.

"Good morning, sir." Teancum greeted his father-in-law with the appropriate measure of military courtesy.

"Good morning, Captain." He seemed overly cheerful this morning. "I thought I would come by and see how the first day was progressing. He looked out at the ground in front of the podium as some of the men started to return from the bunk house and reform into their platoons. "Going to do some physical exercise this morning, I see. Not going to ease them into the life of army training?" The seasoned soldier asked in a rhetorical and sarcastic tone.

"No, sir." Teancum winked. Gid and Teomner both came up to Teancum and the commander and saluted.

"All accounted for and ready for training sir." Teomner advised. "May I ask what the plan is for the morning workout sir?"

Teancum got a sudden idea and looked back at his father-in-law. "In honor of the commander, I thought we could play his favorite exercise game: follow the leader."

Gid and Teomner both looked at each other and shook their heads. They both worked for the commander and they both knew this game very well.

"With your permission, sir?" Teancum turned and saluted his commander, who was grinning from ear to ear.

"Carry on, son."

Teancum dropped his salute and looked over his left shoulder. "Follow me, boys— follow the leader!" He shouted and took off through the gates and into the city like a rabbit.

There was some confusion among the troops. Gid and Teomner looked at each other, shrugged their shoulders and took deep reassuring breaths. "Let's go, boys!" Gid shouted as he and Teomner took off after Teancum. The rest of the unit figured it out and sprinted to catch up. The old commander remained standing alone with a wide grin on his face as the last of the new recruits disappeared around the corner.

"Glad I don't need to do to that anymore." He whispered as he turned his tired old body and walked away.

In the shadows, a pair of watchful eyes kept a very close account of the day's events. The Nehor were scared, and with good reason. One Ghost Soldier was almost too much for them; an entire military group of Ghost Soldiers would mark their doom.

The training Teancum was putting his men through was revolutionary. With an emphasis on physical fitness, Teancum was breaking down the individual and rebuilding the men into a team. There was no way any of them were going to survive out there fighting the Nehor if they did not learn to work and function as one. So everything Teancum had them do was focused on them working together. In pairs, as a small group or all together, toiling at the same time, the emphasis was always on teamwork, accountability and never leaving a man behind.

After several weeks of hard physical training, the men were ready to cycle into phase two of Teancum's plan. The first few weeks were rough, and Teancum made no apologies for it. He lost a few men along the way to injuries and some refusing to continue. Those who were injured were welcome to return and continue training where they left off with the next batch of recruits after they had properly healed. Those who quit were given a hot meal, a warm bath, and unceremoniously escorted from the post. Everyone knew this was going to be demanding on their bodies and

CHAPTER FOUR

minds. So when they quit, they were told they would need to wait one full year before they could re-apply and they would start all over from day one with the training.

All of this was done out in the open where the Nephite citizens could watch and be inspired by the hard work and dedication of the men striving to become Ghost Soldiers. Teancum also did this in the open so the Nehor spies could see the men going through the hard training and report back to the clan's grand council. Teancum knew most of the members of the Nehor clan were cowards. He hoped he could cause a panic among the members and get some of them to quit. This way he could avoid the shedding of blood and still accomplish his mission of dismantling their criminal network.

Weapons and special tactics training came next. Teancum had the weapons experts from the army come and teach the men how to use all of the hand weapons in the Nephite arsenal. Swords both big and small, shields, spears, bow and arrow, clubs, darts, slings, javelins, the small and large axe— every weapon used by the army was explained and trained with. Most of the men were veterans of the regular army, but Teancum wanted everyone on his team to learn and train together. So he started from the very basics and raised everyone up at the same time. This gave the men in his unit with experience an opportunity to assist and help train and lead the other men. Learning and growing together helped in building the bonds of brotherhood within the group.

The days started to blur together for the men as a routine was established. Hard, task-oriented, physical training in the morning, followed by weapons drills until lunch. The afternoons were spent learning the fieldcraft which helped make Teancum so successful at killing the bandits. Camouflage, tracking, stalking, observation, reconnaissance and intelligence gathering, pioneering, map reading and orientation, field medicine— all of it was useful and all of it Teancum had learned the hard way.

Once the men had all demonstrated a basic understanding of the common tasks he would be asking them to perform, Teancum started to introduce them to some of his more unconventional methods of dealing with the Nehor. One morning Teancum had taken them on a long run through the countryside. The run had lasted all morning and it ended when the men reached a large stream near a pasture and some barns. The men were allowed to cool themselves in the water and relax while

Teancum walked over to the barns and spoke to a farm hand. After a few moments the farm hand returned with a large cow in tow. The cow was led into a large corral and the men were all called to gather around.

"Men!" Teancum spoke loudly so everyone could hear him. "What I am going to show you now is highly classified and must not be discussed outside of our unit. Is that clear?"

'Sir, yes sir!' was the unison response. No one was going to violate the code of conduct Teancum had established. They had all come too far and suffered too much to risk being dismissed from the unit. It was more than their jobs at stake if there was a violation of the codes. Their personal honor would be questioned, and to a Ghost Soldier that was a fate worse than death.

Teancum walked out into the middle of the corral and removed a small hollowed out gourd from his satchel. Teancum removed the cover from off the small gourd. It contained a sticky black substance. "Do not touch or inhale, just look and see," he said as he walked past the men showing them the substance inside the container. Teancum reached back inside his well-worn satchel and removed a long hollow reed, and several small fragments of bone shaped and honed into darts. Teancum dipped the sharp end of one of the darts into the black sticky substance, then put the dart into the reed. He held the reed up to his mouth and blew hard on one end, causing the dart to fly out of the other side. The dart traveled quickly across the corral and stuck into the side of the cow's neck. Almost instantly the cow started to bellow as its body began to jerk and spasm. After kicking and bucking for a few seconds, the cow's body stiffened, it snorted loudly, then it fell over, hitting the ground dead.

There was a collective gasp from the men standing around the corral. Teancum put the reed and the small gourd back into his satchel and walked over to where the famer was standing. Teancum handed the farmer a small bag of coins and patted him on the shoulder. " Thank you again for your assistance." He spoke low enough only the famer could hear him. "Remember, do not eat the meat— it is now tainted with the poison."

The farmer did not look surprised or upset Teancum had just killed one of his animals. Teancum had planned this moment ahead of time and the farmer was in on the example. Teancum left the farmer and walked back to the center of the corral. "What did you all just witness?" He asked the men. Teancum waited for a response but no one committed. They

CHAPTER FOUR

were all still in shock at seeing such a small item like the bone dart kill such a large beast. "Many of you know I was a physician once, and one of my jobs was to find cures for many of the fevers and poxes that plague our people from time to time. During my research I discovered a certain combination of ingredients, in just the right dosage, can be lethal." He gestured toward the lifeless cow. "I am sharing the knowledge of this poison with you because as Ghost Soldiers, you will be asked to fight the enemy in an unconventional way." Teancum was walking in a circle as he spoke and trying to make eye contact with as many of his men as he could. "I have found this method very useful in the wilds, and I know you will too." Teancum gestured toward Teomner who was holding a box in his hands. "Gentlemen, if you will each pass by Lieutenant Teomner and retrieve one reed and a few bone darts we will then begin the training for the day." A line was quickly formed and each man in the unit was given a hollow reed and several polished bone darts. Captain Teancum gave a quick block of instruction on how to load and use the blow darts, then the men broke into groups and practiced hitting different targets like hay bales, or small hunks of metal and wood dangling from trees, all set up by the farmer.

After an hour of practice Teancum called the men back together. As expected, his Ghost Soldiers quickly adapted to the new weapon and they began to challenge each other by adding movement and distance to their attempts to hitting the targets. "Men, the recipe for the poison will remain a secret, but I will make enough for each of you to have a portion." He paused so he could emphasize the next point. "It is only to be used against the enemy, and only for the enforcement of our laws in defense of life and against invasion. Are we clear?"

"Sir, yes sir!" The response echoed off the mountains and rang in the trees.

"Excellent! Now, on to the next item." Teancum reached back into his satchel and pulled out his trusty bola. "Some of you will know what this is, but most of you have never seen this before." He spoke as he loosely swung the ends of the bola out in front of him. "Lieutenant Gid, would you do the honors?"

"Sir...?" Gid questioned. He knew what the bola was but he was unsure what Teancum wanted him to do.

"Run, lieutenant— run." Teancum had a mischievous grin on his face and was swinging the bola faster and above his head.

Teancum Meets Moroni

"Go!" Teomner pushed Gid to start running away from Teancum.

"Oh no!" Gid gasped as he took off at a sprint. He knew what Teancum was wanting to do, and he wanted no part of it.

All of the Ghost Soldiers watched in puzzlement as Teancum planted his feet and let the bola fly right at Gid as he tried to put distance between himself and his Captain. The bola made a swooshing sound as it cut through the air and almost instantly found its mark. One of the weighted ends found Gid's left leg, and started to wrap itself around it as the other two ends snapped and caught up around his right leg. Gid's legs were hopelessly entangled in the long leads and he went down with a thud. A cheer went out from the gathered as they quickly understood what this new device Teancum was showing them could do. Teancum was laughing as he ran up to Gid and helped him untangle the bola from around his legs.

"You could have warned me you were going to do that." Gid spoke under his breath to his commander.

" True…" Teancum responded with a laugh. "But where would the fun be in that?" He held out his hand as an offering to assist Gid up and off the grassy pasture.

"Your toy, my Captain." Gid sarcastically quipped as he held out the bola for Teancum to take back. Gid knew his friend and captain would never purposely try to hurt him, and he was none the worse for wear. The two men had a quick laugh and they returned back to the unit.

"Men, gather round!" Teancum shouted. "We are all charged with bringing the Nehor and Lamanite bandits to justice. We must always stay within the confines of the laws of the land. So every opportunity must be taken to apprehend the criminals and bring them before the judges to answer for what they have done." He pointed back toward the dead cow behind the formation. "This poison, it is a last resort. We will only use deadly force when it is needed." He held out the bola for them all to see. "This is called a bola, and it is a tool used by some sheep herders I met while I was in the wilds. I found it quite useful if I wanted to take a Nehor prisoner for questioning."

There was a snicker among the group when Teancum said the word 'questioning'. They all had heard the stories and legend of the mighty Ghost Soldier and how he dealt with the Nehor. Teancum heard the snickering and responded. "True, I was a bit… *enthusiastic* when it came to dealing with the bandits, but this is a new day and we are going to

CHAPTER FOUR

obey the law— clear?"

"Sir, yes sir!" Again in unison.

In the wood line, too far away to hear what was being said, two spies for the Nehor clan were cloaked and hidden from sight. They were still trying to figure out what happened to the cow when they saw Teancum throw his bola and take down the running Nephite.

"Did you see that?" One whispered to the other.

"It looks like he means to capture some of us..." The second one spoke and trailed off in thought. "Keeping us alive... But why?"

"So he can torture us for information, then take us before the judges and put us in prison." The first bandit put the pieces together. "Well I, for one, would rather face the executioner than wallow in a cell the rest of my life."

"The Grand Council must know of this!" The second bandit whispered in an excited voice and started to crawl back out of the bushes. The two men made their way back several yards through the brush and undergrowth to where their horses were tied up. They walked their horses for several hundred yards away from the open meadow where the Ghost Soldiers were training to ensure they would not make any noise and give away their position. Once they were sure they were out of sight and sound of the Nephites, the two bandits mounted their horses and galloped away at top speed. They knew the others in their clan must be made aware of the new tactics.

Over the next few weeks Teancum demonstrated several new methods for the Ghost Soldiers to use in their mandate to hunt down and end the scourge of the Nehor brotherhood. The difficult training continued, and Teancum lost a few more men to injuries and inability to keep up the rigorous pace. It was a hard lesson to learn for some of the Nephites who, physically or emotionally, could not keep up with the rest of the Ghost Soldiers. Some of those men who failed had friends and family in important positions within the government. Teancum was continually pressured to lower the standards and level the field, so those who were not strong enough or did not have the desire to work as hard as the rest of his men could still enjoy the benefits of being a Ghost Soldier.

"Absolutely not!" Teancum was almost insulted that someone would even suggest it. "I will not lower the standards, and I will not accept anything less than the very best from my men."

"Captain Teancum, be reasonable." A very well-dressed and manicured man sitting behind a table spoke to Teancum in a condescending tone. There were several more men and women, all well-dressed and sitting around the large table while Teancum was standing up at the far end. His two lieutenants were also standing but behind him, near the door.

"Ladies and gentlemen." Teancum kept his tone low. He was frustrated he even had to explain this to the leaders of the city. But he was once a politician and he knew how to play the game. "I understand your concern and I appreciate your eagerness to resolve this matter. But the simple fact is I will not change the method I have chosen to train and prepare the men." Teancum looked at his father-in-law who was sitting near the head of the table. "I was told if I chose to walk down this path I would have complete discretion over the recruitment and training of the men; has that changed?"

"No, Captain Teancum, it has not." The old commander sat up straight in his chair and projected his authority through his words. "That was the agreement and you are completely supported by the army."

He smiled and winked at his son-in-law. This was the closest the old soldier would ever come again to combat. He was past his prime and a figurehead now, but he still pulled considerable weight on the city's council, and he knew and supported what Teancum was trying to do.

"Does the city council understand what must happen if I am to change the standards and, as you say, level the playing field?" Teancum looked around at the people seated before him. *Most of them already know the answer, those pompous self-serving politicians.* Teancum wanted to say it out loud, in front of them so there would be no misunderstandings. He could scarcely believe he used to be just like them.

Teancum held up his right hand at eye level and put it parallel to the ground. "This is the point my Ghost Soldiers are at. They are extremely well-trained and equipped. I am not boasting, but stating a fact. The men under my command are elite in every sense of the word." Teancum then held his left hand down by his navel. "For demonstration purposes, this is where the rest of the Nephite army is. Most of the soldiers are basically trained and basically prepared for combat. A few have some skills and abilities beyond their companions, but for the most part the army exists at this level. The men of the Nephite army are brave, but they also lack advanced training."

Teancum stopped speaking for a moment to allow the members of the council to absorb his object lesson. "The only way to allow all these men here," he shook the lower hand," to become Ghost Solders would be to lower the standards of these men." He then moved his right hand down toward the left one. "Leveling the playing field means changing the standards from elite to basic levels. You cannot level the playing field by decreasing the standards for the lesser ones. If those basic soldiers could all rise up to the elite level then there would be no need to level the field." He looked at them with disdain in his eyes. "There was an open invitation for all who wanted to join my team. No one was denied the opportunity to excel. The rank of Ghost Soldier is won through personal achievement only. I will not lower the standards or allow someone who cannot or will not keep up with the best to be a member of my unit. No one gets a special pass or is treated differently; there is one standard for the Ghost Soldier, and only one standard." Teancum put down his hands. "The training to become a Ghost Soldier is tough, rigorous and intense—I will admit to that, guilty as charged. I do not ask the men to do anything I am not willing to do myself and I lead them over, across and through every obstacle."

He looked at the gathered assembly for any sign of understanding. Not seeing anyone disagreeing with him, Teancum finished speaking. "Those who failed to measure up are more than welcome to try again at the next open enlistment. I don't need more unqualified men to swell my ranks. I can do more with twelve well-trained, well-equipped, and well-motivated men then with one hundred soldiers who don't want to be there. The standards stay… Or I walk." Teancum stood up to walk out of the meeting.

His last few words got the attention of the leaders of Zarahemla. They all suddenly became very adamant Teancum remain as the leader of the Ghost Soldiers. Teancum knew what he was doing when he had his men train and exercise in full view of the citizens of the capital city. If this radical new idea was going to work, he would need the support of the people, and the only way to gain their support was to give the people what they wanted— good, capable, hard-trained men ready to fight the Nehor robbers or the invading Lamanites if necessary. And the only way to display their skills to the people was to train out in the open.

The people loved it. They loved seeing the men of Teancum's army run past their shops and homes. They cheered as their new guardians would train and sweat and display their abilities for all to see. The love the common people felt for the Ghost Soldiers was brought to the attention of the elected officials, who in turn made sure the voters saw them supporting the warriors. So the thought of Teancum disbanding the unit and walking away over something so trivial made the governing body very nervous. Teancum was a smart man, he knew how to play the game; but this council had gone too far. Now they wanted to soften and weaken the only real response they had for the Nehor. Some of them were on the take and lined their pockets with the bandits' blood money.

No one here is asking you to resign, Captain Teancum." One of the more prestigious members of the council spoke out. They needed to calm the situation before he did quit. The people would riot if they found out Teancum left because of them. "We understand what you are saying, and are grateful for your commitment to keeping this city and the Nephite people safe." The man speaking had his hands out, and he sounded like he was almost pleading with Teancum. "Please, tell us what you need from us."

Teancum sat back down stone-faced, the veins in his neck pulsing and his jaw muscles were tightly clenched. It took him a moment to find his calm. He was not the same person who sat in those chairs across from him just a few years ago. His personal struggles with the Nehor and the demons in his head had turned Teancum into a hard man both inside and out. The next few words hissed out of his mouth. "I do not require anything different then what this body has already committed to— your continued support for the plan already in effect."

"On that, we can all agree." An elderly white-haired lady with her head covered in a large scarf spoke up. "Please keep us informed of your progress."

Teancum stood back up. "I will continue to personally deliver my reports to the council." He stood motionless looking back at the soft and pampered faces. "If there is nothing else then may I have your leave to return to my company? My core leadership group is ready and we start the next recruitment process in the morning."

"How many do you hope to find tomorrow, Captain Teancum?" A young and well-dressed nobleman asked from the back of the room. It was no secret he was involved with the Nehor. Teancum felt this question was a way to gather intelligence on the Ghost Soldiers.

"I am expecting as many, if not more, to apply tomorrow as came

CHAPTER FOUR

on the first recruitment. Out of that lot I found fifty who passed the initial phase. Thirty made it all the way through the training." Teancum answered his question but did not tell him anything that was not already common knowledge. The man shook his head and sat back down. Little did the nobleman know, but Teancum had already set some of his men to do surveillance on his movements and gather enough information to charge him with sedition and conspiring with the Nehor.

The next day went exactly as Teancum had hoped. Hundreds of men came to try their luck at becoming a Ghost Soldier. In the end, they had just over sixty men who passed the interviews. The next morning Teancum greeted the candidates, told them of his expectations and then turned the training over to his cadre of instructors he personally trained. Over the next few weeks the training went well. Teancum supervised and led some of the training, but like any good leader he trusted his subordinates and let his officers and sergeants do their jobs. The team was growing and growing well.

A third and fourth recruitment was conducted, and in just a few more months Teancum had a working unit of 300 men. All the men were expertly trained in weapons and fieldcraft, but some of the men showed a particular aptitude for certain aspects of the job like horsemanship, archery, scouting and surveillance, and intelligence gathering. Teancum recognized the advantage of having men specialize in those aspects and he encouraged them to become even more proficient.

Teancum was now ready to take the fight to the Nehor. He started his men off with small assignments first. Teancum wanted to let his men gain experience and confidence by accomplishing simpler tasks before he confronted the bandits in open conflict: setting traps for the bandits, watching people who were known collaborators, responding to robberies and tracking down those responsible, surveillance and intelligence gathering on known Nehor hideouts; these jobs were just the start of the master plan Teancum had for his Ghost Soldiers.

Once they had gained experience, Teancum would turn his attention to the infestation of Nehor in the city of Zarahemla. Teancum knew the markings and symbols of the Nehor; finding their safe houses was a matter of knowing where to look. It was during one such operation that the Ghost Soldiers experienced their first death in the line of duty. It came when they raided one of the larger safe houses located in the western district of Zarahemla. The west side was a rough neighborhood,

Teancum Meets Moroni

but good, hard-working people lived there. Teancum led the assault himself, but one of his men triggered a Nehor trap and he was killed.

Teancum took the death hard. There was a very public funeral, and the man was buried with full military honors. Following this casualty, Teancum refocused on his duty and trained his men even harder. "If one cup of sweat can prevent one drop of blood, then it will all be worth it!" he shouted as he grunted and groaned through the training.

The fight against the Nehor continued on for two more years. There were several high profile arrests and successful raids on bandit hidouts and safe houses. Teancum was beginning to unravel the web the Nehor had wrapped around the Nephite people and it was making some in positions of power very nervous. The fight continued until one day, Teancum was recalled back to the military command center for Zarahemla. He reported to his father-in-law, who was about to conduct a war council with his officers.

"It's open war, gentlemen." The old soldier held nothing back. "The Lamanite dogs have invaded near the land of Jershon. Chief Captain Joshua and his son Moroni have taken their forces and joined with Chief Captain Lehi near the river, over here." He pointed on a map at a section of land near a large river cutting through the countryside. "They have requested reinforcements and I have asked the city elders to call up the militia."

There was an excited grumbling among the gathered military men. The garrison commander looked right at Teancum. Teancum felt a rush of adrenaline spike though his body. *Finally, a chance to display the full might and skills of the Ghost Soldiers on the battlefield agianst armed troops, not just cowards and criminals, but actual soldiers.* he thought.

"I am glad you are here son. I have orders for you and your Ghost Soldiers."

"Yes, sir." Teancum responded like a good soldier. This was it, the moment he had waited for— deployment of his elite soldiers to the front lines of a war with the Lamanites.

"Your fight with the Nehor will need to wait while we repel this new threat." The commander put his hand on Teancum's shoulder as he spoke. "Take your men and secure the main merchant road between us and Jershon." He pointed down to the map where the road was marked. "There are reports coming in of Lamanite raiding parties; it is possible they will ally with the Nehor, and we can't allow that to happen. If we can't control the roads between the cities and the army, then our supplies will not make it to the front lines." He stepped away from Teancum and waved his hands over the map.

Teancum looked like he had just been punched in the gut. "I know it's not the most glamorous assignment, and you and your men are chomping at the bit to see some proper action, but this assignment is vital to the cause." The old soldier could see the words had no comfort and there was disappointment in Teancum's eyes. He knew Teancum wanted to prove the value of the special training his men had done to the rest of the army. He wanted to explain his reasoning to Teancum, but now was not the time. There was a war being waged and orders needed to be followed.

The commander continued, "I will march at the head of our forces and meet up with Chief Captain Joshua." He pointed to the other officers in the room. "You men are to rally the militia, arm them and march them to the front lines while escorting the relief wagons. Questions?" He waited for several seconds but there were none. "Excellent. You have my leave to do your duties." The commander saluted the officers in the room and everyone moved toward the exit. "Captain Teancum, may I have a word in private?"

"Yes, sir." Teancum was curt in his response. He was upset over being denied his chance to lead his men into a real battle and instead got stuck with doing patrol duties on the main roads. But he was a true warrior and he knew that he must do his duty. *Oh well*, he thought. *At least I might still get to hunt some Nehor along the way.* He turned around and came up to his father-in-law. "You wanted to speak to me, sir?"

"Look son, I know you are disappointed about being left behind; believe me, it was not my choice to make. I am the garrison commander, yes, but I answer to the civilian authority." The old man was trying to apologize in his own way. "Each one of your special soldiers are worth ten regular infantry men in a fight." Teancum was looking down and the commander tried to look him in the eyes and smile. "I don't have a single man to spare in this fight, and it would take a force much greater in size to do what your men can do on those roads." He patted Teancum on the back and tried to give him some manly encouragement. "Besides, you have been ruffling some very influential feathers out there with your raids and arrests. If you leave Zarahemla now, the Nehor will have time to replenish their ranks and move back into the communities you have swept clear." The commander walked back over by the map table and took a deep breath. "Wars are not just fought on the front lines, Captain Teancum. If these intelligence reports are correct, the Lamanites have amassed a massive army of men. It will take a concentrated effort on everyone's part to overcome the forces gathering against us."

Teancum smiled. "If my men had gathered that intelligence, you would *know* it is correct."

The old commander looked up at Teancum with a stunned expression. He held his expression for several seconds then burst out in a full belly laugh. Teancum could not hold back his own laughter and joined in with his father-in-law.

Teancum did his duty. He did not like it and neither did his men. He knew the Ghost Soldiers were capible of so much more, but they were all good soldiers and performed their assigned tasks to the best of their abilities. There were some skirmishes with Lamanite raiders and it was nothing the mighty Ghost Soldiers could not handle. Meanwhile Teancum kept a small but productive force of men in Zarahemla as insurance against a resurgence from the Nehor bandits.

As captain of the Ghost Soldiers, Teancum was privy to the intelligence reports delivered almost daily. He could see the war was going badly for the Nephites and the losses on both sides were staggering. After months of fighting a report came that the Nephite army was in full retreat and Chief Captain Joshua and most of his command staff, including his only son Moroni, were missing in action. "It says Captain Lehi has consolidated the remaining Nephite forces by the river and is hoping to put up enough resistance to allow the army to escape to the other side before they are completely overrun." Teancum was reading a dispatch to some of his men.

One of his men spoke up. "It's a hard two-day ride on horseback from Jershon to Zarahemla. This report is at least three days old now." The Ghost Soldiers were all professionals and very close; closer than brothers in some cases. In a setting like this, the formality of the traditional military customs and courtesies had been set aside. Informal talk among the ranks was accepted. Besides, everyone knew Teancum was in charge.

"The fact a new dispatch has not yet arrived is a bad sign, too." A second soldier spoke from the back of the group.

Teancum nodded his head in agreement. "I need two men to ride to the front and get an update. Any volunteers?" Every hand shot up, just as Teancum had expected. These were good, brave men. He was proud

CHAPTER FOUR

to be among them. Teancum pointed to two men and in less than thirty minutes they were on their way.

A few days later the two scouts returned from the front lines with an amazing story of how Chief Captain Joshua had been killed in a daring raid on the Lamanite command post. They told how his son Moroni had assumed command of the army, led a surprise attack on the Lamanite king's own camp, captured all the Lamanite chief captains, and a how treaty was made with the Lamanite princess after her father killed himself, rather than accept defeat. "Moroni is coming here to make his report to the Grand Council and chief judges." The men explained to Teancum. "You should see this guy! He's just a kid, but man, is he huge."

The second scout agreed with his partner's assessment of Moroni's physical size. "He's like a giant tree wearing sandals."

"So the war is over. That is very welcome news." Teancum expressed his relief no one else needed to die because of the Lamanites.

"Should we recall the patrols?" Gid asked his Captain.

Teancum thought about his question for a few seconds. "No." He responded. "Keep them on patrol until the army is on the road and moving back home. If there are any more Lamanite raiding parties left they probably have not heard the news of their surrender. We need to keep the roads open so the wounded can get home safely."

Teancum and his men stayed true to their assignments and the roads were kept free of bandits and Lamanite raiding parties.

Moroni eventually made it back to the capital city and, in a general session with all the elected leaders of the Nephites, he addressed the Council of Judges on the amazing victory over the Lamanites. Moroni made sure to give God and his father all the credit for the outcome of the battle. When Moroni was finished speaking, Teancum's father-in-law introduced Moroni to Teancum. The two became instant friends and Moroni attended several training sessions with the Ghost Soldiers. It was during one such training session that Moroni was able to demonstrate the advantages of his great size and incredible strength.

During hand-to-hand combat training, Moroni was tossing grown men in the air and wrestling three soldiers at one time. Moroni saw the value of the elite unit Teancum commanded when the men stopped trying to challenge him in single competition and worked together to bring the big man down. He grew to respect their revolutionary ideas for training and looked forward to deploying Teancum's new force.

"I want to tell you something in confidence, Teancum." Moroni spoke as the two sat on the porch of his father-in-law's home one night after a good family dinner.

Teancum looked inquiringly at his friend. "Okay…?" He replied as he adjusted his position in his seat.

Moroni took a deep breath and slowly let it out. "There is talk of consolidating the different commands for the army into one central leader: a general."

"I have heard that talk myself." Teancum acknowledged. "It makes sense to have one person in charge. We could have avoided what happened at Jershon if there was one person giving the orders, instead of several clan leaders failing to coordinate efforts and not working together."

"Agreed." Moroni spat out. He was surprised at how much Teancum knew about what happened during the battle of Jershon even though he was not there. "So many men died because we could not agree on tactics and who was in command." Moroni shook his head. "Hopefully that will change if and when they call for a supreme commander of the entire army." He shifted in his seat and the wood creaked and groaned under his weight.

"Don't you dare break my mother-in-law's chair!" Teancum seemed to be joking, but there was a hint of seriousness in his voice. He did not want to be the one to explain what happened to the matching deck chairs. They both had a laugh.

Over time, Moroni gained much favor with the local civilian leadership as he worked and trained with the Ghost Soldiers. He even joined them on some of their expeditions, when his own command duties did not get in the way. The Nephites had all but lost the previous war, the army had been in full retreat and most of the experienced military leadership had been killed. If not for the daring raid by Moroni and his father on the Lamanite command camp and the capture of the princess, their cause would have been lost.

Then one day word came to Teancum regarding movement along the Lamanite border. Teancum had wisely established his own network of supporters among the Nephite population. These were people who wanted to help the Ghost Soldiers fight the Nehor but were too old, unable to try out, or did not have the skills needed to join the team. Teancum employed some of them as his secret eyes and ears.

Teancum made sure no one knew who was feeding him information about the Nehor or who were involved, and he always verified the information from more than one reliable source. So when he came to Moroni with the news the Lamanites were massing troops and equipment along the border, and that there was a Zoramite leading the Lamanites, he knew the information was accurate.

Moroni took the information of the Lamanites preparing for war to the civilian leadership. Panic set in after Moroni and Teancum explained what was happening on the frontier.

"It has been less than two years, and we have not even recovered from the last war with the Lamanites." Moroni reminded the Council. "We— this city and the surrounding areas— are not prepared for war. At best, with the forces at my disposal and with Captain Teancum's Ghost Soldiers, all we can hope to do is fight a delaying action. Unless this council agrees to combine all the clans and cities forces under one banner, and name a general to govern and manage the war, we will be overrun."

The leadership agreed, Moroni was given command of the army, and with Teancum's help, the outnumbered Nephites fought a desperate battle for the city of Manti and were able to repel the invaders.

Because of their involvement in the battle for Manti, especially how Teancum defended the city and how the Ghost Soldiers held the bridge during the Lamanite retreat, the legend of the Ghost Soldiers grew until they were known from one end of the land to the other. When the war ended, Teancum and his men returned to Zarahemla and assumed their primary duty of dealing with the Nehor. But they were always ready to assist Moroni in keeping the Nephite country safe.

Thanks to Moroni and his army's efforts, the Nephites enjoyed a time of prosperity and peace.

Until an evil arose among the Nephites in the land of Morianton.

CHAPTER FIVE

Morianton Goes Too Far

"I tell you my brothers; the people in the land of Lehi have been robbing you of your divine rights!" The gathered crowd of dirty and unkempt men and women murmured and agreed with the large, red faced and sweaty speaker. "How long will we stand for this injustice?" He continued with fire in his voice. The crowd gathered around him to hear him speak started to gain encouragement from his showmanship and enthusiasm.

The large wooden-framed tavern where he was speaking was dimly lit with candles and a large fire in the hearth. The smell of dirt, sweat, burnt food, rotten wood and alcohol filled the air. "How long have we toiled up here in the highlands under these harsh conditions and tilled up this rocky ground to plant our meager crops, while those lazy dogs in the land of Lehi enjoy the good water, flat ground and dark soil." He pointed out to the crowd. "You gave no offence to earn this harsh punishment, but the gods have cursed you with this life. Why? Are the flatlanders of Lehi better then you?"

"No!" The rough and dirty group shouted in unison. Some even waved their farming tools, or sharp weapons in the air.

"Are they more deserving than you?"

"No!" The crowd replied with even more vigor.

The speaker leaned forward into the crowd. His voice was low at first, but it got louder and he got more animated as he continued to talk. "I'll tell you what I think… I think the forefathers of the flatlanders set this whole thing up. I think when the lands were divided and settled, they set it up so their posterity would thrive while you and yours would suffer!"

CHAPTER FIVE

The gathered group of poor farmers and herdsmen looked at each other and murmured in questioning tones. "As your leader, I have gone before the so called judges in the land of Lehi. I asked to see the original maps showing the divisions of land and the documents showing the deeds. And do you know what I was told?" He paused for effect, and then spoke dramatically, in a high pitched, funny tone, mimicking the judges. "We're sorry, Morianton! We can't find the maps, they just all conveniently disappeared!" He waved his hands out in front of him to emphasize the point.

He knew it was a bold-faced lie, but Morianton did not care. He wanted power and he was willing to do anything to get it, except hard work. Morianton was a large man and he learned early on in life that he could use his physical size to intimidate and scare other obliging and timid folks into doing his will. But he knew, deep down in the dark places of his heart, that he was lazy and a coward. He knew he was not a good or honorable man, and he needed to control others to feel better about himself. He'd failed in his business ventures and in farming, so now he was trying his hand at community organizing. Finally, he found a job requiring no credible skills, where everyone else does the work, and he takes no responsibility if it fails and all the credit if it succeeds.

"Interesting?" He continued on in his normal angry voice. "They demand we live by the boundaries established by their forefathers, but as soon as someone like me shows up with the guts to question the all-powerful judges, their proof conveniently disappears." He took a step back and paused while he wiped large beads of sweat from his balding head. "I say no more!" He bellowed as he tossed the sweaty rag on the ground. The drunken crowd cheered with him. "It's not fair they get the easy life while we work hard. No more!" A cheer rose from the crowd. "It's not fair those flatlanders have the best property and we have rocks and mud… No more!" Again the cheers ring out. "It's not fair they have fancy clothing, jewels and an easy life… I have had enough!" Morianton pounded his fist on the table in front of him. The gathered mass of drunken ruffians fed off of his emotions and screamed in unison. Morianton held up his hands and waved them over his head to try to get the mass to quiet down. "My friends!" He yelled over the noise. He felt the emotions in the air. These simple people were ripe for the plucking. So long as he can keep them fired up and a bit drunk, they would do whatever he asked of them.

Morianton Goes Too Far

"My friends, I am going down from the highlands and walking up to the first flatlander village I come to. I am planting my standard in the village square and declaring that all the land before me belongs to the people of Morianton... Who is with me!?" Cheers went up as Morianton waved to the crowd to follow him as he walked out of the tavern and into the muddy street. The gathered mass had grown during the evening to well over one hundred drunken men and women. All of them were armed with some sort of farming tool or rough-made weapon. They all followed him out into the cold mountain air.

As the people exited the tavern they formed a circle around Morianton who was standing in the middle of the street holding a large burning torch. "Listen to me!" He shouted several times over the ruckus from the riotous mass. As they began to calm down he continued "My people! Down this mountain road, not five miles away, is the village of Heth. There is good water and plenty of grain fields. We deserve it, the people of Lehi have more than they need and we want it, so we are going to take it. Follow me!" Morianton waved the torch over his head like some grand military leader inspiring his men to march into battle. He started to walk toward the peaceful unsuspecting village at the bottom of the mountain while the drunken gathering fell in behind him in an unorganized formation. Most still had clay jugs or goblets of wine and ale in their hands. They continued to drink as they walked.

The conditions that night were not very favorable for Morianton and his drunken band. There was a cloud-covered, moonless sky and it was very cold, almost freezing, with drizzling rain all night. In their drunken logic, the mountain people now blamed the flatlanders from the land of Lehi for their current misery.

"Look there." Morianton pointed to the thatched roofs and wood framed homes of the village of Heth accented in the first light of dawn. They were gathered in a tree line about 100 yards away. "We must move quickly before the farmers waken. You..." He pointed to a man next to him. "Take a group and go over to the water well." Great puffs of warm steamy air came out of his mouth as he spoke. "You..." he pointed to another. "Take those with you and move to the stables over there." He directed them to a large barn at the far end of the village. "I will take what's left with me and move on the middle. Work your way toward the center of the village. Go into their homes, get the people out of their beds and gather all the villagers up and move them into the village square.

CHAPTER FIVE

Be quick and brutal if necessary." He looked around at those closest to him. "Speed is the key. We must move quickly and keep the element of surprise. Don't let anyone escape. We don't need others coming to the rescue until we are ready to negotiate terms." He paused for effect.

He wanted to be dramatic to make the people with him think he truly cared for them. "If we do this right, none of us get hurt. Okay?"

Those with him rocked their heads to agree with him. Those drunken fools really thought Morianton had their best interest at heart. If only they knew he was willing to sacrifice their lives and freedom for his own gain. "Go, and may the blessings of the mountain gods be with you."

Morianton knew this was his moment. He watched as those he ordered to move to the outer edges of the village left to take their places. Clumsy and undisciplined, the horde of drunken mountain men and women left the confines of the tree line and advanced from their hidden positions.

One of the many things Morianton had failed to consider in his ill-conceived plan to steal what was not his were all the farm dogs in the village. As soon as the intoxicated raiders left the cover of the tree line and moved toward the village, the dogs all started to bark. A true military professional would have done a detailed battle plan, and considered who and where he was assaulting. A real soldier would have known a farming village will have dogs, and they will bark at anything they think is a threat to their families. Morianton was no soldier, and he was a poor leader at best, so there was no plan for dealing with the barking dogs.

"Move!" He shouted when he saw the surprise assault falter. Some of the drunken rabble turned and ran back to the safety of the tree line; others froze in place not knowing what to do. Others continued on to their assignments. Morianton had a very quick temper and he grabbed the closest mountain man next to him and shouted in his face. "Take the rest straight into the village and shut up those blasted dogs!" Those who remained in the tree line with Morianton rose up in unison and charged ahead, shouting as they ran.

One or two dogs barking during the early morning hours was a common thing for the villagers. But all of them barking at once and getting aggressive was a warning that danger was approaching. Life on the frontier was hard, and you learned quickly danger comes in all shapes and sizes. Not knowing the nature of the threat, the men of the village jumped out of their beds and grabbed whatever tool or weapon was close to them. Some had old swords, others had shovels or pitch forks, but all of them tried to find a way to defend their families from danger. The attackers were barely reaching the village when the first of the villagers emerged from their homes. If they'd had a few more seconds of warning they might have put up a stout defense against the hill people, but everything was happening too quickly. As they emerged from their doorways, the villagers were overpowered by the drunken attackers. Some were clubbed over the head and knocked unconscious, others were threatened with harm if they did not drop their weapons, and a few were stabbed or sliced with a sharp edge of a sword.

Morianton was a true coward. He knew if he entered the village with the hill people he might be challenged by a villager and hurt or killed. He remained in the tree line well after the rest of his band had entered the village and rousted those living there. After waiting several minutes, and after drinking the entire contents of his wine jug, Morianton walked calmly into the town square.

Most of the villagers had been disarmed, rounded up and moved into the town square. A young stable boy was hiding behind some hay bales as members of the mob crashed into the large barn at the far end of the village and grabbed the stable master out of his warm cot. The old man refused to comply with the rogues and was jabbed with a pitchfork in the backside to get him moving faster out the doors. The old man was fussing, complaining and pulling away from his captors as he slowly walked in the direction of the barn doors. Through the open barn doors, the old man could see what was happening outside in the square. He saw the entire village gathered in the square and under guard. Some of the men were injured and most of the women were crying or holding on to their children.

Just before he exited the barn the old man and the stable boy made eye contact. He was relieved to know the stable boy was safe for the moment. But he also knew it would not last. Those uncouth hill people would eventually find the boy, and someone needed to go for help. The old man knew what he had to do. Walking outside and several yards away from the barn, the old horse master suddenly turned and shouted back into the barn.

"Run, boy! Run to General Moroni's camp! Tell him what is happening here. Take the mare, go!"

But before he could say any more, Morianton, who had just arrived

CHAPTER FIVE

in the center of the village, clubbed him in the back of the head with a shovel. The old man fell hard to the ground and let out a pained moan.

"You two, go check the barn again!" Morianton ordered as he pointed to the closest two men standing next to him. The two men moved quickly toward the open barn doors. Morianton dropped the shovel on the ground next to the old man. "Get him up and move him over with the rest of the people." He barked to the remaining men. They quickly reached down and grabbed the wounded man under both arms and dragged him over to where the other villagers were.

The sun had risen above the horizon and the stable boy could clearly see two of the attackers moving back toward the barn. He knew they were going to search for him and he had to act fast. Following the instructions from the stable master, he ran to the far end of the barn and jumped on the back of the tan colored mare in the last stall. Riding bare back was easy for him. He had been working with horses for most of his young life. He had learned that because he was small, he could hold his weight with his hands wrapped in the horse's mane. Urging the horse forward, they walked over to the back doors of the barn. The boy reached down and unlatched the lock just as the two bandits' entered the barn.

"Hey!" One of them shouted out as they saw the boy kicking open the back door and urging the horse outside. "Stop!" The second dirty hillsman called out as they both took off running after the boy and his horse. The boy kicked the horse in the ribs and in three steps the horse was at a full gallop.

The boy guided the horse through the open fields behind the village and onto the main cross roads leading to General Moroni's camp. Those who were being held against their will all started to cheer and encourage him to keep moving. They, along with all the drunken captors, had heard the old man shout to run to Moroni and tell him what had happened. They knew their only chance for justice was with the brave young boy riding like the wind to plead for help from Moroni.

The two men who were in the barn tried to get horses of their own to ride after the boy. "None of these are saddled!" One of the men shouted to the other as he went up and down the row of stables.

"Just get on one and let's go!" The other shouted back as he tried to get a horse out of its stall. The first man tried to climb up onto a horse, but he was too fat to even get on. The second man fell off his horse trying to ride bareback after only a few steps.

"I think my arm is broken." The overweight man who fell off the horse lamented as he struggled to stand up while holding his injured arm with his good one.

"That will be the least of your problems when Morianton learns how you let that boy escape." The second man spoke with a judgmental and accusative tone as he walked past the injured man. "I was ready to chase after him when you fell off, scaring my horse half to death, you big dumb fool."

"It's not my fault! The horse, it bucked me off. I tried…" The fat, injured man whined in his drunken voice.

"Save it for Morianton." The other spoke back waving his hand to silence the injured one. As long as he could keep up the ruse and let the fat man take the blame for losing the boy he would stay out of trouble. No one needed to know he fell off his own horse, too.

"What happened?" Morianton demanded as the two clumsy drunks returned to the center of the village where the rest waited. "I told you to find the boy before he could escape!"

Before they could give an explanation an elderly woman's voice rang out from where the villagers were being kept.

"When word of your crimes reaches Moroni's ears, he will come and justice will fall upon you!"

Morianton and all who were with him turned to see who dared to make this statement. The villagers all moved out of the way and Morianton saw a skinny old lady with silver hair sitting on the ground with the bloody head of the stable master resting on her lap. She had torn off the hem of her sleeping gown and used it to wrap the wounded man's head.

"You got something to say, grandma!?" Morianton barked at her in defiance.

"Yes!" She pointed with a blood-stained finger at a large banner flying from a pole on top of the community building next to the town square. "That is the Title of Liberty. This village and all who live here are under the personal protection of General Moroni! You have attacked a peaceful people without cause. This is naked criminal aggression, and it will not stand. Justice is coming for you and all your men!" She pointed at Morianton as she finished speaking.

The rest of the villagers all mumbled in agreement. A second villager, one of the other wounded men, spoke up next.

CHAPTER FIVE

"What do you think Moroni and his men will do when he hears of your treachery? Who do you think he will send to deal with you? Amiha, Captain Lehi?" There was a pause for the effect. "No... Moroni knows there is only one man who hates criminals like you with a passion few will ever understand. There is only one man who he will send to deal with dogs like you— Teancum! Teancum and his Ghost Soldiers will come and avenge us!"

The name of Teancum caused all the captors to immediately shiver and shake. Everyone knew who Teancum was and what he could do. The alcohol was starting to wear off, and the true realization of what they had done was starting to come over them. Nervously, some of them started to look at Morianton for guidance, but he was just as scared as the rest of them.

Others among the villagers could see the shift in Morianton's countenance. A third villager spoke up. He was older and had a cane to help him move around.

"We all know what Teancum and his men are capable of doing. They won't need much to deal with the likes of you." He spoke as he turned around to address all of his captors surrounding the villagers like a pack of wolves herding sheep to the slaughter. "I got this crippled leg fighting alongside men like Teancum." He shook his cane in the air. "I know what they can do. They will travel light and fast." He continued to talk and look around at the bandits. "If they move all night, by my reckoning, Teancum and his men should be here by first light tomorrow." He stopped moving and turned to look at Morianton. "And you will all be dead shortly after."

"Morianton...?" One of the captors called out for guidance.

"Quiet! I'm thinking!" Morianton was panicking. The old man was right; he had no plan for a counterattack by Teancum. Another amateur blunder by a drunken fool who thought he could lead men. A good strategist would have been thinking three or four moves ahead and have contingency plans ready to go in case there was a change.

"Morianton? From the land of Morianton?" Another of the village elders questioned. "I knew your father, he was a just man. What is the meaning of all this?"

"Shut your mouth, old man!" Morianton demanded as he pointed at the elder who spoke. He was quickly losing control of not only himself but the situation.

"That man is right. We need to establish a defense if Teancum is coming!" A second bandit moved next to Morianton and barked in his face. Morianton turned to face the man yelling at him.

"No!" A third bandit spoke up. "We need to run back to the hills and hide! We cannot fight the Ghost Soldiers out here in the open!" Several of the others agreed with him and started to talk amongst themselves. Morianton spun around and glared at the man who just spoke.

"You will do as I say!" Morianton shouted with more than a hint of panic in his voice. "I am your leader and you will respect me!" The gathered hill people did not like hearing his response.

The second villager continued. "The only way you are going to survive this is if you lay down your weapons and surrender to us now, or if you flee to the wilderness and hope Moroni and Teancum can't track you down."

Then an idea came to Morianton. "My people..." He waved for them to come closer. "Once again we have been shown how those who wish to hold you back and keep you from reaching your full potential will do whatever is necessary to keep you poor, sick and helpless. Go, grab what valuables you can from the houses and get back here. We are leaving for the highlands in ten minutes."

"What about the villagers, who is going to watch them? Who will keep them from following us?" One of the more sober criminals questioned.

Morianton looked around for an answer and suddenly realized it was sitting right in front of him. Calmly, he walked over to where the villagers were kept and quickly grabbed a small girl out of her mother's arms. The mother cried out and tried to grab her child back from Morianton. Her husband was one of the wounded and he lay unconscious on the ground next to her. Morianton cursed as he slapped the mother with the back of his hand, knocking her to the ground. Several other men from the village started to move forward to challenge Morianton and he pulled out a large knife from his waistband. The weapon looked more like a meat cleaver than a knife, with jagged edges and a leather wrapped handle. "If any villager tries to interfere," He held the weapon over his head. "I will cleave her arm off!" Morianton pulled the child's arm straight up and gestured like he was going to deliver a downward slice as he stared at the men from the village who stopped moving.

"Coward!" Someone from the crowd shouted.

CHAPTER FIVE

"Your pretty trinkets are not worth her arm… Now stay back, all of you!" Morianton commanded as he slowly waved the knife from side to side. The men of the village moved back and the highlanders took it as a good sign. With Morianton keeping watch, the village was quickly ransacked. Two wheelbarrows were found and loaded up with any of the villager's meager items of value the bandits could find.

As the robbery continued, Morianton was getting nervous. He could see the men of the village whispering to each other and looking at him. In his mind he could see them plotting a sudden attack with him as the target of their anger.

"Let's go, hurry up!" He shouted as the looting continued. After a few moments, Morianton's paranoia began to kick in. Morianton had not slept in over 24 hours and he spent most of that time drinking alcohol. This was a dangerous combination and now Morianton was starting to have hallucinations. He imagined off in the distance a mass of Nephite calvary charging down on them. Then the haunting voice of the old lady from the village echoed in his mind as shadows darted from hut to hut all around him, *Justice is coming for you and all your men…*

Panicked, Morianton shouted out, "Let's go! We are leaving," and dragged the crying girl with him toward the village barn.

"Where are you taking her?" The young mother cried out.

"She is a little motivation to keep you from following us!" He shouted back.

Hearing this, the men of the village surged forward but Morianton slashed the large knife again and they stepped back. As he got closer to the barn Morianton realized that trying to bring this child kicking and screaming with him was a very bad idea. She would slow him down and keeping her only increased his chances of being hunted down by an angry mob or worse. Looking around for an answer he saw the barn full of animals behind him and he had an idea.

"Bring me a torch!" He barked to his men. One of them came running up with a large burning torch in his hand. He was also carrying a candle stick and had a lady's gardening hat on his head that he'd taken from a home he ransacked. Grabbing the torch he said, "Take her," as he shoved the arm of the little girl into the chest of the man with the hat.

"Get moving!" Morianton called out to the rest of his band. "This way," he waved as the robbers rallied around the two loaded wheelbarrows and moved toward the barn.

"The girl is coming with us!" Morianton shouted to the villagers. "I will release her when I and my company are safe. Now, you can chase after us, or..." He turned and tossed the lit torch into the barn. "You can put out the fire and save the animals, your choice." He turned to those around him. "Let's go!" he pointed at the mountains. "Bring her." He looked back down at the girl and then turned and ran for the tree line with his band carrying the loot they stole following close behind.

The men of the village were panicked. Do they rush after the girl and try to save her, or do they save the animals and put out the fire? After Morianton assaulted them, took them hostage and robbed them, no one believed him when he said he would set her free. But if the animals die, then they can't harvest the crops in the field, or do anything necessary to keep the village alive. Smoke was starting to billow from the open doors and Morianton was quickly getting away. It would take all the remaining healthy men of the village to chase after and fight the bandits to get the girl back. It would also take all the healthy men, and some of the women, to fight the barn fire. If Morianton reached the wood line without them following, then she would be lost to them. If the barn burned with the winter stock and the draft animals inside, then the village would be lost. Sensing the moral dilemma, the child's mother spoke out.

"She is an innocent child, blameless before God." Everyone turned to look at her. "He will protect her and return her to us. If the animals die, then the whole village will die. Save the animals!"

As if on cue, every man and strong boy still able to stand broke for the barn. The boys went for the animals while the men grabbed tools, buckets of water and blankets to fight the flames.

Reaching the tree line, Morianton stopped running and looked back to see if they were being followed. Breathing heavily, he scanned the village below for several seconds. No one was moving toward them and most of the activity in the village was centered on the smoking barn. Smiling he turned to his mob and spoke. "Looks like we gave them the slip."

A less than enthusiastic cheer went up from the crowd of robbers and drunks, they were all worn out from the last several hours. Everyone was exhausted, and they all knew it was still a long walk home carrying all the valuables they'd stolen.

"What about her?" The man who was responsible for the young hostage questioned as he pushed his way up near Morianton. He dropped her at Morianton's feet, and she curled into a ball and started to cry again.

CHAPTER FIVE

"She is too heavy to carry all the way up the mountain, and will slow down anyone who tries. I'm not dying because I had my arms full of a wailing child."

The two men locked eyes.

"Let her go." One of the women in the gang spoke up. There was pity in her voice. "She is of no use to us now. He is right; she will only slow us down."

"No…" a large man objected and moved closer to Morianton. "She is the only reason they do not follow. She will run back to the village and tell them where we are! We take her with us, or we kill her and hide the body!" The bandit who was carrying her agreed with the notion of killing the child. He pulled out a long, thin knife from his belt and smiled.

"Let them come!" The woman responded, moving to the child and pushing the bandit with the knife away from her. "They want to climb the mountains and face us highlanders on our own ground, then so be it! She kicked the young girl in the back. "Get up, child!" She ordered.

They are challenging your authority, a dark voice rang in Morianton's ear. Morianton stepped up between the crowd and the child. He pushed the protective woman away and looked down at the crying child, then up the mountain trail leading to his own village. "Put her in the wheelbarrow and let's keep moving!"

"What are you doing?" The woman spat at Morianton as she pointed at the weeping child.

"She is our ticket to safety! She comes with us back to the tavern!"

"Then what?" The woman stepped closer and challenged Morianton.

Morianton was outraged and he had enough. With one swift motion he struck the woman right across her face with the back of his right hand. "I'm in charge, and I give the orders here! You don't like it then you got two choices, challenge me or walk away!" He yelled as he pointed one of his fat fingers at her. Several of the men stepped forward to come to the aid of the woman. Morianton pulled out his massive knife. "Back, or the first thing I will do is gut her before I turn on you!" Morianton was losing control of his band of marauders. He had to act fast to maintain control.

Get them to think of something else. The cold whisper was speaking in his mind. *Moroni is coming, you must move your people to safety.*

Morianton knew what to do. Changing his tone and tactics he lowered his weapon and announced, "Attacking the village like we did may have been ill-conceived, I can admit that. Nevertheless, we did make our point known. We are tired of being treated like second class citizens by those who mean to rule over us. My father was the brother to King Noah, I have the blood of royalty in my veins." He was back to being a showman again. "We are all fugitives now and we need to move fast if we are going to get away from the long reach of General Moroni's authority."

In a moment of passion, Morianton looked around at his followers with fake concern in his eyes. "We are no longer safe in our own lands, I'm going north to the frontier past the land of Bountiful. I have heard there is a man who could help us break the chains of this false, so-called republic and establish a kingdom again, so we may all reap the rewards of a true monarchy." Morianton dramatically picked up his sack of stolen items and flung it over his shoulder, and then walked to the wheelbarrow where the child was sitting on top of some additional stolen items. "This child will guarantee us safe passage from the people of that village until we get back to our own homes. Once there we will release her. Who's coming with me?"

There was a grumbling among the gathered as they all came to realize they are now wanted criminals with no choice but to follow Morianton.

"This man in the north, what is his name?" A voice called out from the back.

Morianton turned back and replied. "His name is Pachus."

Morianton and his band were now on their second full day without sleep. Most had not eaten since the night before, and they had run out of water hours ago. So trying to walk uphill to their own homes, all while carrying the precious few items they took from the farming village during the raid was a monumental task. Some of the less valuable stolen items were being discarded along the way to help ease the burden of those carrying them. The stronger ones were still making good time, but those weaker members of the raiding party were quickly falling behind.

Morianton stopped at a bend in the steep trail to catch his breath and looked back at his followers who were straggling behind. "You need to keep up!" He shouted down the trail to those at the end of the formation.

"If the villagers track us up the mountains, those still below us will be easy prey for their vengeance." One of Morianton's closest allies whispered as he joined Morianton on the overlook.

"If that is the case then their cries for help should give us plenty of

CHAPTER FIVE

warning before they get to us." Morianton whispered back with a smile and a gesture to keep the comment between them. Morianton motioned for both of them to keep moving. Readjusting their own heavy burdens the two men rejoined the long train of weary bandits moving farther up the mountains.

It was well past noon when Morianton and the stronger men of his band reached the tavern where the plot to raid the village below had been hatched. The large thatch-roofed structure was made of wooden beams and was the focal point for the entire village. It was one of the largest buildings in the village square, and on any given night you would find almost all of the local men and some of the women walking in and out of its doors. Morianton came crashing through the front doors of the tavern and dropped his heavy sack of swag down on the closest table top.

"Diaya!" He called out gasping for air and falling into a chair next to the table. "Diaya, you worthless girl, bring me something to drink and some food!"

A young girl not much older than sixteen quickly emerged from a room behind the bar and moved toward Morianton. Wiping her hands on a large rag, she came up to him. She was tall for her age with curly brown hair and good posture. She was a natural beauty with a light in her eyes to match.

"My lord, what would you like?" She asked with a hint of fear and hesitation in her voice. She learned not to make eye contact with the clients in the tavern, or appear too happy. This tavern was a dark place with a foul spirit and anything bright or uplifting was quickly crushed under the weight of the dreariness.

"What took you so long?" Morianton bellowed at the waitress. She backed up a few steps with fear in her eyes. Lowering her head she apologized for her tardiness in a voice barely above a whisper.

"Ugh… Useless." Morianton waved his hand in disgust at her. "Ale. in a large goblet." He shouted as he pounded on the table with his fist. "And some meat and bread!"

"My lord, what kind of meat would you—?" She was cut off by Morianton jumping from his chair and pushing her to the ground. This was more for show as several members of his criminal band entered the tavern. Morianton could see them out of the corner of his eyes and upped the vulgarity at the small girl as entertainment value. In the difficult environment they lived in being harsh and rude toward those weaker

CHAPTER FIVE

and smaller was a way of life. "You worthless cow!" Morianton shouted. Moving way too close to her he continued in a deep and provocative voice. "Does it look like I care what kind of meat you bring me?" he sniffed her hair and walked around her examining her figure. "Kill it… skin it… cook it… and get it here… Now!" He looked back up at those other bandits in the room with him and smiled. The little waitress tried to move past Morianton but he blocked her path with his fat body and grabbed her by her arms. "Unless you can think of something else I might like to have for lunch?" He said in a soft and disturbing tone. He tried to smell her hair again but she quickly spun around out of his grasp and moved for the cooking area in the back of the tavern. As she moved past him he put his meaty hand on her back and pushed her toward the counter. "You can't find good help anymore." He laughed and sat back down in his chair. "And bring us some ale!" Morianton shouted as he gestured for the other men to sit with him. The men all came and sat down next to Morianton.

"So, now what?" The bandit who wanted to kill the young girl earlier asked as he wiped the sweat from his face.

"Where is the girl?" Morianton asked back.

"Tied up on the porch like a dog." A second hillsman responded to the question.

"Forget the girl, Morianton." The first criminal interrupted. "We followed you down to the flatlands with the promise of hope and change. Now look at us… Nothing but common criminals, kidnappers and thieves."

"You don't seem to be complaining about the sack of loot you pulled out of the village." Morianton responded while pointing at his companion.

"And I am going to need to spend every bit of it and more to find a way to avoid Moroni and his men when they come looking for us!" The man responded to Morianton.

As they continued to quarrel, more and more of Morianton's band of thieves wandered into the tavern. They were all exhausted, confused and everyone was thinking the same thing— 'What do we do now?' They all looked to Morianton for answers, and all he could do was get more excited and angry as the time progressed. No real answers or resolutions; only finger pointing, blame and excuses.

As the conversation continued and got more heated, Diaya, the young barmaid, kept the drinks flowing as best she could. The owners of the village's only real tavern never had this many patrons at one time during the day, so the poor girl was the only one there to help serve and make food. The problem with drunkards is the more alcohol you serve them, the more they want to drink and the more obnoxious they become. At one point during the heated discussion Morianton stood up on the table where he was sitting and shouted over everyone else to quiet down.

"Enough!" He bellowed. Everyone stopped arguing and looked up at him. "I am very tired and very drunk, so I don't have the patience for this bickering anymore!" He was swaying back and forth from the strong drink. Slurring his words, he tried to continue. "The fact of the matter is… Moroni will send his soldiers here… It is only a matter of time. We need to flee with our families now before they arrive, or we will be imprisoned or worse." He stopped to gain courage by taking a big drink from his goblet. Wiping the drippings from his beard he continued with his plan. "Go, gather your belongings and meet back here. We leave at dawn for the North Country!"

"Abandon our homes!?" Someone shouted from the back.

Morianton squinted to try to see through his drunken haze and find who spoke up. "Yes, we have no choice now. If Moroni and his men don't find us, those people down the mountain will come. But like I said, I have the blood of the kings in my veins. With the help of Pachus and his friends I will be crowned the rightful ruler of this land and we all will benefit… You will all have villages of your own by the time I am done." He held up his hands like he was waiting for the gathered to acknowledge his generosity. A shout went up as all of the drunk and greedy people in the tavern with him rejoiced at the possibility of changing the status of their lives by helping to overthrow the legitimate government.

Diaya was working her way through the excited crowd, gathering up empty goblets and plates covered in crumbs and bones. She had been working there long enough to know that eventually someone was going to start a fight and if she did not get the dishes cleared quickly, most of them would be broken during the struggle. Her father had been killed by Lamanite bandits several years before and her mother was indentured to the tavern owners until she could pay off the money she'd borrowed to help support her children. Although Moroni had outlawed indentured service and slavery, it was hard to enforce those rules in the outlying

CHAPTER FIVE

towns and villages. She was the oldest child, and as such she helped her mother with raising her younger siblings and working at the tavern so her mother could be at home when there was a sick child or to plant the crops. Just like any other girl her age, she dreamed of bigger and better things, but the reality was that people like her and her mother were expendable and only valuable if they could work hard.

As Diaya was walking past the doors of the tavern with a load of dishes in her arms, she heard the muffled cries of a child coming from outside on the porch. She set the stack of plates and cups on the counter and slowly peeked her head outside. She knew better than to get involved, but she was curious to know why there was a child crying. She had to stick most of her upper body out of the doors to get a look at the sobbing child. The little girl was shivering from the damp air, and she had her hands tied behind her back. The other end of the rope binding her hands was tied to the porch railing, and she was in the fetal position. Diaya's heart instantly broke and, against her better judgement, she carefully snuck out of the tavern and after ensuring the tavern doors did not slam shut, she moved quietly up next to the little girl. When she got close enough Diaya could tell the child was not from this village or the mountains. Her clothing looked like it was patterned after the flatlanders from the village at the bottom of the mountain.

"Are you okay?" Diaya whispered in the child's ear.

The small girl reacted to the sound of Diaya's voice and tried to wiggle away from her. She was so frightened and confused that any contact with someone from the mountain tribes was terrifying to her.

"Shhh... It's okay." Diaya tried to calm her and reassure the child she was not going to be harmed. Diaya stroked the girl's blond hair and gently placed her other hand on the child's arm. "My name is Diaya, and I work here. I don't like these people very much, and I bet neither do you?" She spoke softly so as not to attract attention to herself. The little girl snuffled and looked up at Diaya. Shaking her head no, she agreed with Diaya and then laid her head back down on the hard wood floor. Diaya smiled and then looked at the ropes holding her hands and the knot at the other end. "How did you end up here?" She asked.

"The men came in the morning and took me." The girl responded in a weak voice. "Where is my mama? I want my mama..." She started to cry again.

Something deep inside of Diaya snapped as she heard these words.

They took me, echoed inside her soul. She was not going to stand for it.

Before she could rationally consider her next move, she sprang into action. Like every other villager, Diaya had a small knife tucked inside her waistband. She pulled it out and made quick work of the ropes holding the little girl's hands tight. Once the child was free, Diaya untied her apron and wrapped it around the child's shoulders. Helping her to her feet Diaya then held her close as she tried to quickly walk the child past the doors and around to the back of the tavern to where the distillery was. At that exact moment, inside the tavern, Morianton had concluded his speech and several of the drunkards were walking out the doors to go and collect their belongings for the journey north.

"What is this?" One of the men shouted as he came upon Diaya helping the child escape.

The emotions inside of her burst out and as the mountain man reached out for the child. Screaming, Diaya slashed the palm of his hand with the sharp edge of her little knife. The man cried out and reacted to the wounding by pulling his hand back and up against his own chest. Another man stepped forward and Diaya slashed at him but just missed his arm.

"Get behind me!" She spoke as she pushed the child behind her and moved toward the stairs leading from the ground up to the porch. More men and women poured out of the doors to see what the commotion was outside. Diaya knew she was now in very real trouble. "Go down the stairs." She told the child, her eyes were alive and flashed with hot anger. "Anyone moves at us and I will cut them!" She snarled back at the collection of village folk. She was shaking and the knife was trembling in her hand as she held it out in front of her. Running on pure emotion, Diaya was not thinking logically. She had been abused and mistreated by this lot for long enough. Seeing the little child in jeopardy woke something inside of her and she was responding to her pent up emotions the only way she could. "Run!" she yelled over her shoulder at the child. "Run home! Follow the path down the mountain and don't stop!" Without a word the child was off, her little legs moving as fast as she could.

"Stop her!" Morianton shouted from the door way of the tavern. Two men made a move to get past Diaya and chase after the lowlander child. One jumped over the railing and Diaya moved to slash at him. He spun to his right, and she missed the first strike. When Diaya had moved from

CHAPTER FIVE

the front of the stairs to confront the villager who jumped the railing, the second man ran down the stairs and past Diaya. She let out a scream and tried to jump on his back. The first man grabbed her and she wrapped her arms around the second man's head and shoulders, biting, scratching and screaming. She refused to let go and all three fell to the ground and landed in a cold puddle of mud.

"Run!" Diaya screamed as she struggled with the two men in the mud. It was a losing battle and she knew it. She was much smaller and weaker than the grown men, but all she needed to do was distract them long enough to give the child a chance to make it to the trees. The little girl was terrified and her legs were moving as fast as she could make them go. Quickly, she made her way past the last of the shanty buildings and into the thick mountain forest. Not stopping or looking back she kept to the thick woods, but tried to follow the merchant trail leading down to the flatlands and her home. She knew enough to know that downhill led to safety, so she ran for several minutes and stopped only to catch her breath. She knew the village was still close and the evil people who took her would try to find her. She was smart enough not to run on the main trail and continued to move down the mountain as quickly and quietly as she could.

"She got away, boss." One of the muddy men looked up at Morianton after spending several minutes searching for the little girl. With more help he might have been able to track her little footsteps but he was still hung over and exhausted from the events of the last day. Besides, he did not want to be the only one looking for her as the rest of his criminal band packed their belongings and made ready to leave. Morianton stood at the top of the tavern stairs looking down at Diaya, who was being held down on her knees by the second man she tussled with. Morianton was holding his goblet and posturing like he was the lord of the village and preparing to cast judgement on Diaya. The man with the wound to his hand was standing next to Morianton with a fresh bandage wrapped around it. He was holding and rubbing the wound like he was in severe pain and looking at Diaya with hate in his eyes.

"Kill her." He whimpered as he held his injured hand out for Morianton to see. Several of the other villagers were close by but all were giving Morianton his space.

"So…" He spoke after taking a long drink. "What to do with you?" He handed his goblet to the wounded man next to him and made his way down the wooden stairs. His footsteps were heavy and slow as his boots took the full force of his weight on each step. Reaching the bottom, he walked up and slapped Diaya across her face with the back of his right hand. "Just like your mother... Nothing but trouble." The strike to her cheek caused a flash of hot pain.

"You leave my mother out of this!" Diaya cried out. Her lip was split open and the blood was running down her dirty face. There was a long and dark history between Morianton and Diaya's mother. He was infatuated with her, and had made several unwelcome physical advances toward her in the past. Every time she refused him, and Morianton took the repeated refusals as a personal insult. Instead of being a gentlemen and honoring her wishes to be left alone, he reacted by trying to make life as harsh as he could for her and her children. Diaya was not spared from his wrath. Morianton was a pig in both body and soul. It was no wonder someone as lovely and kind as Diaya's mother wanted nothing to do with him.

"Shut your mouth, trash!" Morianton barked. Morianton instantly reacted to Diaya's contempt and slapped her again with his left hand sending another shockwave of pain shooting across Diaya's face. She gasped for air and her legs buckled underneath her.

"Hold her up!" He gestured with his hands to the man holding the girl by her arms to lift her back up to her feet. She was stunned and her head was bobbing up and down as she floated in and out of consciousness.

"Look at me!" Morianton shouted. He got in close to her and shouted again. "Look at me!" In a fit of pure drunken rage he grabbed her by the hair on the back of her neck and shook her until she had regained her senses and was looking him in the eyes. No one knows if what happened next was done intentionally, or just a spontaneous reaction, but when Morianton got close to Diaya's face she smiled and then spit a large amount of blood-soaked spittle all over his face and beard. Morianton outweighed Diaya by at least two hundred pounds and was old enough to be her father. This did not stop him from reacting viscously as he punched her several times in the face. The last punch was particularly brutal and her head violently snapped back, her eyes rolled back in her head and she went completely limp. The man who was trying to hold her up dropped her into the dirt and she crashed to the earth like a rag doll.

"Tie her to the hitching post!" He spat as he tried to wipe the blood from his beard and eyes. Two more men came down the stairs and grabbed her by her leg and arm. They pulled her limp body over close to the stairs where a

CHAPTER FIVE

post had been set up for people to tie off their animals before going up the stairs and into the tavern. Morianton, still raging from the loss of his hostage and the blatant disrespect from the slave girl, moved up next to Diaya and kicked her twice in the ribs as she lay helpless on the ground. He spat down on her and cursed her. "Ungrateful wretch!"

"What are we going to do now, Morianton?" A woman from the crowd at the top of the stairs called out. There were grumblings from the gathered villagers. Most of the folks liked Diaya. She was a good servant girl and made the dreary tavern a bit more cheery. The beating from Morianton was completely unnecessary, but no one had the courage to say something or try to stop it.

"I said tie her to the post!" He shouted back up at the crowd and pointed down at Diaya. Someone tossed down a section of rope and she was sat upright and lashed to the wood post. His plan was falling apart and he was losing control. He was a complete coward and a childish drunk who never accepted responsibility for his actions, and he blamed others when things went wrong. Right now his anger was focused on Diaya. Morianton walked in a circle in front of her motionless body and shouted in a fit of rage as he kicked her one last time.

"All right, you made your point." The same woman who tried to save the kidnapped child in the woods the day before finally stepped forward and confronted Morianton. "We are wasting time here, we have some packing to do." She looked directly at Morianton searching for some clarity. After a few seconds Morianton shook his head and agreed with her.

"Gather your things and make ready to flee to the north country. Meet back here at dawn!" He shouted.

"What about her?" The brave woman questioned as she pointed down at Diaya.

"Leave her for the dogs." He responded as he walked away without looking back. The woman looked down at Diaya sorrowfully and pondered for a moment her next move. When she saw everyone else move from the tavern toward their own homes to start gathering up their belongings she slowly turned her back on the poor child tied to the post and walked away.

The little lowland girl was growing very tired and hungry. She had been moving for several hours following the main trail down the mountain and was deep in the forest. She eventually came across a small but fast-moving stream filled with fresh rain water not far from the trail. There was a clearing near the stream by the trail, and it looked like a good place for travelers to stop and water their pack animals and take a break from their efforts. She was very thirsty, but cautious at the same time. Looking over the top of a small hedge, she scanned to see if anyone was in the area. Holding very still she tried to listen for any sounds that might tell her it was unsafe, but the only noise she could hear was the pounding of her own heart and the thumping of the blood in her temples.

    Satisfied she was alone, she carefully stepped out into the open and moved to the edge of the stream. Kneeling down, she scooped her right hand into the ice-cold water and brought a measure of the cool liquid to her lips. Sipping at first, she tasted the water and it was sweet and refreshing. She hurriedly brought several more scoops up to her mouth but then abandoned that technique and stuck her face down into the water and drank deep and long from the life-giving stream. After several seconds of drinking she sat back up on her knees, took a few deep breaths and tried to wipe the sections of hair that got wet from her eyes. Then she heard rustling behind her and she quickly turned around to see what was making noise.

    The air in her lungs was snatched from her chest and all the blood in her face was drained as she looked up at the figure of a man standing behind her in the middle of the clearing. He was armed with a long wooden pole sharpened to a rough point on one end. His clothing was made of the lowland homespun material, his face and shoulders were covered with a large scarf and a woodsman's cloak shrouded his body. She tried to scream, but could only let out a squeak. The man brought his finger up to where his lips would be behind the scarf and gestured to her to not make a sound. He then motioned with his hand for her to calm down and he carefully covered the distance between her and him without making a sound. She was frozen in place as the man knelt down beside her and pulled down the scarf, reveling his face.

    "I am from the village." He whispered. "Are you alone?"

    She recognized his face but she was still in such a state of shock and exhaustion her little mind could not process what was happening.

    "Are you hurt, are you alone?" He asked again with concern in his voice. He kept looking over his shoulders and checking the surroundings.

CHAPTER FIVE

"I want my mama." She choked as the tears started to flow down her cheeks. The little girl was in terror and cried out for the one person who could make it all better.

The man's heart broke and he tried to comfort her the best he could. "That's why I am here, to take you back to your mama. My friends and I have been looking for you for a while now." He tried to readjust his position to make himself seem less threatening to the child. " The men who took you… Do you know where they are?" He continued in a reassuring whisper.

She nodded her head and pointed back up the the mountain.

"So they are not here. Are they still in the village?"

She nodded her head to confirm his suspicions.

"Did you escape?"

She nodded her head again. "The girl helped me." She spoke more clearly. "I think they are going to hurt her for helping me."

Suddenly two more men and a tall boy, all dressed like the first man and armed with farming tools, emerged from the woods. The little girl instantly recognized the tall boy as her brother and squealed out his name. She got up and ran to his arms. The two of them moved to one side as the three men huddled and spoke quietly.

"Any sign of them?" The first man to find the girl asked.

"No, nothing." The older of the two other men spoke. They all turned and looked at the tall boy cradling the child in his arms as she cried with relief. "What are the chances we would have come across her this far up the trail?" He shrugged in disbelief. "God is good."

The tall young man walked up to the other three men. "She keeps going on and on about some girl who helped her escape. Did you see anyone else?"

"No." The child spoke with the innocence of youth. "She is still in the village and they are hurting her for helping me. You need to save her."

"What are you saying, child?" The oldest man and clearly the leader questioned.

"The girl with the smile and curly hair… She let me go and told me to run when the bad men came. Please go and help her…" She looked up into her big brother's eyes. "Please go and help her."

All of the men looked at the leader for guidance.

"I know the way." One of the other men volunteered. "We can at least get a look at the village and see if they have abandoned it. Maybe even get some of our stuff back."

The oldest man nodded his head in agreement. "Call the others in and rally here." He spoke as he looked at the man who walked in with him. The villager moved toward the main trail and whistled for the others in the area to come to him. In no time there were at least two dozen men all dressed in the same manner and armed with various farming tools like axes, shovels and pitch forks. The bandits took all the personal weapons from the village they could find when they robbed the lowlander's homes. This could not keep the men of the peaceful town from trying to save one of their own or exact revenge on those who assaulted them. Armed with what they could find they slowly were making their way up the mountain in hopes of rescuing the child and finding the bandits.

When everyone was assembled around the older man, he spoke slowly and calmly. He clearly was a village leader and respected by everyone there. Pointing to the boy still holding his rescued sister he spoke, " Take your sister back to the village. You should be safe on the trail, it will be the quickest route home." He brushed a lock of hair from her face and smiled. "I am glad you are safe little one, we all were so worried about you." She cracked a slight smile and blinked back at him. "Are you hungry?" She nodded her head yes. "Give him an extra ration pack and waterskin." He spoke to the gathered villagers. Almost instantly a small knapsack was handed to the boy along with a water skin. He took the knapsack and water skin and draped their long straps over his shoulder. "Hurry home, boy… Your mother must be beside herself with worry."

"Yes sir, thank you sir." And he was off, moving out of the clearing and onto the trail leading downhill and home with his sister safely in his arms.

The gathered men all watched as the boy disappeared around a bend in the road then, almost as if on cue, they all turned back to look at their leader.

"How far to the village?" He asked.

"If we hurry, we can make it there by sundown." The man who knew the way responded. "I know a location about one hour's walk from the mountain village where we can camp and then make our move at first light."

"Sounds good," the leader answered. "You have point. Lead the way." He pointed up the mountain trail. "The rest of you fall in behind him in a single file. No noise, no talking."

CHAPTER FIVE

They walked the rest of the day in almost complete silence. They reached the small, secluded grove as the sun was making its descent behind the western mountains. Looking around, the leader liked the location. "How do you know about this place?" He asked the man who led the war party to this spot.

"I made poor choices when I was young and used this place to hide from my parents, and the law." He responded with a grin.

"Yeah... I remember." The older man winked back, indicating they had known each other for a very long time. "Okay." He continued. "The rest of you get settled and post a guard. No fire tonight, we don't need the mountain men coming to see what is burning." Some of the folks who were with them looked up with concern in their eyes. Sleeping outside without a campfire was something they were not prepared to do. "We will be back after dark." The leader turned back to his companion. "Let's go have a look at the village."

Moving quickly the two men made their way through the dense forest until they reached the edge of the criminal's village. Very slowly, the two men moved up to the the tree line and positioned themselves to where they could overlook the main part of the village.

"Looks empty." The younger whispered. "Maybe we are too late?"

The older man was quiet as he scanned the village. "Movement." Was all he said as he pointed to the large thatch covered tavern near the center of the town. It looked like something or someone was tied up at the base of the tavern's wooden balcony and was trying to move.

Diaya was unsure how long she had been alone. The late afternoon sun was starting to dip behind the western ridge and the glare from the hot sun was in her eyes. One of her eyes was swollen shut and the second was not much better, but she could still see out of it. Every part of her body hurt and her throat burned from a lack of water. Swallowing hard, she forced open her one good eye and tried to look around. The village was completely empty except for two scrawny dogs sniffing around the outlined buildings and shanties. Her hands were numb, and her shoulders ached from the ropes holding her fast to the large wooden post. Breathing was an uncomfortable struggle. She had shooting pain in her side as she inhaled and tried to readjust her position. The only thing that did not hurt on her body were her toes. She looked down at her feet as she saw someone had taken her sandals. She grunted and winced in pain as she thought about one of the scoundrel villagers removing her shoes while she was unconscious. As she tried to clear the fog from her mind and focus on her condition, a faraway voice calling out her name, was sounding in her ear. At first she did not recognize the voice calling out her name over and over again. Then the tone and pitch struck a chord in her mind. "Mother…?" Diaya could not be sure. She was in such pain, she thought she might be delirious. Then the voice grew louder.

"Diaya!" A stunning woman with long black hair and rough clothing came running around the corner, followed by two small children, twins—a boy and girl.

"Mother!" Diaya cried out. She could not move her mouth very well but managed to get the word out loud enough for her mother to locate her.

The woman turned to face the sound of Diaya's voice and cried out in horror when she saw her beloved child bloodied and secured to the wooden post like a beast. "Diaya!" She shouted as she hurried to her daughter's side. Flopping down to her knees next to Diaya, the woman struggled to comprehend her daughter's condition.

"Mama…" Diaya cried when she felt her mother at her side. "Please cut me loose!"

Diaya's mother pulled out her own knife and made quick work of the ropes binding Diaya's hands and arms. Feeling the pressure being released from her bonds, Diaya cried out in pain as she tried to move her shoulders and get blood flow back to her hands. She fell into her mother's arms and they cried together.

"Who did this?" The lady asked as she brushed the mud and blood-caked hair from Diaya's eyes. The tears welled up in her eyes as she watched her oldest child struggle with the pain of her injures.

"Morianton…" Diaya whispered before falling back into unconsciousness.

The two men watching from the tree line looked at each other with puzzlement in their expressions. They were too far away to hear the exchange between Diaya and her mother, but they could see everything.

"What is going on?" The younger man wondered aloud.

"The child spoke of a young girl with dark curly hair who helped her escape." The older man looked back at the scene before them and responded as he pointed at Diaya. "That might be her."

CHAPTER FIVE

"We should go help her!"

"Easy..." The leader reacted to the sounds of horses and pushed the younger man down into the dirt. "Someone is coming."

Morianton came around the corner of the village road riding bareback on a bulky, but old plow horse. He had two mules in tow and they were loaded down with supplies. Several other men and women were following with their own pack animals and gear.

"That's him!" The young lowlander almost shouted when he saw Morianton ride into the mountain village. "He was the man leading the bandits!" He pulled out his knife and tried to rise up to his feet. He was going to kill him.

"Stay down!" The older man ordered, as he grabbed the young man's arm and yanked him back down behind the dirt mound. "Don't be a fool. I know him." He gestured with his head for the younger man to look back at the village. "He is a drunkard and a coward." He did some quick math in his head and came to the obvious conclusion. " There are too many of them for us to make our move now. We wait and see what transpires. He will make a mistake, and then we will exact our revenge. But not now."

The younger man felt slighted but also understood the need to be still and wait. His emotions had gotten the better of him and it was lucky the older and wiser man was with him to temper his actions.

"Morianton! You monster, look what you have done!" Diaya's mother was livid. She was holding Diaya in her arms and held her out for all to see his work. "You are all monsters!" She screamed as she scanned the other villagers who came back with Morianton.

"Now, now, my love." Morianton sarcastically answered as he slid off the back of his draft horse. "Is that any way to speak to your future king?" He grabbed Diaya's mother by her arm and pulled her to her feet. She let go of Diaya as she was being jerked up and Diaya dropped to the ground like a sack of oats.

"You let me go!" She tried to pull free from his grasp but he was holding on too strong.

"Oh no, my dear… You are coming with me." Morianton spat as he struggled to hold onto her arms. "Settle down now or I will be very unkind to the little ones there." He gestured toward her two small children who were standing nearby and crying for their mother while looking very sacred and confused.

She knew Morianton was telling the truth. He was capable of anything. She stopped struggling and he released his strong grip on her arms. "There now…" He smiled exposing his stained teeth. "That's much better." He looked back at the others still with him. "My new queen will need a ride. And fetch the little ones, they are coming along with us."

Great big tears were falling from her eyes as she watched rough men pick up her two babies and put them on top of a pack animal. "What about Diaya?" She choked out in a gasp.

Morianton looked back down at the motionless body of the teenager lying at his feet. "She stays. She is nothing but trouble anyway, and I am done with her."

"At least give her some water…" She pleaded.

Morianton moved much quicker then she thought possible and had grasped her throat in his rough and dirty hand. He was squeezing hard and hissed as he spoke. "Ask me nicely." He was inches away from her face, and his hot breath blew across her lips. She gasped and grabbed at his wrist with both of her hands. "You need to ask me nicely… I am your king now." He smiled an evil smile. "Understand?" She tried to shake her head but his hand was in the way. The best she could do was a slight nod up and down. "Good." He released his grip and took two steps back.

Gasping and grabbing at her throat the poor woman lost her footing and went to one knee. Hacking and coughing she tried to regain her breath and her balance as she stood back up. Once on her feet, she flipped her long hair out of her dark eyes and with a defiant look contemplated her situation. Morianton was holding her two younger children hostage. She knew they were helpless without her, and he would kill them or sell them as slaves to the Lamanites if she did not cooperate. She was going to travel with Morianton whether she liked it or not. She looked down at Diaya and her heart sank. She was helpless to aid her oldest child lying in the mud. "What am I going to do about you?" She fretted softly. She knew the journey alone might kill her, as injured as Diaya was. "Or Morianton will kill you outright to spite me…" It did not take her long to realize the only workable solution to this problem was to leave her here. Bending down she stroked the matted hair of her lifeless child. "I am sorry, please forgive me." Standing up she turned back to Morianton. "Please give her some water." She begged softly.

He brought his hand up to his ear and spoke in a sarcastic tone. "I'm sorry, are you addressing your king?" Some of the people traveling with

CHAPTER FIVE

Morianton started to giggle at the snide way he was dealing with her.

Clenching her jaw in anger and flashing hot fire in her eyes, she took a deep breath and spoke again, her teeth clenched together in anger.

"My king." The words formed and moved like poison dripping from the edge of a needle. "Would you show this poor subject mercy, and please give her some water?"

Morianton stood still for a moment then smiled back at her. "Never let it be said Morianton failed to show mercy to his subjects." He turned and faced his cohorts and signaled to one of them to toss him a water skin. Grabbing the water container in midflight, Morianton uncorked it and walked up next to Diaya's body. He smiled at the beautiful woman standing next to him and without breaking eye contact, he poured the entire contents of the water skin over Diaya's head and body.

The gathered crowd all broke out in laughter. When the water skin was empty, Morianton tossed it back to the rider who gave it to him. Holding out his arms like a victor he turned and acknowledged the response from his men. Diaya's mother was furious. When Morianton turned back around to face her she slapped him across the face with her right hand. The crack of skin could be heard across the open ground and Morianton brought his own hand up to rub his cheek. The slap was more symbolic than damaging. It would take more than a slap from a woman her size to really hurt a large man like Morianton. "Feisty…" He said smirking. Then a dark cloud covered his face and anger welled up in his eyes. With the same hand he used to rub his face, he balled up his fist and struck the woman square in the mouth. She fell to the earth, landing on top of her child. The water previously poured over Diaya had helped to revive her and she was starting to wake when she felt the weight of her mother crash down upon her. The pain of her mother's body smashing down on hers instantly brought her to full consciousness, but she dared not move anything but her eyes.

"Pick her up and put her on the mule." Morianton commanded as he pointed at one of the pack animals next to where he was standing.

Diaya felt the weight of her mother's body come off of her as three men from Morianton's horde picked her up and straddled her across the flanks of the mule. She could hear what they were saying but dared not move her head to see who was talking.

"How much longer do you want to wait?" One of the men with Morianton asked him. They both looked over the mass of bodies and animals gathered in the street. They could see in the faces of some villagers the anxiety and fear of leaving their homes. Most of the village had gathered and were prepared to move. Although many did not go on the raid and some had even condemned it, they all knew when justice came for Morianton and his band of robbers they would not be spared Moroni's wrath. They were just as much to blame for allowing evil men to have that much control over their lives. They should have put a stop to Morianton and his evil ways, but they were cowards, or they just did not care, so now they must flee. "Most are here, so we should get moving. I want as much distance as possible between us and this cursed village before Moroni and his men arrive. The rest can catch up." Looking up at the evening sky Morianton continued. "Until it rains again, our tracks won't be hard to find and follow." He looked back at the crowd and shouted. "We make our way to the northern road and the narrow pass to the frontier!"

Diaya could hear everything that Morianton said, but remained motionless. She knew the only chance for her family's survival depended on Morianton leaving her for dead. Then she could go and get help. She lay still for several more minutes as the large group of criminals and their families moved past her in a long slow single file. They were headed up the mountain trail and down the other side where it would eventually connect with the northern trade road.

The two men in the trees waited until the village was again empty. It was almost dark as they emerged from the woodline and made their way toward Diaya. They'd seen everything and heard most of it. They knew Diaya had infuriated Morianton, and along with the description given by the kidnapped child of the young lady who helped her escape, they were sure the injured girl was the same person. With their dark-colored cloaks covering their bodies and faces, the two men moved from building to building until they were next to Diaya.

"Child, can you hear me?" The older man asked as he gently placed his hand on her shoulder. Diaya had fallen back asleep and was startled by his touch.

"Please don't hurt me…" She begged.

"We are here to help. Can you sit up?"

"My mother, my family… Please help them." Diaya begged with tears in her eyes. She was trying to roll over to be able to see the man speaking to her.

CHAPTER FIVE

"I am going to check inside." The younger man pointed up into the tavern and started to move up the stairs.

"Child, we need to move you off the street before they come back. Can you get up?" The older man was as gentle as a loving father as he coaxed Diaya up to a sitting position. She wailed in pain from the numerous injuries to her face and body caused by the vicious beating from Morianton. She sat still, leaning against the lowlander for support. The pain of it all was taking the breath from her lungs.

"Did you see where they took my family, my mother?" Diaya asked after gaining some control over her breathing.

"They continued on up the trail." The man responded as he cautiously looked around for any other highland villagers who might still be lingering in the area.

The other lowlander came bounding down the stairs with a bundle in his arms. He handed the older man a thick blanket he had found inside. "Here…" He said giving the blanket away. "Wrap this around her." He then uncorked a bottle and held the rim close to Diaya's mouth. "For the pain." He whispered as he tried to get Diaya to drink some potent alcohol. Diaya could smell the fermenting liquid and pushed it far away from her face. It was the drink that plagued her every day, the drink that fueled the anger in the upland villager's hearts— and it was the same drink on Morianton's breath when he almost beat her to death and the same drink giving courage to the criminals who took her family. She was going to have nothing to do with the vulgar, intoxicating substance ever again. The two men saw the effort Diaya made to keep from drinking the alcohol and looked at each other. The younger man shrugged his shoulders and tossed the bottle under the stairs.

"Can you stand up?" They asked Diaya.

"I think so…" She said. "Can you please help me?"

The older man wrapped the blanket around her shoulders and each man took an arm. With their help, Diaya managed to get to her feet and tried to stabilize herself but she was still too dizzy and weak to walk on her own power.

"Are you the same girl who helped the lowlander child escape this day?" The older man asked as they tried to walk her over to the stairs so she could sit down.

"Yes, and I paid a high price for my deeds." Diaya groaned as she sat on the hard wooden planks. Moving the short distance was exhausting for her.

"The child is from our village. We owe you our gratitude and thanks." The younger man spoke. He'd found some cheese and bread while he was rummaging around in the tavern. He offered her a small hunk of the soft, dark-colored bread. She took it and tore off a tiny bite. Working the piece of bread inbetween her swollen lips, she chewed gently and swallowed hard.

"Water?" She asked. A waterskin was handed to her and she gingerly poured a helping of the cool liquid down her throat. She took a second drink and then bit into more bread. After sitting in silence and chewing on the bread for a while Diaya looked at the two men and spoke. "So… Now what?"

The lowlanders looked at each other but neither had an answer. "If you are well enough to travel, we can take you back to our village at the bottom of the mountain. You can rest and heal there." The older man finally proposed.

"They took my family." Diaya replied in a soft voice. Her head was down and she was starting to feel the heartache.

"Those men came into our village to rob and murder us." The older one replayed the events for Diaya. "They took the child hostage to keep us from following them back up here. We sent a rider to inform General Moroni, and then came looking for her." He readjusted his seat on the stairs. "When we found her unharmed in the woods, she told us of you and we are here to help."

"Moroni knows of what happened to your village?" She looked at them both. They both nodded their heads.

"By now the rider should have reached his base camp outside of Zarahemla." The older man responded.

A dog started to bark in the distance and the men both looked around nervously at the abandoned mountain village. "We should go." The younger man said as he stood up and readjusted his pack and gear.

The older man held up one finger to tell the other man to wait one minute. "Do you know where they have gone— Morianton and the others?" He asked Diaya.

"I heard them talk for hours in the tavern. He said something about the pass by the sea and going to the land northward."

"That would explain why they went that way." The younger man spoke as he pointed toward the top of the mountain. In the distance

CHAPTER FIVE

the lone dog barked again. "We do need to move back to the tree line." He admonished.

"Come with us." The older man begged Diaya. "You will be treated very well in our village, and when Moroni's men come you can tell them everything you know about Morianton and his whereabouts."

CHAPTER SIX

A Warrant for His Arrest

"My general?" Amiha called out as he stood at the opening of the large command tent.

"Come!"

Amiha entered a few steps then continued, "Sir, there is someone outside I think you are going to want to talk to."

Moroni put down the papers in his hands, and turned to face Amiha.

"Alone…?" Amiha hinted to Moroni to excuse the other ranking officers, who were in the tent with him. The other soldiers in the tent stopped what they were doing, then turned to look at Amiha. They all wondered what was so important they should not be privy to it, since they were his trusted command staff.

Moroni gave Amiha an inquisitive look. Amiha returned it with a slight nod of his head.

Not breaking eye contact with Amiha, Moroni spoke to the officers and attendants in the tent. "Gentlemen, will you please excuse us?"

Those who were excused slowly gathered up their maps, scrolls and personal items, then walked out of the tent. Amiha could feel the tension and the coldness coming off of each one of the high-ranking Nephite officers as they all walked past him and out into the sunlight.

As the last of the soldiers exited, Moroni gestured for Amiha to bring in the mysterious visitor. Amiha turned and walked out of the tent. A few seconds later, he returned and stood near the opening. He was reassuring a small, hooded figure that she was permitted to enter the tent and speak

CHAPTER SIX

to General Moroni. After a moment, the hooded figure entered the tent, then moved to a corner away from Moroni.

The young lieutenant who had brought Diaya to camp walked in behind her and stood at attention. He was still dressed in his armor and had his cavalry helmet under his arm.

"Forgive us my general, she is scared." Amiha said softly.

"As you were, lieutenant," Moroni nodded to the Nephite officer. He relaxed, but remained standing. "My lady, you have nothing to fear. You are a guest in my tent and perfectly safe. Would you like something to drink or eat?" Moroni motioned to a pitcher of fresh fruit juice along with a hunk of bread with cheese on a table near him.

"I will fetch that, my lord," the voice under the hood called out timidly as she moved toward the table.

Removing her hood, Diaya exposed the fresh bruises and cuts to her face. Moroni's heart broke when he saw the damage done to Diaya's face. Unconsciously, he took one step back so he could get a better look at her face as she picked up the pitcher of juice.

"What happened to you, child?" he gasped. "Who did this to you? Speak the truth." She put the pitcher down then looked away from Moroni as he spoke. "You have nothing to fear anymore. You are now under my personal protection... Tell me, how did this happen?" Moroni moved closer and gently touched her chin. He raised up her head so he could look into her eyes.

"Great one, please forgive me... I am just a servant girl." She blinked, several times, as tears formed in the corners of her eyes. She gently wiped them away, being careful not to touch her swollen eyes. For the first time in her entire life, in Moroni's presence, she felt safe. She instantly knew he was not the kind of man who would strike a young girl, or take advantage of her or her family in any way. All the emotions she was desperately trying to hold back came pouring out in great drops of salty tears.

Moroni saw the tears; he heard the sobs and saw the pain in her eyes. Taking pity on her, he escorted her to a chair, grabbing a small towel from his washbasin. Kneeling down in front of her, he handed her the towel and gave a caring smile. "I will have my personal physician tend to your injuries. Now, please tell me, who did this?" Wiping her tears, Diaya looked into Moroni's eyes. All the stories about the young general were true. He was a giant of a man, like a great bear, but so gentle and kind. *He truly is handsome*, she thought to herself, as she looked up into his piercing blue eyes and saw his chiseled jaw. She tried to smile but winced from the pain.

"It's okay, tell the general about Morianton," Amiha beckoned in a gentle tone.

"Morianton?" Moroni looked up at Amiha. "Last week you brought a boy before me who told us about some disturbance near the borders of the land of Lehi. He said something about a man named Morianton. He was the cause of the trouble. Is this the same man?" Moroni looked back at Diaya.

"Yes, great one... The same man," she sniffled.

"Is he the one who did this to you?"

"Yes, great one." Diaya lowered her head and started to cry again. "What's going to happen to my family?" She questioned between the sobs, then she covered her face with the towel and wept openly.

"Where is your family?" Moroni asked with concern and empathy in his voice. "Why do you think they are in danger?"

Diaya did not answer Moroni, but continued to sob. Amiha could see he needed to interject.

"Sir," he said as Moroni looked up at him. "She explained to me that Morianton is, or was, a very rich and influential man. He and a company of his followers raided a small farming village in the land of Lehi, near the border."

"I remember the report. I dispatched two platoons to investigate and send word," Moroni interrupted. "I'm assuming they have not returned?"

"No sir, they arrived back in camp one hour ago." Amiha gestured to the soldier still standing near the tent opening. "This is the officer who was sent. He briefed me on what he and his men found, then brought this girl with him to make his report. Her name is Diaya."

Moroni looked the solder in the eyes, then turned back to look at Diaya. She tried to smile, but winced, again from the pain of the cuts and bruises to her face.

"Sir, she was insistent she speak to you alone," the Nephite officer stepped forward, speaking without being prompted. "She has information on the criminal's whereabouts and plans. From what I gathered there at the village, as well as the little she has told me, Morianton is not done yet." Moroni looked back at Diaya, who was sitting with her head down.

"Very well, lieutenant," Moroni spoke slowly as he looked at Diaya,

CHAPTER SIX

trying to judge her on his first impressions. "See to your men and have your full report ready for me after dinner."

"Yes, sir!" The young leader snapped, putting his helmet back on his head. Saluting quickly, he left the tent, relieved he would have time to clean up and prepare his notes before he accounted for his actions and those of his soldiers. "Now," Moroni spoke as he moved back over to Diaya, "what do you have to tell me?"

Diaya slowly turned her head toward Amiha, then back at Moroni and looked him in the eyes. The nonverbal communication was very clear. Diaya did not trust anyone, and with good reason. She knew Morianton had friends everywhere, possibly in this camp. She was only going to share her information with the general himself because she knew he was the only one who could guarantee her safety and bring her family back unharmed. "Great one, the words I have are for you alone. I trust no one else with this information."

"I will honor your wishes, but know this," he said as he pointed to Amiha. "Chief Captain Amiha is my aide de camp and personal assistant. Everything you tell me, he will know the second you leave. He is a trusted ranking officer, and I personally vouch for his integrity."

Diaya looked again at Amiha, holding his gaze for several seconds. "Well..." she raised her eyebrows, then continued, "if the mighty General Moroni says you can be trusted, then so be it." She turned back and looked at Moroni. "Morianton is a very dangerous man." She gestured up to her face as well as pointing to the bruises and cuts. "He is the one responsible for the raid on the lowlanders' homes. I heard him plan the attack. I was there when they all returned with the property they stole." She wiped some tears away from her eyes with the cloth Moroni gave her. "They came back with a child they had kidnapped, from the lowlanders. They were holding her as a hostage. She was tied up like an animal, so I took pity on her. I helped her escape and Morianton, in his drunken anger, beat me almost to death for it." She wiped at the tears again as she relieved the pain, then continued to speak. "He knew you would not stand for such lawlessness and would come with your men to make things right, so he took my mother as well as two of my younger siblings with him. They fled north with those who helped him plan and execute the raid."

Moroni stood up straight, looking at Amiha. One could feel the anger well up inside him as Moroni thought about the crimes and victims of

Morianton's actions.

"Do you know where they were going?" Amiha spoke after a few seconds of silence. He could tell Moroni was getting upset. Amiha felt it was important to keep the conversation going in order to help Moroni focus on the problem at hand. He knew Moroni had suffered a great deal and seen much sorrow as the supreme leader of all the Nephite forces. He knew Moroni's great heart had been broken over and over again at the sight of the victims of the Lamanite aggression, as well as the evil attempts of the criminals and usurpers within the Nephite people. This was one more reminder that, despite his best efforts, Moroni could not stop all the dark powers on this earth. Moroni knew deep down it was more than likely he, along with his mighty friends, would be in close combat with evil until the day they died. But that is the burden and the sacred honor of a true warrior. The duality and contradiction of the life of a noble hero is the stuff of legend and mythology. A warrior will train to fight to the death if need be. At the same time, he prays for peace. A true hero is willing to do what is necessary as well as sacrifice his or her own life for the greater good, but at the same time shuns the trappings that come with the title of champion. Moroni was a true hero Amiha knew it, and he was proud to be at Moroni's side.

Diaya could also see the struggle going on in Moroni's mind. She knew the stories about him— who didn't? He was a mighty warrior, a man to be respected and feared by all. Looking at him now, she knew the stories were all true. He was the biggest man she had ever seen. Morianton was a big man, but he was fat and lazy. Moroni, on the other hand, was not only an imposing figure, but he had an aura of quiet dignity and honor. Moroni did not need to remind everyone in the room he was in charge. But clearly, his heart was breaking all over again with the sad news of the marauding and kidnapping by Morianton and his followers.

Diaya continued, "He said there are people in the land northward who believe the rightful rule of the kings should be re-established, and there was a man there who was trying to organize the north people and seek help from the Lamanites. They were going to take the narrow pass by the sea to escape your justice and join up with this man." She put her head down. "That is all I know."

When they heard the report from Diaya, Moroni and Amiha both made their way to the large map hanging on the back wall of the

CHAPTER SIX

great tent. "Here…" Moroni pointed to the map, after inspecting it for a moment. "The mountain pass, near the inland sea and the Land of Desolation; it leads to the Land Bountiful," he tapped the map to show Amiha. Amiha knew what it meant when Moroni said the Land Bountiful. There had been trouble there in the past. "If they take the mountain road north from their village…" he showed Amiha the possible path that Morianton could take to reach the outlined lands, north of the established boundaries of the Nephite people. There, in those lands, Moroni knew he had no authority. Morianton and his followers would be fugitives and able to escape justice. Then, Moroni felt a sudden chill run down his spine. "Child?" he questioned over his left shoulder. " The name of the man Morianton was going to meet with… What is it?"

Diaya looked back up and took a second as she tried to remember. Then it came to her. "Pachus, he said his name is Pachus." She smiled, relieved she was able to remember this important detail.

It was like the warm air in the tent had been flushed out by a great frost as Moroni and Amiha both looked at each other. "Pachus." Moroni hissed as he clenched his jaw tightly, and stood motionless in anger.

Amiha knew what needed to happen next, but he also needed Moroni to make it so. Amiha was not in charge of this grand army. He did not have the consent of the people to enforce justice and keep the peace like Moroni did, so he prompted Moroni to act. "What are your orders, sir?"

Moroni took Amiha by the arm and they walked over to the far corner of the tent, away from Diaya's ears. "What do our spies say on this matter?" he whispered to his trusted friend.

"They confirm her reports," Amiha whispered back, looking in her direction to ensure she could not hear their conversation. "Morianton is moving with a large body of armed men and their families., possibly the enitre village. He was last seen going north."

"Find Captain Teancum." His tone was low but intense. Not the kind of fake bravado cowards bark toward each other, hoping to scare their adversary and avoid a conflict, but true feeling. This specter named Pachus had haunted Moroni and the Nephite army long enough. There was only one man who Moroni could trust to solve this deadly equation. What Moroni needed now was a hunter, a predator who stalked evil men, a true soldier and someone who hated criminals as much, if not more, than he did.

"Yes, sir!" Amiha replied as he quickly exited the tent and moved through the camp. He was smiling as he walked toward his own horse. "I almost feel sorry for you, Morianton," he said jokingly to himself. Amiha had seen firsthand what Teancum was capable of. In a small way, he wished he could go along to watch.

When Amiha left, Moroni suddenly realized he was now alone in the grand tent with an underage girl. This was most inappropriate. As the leader of the entire army, and high protector of the Nephite nation, his honor must be beyond reproach. He was the moral compass and supreme authority for every soldier in camp. He also knew how damaging a false rumor could be for morale, a scandalous story about the general and the girl would be all his enemies would need to destroy his credibility. He quickly moved to solve the problem.

"Excuse me, my lady," he bowed slightly as he spoke to her. Moroni did not care that she was a lowly servant girl; she was a daughter of God, deserving of chivalry and respect. "I will wait outside until the doctor arrives to tend to your injuries." Stepping into the fresh air and sunlight, Moroni turned to the two fully-armored guards standing near the front of his tent. "Keep an eye on her and don't let her leave," he spoke just above a whisper.

"Yes, sir," they replied in unison.

"Sergeant of the guard!" Moroni shouted, as he turned away and walked a few paces from his tent.

"Sir?" A fit-looking soldier, in full armor and carrying a spear, came up and saluted Moroni.

"Send someone to fetch the camp surgeon. Have him report to my tent right away. Tell the doctor to bring his medical kit and that his patient is a young girl who was physically assaulted."

"Yes sir, is that all?"

"Yes, go quickly now." Moroni returned the salute and watched the young soldier as he carried out his duty.

In short order, the surgeon arrived. He took Diaya away to be cared for by his medical staff. "She is hurt badly, but will live," the doctor whispered to Moroni before he departed with his brave new patient.

"Take good care of her, doc," Moroni spoke. "She has been extremely brave and deserves our gratitude."

The surgeon smiled and bowed slightly before Moroni, then held the tent flap open wide for his medical orderlies, as they moved Diaya on a

CHAPTER SIX

stretcher to the waiting medical wagon.

"Thank you, great one," she spoke in a weak but grateful voice, letting her hand linger for just a moment on his. Moroni had seen the look in her eyes in several other women in the past, causing him to blush as Daiya was carried past him. For as strong and powerful as he was, when it came to dealing with women, Moroni had always felt shy.

As Moroni stood outside the tent, watching the medical wagon move away from his command area toward the main camp, two riders came through the only access point in the wall of wooden pickets around the big tent. The sergeant of the guard waved the two riders past his security detail, and they rode up to the tent where Moroni was standing.

"Captain Teancum, thank you for coming so quickly," Moroni addressed his most capable captain while holding his horse's reins as Teancum and Amiha dismounted. "Please, come inside. I have an assignment for you and your Ghost Soldiers."

Everyone stepped inside the tent, pausing for a moment to let their eyes adjust to the dim light. Moroni gestured to the jug of juice, offering his two captains some refreshment. Teancum accepted a goblet, gave his thanks to his general for the hospitality, and then took a quick drink.

"Chief Captain Teancum, how many of your Ghost Soldiers are here in camp with you?" Moroni questioned, without looking up from his large map.

"Sir, I have both my companies with me; all are accounted for," he responded in his own quiet and stoic way as he stepped forward to stand next to Moroni at the map table.

"Excellent!" Moroni looked up then pointed to a section of the map. "Move your men north, to the pass by the sea, here, north of the lands of Lehi, near the Land of Desolation... just below Bountiful." Moroni gestured to a section of the map, and Teancum leaned in closer for a better look. Moroni lowered his voice as he continued to speak to Teancum. "You are aware of the ongoing problems with the brigand, Morianton?" Teancum nodded his head in acknowledgement. He had his own spies too. "We have just received verified intelligence he is leading a large body of armed criminals north from his lands in an attempt to escape justice, as well as join forces with the king men in the north country."

Teancum looked up at Moroni with questioning eyes. He quickly figured out the direction this conversation was going, but needed to hear it from Moroni, himself. "Morianton is not going to march his men, their families, and all of their possessions north over the mountains during the monsoon season. Not even he is that foolish. So the only other way for such a large group to travel to the Land of Bountiful is to follow the trade route across the small section of land by the sea." Moroni tapped the point on the map with his finger. " Take control of this section before Morianton and his band of followers can cross. If he gets north of the mountains and into the Land of Bountiful, he will be very hard to track." Moroni stood up and took a deep breath. Looking into Teancum's eyes, he continued, "There is dissension between the wealthy in the Land of Bountiful and the judges."

Moroni paused, as if his next words physically pained him to say. Moroni took his eyes off Teancum and looked back down at the map, then tapped his finger on the wooden surface. "Pachus is there." Pachus was a problem Moroni had allowed to spiral out of control. Everyone in the tent was at the battle of Manti. They all knew of Pachus's treachery. "He is inciting others to follow him and his, so-called, king men."

"Pachus!" Teancum sighed in frustration. "That fat toad." Teancum stood upright and faced Moroni, "You should have killed him back in Manti." Teancum was one of a very few who could speak so boldly before the general. In Moroni's eyes, Teancum had more than earned the right to speak his mind when giving counsel to the great Nephite leader.

"I agree," Moroni responded, matter-of-factly. "I take full responsibility for that mistake. It will not happen again." Moroni waved his hand over the top portion of the map. "He is hiding up in the frontier, beyond the Nephite borders, outside of the reach of the sheriff and local judges." Moroni paused to breathe while rubbing his hand on his neck, to release the tension he felt. "My fear is that Pachus and Morianton want the same thing— they want to get rid of the republic and put a king back on a throne. If he makes it to Bountiful with his armed camp, then Morianton will give Pachus an instant boost to his forces." Moroni rubbed his eyes, then walked around the map table. He was exhausted; he had been looking at maps and reading dispatches all day. It was always surprising to Moroni how tired he felt after doing hours of clerical work. "The last thing we need right now is an armed band of usurping Nephites on our Northern border. We are stretched too thin as it is, trying to keep the Lamanites at bay."

Moroni moved to his desk and grabbed a rolled parchment. He

CHAPTER SIX

turned and looked directly at Teancum. "I need you and your men to get up there, arrest Morianton, and turn his followers around. Disarm them and bring them back here to face justice for their crimes, with force if necessary." Moroni dipped his writing quill into the inkwell, writing on the parchment. When he was done, he sealed the parchment with wax. "Here is your warrant." He handed Teancum the arrest orders. They were sealed with a red wax seal bearing the personal emblem of the general of all the Nephite armed forces. Teancum saw the parchment was sealed, but it did not matter to him. He did not need to read the words; he knew what it said. He also realized why he was the only one Moroni could trust with this mission. Moroni had been given consent, by the voice of the people, to do whatever was necessary in order to keep the peace and save the republic.

An arrest warrant, without the review from a high judge, was contrary to the civil laws of the Nephites. Moroni understood this; he also knew Teancum knew this because he had helped write the new laws in his past life, before his family was murdered. But, with the unprecedented powers granted to Moroni during this time of military crisis, including the power to arrest citizens without the consent of the judges, Teancum knew Moroni could be trusted to not exercise unrighteous dominion over the people, as well as not act outside the authority granted to him by the voice of the people.

"Yes sir," Teancum quipped as he reached for the warrant. "If any of them resist the arrest warrant?" It was no surprise to Moroni that Teancum would ask this question. Not only was he a predator, but he was a former common judge and physician. The man was always thinking. He knew Morianton was a criminal, but he was also a citizen of the Nephite nation and entitled to certain rights. He already knew the answer but wanted to know if Moroni had thought this problem through to its logical conclusion.

"They are murderers, thieves and kidnappers, and they are now moving in force to support a man who is provoking agitation. Do what you can to resolve the matter peacefully, but they must face justice." Moroni paused. "And they cannot be allowed to reinforce the usurper, Pachus..." Moroni paused again and was, for just a moment, lost in thought. "The last thing I want to do is make Morianton a martyr to the king men's cause." Moroni waited until he was sure of the feelings he had on the matter. "You understand the laws of this land better than most. You are also my most gifted captain." Breathing deeply, he gave his instructions. "Do everything you can to resolve this peacefully and bring the criminals to justice. If they resist you with physical force, and you are left with no other option, then kill them." There was no more hesitation in Moroni's voice.

Teancum almost smiled as he looked his friend and general in the eyes. "For a man with no legal or political training, you understand God's laws and the laws of this land very well, my general. As long as we have someone as honorable as you running this army, we cannot fail."

CHAPTER SEVEN

The Kill, Capture & Rescue

Morianton and his followers were moving more slowly than usual on this crisp, drizzling morning. The sun was barely breaking through the thick fog, burning away some drizzling rain rolling in from the sea. The weather conditions would have made traveling almost impossible if it weren't for the wide, well-marked merchant road running north and south, right through the heart of Nephite lands. The lamenting of the beasts pulling the heavy wagons, the squeaking of wooden wheels, as well as an occasional whimper of a child were the only sounds coming from the long trail of wagons full of beleaguered men and women. Morianton's followers settled into another day of mindlessly trudging forward. They had been up well before first light and on the move for over an hour, following their leader who was taking them away from the mess he'd created with the lowlanders, toward the wilds north of the land Bountiful.

Morianton, along with several of the men were in front of the wagon train riding their horses when the fog covering the mountainside lifted. They were finally able to see where the road was leading them.

"Look there," Morianton spouted, as he pointed north. "See how the mountain comes right up to the edge of the water? Just like I told you… This is where the road takes us." He looked around at those who were with him. He needed them to validate his leadership as well as acknowledge the fact he had led them to this point. Everyone knew where they were going. The merchant road was so well-used, a wandering cow could have made it safely to this point.

Morianton had no real leadership skills. He was a brute. As the days

CHAPTER SEVEN

went on, more and more of those who had chosen to follow him started to question why. The other men gave each other a cynical look and they acknowledged, somewhat condescendingly, Morianton and his so-called leadership. This spoke volumes about how they felt toward their false king.

Morianton was too engrossed in his own world to see the contempt coming from them. He continued to speak, "Out beyond that point are the forests and Lands of Bountiful." He smiled as he spoke. "We will be safe there from Moroni and his unjust laws." The men with Morianton agreed they were going to make it safely to the frontier wilderness. "Someone ride back and tell the rest of the company to hasten their steps. Tell them," he puffed up a bit and sat up in his saddle, "their king has reached the pass." Morianton spoke as he continued to look northward.

No one wanted to be the messenger. They all wanted to ride ahead with Morianton and be the first to see the lands of Bountiful. After several seconds, Morianton realized no one from his group had ridden back to the wagons. "What part of 'someone ride back' was unclear to you all?" He challenged sarcastically, as he turned around to face the men all around him. Still no one moved. They just looked at each other. "Have I gone mad?" Morianton barked. "Did something happen in the last two minutes to make you all forget I'm your leader?" No one spoke for several more seconds. They all looked around uncomfortably at each other until, finally, one of the older men said something.

"Sir, none of us want to go back with the women and baggage while the rest of the men range forward to inspect the pass and beyond."

"I don't remember this being a committee!" He shouted back, spitting bits of saliva all over his beard. Morianton had long ago lost control of his emotions. The slightest thing now sent him over the edge.

After several more seconds of awkward quiet, the same older man spoke again. "Fine… I will return to the wagon train," he said as he spurred his horse to move. "And enjoy a hot breakfast with your wives!" He shouted and laughed as he galloped away from the vanguard company.

Teancum was crouched down behind a fallen tree, next to the wide road, near the top of the pass. He had his Ghost Soldiers spread out along the tree line skirting the edge of the road and covering the rocky mountain, with their trademark camouflage cloaks and coverings hiding them from view. He could see the large group of men sitting on horseback, gathered in one group a good distance from his location. He watched as there was a heated exchange among the men, then one rider took off down the trail, away from the pass.

"Sir, can you make out what was said?" Gid asked Teancum. Gid was next to Teancum and removed his green and brown-colored Ghost Soldier hood from his head as he spoke.

"No, too far away," Teancum responded matter-of-factly.

"Rider leaving the group, sir," a second man reported to Teancum. "Could be heading back to warn the rest of our presence." He turned to face Teancum. "Should we attack?"

"No," Teancum warned. "We are not here to attack them and they are not our enemy." He held out the warrant for those officers and men with him to see. "We are here to apprehend Morianton and his cohorts, not slaughter our own countrymen."

Those words calmed the men of the Ghost Soldiers. They all looked back down the trail at the men heading up the pass.

"Which one is Morianton?" Gid asked Teancum. A change in subject was welcome.

"Not sure," Teancum whispered, as he squinted to try to see farther. "Probably the one in the lead. I was told he was a large man, and the guy leading the pack is a big fella." They both looked back at the man leading the other horsemen and watched as his fat frame awkwardly bounced up and down as he sat in the saddle.

"Yeah," Gid snickered, "That's probably him."

"Pass the signal. Tell the men to make ready," Teancum ordered, as he crouched down a little farther to stay out of sight. Gid gave a hand sign to the next man and he, in turn, signaled to the man to his right. The signal to get ready was quickly passed all the way down the line of Ghost Soldiers in the typical quiet and efficient manner as was the custom in this elite unit.

Morianton reached the crest of the pass and turned his horse around to look back down the elevation at the train of wagons following behind him. He smiled to himself as he thought about Moroni trying to catch up to him. "Hold me accountable, will you?" He snorted as he sat up straight on his horse. "Your authority ends here, Moroni."

CHAPTER SEVEN

"Actually…" a voice rang out from behind Morianton. It startled him badly, and he jerked in his saddle. Spinning around, Morianton was now facing a lone man standing in the middle of the road. His head was covered by his multi-colored cloak and he was holding a spear. "Moroni is the commander of all the Nephite military forces. His authority extends to wherever it is needed." The cloaked man tapped the bottom of his spear on the ground next to him. "Including this ground, right here."

"You wear the colors of a Ghost Soldier," Morianton stammered. He was making reference to the now infamous camouflaging colors on the cloak. "Who are you?" Morianton barked, as he tried to calm his horse. They were both caught off guard by the sudden appearance of the hooded man. It was one thing to sneak up on a lazy, unaware man, but it was something else indeed to surprise an animal in the open. Several of Morianton's cohorts were now alongside him. They too were all wondering about the identity of the mysterious man standing in their way. The hand signal was given, and the wagon train was stopped halfway up the pass.

"I am a Ghost Soldier; that is all you need to know." The hooded man reached into his shrouded waist, pulled out the sealed arrest warrant. "I hold a signed warrant for the arrest of the criminal, Morianton. I am charged with apprehending him and those with him who are responsible for the attack on the lowland village in the land of Lehi." The man's face remained covered by the cloak's hood so Morianton and the others with him could not see his eyes, but they could tell by his voice he was serious. "Morianton, climb down from your horse, drop your weapons, and submit to this lawful arrest."

Morianton started to snicker. "I am not the man you seek. Stand aside," he waved with his hand.

"How did you know I was talking to you?" The Ghost Soldier responded coldly. The blood in Morianton's face drained and he turned a shade of white. He was caught and needed to end this conversation, quickly. "You have no proof of my identity. Now stand aside!" He was trying to hide behind a false bravado, but there was panic in his voice.

"I don't need your confession; my men are asking those with you to confirm my suspicions."

Every man with Morianton turned and looked back down the gentle slope toward the wagon train behind them. They had left it mostly unguarded, and now realized their fatal error. Several men, dressed just

The Kill, Capture & Rescue

like the hooded Ghost Soldier standing before them, were now moving around the wagon train. The few men who were still with the baggage train were all disarmed and on their knees, with their hands high in the air.

"If any of you try to make a run for it or turn to move back down the hill, my archers will kill you," the hooded man continued speaking in his even and professional tone.

The large group of men with Morianton looked angry and confused. Morianton did not take his eyes off the stranger blocking his path. He did not need to see what was happening with the women and supplies. The reaction from those with him was proof enough things were not going according to his plans.

A lone Ghost Soldier came galloping to the top of the pass from the wagons. He slid off the back of the horse while the horse was still at a dead run and in three steps, the Ghost Soldier was next to Teancum. The Ghost Soldier whispered something while gesturing toward Morianton. Teancum looked up at Morianton, then removed his hood, revealing his true identity. Several of the men with Morianton started to murmur; one even gasped out his name. The change was almost tangible. It was one thing to face a few Ghost Soldiers. It was something completely different to challenge their leader.

"Morianton, this is the last time I am going to ask," Teancum was now speaking without the hood covering his face. "Come down from your horse, drop your weapons and submit to arrest." He pointed to a spot of ground just in front of Morianton's horse where he wanted Morianton to kneel.

Morianton was livid. He could see the thick forests of the north country off in the distance. They were shrouded in mist and the mountain tops had snow on them. He knew Pachus and the other king men were waiting for him inside those woods. The only thing standing in his way was this upstart, so-called Ghost Soldier. "Only two of you against all of us?" He tried to sound insulted as he spoke, "We will ride you down, then turn on your men." Some of the men with Morianton were finding courage from their leader's words, but others were backing away. They wanted no part of a fight between themselves and Teancum the Ghost Soldier, regardless of the odds.

"I don't want to hurt you, Morianton. Don't be a fool." Teancum warned.

CHAPTER SEVEN

"Fool? You dare call me a fool?" Morianton spun his horse in a circle. "I have the blood of kings in my veins, and I intend to rule over you!" Morianton's eyes were glossing over and he was slurring his speech. Clearly, the heavy wine drinking he had been doing the last few days was affecting his judgment. Teancum could see Morianton was quickly starting to lose control of his temper. He gripped the spear in his hand a little tighter, while carefully shifting his weight for a better stance. Teancum realized calling Morianton a fool might not have been the best choice of words. Instead of calming the situation, it had only made things more aggravated, but he could not take it back, so he held his ground and upped the ante.

"Morianton, you are a murderer and kidnapper," Teancum asserted firmly. "If calling you a fool is upsetting to you, then so be it." Morianton huffed and puffed, but had no real response to Teancum's words. "You are under arrest, Morianton, you and those with you! Get off your horse. Now!" This was the first sign of any emotion from Teancum. Morianton was wearing a big, heavy, bearskin coat and it covered his right hand. Teancum was sure Morianton was gripping a weapon, but he could not see his hand.

Gid was still hiding in the tree line, not a hundred feet from the road, along with the remaining squad of Ghost Soldiers. He could see and hear everything going on between Teancum and Morianton. "Come on," he softly muttered as he urged his captain to give the signal for the remaining Ghost Soldiers to make their presence known. Gid could tell the confrontation was not going well, and more than likely blood would be shed. "Archers, make ready!" He loudly whispered toward a group of men waiting nearby. The men who received the order all readjusted their position and readied their deadly, handmade bows. "If the order is given, concentrate your fire on the mounted men first," Gid said as he pointed toward the road. "Two volleys, then draw your hand weapons and move out toward any horsemen who remain or those who are on foot."

Morianton looked around at the so-called supporters, who were with him. Most of them were backing away while trying to increase the distance between themselves and Teancum. Only a few were standing their ground and ready to back Morianton with whatever his next move might be. Morianton looked back at the wagon train. He saw Teancum's men had rounded up anyone who might pose a threat to them. They were disarmed and submissive.

You are alone, a dark voice crept into his thoughts. His mind was clouded by the alcohol and pressure of the moment. *You have been betrayed by those who claim to support you.* The voice was taunting Morianton now. *Show them your power; show them you are a true king.*

Morianton reacted to the voice. "Yes," he proclaimed. "I am a king, and I will not be denied my destiny!" He had his hand on the handle of his big cleaver-shaped weapon. He pulled it out and waved it over his head. "I am your king! Follow me!" He shouted as he kicked his mount in the ribs. The horse lurched forward and Morianton charged directly at Teancum. About a dozen of the horsemen blindly reacted and charged with him, while the remainder, about fifty men on horses or on foot, stayed put.

Gid instantly knew what to do. "Archers, move out and hold those who remain!" He pointed to the large gaggle of men who had not followed Morianton. "The rest of you, with me!" Gid pulled out his hand weapons and started to run from the trees and toward Teancum. He had dozens of Ghost Soldiers hot on his heels. His captain was going to need help. Facing Morianton and several armed men charging on horseback all alone was more than even Teancum could handle, or so he thought.

Teancum saw the charge coming before Morianton even got the words out of his mouth. Knowing the cloak was only going to slow him down, Teancum quickly pulled at the ties holding the cloak onto his shoulders. The garment fell to the ground and Teancum was moving sideways in a flash. He had no choice now. Morianton was attacking him with deadly force while resisting lawful arrest.

Teancum still wanted to take Morianton alive. He believed in the power of true justice. Having Morianton face the chief judges in open court and answer for his crimes would be an important validation of the new government system he had helped create. Moroni knew Teancum would do everything in his power to resolve the conflict without bloodshed.

Teancum's next few moves were instant and flawless. Taking three steps to his right, Teancum spun the long, thick wooden spear in his hands several times in a circular motion around his body, then brought it up as if he were playing stickball. He let Morianton ride up next to him. Teancum, with the metal point of the weapon away from Morianton, swung the wooden shaft, striking Morianton squarely in the chest. When he was hit by the blunt end of Teancum's spear, Morianton let out a gasp

CHAPTER SEVEN

and did a backflip completely off the back of his horse. He landed hard on his shoulder blades with a loud thud, knocking the wind out of him as snot bubbles started to form around his nostrils.

Without missing a beat, Teancum then turned to face the other criminals still charging directly at him. He waited until the next man was almost on top of him, then he effortlessly spun out of the way. At the same time, he took his stout spear and struck the running horse in the front legs, causing it to stumble, throwing the rider off the top. The man riding the stumbling horse shot out of his saddle, screaming. He hit the ground in front of the tumbling horse in a hard face-plant. He was out like a blown candle.

That's two, Teancum counted in his mind. He knew there were still several more coming, and he moved again with the dexterity of a jungle cat on the hunt.

The third rider was almost on top of Teancum now. Still not wanting to kill anyone unless he had no other choice, Teancum turned the metal point of his spear away from the next rider and thrust up toward him with the blunt wooden end. The back of the spear hit the third man right in the chest, and he was knocked off his horse. The third man hit the ground, crying out in pain as his ribs were crushed from the impact.

There were at least ten more riders charging Teancum, but they all pulled up on their reins when they saw him dislodge the first three riders from their horses with very little effort. Teancum stepped into the gap between the three downed riders and the rest. He spun the large spear in his hands, bringing the point of the spear in front of him in a strong combat stance. This move gave Gid and the rest of the Ghost Soldiers time to catch up to hold the men on horseback, as well as those who were on foot, at sword point.

"Drop your weapons!" Teancum shouted. He was as calm as the evening breeze. Even though he had just single-handedly taken out three men on horseback, he was not even breathing hard. This fact was not lost on those who were now his prisoners. They all whispered, gesturing toward Teancum and Morianton, who was still reeling on the ground trying to recover from his fall. No one was going to challenge Teancum now that he had proved his point.

No one, except Morianton. Morianton, rocking back and forth like a fat turtle, finally got to his feet. His face was flushed red, his eyes were wild and full of rage. "How dare you?" Morianton blustered, as he staggered to find his balance. "I am King Morianton! You will pay for your insolence!" Morianton cried, as he jerked at the thick bear skin coat tangling his arms. Teancum knew he had nothing to fear from those other riders, considering his men had them surrounded and disarmed. He turned back to face Morianton. He almost burst out laughing as he watched the fat and drunken man wrestle with the coat while trying to remain dignified.

"Need any help?" Teancum sarcastically asked. He knew it was a low blow and beneath him to comment in such a way, but it was fun to watch Morianton's reaction.

"Curse you, you dog!" Morianton bellowed back. He finally got the burdensome coat off his back, tossed it to the ground, and then kicked it away from him. Looking around, Morianton realized his circumstances. All of Morianton's men had been disarmed, the wagon train was in Teancum's hands and Morianton was on foot and alone. Worst of all, they were laughing— *laughing* at him.

They are mocking you, so you must fight and kill the Ghost Soldier in order to regain any hope of honor, the dark voice sounded like it was almost standing next to Morianton. *Look at how they point and jest. Kill the Ghost Soldier and those with you will follow you again.* Morianton was blinded with rage, alcohol and pain. It appeared all his hopes and dreams had been dashed by this upstart, so-called warrior. *How dare he stop you? You are a king!* The dark voice was moving around him now, goading Morianton on to do a terrible thing.

The two other men who had been unseated by Teancum were not as quick to get up. When the remaining Ghost Soldiers reached them, the men on the ground, as well as the rest of the bandits, had all been disarmed and moved back from Teancum and Morianton. They all knew it was folly now to try to engage the Ghost Soldiers in a fight, all of them except Morianton. Morianton was pacing back and forth now, foaming with rage and hate, his hand holding tight on the handle of his large metal cleaver. His eyes were burning hot, and his spit-filled breath came out in great hissing sounds.

Teancum pointed the tip of his spear at Morianton. "Drop you weapons, Morianton. It is over. You are under arrest... I don't want to hurt you."

"You have taken everything from me!" Morianton barked. He spat again as he shouted, "How dare you say you don't want to hurt me?" He

CHAPTER SEVEN

took his large intimidating blade, holding it down at his side. "I am King Morianton!" Then, like a bully in the park, he gestured for Teancum to close the distance between them and face him in a fight.

Yes, challenge him to fight, the taunting voice in Morianton's head barked, in its dark, evil way. *Show them all you are a big man!*

Morianton's posture and actions were a direct challenge to Teancum and the authority given to him by Moroni. At that moment, something changed inside Teancum. Up to this point, Teancum had tried everything he could to resolve this problem with the least amount of force necessary. It was Morianton who continued to escalate the confrontation. Now, the bandit leader was standing in an aggressive stance with his short chopping blade in his hand, daring Teancum to confront him.

"What say you, Ghost Soldier... Man to man?" Morianton gestured again for Teancum to come closer and fight, the gleam of his blade flashing in the morning sun's light. He was clearly blinded with rage from the reality of the situation. He was challenging, quite possibly, the most dangerous person in the entire Nephite army in hand-to-hand fighting. "Or are you not man enough?" He smirked.

"Morianton, you have murdered innocent people." As Teancum spoke he cradled his spear in his left arm, reaching down with his right hand, he picked up his war cloak and handed it to the Ghost Soldier who was standing next to him. "I have given you plenty of chances to surrender and go peacefully before the judges to answer for your crimes." He took the spear from his left arm, and held it in front of his body. "You leave me no choice. I am forced now to disarm you. If you resist, I will kill you." Teancum started to move forward toward Morianton. Morianton brought his short sword up, then side-stepped to his left, trying to gain the angle on Teancum. By this time, the rest of the wagon train had moved up to where the horsemen were stopped. Everyone was trying to find the perfect spot where they could watch what was about to happen. Teancum's men still controlled the perimeter. The people had been disarmed, so they were allowed to move around in order to witness what the Ghost Soldiers all knew was about to happen.

"Come closer, boy," Morianton hissed, as he lowered his body, raising up his hands in front of him, making himself ready for a fight. "Let's dance!" he shouted, as he lunged forward, swiping at Teancum's spear tip with his big blade.

Teancum was ready for Morianton's attack and parried the blow.

He then jabbed twice at Morianton's fat body, but missed both times. Teancum was surprised at how much dexterity Morianton had, in spite of his heavy frame, as he sidestepped both thrusts, then chopped overheard and down at an angle with his own weapon. Teancum moved out of the way of the swipes, then spun in a quick circle, bringing the hard wooden handle of his spear across the back of Morianton's head. There was a loud crack when the wood met his skin and bone. Morianton was knocked forward, almost losing his balance. Grabbing the back of his head, while shaking it back and forth, Morianton shook the mists from the hard blow out of his mind, refocusing on his opponent. Snorting, he shifted his weight, adjusting his grip on the big metal blade in his hand.

"You're quick," Teancum smiled and winked, as he acknowledged Morianton's skill. Teancum could see how Morianton was moving while holding his weapon. *You know what you are doing*, Teancum reflected. He could see the heavy breathing, along with the labored look in Morianton's eyes. *The once-great warrior is weighed down with fat and wine.* He readjusted his own stance, then fixed his spear tip toward Morianton. "Remember," Teancum spoke softly, his eyes fixed on his opponent, "you can stop all of this. Whatever happens next, you wanted it."

Provoked to rage, Morianton yelled, "Your head on a spike is all I want!" Morianton lunged forward again, swiping at the tip of Teancum's spear. He was trying to get the spear out of his way so he could get close enough to cut and slash at Teancum. Teancum was onto Morianton's plans almost instantly, but instead of trying to back up and parry the blows, he simply side-stepped, spun his body, and effortlessly jumped out of the way, all the while moving the metal tip of his weapon up or down as well as side-to-side. This made Morianton miss the spear or Teancum every time he swung his blade, making it look to his followers like he was a novice with his weapon and demonstrating to all the impressive abilities of the Ghost Soldier to fight, block and move.

This dance went on for several more turns, until Teancum had had enough of it and was tired of the game. Seeing an opportunity when Morianton was gasping for air and caught off balance again, Teancum struck the outside of Morianton's knee with the blunt end of his spear, causing his leg to buckle, and Morianton to cry out in pain. Then spinning the spear in the air and behind his back, Teancum readjusted his angle, and brought the strong wooden staff down across Morianton's sword arm. There was a second loud crack as wood met bone. Morianton's

CHAPTER SEVEN

big blade fell to the dirt with a thud.

"My arm!" Morianton cried out, as he grasped his injured limb with his good hand. Teancum back-stepped, while spinning the spear in the air, settling it a few feet away from Morianton, in a solid combat stance.

"Surrender, Morianton. It's over," Teancum pleaded. "I don't want to kill you. You have a choice. Please, stop fighting."

See how he mocks you, came the strong but quiet statement from the dark voice in Morianton's head. *See how he will even deny you an honorable death. He is toying with you and taking your honor. Kill him!*

Morianton's mind flashed with rage. The pain, the humiliation, the alcohol, the loss of his possible kingdom, all of it was blinding him to the reality of the deadly situation. He looked out over his so-called subjects, seeing only contempt for their king. He was hallucinating. He thought they were pointing and laughing at him. Morianton's eyes went black with hate and anger, the breath escaping past his lips was now putrid. Morianton was completely overwhelmed with his desire to kill Teancum. "Never!" Spit and bile was hanging from his beard. His body quivered with pain and anguish. He winced, while subconsciously holding his broken arm closer to his barrel chest. "I will never surrender to you. I am a king!" he bellowed. "And I will die a king… Aghhh!" he shouted as he sprang to his feet, pulling out his hidden boot knife, charging at Teancum like a raging bull.

Teancum readied himself by bracing for impact. He held his sturdy spear in perfect form in front of him, ready for the final chapter of this saga. At the last possible second, Teancum pulled back on the handle of his weapon, then thrust it forward with all his might. The metal tip of the spearpoint pierced Morianton's chest dead center, and then Teancum drove the spear into Morianton's body. With the combined energy of Morianton's bodyweight and Teancum's thrust, the spear passed completely through Morianton's chest— he was a dead man standing. No power on earth could stop it now. Gasping and moaning, Morianton reached out for Teancum with one last effort to strike at his nemesis, but he was overcome, then fell to his side.

Teancum let go of the spear while watching as the man who caused so much sorrow and heartache fell to the ground, going to his reward in the next world. Screams and lamentations erupted from the wagon train, as those who supported Morianton saw their mighty leader fall. The rest of the Ghost Soldiers quickly regained control of the rabble and got the more vocal supporters back in line.

Teancum stood next to the body of Morianton for a moment, with his eyes closed and his head up, facing the sun. This was the last thing he wanted to do. He needed a moment to try to find his balance. He could hear the commotion coming from the others near the wagons, but he did not care right now. "Misguided fools," he whispered. He could hear his men coming to his side, but he wanted one more moment of stillness before he returned to reality.

"Sir, are you okay?" One of the braver Nephite soldiers asked, as he and several more men ran up to Teancum. Two of the soldiers pulled Morianton's large body away from him.

"I am fine," Teancum said with a sigh. "Report the status of the prisoners."

"They have all been disarmed. Some remained loyal to him and tried to resist." He pointed to Morianton's body as he spoke. "But we have separated those from the others."

"Casualties?" Teancum questioned Gid, as he made his way forward to report to his commander.

"No Ghost Soldiers injured, sir. A few of the men in the caravan had to be knocked around a bit to get them to comply, but they will heal." There was a hint of sarcasm in his voice. They both looked back, seeing the few disgruntled men still on the ground, holding injured body parts and rubbing sore areas.

Teancum stopped looking at the caravan, then looked back up at the sun. "Plenty of time left in the day to get this circus turned around and headed back." Teancum looked back at Morianton one last time, then took a deep breath and pointed at the wagons. "Tell them to quickly pick a spokesman and have him report to me. I don't want to deal with a hundred want-to-be kings—only one man. Are we clear?"

"Yes sir," Gid responded.

"Then have Alpha Company stand watch over the wagons and Bravo Company gather up our equipment and horses from the trees. I want to be ready to move in one hour."

"Understood." Gid paused for a second. "Sir, what do you want done with the body?"

Teancum turned back to look at the wagons. "He was one of them, so I will let them figure it out. Let's get moving. I want to be long gone by sundown."

CHAPTER SEVEN

Standing in the crowd of onlookers was Diaya's mom and her two children. Her face, partially hidden by a shawl, showed the marks from the last beating by Morianton.

"Mama… What happened?" The littlest one asked. She was too small to see past the larger bodies blocking her view.

"Morianton is dead… He was killed by a Nephite soldier who was sent to rescue us." There was relief in her voice.

"I hope you burn in the lake of fire, Morianton," the older boy threatened. He was seven years old and trying to be strong for his mother. But he was scared and confused about what might happen next.

"Son, we should not think that way." She looked down at her only son with pleading eyes. "Wishing that judgement on anyone is not Christ-like."

"But Mama, Morianton hurt you. He was an evil man. He held us prisoner."

"Are we free now, Mama?" Her little girl chimed in before her mother had a chance to respond to her son's statement.

"Yes, my dear, we are free now. Thanks to God and those brave soldiers." She gestured towards Teancum and his men with her head. "And yes, Morianton was an evil man who hurt us." She turned and looked back at her son. "But because Morianton chose to fight those soldiers and not repent, he has died in his sins." She paused to look over at Morianton's dead body lying on the ground. "Now he will face God with full knowledge of his guilt, and suffer the consequences of his deeds." She knelt down and pulled them close, smiling with light in her eyes. "We are followers of Christ," She kissed and hugged her two babies. "We try to love and respect all people, and want everyone to feel the joy of knowing they are forgiven of their sins if they will take His name and love their neighbor." Brushing the hair from her daughter's face, she continued. "I am happy we are safe and free, but sad that Morianton will carry his pain into the eternities."

There was a long pause then the girl spoke again. "Mama, can we go home now?"

"Yes, my love… We can go home now," she reassured as she held her daughter close.

"What about Diaya?" The boy asked.

"God will care for Diaya." The mother squeezed both of her children's hands. "We will pray for her safety, for mercy for Morianton, and give thanks for those brave soldiers who protected us from evil." She stood up and turned to walk back towards the bottom of the rise. "Let's go back to our wagon. I have a feeling we will be leaving soon."

In less than one hour, the Ghost Soldiers had the entire wagon train turned around, with everything ready for the command to move out. A new leader was appointed over the remnants of Morianton's band, and after seeing what Teancum was capable of doing, this new leader was much more congenial toward the Ghost Soldiers than Morianton had been.

"Understand this—" Teancum spoke from atop his horse as he looked down at the man now in charge of the wagon train with several other men standing behind him, "we are not here to babysit you. You are all our prisoners. Our orders are to return you to General Moroni and the council of judges. If there are any internal issues, then you will solve your own problems. If anyone tries to escape, they will be hunted and killed. If there are any attempts to harm one of my Ghost Soldiers, I will hold you personally responsible. Are we clear?"

The older man who had been quickly voted in as the newest leader of the group blinked several times, while sheepishly nodding his head. He was not looking forward to the next few days working with Teancum.

"Good." Teancum could read the man's body language. "The quicker we get going, the quicker we can end this madness. Move your people out. Keep them moving on the road until I call for a halt."

"Yes sir," was his two-word reply.

Teancum pulled on his reins, then left before anything else could be said. The rest of the soldiers with him quickly followed. The defeated supporters of Morianton were left standing alone. After a moment of awkward silence, the new leader spoke up, "Has the burial detail returned from digging a grave for Morianton?"

"Yes, they just finished," the lone woman in the leadership council replied. It was the same woman who had gone with Morianton to raid the village and tried to defend the little kidnapped child in the woods.

"Well, let's say some words over his grave and mark the site. Spread the word— anyone who wants to show their respects to Morianton needs to be there in ten minutes," the old leader instructed. He looked up at

CHAPTER SEVEN

the sun's position in the sky, then over to where Teancum was now. "We need to be quick about it and get a move on. That Ghost Soldier is not to be fooled with."

Teancum and his Ghost Soldiers had been slowly moving the remnants of Morianton's criminal band back to the camp of General Moroni for three days. Because they were traveling with several wagons full of women, children and those wounded men who were foolish enough to try to resist their arrest, the Ghost Soldiers were forced to take the wide and well-used merchant road. This was completely contrary to how they usually did business. Under normal circumstances, they would never expose the entire unit in such a fashion. Usually, they would travel at night, or under the cover of the trees or going over the mountains, following some goat path, all the while staying unknown and unseen by the area's inhabitants. But now, they were acting more like sheepherders than elite warriors. They had little choice, since they would never get these civilians or their wagons through the dense forests. So, they traveled back to Moroni by the most direct and most exposed route.

But this was not a good enough excuse for Teancum to slack off when it came to moving his whole unit safely along with the prisoners. He held daily command briefings every morning before they would start out. He posted roving reconnaissance and security patrols during the day, as well as rotating double guard duty at night. Not only were the Ghost Soldiers on high alert for an attacking enemy, but they also had to deal with their prisoners trying to escape.

Camp was always set up in two squares. One was for the prisoners. They would line their wagons up on four sides. Everyone would sleep on the ground or in small tents set up inside the square perimeter of the wagons. The larger square would line the outside of the smaller one. This was for Teancum's small army. They would have the prisoners build hasty defense pickets, then set them up every night before the sun went down. The horses would be kept in two corrals set up outside the camp and made from rope and small logs. This way, the guards could keep an eye on the horses, but the horses were not kept near where the soldiers slept.

After the third day of travel, Teancum felt the prisoners were getting the hang of camp life and things were starting to run more smoothly. The routine of setting up and taking down the hasty camp was working well, for the most part. The complaining from the prisoners had stopped, or Teancum and his officers had learned to block it out.

On the morning of the fourth day, Teancum finished rolling up his sleeping mat along with his small, one-man tent. He was tying them to the saddle of his horse while trying to enjoy a meager breakfast of dry corn bread with jerky when his sub-commanders approached.

"Good morning, gentlemen," Teancum spoke, with the remnants of corn bread still in his mouth. Back in the garrison, speaking with his mouth full of food would have been completely unacceptable for an officer of his high rank. But out in the field, among his men, the rules of etiquette were a bit blurry at times.

"Good morning, sir," they responded in unison.

"Who is the duty officer this morning?" Teancum asked, after washing the dry corn bread down with a swig of water from his water skin.

"I am, sir," Gid responded to Teancum's inquiry.

Teancum turned to look at Gid. "Very well, Gid; make your report."

"Sir, the night watch reported nothing of consequence happening during their shift. The morning head count has been completed and all prisoners are accounted for. One stallion has gone missing, but we think it was looking for a friend," he cleared his throat, "and it found its way into the other pen with one of the mares. I have men checking as we speak."

"It's true love!" one of the officers belted out. They all chuckled at the joke.

The laughter settled down and the rest of the morning briefing went as uneventfully as the last few days had. When his officers were done speaking, Teancum raised his hand to quiet the men and speak. "Gentlemen, we have one more day of hard riding before we reach the main army camp. These people know they are going to their judgement. If they are planning to make a run for it, it will happen today, so be alert and keep your men vigilant."

The men all nodded their heads in agreement.

"Questions?" Teancum asked. There were none. The men were professional and they knew what needed to be done in order to move this wagon train. "Good. I want to be standing in front of General Moroni, briefing him tomorrow morning, so we have a long day ahead of us. Let's make it happen." He stood up and all of his officers, as well as ranking sergeants, stood after him. "Dismissed."

CHAPTER SEVEN

The rest of the day was uneventful until around supper time. Two men did try to make a run for the thick trees in an attempt to escape, but they were quickly captured by a squad of Ghost Soldiers. One man was slightly wounded when he fell, hitting his head after his legs were tangled up by a bola tossed at him by one of Teancum's men. They arrived at the main Nephite army camp just before night fall. Teancum had his men set up their own camp, just like they had on the road, then he made his way to Moroni's tent.

He was escorted inside, finding Moroni and Amiha. Both of them were dressed in armor, looking dirty and tired.

"Come in, Captain Teancum!" Moroni roared, as he removed his breast plate so he could hang it on his armor stand. Sitting down, Moroni started to remove his shin guards while continuing to speak, "Please have good news for me."

"General, did I miss something?" Teancum questioned, as he stepped closer to Moroni. He could see both Moroni and Amiha looked exhausted and noticed there was concern in their eyes.

"Long days while you were gone, my friend," Amiha said as he walked past Teancum, patting him on the shoulder. Amiha poured three large glasses of water, one for himself and one for Teancum, as well as one for Moroni. He handed Teancum his glass then moved back to hand the other goblet to his commander.

"We were summoned by Chief Judge Pahoran to return to Zarahemla. The king men are making trouble. Our presence was requested to help ensure order," Moroni explained between gulps of cool liquid. The refreshing water had an instant effect on him. His shoulders relaxed as Moroni sat back in his chair.

"What happened?" Teancum questioned. He knew there was more to the story.

"The king men made a political move to try to take power from the judges. It has been resolved for now." Moroni was totally spent and took another drink. "But, I am sure we have not heard the last of them."

"Was Pachus there?" Teancum asked in a low tone.

"No," Amiha spoke up. "The coward sent his lap dogs to speak for him. He knows Moroni would arrest him, or worse, if they ever met again."

"What news of your mission?" Moroni asked, in order to change the subject.

The Kill, Capture & Rescue

Teancum cleared his throat, then spoke. "As you instructed, I met up with Morianton and his band at the pass by the sea. Morianton refused to submit to the lawful arrest and attacked me. I was forced to kill him in single combat, but my Ghost Soldiers were able to capture the entire wagon train intact. We returned the lot here, to face the voice of the people's judgment."

"Where are the wagons now?" Amiha asked. "I think I know someone who would like to see if her mother and siblings are among the ones you brought back." Moroni nodded and raised up his goblet to salute Amiha for his quick thinking.

"My soldiers have them detained just outside the camp, near the main road," Teancum had a questioning tone when he answered. He saw the interaction between Moroni and Amiha.

"The girl who brought the intelligence report about Morianton's exploits and his attempt to escape. Her family was kidnapped by Morianton and forced to join him," Amiha explained.

"I think I know who you are talking about," Teancum nodded in understanding. "If it's the same woman, then she is safe and healthy."

Moroni stood up, putting his cup down on a small table, near his cot. "Excellent news for Diaya. We will address this further during the morning briefing. Until then, Captain Teancum, well done. What do you need from us?" The last thing Moroni wanted was more bloodshed over an arrest of a Nephite citizen, but he trusted Teancum. If Teancum said he had tried everything to avoid killing Morianton, then it was good enough for Moroni. He knew Teancum had lived his life with honor and integrity. He knew Teancum was, first and foremost, a true friend to freedom, and only fought to defend the rights and liberties of others. Morianton needed to face justice for what he and his men had done. According to the law, Teancum did what he had to do to bring the fugitive back. It was Morianton's actions which led to the fight and his own death, not the law or the person enforcing the law.

"Some of your soldiers will need to replace my men in guarding them. They have been going hard for several days now. They could use some rest," Teancum responded to Moroni's question.

"Amiha, see to it. The Ghost Soldiers are relieved of the responsibilities of guarding the people of Morianton. Make arrangements to have the wagons moved back to the land of Lehi and the custody of the people turned over to the local judges for trial." Moroni turned back to face

Teancum, "Did you bring Morianton's body back with you?"

"No, sir. I had his followers prepare a simple grave for him. We buried him in the woods, near the spot where he fell."

Moroni nodded his head in understanding. He took a deep breath of air, then slowly let it out in a long sigh. "Senseless," he whispered, loud enough for the other men in the tent to hear. Moroni understood Morianton was a murderer. But it did not make his job any easier. Sending other men to face evil, knowing the outcome would most likely lead to the shedding of blood, as well as the loss of life, was the hard but important job of the man anointed by the prophet of God to defend liberty and justice. Moroni knew he could not fight every battle, personally. He could not be in every town and village to face every criminal or attacking Lamanite. He had trusted leaders along with well-trained soldiers for that. Moroni's job, as the general, was to lead, direct, train, and inspire those men when the call went out for the guardians to protect the innocent. It was his responsibility to recognize the need and send the appropriate response.

In this case, the right thing to do had been to send Teancum with his Ghost Soldiers to intercept and arrest Morianton before he could escape justice. Moroni also wished to keep Morianton from reinforcing the king men and their usurper allies, like Pachus. The biggest problem Moroni had with all of this was trying to understand the thinking of people like Morianton. It was hard for a man like Moroni to comprehend how someone could be so evil, and care so little for their fellow man. "Senseless," he said again while shaking his head.

CHAPTER EIGHT

Pachus Makes a Deal

Pachus sat in a large chair, at the head of the long wooden table, eating hunks of bread and meat from a large plate. His unhealthy body was sweating and his breath already stunk of too much wine. There was a solid band of gold set on top of his head, accented by his greasy hair. The room was crowded. It was full of high-born Nephites whose blood lines could be traced back to the time before the judges, to the royal lineage who ruled the Nephite people for hundreds of years. They were all sitting quietly, listening to the messenger's account of the events which took place at the great capital city of Zarahemla.

"The debate was going in our favor, my king," the disheartened man explained, with his head down, nervously fidgeting with his hands. "We used the flattering words and phrases you told us to use. We were winning over the people, ready for the final vote, when Moroni and his entourage arrived." There was a murmur among the gathered. If there was one person in this land who was hated by Pachus and his king men, it was General Moroni. Pachus rubbed the large scar on his hand, given to him by Shem during the battle for Manti.

"That oversized choir boy!" Pachus barked. Those gathered tittered in response. "Let me guess the rest," Pachus spoke, as he stood up and started walking around the large table. Bits of food fell to the floor from his tunic. With his wine goblet in one hand, he waddled past the others, who stood up respectfully as he passed. He waved for them to be seated as he continued to move about the room. "If I know our friend Moroni,"

CHAPTER EIGHT

Pachus cleared his throat, and took a swig from his goblet, before he continued, "he gave some passionate speech about God and the rule of law," Pachus looked at the messenger, who nodded his head in agreement, "Then told the judges he would spill blood before he allowed the great republic to fall into the hands of the nobles?"

"Yes, my king. He did just that."

Pachus snorted, then took a second, long drink of wine. "And after he spoke, the opinions of the lower judges, the ones we could not bribe or blackmail, changed. The final vote was unfavorable toward our cause?"

"Yes, my king, it was a close vote, but not in our favor." The unfortunate messenger acted like he did not enjoy being the one to deliver the bad news, but there was evil in the messenger's eyes.

"Anything else?" Pachus demanded loudly, wondering what else could have gone wrong.

The messenger took a calming breath. He knew the answer to his king's question would not come as welcome news to those in attendance. "My king, after the vote was taken and we lost the challenge, several of our brothers gave up the fight and left the cause to return to their homes. Moroni has demanded this new Title of Liberty be hoisted above every city, town and village within the jurisdiction of the judges." The messenger paused to make sure everyone was still listening to him. "He has brainwashed the masses into thinking they have the right to self-governance. Moroni declared that all those who would not support the republic and allow all men to live free were to be imprisoned and tried as traitors." The messenger stopped before he finished his explanation of the events which had taken place.

Without asking for permission, he grabbed a goblet full of wine from the table in front of him. He drank the entire contents in one big gulp. The air suddenly got very cold in the large meeting room. Everyone in attendance saw the messenger drink the wine. They all knew he had some very bad news to relay, so they braced for it.

"Go on," Pachus spoke, as he gestured toward the nervous messenger with the goblet in his hand.

"My king," he paused, trying to find the right words to use to describe what happened next. He could not find an eloquent way to describe the events, so he just blurted the words. "Your royal envoy, and most of the men who went to Zarahemla with him, were then imprisoned by Moroni."

CHAPTER EIGHT

There was an audible gasp from the people in the room, then silence as the people all turned to look at Pachus.

"On what charges?" one of the high-born shouted from his seat in disgust.

Pachus raised his hand to calm the room. "Explain to me, in detail, what took place," Pachus whispered, as he winked at the messenger. No one caught the signal or even suspected Pachus was directing the words from the messenger. Pachus knew the truth, but he craved power, so he was willing to lie, cheat, steal and even murder to get position over his fellow man. The messenger had briefed Pachus on the truth of the king men challenging Moroni before the meeting started. Pachus had made a secret pact with the messenger to tell the lies Pachus had fabricated so he could win over the consent of the other nobles, as well as enlist them to help Amalickiah and the Lamanites in overthrowing the Nephite government.

"Sire," the messenger spoke, looking back at Pachus with his eyes telling Pachus not to betray him. "Those of us who would not pledge to the republic were gathered in a field, waiting to march home, when Moroni and his soldiers rode in on us. They killed many and captured the entire company, taking them all prisoner. I barely escaped with my life." The gathered were stunned at the news. "Your royal envoy was killed by Moroni himself. He raised his hands, begging for peace, but Moroni took him and cast him down into the dirt, and killed him with his big sword."

"How many were lost?" One of the other rebellious nobles asked.

"Four thousand men are in chains." The messenger faked a tear of sadness, lowering his head again, pretending to be unable to continue his explanation.

It was all lies, lies created by Pachus to influence the others into making him their king. Moroni had begged the men to disarm and comply with the will of the people. Only when Moroni was physically challenged did he give the order for his men to defend themselves. The men in the council meeting would never know the truth. The damage was already done. The real story died in their grand tent, and Pachus buried it under a mountain of lies.

"This is outrageous!" One man shouted, as he shook his fist in the air. Several other men shouted after him in agreement.

"With all of those men taken, we would have a difficult time

Pachus Makes a Deal

defending ourselves, if Moroni turned his army on us. What shall we do?"

Pachus almost smiled when he heard those words. He had created this master plan to trick the nobles into giving him complete power. He could see his work coming to life. "Gentlemen," Pachus raised his hands, trying to quiet down the room. The others were clamoring back and forth, trying to figure out the king men's next move. "Gentlemen, please, settle down." The room slowly grew quiet as they all turned to look at their leader. " The time for talk and half-measures is over. Moroni has declared war on us for simply wanting to be governed differently than him, as well as his conspirators. He would see us all dragged down into the dirt and labor like commoners in the fields, rather than recognize our God-granted birthright and rightful claim to rule." Pachus paused to let the emotions of the gathered simmer. He knew how to use flattering words and fancy speeches to influence large groups of people to do his bidding. A fat, toad of a man like him could never survive the difficult work of being self-reliant, so he learned to influence others to do the work for him. "Gentlemen, we are not the only ones to have been persecuted by Moroni and the judges. In this time of great trial, I believe we must look to our brothers for assistance." The gathered men in the meeting room, all looked at each other for some understanding to the words Pachus was speaking.

"Whom do you mean when you say 'brothers'?" One of the more outspoken nobles questioned. "We are all gathered from the far reaches of the Nephite nation. Who is missing?"

Pachus responded to the question by walking over to a far corner of the room. He pulled back on the curtain over the doorway, revealing a man standing outside. As the man came into view, the entire room gasped at the sight of his leopard cloak and large, jeweled cimeter hanging from his side. They all knew who he was and some of the men instinctively stood, grabbing the hilts of their own swords.

"Amalickiah!" Several men in the group gasped, as he came into the light. They all knew of his treachery and open warfare against the Nephites.

"Now gentlemen, before you react out of fear, let him speak." Pachus stepped in front of Amalickiah with his hands raised. He was taking quite a gamble letting the leader of the Lamanite army into this meeting, but after Amalickiah approached him with a peace offering, Pachus saw the big picture and knew the only way to topple the current Nephite

CHAPTER EIGHT

government was to ally himself with the Lamanites. Amalickiah had been the leader of a popular uprising to make himself a king, but he was also defeated by Moroni. He had attracted the attention of Pachus. The two had worked toward the same goals for quite some time. They both were chased from the Nephite lands by Moroni and they both wanted him dead. When he heard about Pachus and his plans to overthrow the current government, Amalickiah made contact with Pachus and proposed an alliance, to fight their mutual enemy— General Moroni and his army. The men in the meeting nervously settled down and sat in order to listen to Amalickiah speak, though they remained wary of his words. Amalickiah could sense they were all cautious, so he addressed that first. After all, Amalickiah was the leader of the Lamanite army now.

"My brothers, we fight a common enemy," Amalickiah began his remarks. He was trying his best to sound and look sympathetic to their cause. But deep down in his heart, he hated all Nephites. His master plan was to use these rebels as fodder, to weaken Moroni's army, thus ultimately conquering the entire Nephite nation. "A wise person once said that the enemy of my enemy is my friend." He smiled and looked over the gathered crowd. "I am here to pledge to you the support of the Lamanite army in order to help you retake, by force if necessary, your lands, restoring the rightful bloodlines back into power." He walked over to the map hanging on the wall. He got right to the point. "Gentlemen, I will march the bulk of my army directly toward Zarahemla. I will attack, conquer, and hold these cities along the route." He drew his finger along the path he was going to march with his Lamanites. "This will draw Moroni and his men out from behind his high walls and pickets, forcing him to face me on open ground. You can then free your men being held as prisoners and take the capital, holding it until I arrive."

He looked around again at the men sitting in the council. He could see them nodding with smiles forming on several faces. "When I arrive in the capital, I will declare the Nephite nation is to be again ruled by a king. You will then place the crown on whomever you choose. You will again govern your own lands, and, for a small tribute, I will maintain the peace."

" Tribute? What sort of tribute do you speak of?" the oldest man in the meeting spoke up.

"Nothing you cannot afford," Amalickiah smiled, with a darkness behind his eyes. "Simply tax the people more to pay for your tribute. You

Pachus Makes a Deal

will still be able to maintain your expensive tastes." He looked around at the council. "After all, are you not royalty? Does not the blood coursing through your veins grant you dominion over the commoners? If there is a problem, or the Nephites resist your attempts to have power over them, my army will step in, quelling any uprisings." Amalickiah could see his words were having the desired effect on the men sitting before him. He looked back at Pachus. The two shared a quick smile. "I do have one specific request…" his tone lowered and his facial expressions turned dark. The hilt of a Nehor snake blade could be seen under his robe.

"I want the head of the Ghost Soldier." A deal was made. The men in the council sold their souls to the devil for a bag of gold, with the promise the devil would be fair with them, and would keep his end of the bargain. Amalickiah returned to the Lamanite lands and mustered his forces.

The invasion of the Nephite lands began on the first day after the new moon. Amalickiah woke early and stood at the head of a great host of soldiers. "Men!" He shouted for all to hear. "I now make an oath to you all." He held up a golden, jeweled goblet, lifting it high in the air for all to see. "I will conquer the hated Nephites, then I will drink the blood of their leader, Moroni!" Amalickiah tipped the goblet back, consuming the entire contents in one big gulp, as the massive throng cheered him on. Holding the empty goblet up, he shouted, "On to glory!"

Amalickiah's first move was to attack the newest Nephite city established near the borders of the two nations. It was not a coincidence Amalickiah chose that city to attack first. After all, it was named after his nemesis, Moroni. The city fell quickly to the Lamanites. The protective walls were still being built, and, with no way to keep the Lamanite hordes from spilling into the city itself, the people of the city of Moroni fled for their lives. Several hundred Nephites were captured. They were held as prisoners and forced to work all day finishing the protective wall, making the city secure for the Lamanites. Amalickiah randomly picked one of the older boys from the captured city. He was told to ride to General Moroni's camp. He had a simple message for the boy to relay to the Nephite high commander.

"You tell him," he sneered at the boy, as he gave him the message for Moroni, "I am coming for him as well as for Zarahemla." Amalickiah

CHAPTER EIGHT

grabbed the young boy by the collar of his tunic and barked, "Do you understand?"

"Y-ye…yes, sir," the scared boy responded.

"Then go. Remember, if you do not deliver the message, I will kill your parents." Amalickiah let go of the boy's collar, pushing him away.

The boy took off running. Several of the Lamanites snickered and jeered as he ran by.

"Your orders?" One of the Lamanite lieutenants asked Amalickiah after the boy was out of earshot.

"Gather up what precious items can be found. Send them back to our lands in the wagons with the wounded. Leave a small force here. Have them get these lazy Nephites to finish the wall along with the inner buildings. Assemble the rest of the army, and make ready to move out in the morning. There are plenty more cities to attack on our path to Zarahemla."

"My king, it is not my place to question you or your tactics. I am just hoping to gain wisdom. Why did you reveal our plans to take Zarahemla to that boy?" The lieutenant asked.

"When news of our advancement reaches Moroni, he will deploy his entire force to try to stop our assault. The Nephite army leaving Zarahemla will be the signal to the Nephite king men, to free their brothers from prison and capture the city." Amalickiah looked up from his large chair, then smiled. "We will let those Nephite king men do all the fighting and dying in the city themselves. When the dust settles, and the city guards are decimated from the fight, the Lamanite army will walk unopposed through the front gates." The man speaking to Amalickiah smiled then nodded his head in agreement. "Now," Amalickiah continued, as he stood up from the large padded chair, "on to the city of Nephihah."

Teancum was working on his archery skills with some of his men outside of the Ghost Soldier camp, when a rider approached at a full gallop. The Ghost Soldiers were enjoying some much needed relaxation from their almost constant contact with both the Lamanites and the bandits who still had a presence in the mountains. The mood on the firing line was jovial. Teancum was challenging one of his best archers to a marksmanship duel.

Pachus Makes a Deal

"Captain Teancum!" The messenger boy on the horse called out to the men standing in line with their bows and quivers of arrows at the ready. None of them were wearing any armor or were armed, except the longbows and their personal knives.

"Here," Teancum responded to the messenger, while raising his hand so the boy could see who spoke.

"Sir," the slightly-built teenager jumped from his horse then trotted to Teancum's side. Saluting, he handed Teancum a sealed note. "An urgent message for you, sir, from General Moroni." Teancum took the note, then took one step back to give himself room to read the message in private. Before he could open the note, he noticed the boy did not move, but stood there looking at him.

"Was there more?" Teancum asked curiously.

"No, sir. My orders were to deliver the message, wait for your reply, then return and report directly to the general."

Teancum furrowed his eyebrows in response to the messenger's order. "This must be important." Teancum broke the wax seal, then opened the note. Turning it right side up in his hands, he quickly read the few words on the parchment. Once he read the words from Moroni's own ink quill, he took a deep breath while holding perfectly still for several seconds.

"What is it, boss? Moroni finally get tired of us killing all the bad guys, so he is reassigning us to kitchen duty?" One of the Ghost Soldiers joked, as he leaned on his bow. There was a laugh among the men with Teancum. They knew they were a very valuable asset to the war effort. They took great pride in being the best fighters on the field of battle.

"No, not kitchen duty. We are going hunting again." Teancum looked up from the message, then scanned the group standing before him. They could see the look in his eyes. They knew what it meant. The jovial mood of the men quickly changed. "Report back to camp, make ready to move the entire unit back to the city. I am riding for a war council, and I will meet you all there. Go!"

"Captain, what is happening?" A second member of his archery group questioned.

"War! It's time to earn your pay, gentlemen. The Lamanites are moving on Zarahemla." Teancum turned to address the messenger boy. His demeanor was calm, but intense. "Go tell the general I am coming with all haste. Tell him the Ghost Soldiers stand with him and are ready for his orders."

CHAPTER EIGHT

"Yes, sir!" The boy shouted as he mounted his steed, then kicked his horse in the ribs to get the beast moving toward the capital city.

"Any specific information, sir?" A voice from the gathered men standing before Teancum questioned.

"No, nothing other than he is recalling all his units and consolidating his forces around Zarahemla." Teancum paused to think. " This tells me this is no ordinary Lamanite raiding party. He would have dispatched the local forces to deal with them and sent a reserve component to support them." He held up the paper in his hand and continued, " This is a full recall notice. He knows they are moving on Zarahemla." Teancum paused again to reflect. "Something is happening, something big." He looked again at his men, then spoke with a sense of urgency in his voice. "Return to camp and get the unit moving. I will meet you all at Zarahemla. Make camp outsie the city walls and what there until I figure out what is happening" Teancum walked over to his horse and swung into his saddle. "Don't forget to pack all my belongings in the same wagon this time!" He barked from the top of his mount. " The last time we tried this, I was wearing the same set of clothes for a week, until you guys could find my trunk you packed on a different wagon." The men all laughed softly, and rolled their eyes in remembrance of that moment in the past.

Teancum made good time, reaching the massive gates of the capital, Zarahemla. He saw a clear spot for his camp not far from the city. and knew his men would set up there. He wanted his ghost soldiers rested and healthy before he moved them into the wilds again, to hunt for bandits as well as raiding Lamanites. As with most things, when he reached the gate, Teancum could instantly see something was different. Normally, there would only be a squad of city guards standing at the open gates, but today there were at least twenty well-armed men. They were inspecting every wagon arriving as well as leaving the city. Along the tops of the high walls, Teancum could see several archers standing vigil. *Moroni has put the city on alert*, he thought to himself as he reached the massive gates. After being challenged by the guards, Teancum continued past the gate and into the city itself. Teancum continued riding until he reached a large building at the center of the city. Along the way, he saw soldiers and city guards running in every direction, people closing their shops and getting off the streets. The central building was the justice center, where the lower judges would hear complaints from the citizens as

Pachus Makes a Deal

well as where the sheriff of Zarahemla conducted his business. The streets were almost vacant now, as Teancum dismounted his horse. He gave the reins to a boy who was waiting near the main entrance of the building. "Water and a measure of oats, but keep her saddle on." He looked around as the last of the Nephite citizens moved to shelter. "I might need to leave in a hurry." He gave the boy a small copper coin, and the boy moved Teancum's well-bred mare around to the side of the building.

"Teancum! You made it," Amiha called out to him. Teancum turned around and saw Amiha walking up from behind him. Amiha was in full armor. He was escorted by two massive soldiers who were carrying spears and shields.

"Amiha, what is happening?" Teancum looked the soldiers over, then waved his hand toward the empty streets.

"Trouble," Amiha responded. He grabbed Teancum's upper arm and they moved toward the main doors. "Moroni will feel better knowing you are here now. Come, I will let him bring you up to speed with the situation."

The two warriors walked briskly through the halls of the building, then entered a large windowless room. It was a drab, colorless room, with no tapestries or decorations of any kind, just several large candle holders, along with oil pots, all burning brightly. Moroni was standing at the head of a long rectangular table in the center of the room. There were several ranking army officers, as well as the city guard's force, with the sheriff and his chief deputies. They were all wearing armor and had their swords. Moroni was speaking to the men who were gathered around a map spread on a table. Moroni was pointing to the map so he did not see Amiha and Teancum enter the room.

Amiha cleared his throat and spoke. "General, Chief Captain Teancum has arrived."

The conversation stopped and Moroni looked up from the table. "Captain Teancum, thank you for responding so quickly to my request… Please," Moroni gestured with his hand for Teancum to join him at the head of the table.

Teancum started to walk toward the table, while speaking at the same time, "Sir, the city is empty. All the citizens have returned to their homes and the shops are boarded up. There is a strong guard-force presence at the gate, and it looks like the army is making preparations to move out. What has happened?" Teancum was handed a goblet of fruit juice by a

CHAPTER EIGHT

small woman in a plain apron as he approached the table. He drank it in one gulp, then handed the empty goblet back to the woman.

"Please bring Chief Captain Teancum up to speed on what is happening," Moroni said, as he gestured to one of his officers, who had been informing the gathered leaders of the status of the Lamanite invasion thus far.

"Yes, sir. Amalickiah has made his first move. The city of Moroni has fallen. Most of its occupants have been reduced to slaves being forced to finish shoring up the incomplete protective walls," the army officer pointed to the map as he spoke. "Our spies have advised us, Amalickiah is marching the bulk of his army toward Zarahemla. Most likely, he will lay siege to these smaller cities and towns along the way." The man speaking then pointed to specific locations on the map indicating the cities and towns along the road leading to Zarahemla. "This information was confirmed by at least two separate sources." The man made eye contact with Teancum, then continued, "A young boy, from the city of Moroni was given a message to deliver to General Moroni, personally."

"What was the message?" Teancum asked first looking back at the briefing officer, then to Moroni.

"Amalickiah said he is coming for me and this city," Moroni answered matter-of-factly.

"Why would he show his hand like that?" Teancum asked. "Why tell us his battle plans? Why tell you where he is going? It must be a trick."

"My thoughts exactly," Moroni responded. "He is trying to lure me and the main army away from Zarahemla, but why?"

There was a commotion in the hall outside the war room. The door suddenly flung open. "Apologies, sir," one of the guards standing watch outside said, as he stood in the doorway. " There is a man from the jail who says he needs to speak to the sheriff right away. He insists it is an urgent matter." Moroni looked at the sheriff, nodded for him to leave and inquire about the interruption. The sheriff walked outside. Almost instantly, he reappeared with a second man in tow. The messenger had on tattered, bloody clothing, and was still trying to catch his breath.

"Give the report again," the sheriff commanded. He clearly wanted all in the room to hear what the man had to say.

"My general," the haggard messenger paused and swallowed hard, " There was an attack on the section of the jail where you were holding the king-men. The fence was torn down and they have escaped. They are now

Pachus Makes a Deal

loose in the city." Before he could finish his report, the large bell kept in the tower of the justice center started to ring. It was a recall alarm for all the city's guards, telling them there was trouble and to return to their posts.

"We don't need this right now!" Moroni declared, as he moved around from the front of the table. "Teancum," he spoke harshly, "I will deal with this. You take the Ghost Soldiers and scout the Lamanite army. Find out what you can, and do what you must to slow or stop their progress. Keep me informed. I will come as soon as I can." Moroni continued barking orders as he started to move for the door. "Sergeant Major, please find out what is keeping Captain Lehi. Sheriff, you are with me!" He shouted as he exited the war room and disappeared down the hallway with his aides, as well as other officers trying to keep up. Teancum and Amiha were now left alone in the room.

"Want to come with me?" Teancum asked Amiha evenly.

Amiha gave Teancum a look expressing his thoughts that having the opportunity to join him out in the field hunting Lamanites would be a much better option than the daily grind of life in Zarahemla. They both laughed and shook hands.

"Godspeed, my brother," Amiha spoke, as he moved to exit the room and follow his General.

"Until we meet again." Teancum responded.

The Ghost Soldiers had been moving fast through the thick forest for most of the morning. As they made their way through the trees, they were not moving in a traditional military formation; rows of men marching in step, drudging along. Instead, they fanned out, moving like a giant pack of wolves on the hunt at a light jog, moving loosely, steadily, and quietly. Bounding over logs, moving around trees and large bushes, and rushing across open ground, Teancum and his men traveled farther, faster, and more efficiently than any other body of soldiers in the entire Nephite army. Each man was focused and fixed on the task at hand—hunting the Lamanite invaders. Teancum had trained his men to move through the thick growth as silently as the creatures who lived there. It had been an easy transition from fighting the Nehor to fighting the Lamanites. They made very little noise considering they were over two hundred well-armed men, all carrying their own supplies and moving

CHAPTER EIGHT

quickly on foot in the same direction. A grunt here, a snapped twig there, the scraping sound of a section of leather britches brushing across the bark of a tree; unless you were right in the middle of the movement, you would have no idea how many men were out there, or what direction they were heading.

Teancum held the center of the advancing line. His men spread out to his left and right. He kept the pace and his Ghost Soldiers cued off his movements. Hand signals and chirps were used to tell the unit what to do and they instantly responded. No debate, no questioning, no consideration for anyone's personal feelings, the Ghost Soldiers were true professionals and warriors, each and every one.

After a while, Teancum signaled for a halt. The line of men came to a stop. The thickness of the brush made it almost impossible to see anything past a few yards, so Teancum halted his men every so often so they could listen for the sounds of the retreating Lamanites. Every man was sweating and breathing heavily, while scanning the area in front of them for any signs of the enemy. They had been moving like this for hours, but they showed no sign of quitting. Teancum was looking down the line checking on his men, when he heard a snap of a branch just to his front and a bit left. Turning his head slightly, he tried to catch any sounds or smells coming from that direction.

Teancum sniffed the air twice. He turned to face forward while holding up his hand to tell those around him to stop and pay attention. Those around him knew what this meant— Captain Teancum had picked up a scent.

Teancum scanned the area in front of him while he adjusted his stance. Something beyond his reach had caught his attention. He held still, focusing his senses on the surrounding area. Suddenly, he brought his fighting spear out to the ready. "There!" he shouted, as several wild-eyed Lamanites came crashing through the brush, as well as from around the trees, with their weapons swinging wildly and shouting their war cries. It was a large band of enemy fighters, set in a defensive skirmish line to ambush Teancum and his men. Clearly, they were left there hoping to inflict some serious damage in an effort to get the Ghost Soldiers to stop pursuing the main body of Lamanite soldiers. It was not the first time this day the retreating enemy had tried to set a trap for the Ghost Soldiers. They were almost directly in front of Teancum and charging fast. Teancum set himself in a strong stance, while focusing on three of the men coming right at him. He had no worries about the dozen or so Lamanites next to the ones attacking him.

His Ghost Soldiers knew what to do. Arrows, quickly and expertly shot out from both sides of the Nephite line, cut down six of the attackers and reducing the advancing enemy by a third. Teancum engaged the charging Lamanites closest to him. While thrusting with his spear, spinning then blocking, slicing with his short sword, kicking and throwing bodies as he went, Teancum passed through the advancing enemy line, killing at will. The Ghost Soldiers closest to Teancum joined in the fray. The unfortunate Lamanites never had a chance against the Ghost Soldiers. The intense battle was over quickly; Teancum signaled for his men to stop.

"Check them for intelligence," Teancum ordered some of his men, as he pointed at the bodies of the dead Lamanites with his sword. He moved over to where he had left his spear in the body of one of the enemy, pulling it out as he continued, "Scout ahead to make certain none remain," he barked at the other soldiers standing close by, and his men all moved to accomplish their tasks. "Gid, get me a head count of the men. Any wounded or killed?" Gid walked up to Teancum as he was wiping blood from his own blade.

"One with a wound to his arm. Not serious; it has been bound tightly and he is ready to travel. No loss of life. By my count, there are eighteen dead Lamanites." Gid paused as he scanned the carnage. "We are decimating them in small groups. Why are they attacking like this and not standing against us in force?"

Teancum looked up at Gid, "My guess is, they are desperate. We are pushing them so hard, they don't have the chance to stop and organize a proper defense. They're most likely hoping, with night approaching, we will stop and allow them time to pitch their tents and regroup." Teancum stopped talking and thought for a moment. "Let me see the map," he commanded excitedly.

One of the first things Teancum insisted his men do, once they were trained to fight as a unit, was to go out in small groups and create accurate and up-to-date maps of all Nephite lands. These new maps were of great value to the Nephite army. They helped General Moroni and his war chiefs by giving them a much better understanding of the terrain.

As Teancum examined the maps, he reflected on how the engagement had originally started early that morning. Teancum had been moving

CHAPTER EIGHT

his men over the main road toward the last reported sighting of the Lamanite army, when his lead elements happened upon the vanguard for the entire Lamanite force. The Lamanite king Amalickiah was brazenly marching his entire army right down the main merchant road, sacking villages and taking possession of smaller towns and cities along his path to Zarahemla. Teancum was hoping to spot the Lamanite army in order to spy on its movements, then report to Moroni who could respond with his army. The chance meeting on the road that morning led to a short, but intense battle between the leading elements of the Lamanites and the Ghost Soldiers. The Lamanites were completely overwhelmed by Teancum's brave men and were driven back toward the main body of enemy soldiers in a panic. That started a chain reaction and soon the entire Lamanite army was moving away from Teancum. Teancum took advantage of the sudden shift in momentum, as well as the updated knowledge the new maps brought them. That part of the merchant road crisscrossed through some smaller mountains and forested areas. Teancum did not want to lose the initiative from his first encounter with the Lamanite army. He was able to plot courses through the woods and over the hills, to be able to attack the retreating Lamanites at key points. This tactic gave the Lamanite commanders the impression that Teancum's force was ten times the size it was. In desperation, they kept falling back, hoping to find open ground to reorganize and conduct a counterattack. That gave Teancum time to send a message to Moroni so he could rally his forces.

"Look, right here," Teancum pointed to the map, so those around him could see. "They are going to want to stop for the night. So, let's keep pushing them back until they reach this point here." He pointed to a spot on the map, near the edge of the sea. "There is fresh water and open ground near the shoreline. They will think they got lucky. We can spy on them from the hills above, gaining a better understanding of their strength." All the men with Teancum nodded their heads in agreement. "We move in two minutes," Teancum ordered. "The next stop is the top of this rise, above the bend in the road, right here."

Teancum pointed to the next point on the map for all to see. The men were sweaty, breathless, and bloody from the fights all morning, but they were excited and energized to be part of this moment in history. They knew being a Ghost Soldier was so much more than wearing a matching cloak and using lethal weapons. It was about fighting against impossible

Pachus Makes a Deal

odds and prevailing through honor, courage, strength and discipline.

Teancum carefully rolled the large map back into its metal tube. "On my command, men!" Teancum looked left, then right, to make certain his sub-commanders were focused in on his orders. "Move! Follow me!" He waved with his hand for his men to follow. The Ghost Soldiers were back on the hunt.

Precisely as Teancum had predicted, the Lamanite army continued to move backwards on the wide merchant road, until it reached the open ground near the sea. Thinking it was a strategic, defensible location to camp for the night, the evil King Amalickiah ordered his men to set up camp and prepare to rest for the night. Teancum was informed by his scouts of the Lamanites' location. He wanted a firsthand look at the enemy camp as well as the defenses the Lamanites had erected around it. Teancum asked Gid to join him on his reconnaissance. He told Teomner to keep the men out of sight, letting them rest, but to be ready to advance at a moment's notice. Teancum was not about to let an opportunity slip by: if he spied a weakness in the Lamanites' defense, his Ghost Soldiers could exploit it.

Teancum and Gid applied a fresh coat of green and brown paint to their faces and hands, then covered themselves with their forest-colored cloaks. "I don't know how long we will be gone," Teancum said to Teomner. "If you don't hear word from us by dawn, send a party to look for us. We will be observing from the tops of those hills, there." Teancum pointed toward the tree covered hills behind him. Teomner nodded his head in understanding. He knew what to do, and he understood he was in charge until Teancum returned. Gid and Teancum readjusted their packs, then headed off through the thick growth, as quiet as the night.

It took them about two hours to find the best vantage point overlooking the Lamanite camp below. They settled into their observation position. As the two men looked down at the Lamanite camp, Teancum was the first to speak.

"See how they set their camp?" He said to Gid as he pointed toward the enemy stronghold. " They set their tents with their backs to the cliff face on the north, with the seashore on the east. Two natural barriers they assume don't need to be defended." A thought came to Teancum. He quickly checked his map and then he smiled.

CHAPTER EIGHT

"I'm pretty sure they are not concerned about a Nephite army dropping from the sky or rising out of the ocean to attack them," Gid quipped, as he scanned the camp.

"An army, no." Teancum paused for several seconds as he laid motionless, staring at the camp. Then he moved back from his vantage point, and began to rummage through his pack. "But one man can."

"What?" Gid said, as he looked back at Teancum. "Sir, what are you thinking?"

"I'm going down there. I'm going to put a blade in King Amalickiah's heart," Teancum said matter-of-factly, as he gathered items from his pack.

"Captain, it's not my place to tell you what to do, but that's the camp of the Lamanite king. He is going to be well-guarded, sir, *very* well-guarded."

Teancum looked back up at Gid, then smiled. "It is a hard nut to crack, there is no doubt. But there is a way in," Teancum said as he pointed toward the direction of the Lamanites. "Look again at the camp and tell me what you see."

Gid blinked several times as he looked at his captain in disbelief. While he watched Teancum prepare his personal gear for a lone assault on a fully-armed and well-guarded Laminate camp, he knew if it could be done, Chief Captain Teancum was the only man who could pull off such a feat. Moving back to his observation position, Gid looked again, running the question over and over in his mind— how was he going to get inside the camp? Climbing down the cliff face was out of the question. It wass not solid rock, but dirt and stones packed on top of each other. There was nothing solid with which to anchor, and if even one rock or a handfull of dirt were dislodged during the descent, the guards would be alerted and waiting for him at the bottom. Coming across the beach sand was impossible. It was at least one hundred yards of wide open ground from the sparse tree line to the edge of the camp. He would never make it across without being spotted by one of the several roving patrols or posted sentries. The tree line was being heavily patrolled by Lamanites on horseback. Only one possible direction from which Teancum could attack remained. " The water? Go in by sea?" Gid questioned out loud.

Teancum snorted, while continuing to prepare. Never one to miss a teachable moment, Teancum continued the discussion, "How will I do it?"

Gid turned around, and sat up to face his captain and mentor. He

Pachus Makes a Deal

thought over the various tactics of the Ghost Soldiers forming a plan in his mind. "You will attack at night, very late at night."

"Why?"

Gid thought for a second, then it came to him. " The moon. There is no moon tonight, so it will be the darkest of nights for a cycle."

"Good, and...?" Teancum goaded him for more information. "What is special about tonight to the Lamanites?"

"It's their New Year's Eve!" Gid burst out happily, as he figured it out. " They will be celebrating and drinking toasts to their gods and ancestors."

" They are also licking their wounds from the fight earlier today with my Ghost Soldiers," Teancum continued. "So, those not on guard duty will be in a deep sleep from wine and exhaustion. Those on guard duty will be trying to stay awake with their senses dulled by hot food in their bellies, as well as more wine than they should have drunk." Teancum went quiet and reflected. Then he spoke again." That will make it much easier to move around inside the camp, but I still need to get to the camp. So how will I do that?"

Gid looked at the sea off in the distance. "You will need a boat. Something small enough that it does not cast a shadow against the night sky, so it won't be seen from shore."

"Go on."

"If it is seen from shore, it will need to look natural, like it belongs there."

"Yes," Teancum responded.

"You will need something you and I can handle, like two men in a small row boat, on a night fishing trip."

"Well done, Gid. Anything else?" Teancum questioned.

"You're going to need to escape after you kill the king."

"Very important part of the plan," Teancum said, with a bit of humor in his voice, while wagging his finger in the air, as he continued to rummage through his pack.

"You can't go up the cliff face or cross the sand to escape, so you will need to go back into the water and swim away from shore."

"So how will I find you in a small boat, in the dark, in the middle of the ocean?" Teancum asked.

Gid was expressionless as he worked the problem out in his mind. He sat thinking for a while, but could not come up with a viable option. Giving up, he conceded to his leader his failure to come up with an idea.

CHAPTER EIGHT

"I don't know, sir. That one's got me stumped."

"Look at the cliff. See how it extends out into the water?" Teancum pointed to the massive wall of rock and dirt. We will row the boat out until we are far offshore and parallel with the cliff. There we will drop anchor and you will wait for me. When I have killed the Lamanite king, I will swim out, using the cliff as a guide for my direction. There is no wind or moon tonight, so there will not be big waves. You will hear me splashing as I swim. We will find each other easily enough." Gid nodded at the plan. "If I do not return by dawn, then assume I have been captured or killed. Row back to shore, take command of the Ghost Soldiers, then return to Moroni's camp and tell him what took place."

"Wait— sir, does the general know we are doing this?"

"No," Teancum responded, in his usual matter-of-fact manner.

"Oh, great." Gid threw up his hands. "Well, you'd better come back because I don't want to be the one to tell General Moroni that Chief Captain Teancum was killed as he single-handedly attacked the Lamanite king's camp without his permission."

"Okay," Teancum sarcastically responded, as he finished gathering up his gear and stood up. " There is a fishing village about two miles back that way." Teancum pointed along the shoreline and away from the Lamanite camp. "We will wait until dark, then we will borrow a boat."

"Are we going to ask the villagers if we can borrow a rowboat?" Gid questioned, with a slight smile.

"Sure… when we return it in the morning," Teancum winked back.

The sun had been down for about an hour, and the village was quiet. Fishermen had learned long ago to keep the place where you sleep far from the place where you clean the fish, as well as where you keep the boats and the nets. The smell alone could be overpowering if the flies didn't drive you mad first. So, it was not difficult for Teancum and Gid to find a suitable vessel for their needs without raising the alarm in the village. They quickly moved a small wooden boat with a single sailing mast from its mooring and away from a long wooden dock.

"Once we are clear of the breakers, we will put up the sail, then move farther out to sea. When we are within sight of the camp, we will drop the sail and row again until we are off the point of the cliffs," Teancum instructed as the two moved in rhythm, rowing the small boat farther from shore.

It did not take them long to clear the natural underwater barriers of

Pachus Makes a Deal

coral, where only small vessels could maneuver. Gid grabbed the ropes hoisting the small sail into place as Teancum moved to the rudder.

"Lucky for you, my captain, I know what I'm doing," Gid joked, as he skillfully raised the sail and secured the ropes to the mast. The gentle evening breeze quickly filled the single canvas sail, making the boat cut through the water under the ancient power of the wind.

Gid sat down across from Teancum and the two made eye contact. Teancum gestured for Gid to hold open his hands and he poured a large helping of his famous nut and dried frut mix into Gids hands. "Going to be a long night, eat up." Teancum said. After feeding his soldier, Teancum filled his own mouth with the food and chewed. Holding onto the wooden rudder, Teancum looked up at the sail full of wind, then back down at Gid. There was a question in Teancum's eye.

"My grandfather was a sailor and a fisherman. When I was a boy, after the summer harvest, I would go stay with him at his home near the mouth of the river Sidon," Gid responded. "Do you sail, sir?"

"I have no idea how to sail. I just figured we would work it out as we went," Teancum said with a straight face, still chewing on his mix. He looked away from Gid, staring at the shore line in the distance.

Gid sighed, then wondered to himself if Teancum was just joking with him. He knew his captain had a sense of humor, or was he telling the truth? It was so hard for Gid to tell. How could he leave something so vital to the mission, like the method of entering the camp, to chance? Or was he? He also knew a vital part of the Ghost Soldier training was to learn the ability to adapt, improvise and overcome. Frustrated, Gid just sat there, trying to enjoy the rest of the trip in silence. Upon closer inspection, one could see the corners of Teancum's mouth turning up in a slight smile. Teancum knew Gid was trying to work things out in his mind. This was why he liked his two lieutenants, Gid and Teomner, so much. They were not just excellent soldiers, but they were also thinking men.

After about an hour of moving under the power of the wind, Teancum told Gid to lower the sail and get the anchor ready. Gid could see in the distance at the shore line, the light from the fires around the Lamanite camp. "How will you know the best time to strike?"

"If you look closely, you can see their fires twinkle in the darkness," Teancum observed, as he pointed toward the shore. "When they do that, it means someone is walking in front of the fire, blocking the light for a

CHAPTER EIGHT

split second. When you see lots of twinkles, it means the camp is awake and people are moving about. If there are no twinkles, then the camp is asleep." Teancum looked back at Gid. "We will wait until the camp quiets down before I make my move."

All the many months Gid had been serving Chief Captain Teancum, he had never stopped being amazed at the amount of tactical knowledge Teancum had, as well as his willingness to share it with his men. "Yes, sir," Gid replied, almost out of awe for his commander and friend.

They rowed a few more minutes, until they were lined up with the point of the cliff, but far enough from shore so the darkness would mask their presence.

"Here. Drop the anchor," Teancum ordered. Gid grabbed the heavy chunk of rock attached to a rope sitting at the bottom of the boat near the bow, and dropped it over the side. Letting the anchor free fall to the bottom, Gid held loosely onto the rope as it uncoiled, following the anchor to the bottom. They were both surprised at how soon the anchor stopped falling and the rope became limp.

"We must be over some underwater rocks," Gid said, as he tied off the anchor rope to the boat. "All secure, sir," he advised Teancum, shaking water from his hands.

Teancum took off his shirt, then removed his sandals from his feet. He kept his leggings on, but removed his equipment belt. Taking his dagger out of its sheath, he tucked the weapon into his waistline, then grabbed his bolas from his satchel. He wrapped the bolas around his waist, tying the blunt ends in a quick knot over his belly. Setting the remainder of his clothing, equipment and special weapons aside, Teancum adjusted his position in the boat to where he would be able to face the camp and watch his enemy with an unobstructed view.

"Only your knife and the bolas? Are you sure, sir?" Gid asked, as he watched Teancum prepare for the swim and the assault on the camp.

Without taking his eyes off the shoreline, Teancum responded, "Any more stuff weighing me down and I will have a hard time swimming. Besides, there will be plenty of weapons in the camp for me to grab and use."

Gid nodded his head in a silent agreement, then returned to watching the camp.

After a while of quiet observation, they could see the sparks shoot from a very large fire near the waterline. Someone had moved the

Pachus Makes a Deal

wood while adding more fuel to the fire. "Did you see that?" Teancum asked Gid.

" The sparks from the fire? Yes, sir. Is that a good sign or a bad one?"

"Considering it's the only fire growing in size and the others are not blinking any more, I take it as a good sign," Teancum returned. "It tells me the person who put more wood on it is settling in for a long night. He wants a big fire because he is not planning to wander around the camp or very far from its light and warmth." Teancum looked back at Gid. "Good news for me; bad for him," he smiled. " The bright fire's light will mess with his ability to see in the dark. The noise of the burning logs will mask any sound I might make coming out of the water." Teancum turned his body around to face Gid. "It's time for me to go. I want you to say a prayer for our success and safety."

"Me, sir?"

"Yes, you. You're a good man with a good soul. We need the Lord on our side if this is going to work. I need to hear your words out loud, as I prepare myself for this task."

Gid sheepishly folded his arms, searching his thoughts for the right words to say. Gid was not an overly spiritual man. His father was a soldier and had been killed when Gid was just a child. His mother never remarried, raising him and his siblings the best she could, but he never really understood the whole 'church' thing. He was always uncomfortable praying out loud. He would participate in church when it was convenient, or when the youth activity looked like fun, especially when girls were involved. "Father," he started. It was clear this was awkward for him. "Protect us and guide us this night." There was another awkward pause. Gid took a deep calming breath. He thought to himself, *I'm a Ghost Soldier, why do I fear simple words?* Finding his courage he continued, "Father, Captain Teancum is going to sneak into the enemy's camp to kill the man responsible for all the horror, suffering, and death your children have endured. If you want the bloodshed and pain to stop, then will you help us? in Christ's name, Amen."

Teancum snickered when he heard those words. Patting Gid on the leg he said. "Fine prayer. Honest and to the point. I bet He does not hear such sincere and truthful words very often."

Gid smiled back. He felt lightheaded and wondered if it was the Spirit affecting him, or the fact he had not eaten all day.

Teancum swung his legs over the side of the boat and gently lowered

CHAPTER EIGHT

himself into the water. He did not want to jump in because he could not see the bottom and he did not want to hit an unseen rock and injure himself. He also did not want to make a big splash that might be heard from shore. He knew sound travels far at night, as well as over the water. Holding onto the side of the boat as it rocked from the ripples, Teancum spoke to Gid. "Remember, if I am not back by the time the sun breaks over the eastern mountains, set sail and head right for our camp. Don't look for me or wait. That's an order, do you understand?"

"Yes, sir," Gid reluctantly whispered back. "But, sir, what if...?"

Teancum let go of the boat with one of his hands cutting Gid off.

"I might need to escape through the forest or some other way. I can survive as long as I know I don't need to worry about your safety. Do you understand?" he asked again, more forcefully.

Feeling better about Teancum's chances, Gid agreed to leave at first light. "Godspeed, my captain," Gid quietly called out as Teancum pushed away from the boat, then started to backstroke toward the shore and the armed enemy camp. Gid watched, as Teancum swam with strong and determined strokes, until he was almost out of sight. Gid was left alone with his thoughts as the boat gently rocked in the waves. He suddenly realized how alone and exposed he was in his tiny boat in the middle of the great sea. This made him feel very unsteady, He started looking around in the boat to find something to keep him busy. Fumbling in the darkness, he found the cane fishing pole he had moved to make room, and picked it up. "I might as well do some fishing while I wait," he thought to himself as he squinted to inspect the small colored lure, at the end of the fishing line. Turning in the boat to face the enemy camp, Gid dropped the line in the water, sitting very still, watching the shore for any hope of seeing his captain again.

CHAPTER NINE

ASSAULT FROM THE SEA

Teancum was having a hard time judging his progress as he continued swimming toward land. It was very dark and there was a surprisingly strong current pulling him across the water. Twice he had to stop to tread water, so he could get his bearings, then continue on. "This is harder than I thought it would be," he whispered. The second time he paused, he could see the edge of the shore much more clearly. "I'm getting closer," he thought out loud. Then he saw a small depression in the sand, just to the right of the main camp. *Wait*, he thought. *What is that?* Teancum tried to concentrate on the unknown change in topography, but could not get a clear view of what the depression in the ground really was. *It looks like it might be a freshwater stream cutting through the forest and emptying into the sea.*

His guess was confirmed as a Lamanite walked out of camp heading toward the location in the trees where part of the stream would be. The Lamanite had a small torch in one hand and a large black kettle in the other. Teancum could see the Lamanite was lazily swinging the kettle in his hand as he walked toward the darkened area inside the tree line near the cliff face, where the stream might be. Then, a few seconds later, the same Lamanite walked back toward camp. It was clear by the way he was holding the kettle that it was heavy and full of water. *He got water, so there is a stream*, he thought. Teancum looked over the entire camp again, making a quick calculation in his mind. *I can crawl up the stream, using it to cover my movements. I can get close to the center of the camp, while staying out of sight of the guards.*

CHAPTER NINE

Teancum was very encouraged by this development. He also realized the current he had been battling was no longer an issue. He was actually drifting toward the location on the beach where the stream flowed into the sea. Looking over the camp one last time, before he made his final approach toward the shore, Teancum observed the camp was quiet and dark, as most of the camp's occupants were asleep. He watched as the few guards who were awake and on duty were not really patrolling the perimeter, but huddling close to a large fire, talking loudly, and drinking from large wine skins. Smiling to himself, Teancum knew they would pay the price of failure when the Lamanites woke in the morning and found someone had snuck into camp and killed their king right under their noses.

Teancum knew by attacking from the sea, covering the last hundred feet of distance before he reached solid ground would be the most dangerous. He would be exposed, and it would very difficult to move quickly considering he was half in and half out of the water. After he found the stream, he planned how he was going to get out of the water and move along the shore undetected. Teancum swam forward, using a modified sidestroke, keeping his head out of the water, so he could hear the alarm if it was raised by the guards, or if there was movement on the beach. He also did not want his arms and legs splashing and making noise. Getting as close as he dared, Teancum took one last massive breath in, and dove down to the bottom. Reaching the sandy bottom, Teancum used the momentum of the waves to drag himself along like a large crab and clawed his way forward along the bottom of the sea toward the waterline.

As he moved, his lungs started to feel like they were going to burst. With the physical exertion of swimming underwater, along with the excitement he felt of the coming operation, he was quickly burning up the limited supply of oxygen in his lungs. A quick shot of fear bolted through Teancum's mind as his body's natural survival instincts kicked in. *Don't panic*, a tender woman voice whispered in his mind. *Remember your breathing exercises.* Teancum listened to the voice. Fighting the urge to surface to gulp fresh air, he slowly let the trapped air in his lungs escape, while he continued forward, buying him more time. The water was quickly becoming shallow, and Teancum could feel the temperature of the water change. It was the effect of the cool mountain rain water from the stream emptying into the sea. He knew he was very close to the mouth of the stream now. Teancum waited for the right timing of one more wave to push him out of the water. Teancum felt the pressure of the water pushing him forward. With a thrusting kick, he lunged out of the sea, wiggling his way up the muddy depression created by the eroding effects of the cool stream. He carefully crawled on his belly for several feet until he was deep into the stream bed and out of the guard's sight. His movement now was covered by the path cut into the ground by the continuous flow of water and the thick foliage of the forest.

Getting to his feet, while hunching over, Teancum started making his way farther inland. After moving another fifty yards, he found what he was looking for, then stopped at one side of the stream bed. It was a large section of rich dark mud. Teancum held still for a minute, listening for any sounds of Lamanites moving in the woods. When he felt it was safe, he quickly and quietly covered himself with mud to hide his exposed skin, helping him blend into the night. As he was applying the mud to his arms and legs, there came from the opposite side of the stream, not far from where he was, the sound of a large piece of wood cracking in half. Teancum carefully laid down in the mud and reeds, holding perfectly still for several long and tense moments. He waited to make certain he had not been seen or heard by the Lamanites, or whatever had made that sound. Even the insects stopped buzzing as the air grew tense and heavy. He could hear them approaching long before he could see them.

It was a squad of well-armed Lamanites, walking toward him from the opposite side of the stream. He could hear the squad leader giving orders, and their metal weapons clanking. It was a security patrol. Teancum knew from his many adventures that if he stayed perfectly still, most likely they would walk right by him. He knew he was well-camouflaged in the mud and brush along the bottom of the stream bed. It was very hard to see something like him hidden at night, as long as he did not move or make a noise. *Unless they walk right on top of me...* With this thought, Teancum slowly drew his knife, holding it down low by his body, so the metal edge would not gleam in the starry light of the night.

As the sound of the patrolling Lamanites came closer, Teancum had to force himself to concentrate in order to slow his breathing. He could feel his heart pounding, while his temples throbbed, and surges of adrenaline-filled blood shot through his veins. He knew even the sound of a man trying to control his heavy breathing is enough to give away a position.

Suddenly, they appeared. There were four of them, all well-armed with

CHAPTER NINE

spears and short swords. Teancum could make out the leader. He had on a thick leather top, and was pointing as he talked to the other soldiers with him. The rest of them carried packs, but were shirtless. They were only wearing their leggings and sandals. The squad leader looked to be about Teancum's age, but the rest were just kids, maybe eighteen years old. Teancum understood the Lamanite language fairly well, but the one giving the orders had a heavy, gruff accent. Teancum could make out that two of them would stay until dawn, and then they would be relieved. The guard force leader posted two of the young Lamanites on the far side of the stream bed, then quickly moved on, with the last young Lamanite following behind.

I would have posted them on the near side of the stream, closer to the camp itself, Teancum thought. *That way, they have the stream, a natural barrier, between them and any attacking force.* Smiling to himself, he realized he was not dealing with the most tactically sound group of soldiers.

Teancum continued to watch the two young Lamanites as the guard leader left his view. After several seconds of silence, one of the two Lamanites made a grunting sound, puffing out his chest. Walking around the other Lamanite, he did a campy imitation of their leader, making the other Lamanite laugh out loud. The two laughed a bit more, then talked in a low tone as one of them grabbed a sleeping mat from his pack, spreading it out on the ground. The second guard took a long drink from his wine skin, then handed it to the guard who was lying down on the sleeping mat. They figured with the cliff to their front, the great sea to their right, and the woods to their left being patrolled by their own cavalry, they were safe. They considered the task of guarding the stream a break from the daily duties of a soldier. They were going to relax for the remainder of the night while drinking the rest of their wine. Had they known Chief Captain Teancum, the Ghost Soldier himself, was not more than twenty feet away, things would have been different.

Teancum did the math in his head. He knew if he tried to move over the top of the berm, the guard closest to him would see him, then sound the alarm. *Too risky*, he thought. He also knew he could not sit and wait until they both fell asleep. The sun would be up in a few hours. He did not know how much time he would need in the camp itself to find the king's tent and do what he came to do. *I can't take that chance*, his inner voice spoke. *I'm going to need to quickly remove these two guards from the equation if this is going to work.* He did not know how he was going to do it, but he did know he needed to act soon.

Waiting a few more minutes, Teancum allowed the guards to get comfortable and a bit tipsy from the wine. He needed their senses to be dulled from the alcohol in order to get close to them. As he watched and waited for his moment, one of the guards let out a loud deep belch. As both of them laughed at the rudeness of the burping guard, Teancum knew this was his moment. Slowly he rose up from the mud, bringing his legs up underneath himself. Waiting for any water to drain off of him before he moved, Teancum's demeanor changed from someone hiding in the mud, to a dangerous predator stalking his prey. His senses were alive, every muscle in his body was tight and ready to spring into action. Crouched over, his eyes were focused and locked onto his victims as he gently made his way from the mud bank, over to the other side of the stream bed. He knew, using the angles of sight from him to the Lamanites, he could get right up next to them if he followed the far stream bank, using it as cover. Stepping very carefully around the loose rocks and debris, he rolled his feet from heel to toe as he moved closer. This method of walking while stalking his prey allowed him to keep from snapping a small twig or losing his balance, thus giving away his position. He put his knife away, so he had the use of both hands as he slowly made his way ever closer to the unsuspecting Lamanites. As he moved while crouched over, Teancum felt his legs start to quiver. Wondering what was affecting him, he suddenly remembered he had not eaten since before the first skirmish earlier in the morning, when he and his men ran into the Lamanite army on the main road. Then his stomach growled from hunger.

"What was that?" The more sober of the two Lamanites cried as he jumped up, reaching for his spear. Teancum knew he needed to act fast. He quickly loosened the bolas from around his waist, then started to spin the two ends in the air over his head, while he held the third end in his hand. The Lamanite with the spear started looking out from around a small tree to see what was making the noise. As his face came into view from behind the tree, Teancum let the bolas fly. He was hoping the bolas flying through the air would cause the Lamanite to duck and flinch long enough for Teancum to close the remaining distance so he could take him out. What the bolas did was very lucky, unexpected, and welcome. One of the long cords of the bolas caught the small tree and the Lamanite's neck at the same time. The other two wrapped around

CHAPTER NINE

both of them. As one of the heavy weighted ends was spinning around the Lamanite and the tree, it smacked the Lamanite in the face, knocking him instantly unconscious. As the Lamanite started to fall, his neck was wrapped tightly in the bolas, and he slowly and silently hung himself with his own weight.

    The second soldier was very drunk and almost asleep, so he was slower to react. Teancum was moving as quickly and quietly as he could to reach the second soldier before he could call out. With one mighty leap, Teancum jumped out of the stream bed, landing only a few feet away from the drunken soldier. The Lamanite was reeling from the wine as he tried to stab at Teancum with his spear. Teancum easily avoided the spear thrust, and grabbed the wooden shaft near the blade tip. Jerking it violently, Teancum pulled the weapon out of the hands of the Lamanite, causing the young soldier to fall forward. The guard was completely off balance. He helplessly stutter-stepped toward Teancum. Teancum moved to his right, out of the way of the tripping Lamanite. As the drunken soldier fell past him, Teancum used the Lamanite's momentum to his advantage. He swung his left arm up and under the guard's chin and around the Lamanite's neck. Squeezing tightly, he violently pulled the Lamanite in close to him so his chest was against the Lamanite's back. The Lamanite reached up with both arms trying to claw at the arm that was quickly choking the life out of him. Teancum knew he could not risk being detected. The longer he struggled with the Lamanite, the more his chances of being discovered increased. He knew what he had to do, so he, instantly brought up his right arm, moving it behind the Lamanite's head. In one fluid motion, Teancum twisted hard on the poor Lamanite's head, snapping his neck, instantly killing him. The body went limp in his hands, and Teancum gently lowered it to the ground.

    Certain all the noise from the fight would send others running toward him to investigate, Teancum spun around, grabbing one of the Lamanite spears from the ground. Dropping to one knee, he held the spear out in front of him in a defensive posture, ready to fight any additional Lamanite guards. Teancum waited for several seconds in his fighting position until he was convinced the killing of the two guards had gone unheard. The only other sounds around him were the water running in the creek and a distant frog, croaking in the night. Confident he had avoided detection, Teancum lowered the long spear, then took a relaxing breath. *I need to hide the bodies*, he thought, as he looked back at his handiwork. Both Lamanites were dead, but there was no blood trail to cover up, a lucky break. He quickly untied his bolas from around the neck of the first soldier. Controlling the lowering of the limp body, Teancum laid the dead Lamanite on the ground. Looking around, Teancum spied a large clump of grass and a few leafy shrubs, a short distance away from him. *I don't need to make them disappear, I just need to get them out of sight until I'm done here*, he thought to himself. Grabbing the arms of the first Lamanite, Teancum crouched over and grunted quietly, as he pulled the dead body into the high grass. Returning for the second one, Teancum moved the second lifeless body next to the first. Walking backwards out of the high grass, Teancum pushed the matted clumps of grass back up to keep passersby from noticing someone had walked through the site.

    He returned to where he had left the spear, then noticed he had forgotten to deal with the Lamanite soldier's backpacks and sleeping mats. "Great… Nice move, rookie." Teancum was hard on himself, thinking he almost left those clues behind. Then it dawned on him he could use those packs and the Lamanite spear to sneak into the camp undetected. He looked at his exposed chest and arms and realized that most of the mud had been rubbed off when he fought with the two guards. He knew he needed more mud to cover his light skin before he could continue. Moving quickly back to the mud-covered creek bed and dropping to his knees, Teancum rubbed thick globs of cool mud on his chest and arms. Then standing up, he rubbed mud on his leggings and finally, a bit of mud on his face.

    Confident he was adequately covered, he moved back to the packs and spear he left on the bank of the creek. Teancum put one pack on while holding the other in his left hand. Grabbing the spear in his right hand, Teancum then paused and closed his eyes. *This will only work if I make them think I am a Lamanite who belongs in the camp.* He opened his eyes, then hunched over slightly to look like a worn-out soldier returning from guard duty. Waking slowly with his head down and dragging his feet, Teancum moved into the open ground next to the large encampment, making his way toward the first set of tents. He was moving much slower than he wanted to, but he needed to make the other guards think he was just another exhausted soldier.

    Teancum had traveled about halfway across the grassy open area, when two Lamanites appeared from behind a wagon. Teancum realized they could see him, and one of them called out to him, asking what he was doing. "Bed," Teancum responded, in his best Lamanite dialect, pointing to a set of small sleeping tents. Teancum understood the Lamanite tongue better than he could speak it, and he hoped his attempt at communication would pass. He kept moving while keeping the other Lamanites in sight out of the corner of his eye. The Lamanite who had called out to him raised his hand, waving him on. The two of them were too busy talking and drinking wine to care about stopping one lone soldier returning from guard duty. Teancum raised his spear in a thankful gesture, then continued to move toward the tents, as if he belonged there. Keeping his head down, and staying in the shadows as much as possible, Teancum passed by several small campfires and saw most of the Lamanites outside the tents were passed out drunk from the New Year's Eve celebration. He knew there were many more enemy soldiers asleep in their tents, or still awake and on duty, as he carefully kept moving.

Teancum was surprised how easily he was able to maneuver through the camp without being stopped and questioned. He passed several soldiers and camp attendants who never even gave him a second look. *I guess people see what they want to see*, he thought, remembering the time before when he fought the Nehor as he slipped from one dark shadow to another, avoiding eye contact and confrontation with anyone.

The tension was building as Teancum carefully advanced a few more yards toward the inner part of the camp. Every step brought him closer to the bed of the king, but it also meant he was exposed to the enemy and certain death. Suddenly, he heard the clanking of metal and the pounding of feet coming his way. He stopped near a few wagons still loaded with food and kegs of wine and water. He knelt down behind one of the wagons and was hidden in almost complete darkness. He was just in time, as an entire platoon of armed Lamanite soldiers came trotting past him in formation. " That was close!" He whispered in a relieved gasp. "Maybe I need to rethink this." He quickly reflected on his vast knowledge of Lamanite tactics and what he had been through in his life to get him to this point. Then the smiling image of his beautiful wife came into view. He missed her desperately, and his heart ached every time he thought of her and the joy she had brought to his life.

Shaking from the sudden melancholy emotions from the pain of his past, Teancum refocused, working out the current problem in his mind. *The Lamanites always set up the commander's tent first, then build the camp around it. I need to find the center tent and make my way toward it.*

Looking up, Teancum took his bearings and saw the top of the evil King Amalickiah's tent in the distance. From the light dancing off the sides and the top of the tent, he could tell there were several large fires burning around the perimeter of the tent. Teancum tried to get closer without exposing himself in the firelight. He wanted to get a better look at his destination, along with the security around it. Moving around the back of the mess tent, he found a large tray of freshly baked biscuits with some broiled meat, sitting on a bench, cooling in the night air. Teancum took one sniff and almost spoke out loud. *That's venison!*

"You coming off guard duty?" an old woman's voice cracked the silence.

Teancum almost jumped when she spoke. He lost focus for one second, allowing himself to get distracted by the smell of cooked meat and baked goods. He was better than that. Cursing to himself, he turned to face the camp cook.

"Just finished," he spoke in his Lamanite accent.

"Have all the biscuits you want, but go easy on the meat; there might not be enough for everyone," she told him, as she stepped out from the shadows, handing Teancum a round metal plate. Teancum discovered the old lady was not a Lamanite, but a Nephite.

"You're a Nephite," he said, forgetting his attempts at deception as well as the Lamanite accent.

Stepping closer and squinting, she looked him over and exclaimed, "So are you!"

There was a long pause. Teancum tightened his grip on his spear. He looked her over and saw she was short with silver hair pulled back into a ponytail. Her face was weathered and her brown eyes were tired, but there was still a spark in them. She had not yet succumbed to hopelessness of the life of a slave. He could tell she could get feisty if she needed to. He did not want to kill an old woman, but if she tried to call out for help, he was ready. She stood motionless, staring right back at him.

"I'm just guessing that because you're covered head to toe in stinky creek mud, you don't want anyone else to know you're a Nephite?" She put her hands on her hips and winked at Teancum. "Or, you're completely insane."

Her comment caught Teancum completely off guard. He let out a quick laugh, and she responded by laughing back. They both quickly realized the mistake they made by laughing out loud, so she covered her mouth. Looking around for anyone who might have heard the outburst,

CHAPTER NINE

Teancum grabbed her arm. He moved her into the darkest shadows he could find. "What are you doing here? Are you a prisoner?" Teancum asked in a whisper, while checking for any signs of the enemy.

"A slave is more like it," she replied. "I was captured several weeks ago, when the Lamanites overran my village outside the city of Nephihah. There are a dozen of us women who are being held here. We are forced to do the cooking for the camp, as well as the laundry for the Lamanite officers. We have been traveling with the Lamanite army ever since."

"Where are the rest of the women?" Teancum asked.

"We cook in shifts, to give each other a break— six on, six off. We rotate every twelve hours. I'm in charge of the night crew. They are all still in the tent, prepping for breakfast. The rest are asleep over there, under that tarp." Teancum looked in the direction she was pointing and saw several women lying on the hard ground asleep under a large shade tarp. "Are you here to rescue us?" there was a hint of hope in her voice as she asked Teancum the most important question in her life.

Teancum quickly turned back around, then looked her in the eyes. "No one in the Nephite army knows you were taken, or that you are here. I came for a different purpose, but I swear to you, when I have completed my task, I will do all I can to free you and your friends."

She had been promised things before, only to be let down. Now she was being told that she and her friends were not the most important thing this Nephite soldier had to worry about. She was devastated. It showed in her eyes and facial expressions. "Well, Godspeed on your mission, young man." She turned to walk away, dabbing the corner of her moist eyes with her apron.

"Wait." Teancum reached for her arm, then turned her around. "Do you not believe me when I say I will help free you?"

There was true sadness in her expression, as well as in the tone of her voice "You're a soldier, and you have your duty to perform. We are just a handful of women, most of us too old to bear children anymore. We are not worth the time and resources it would take to get us out of here safely." She smiled, "Besides, how can I trust you? I don't even know who you are."

Teancum almost blurted out his name, but he caught himself. She would be tortured for sure if the Lamanites knew she had information on the whereabouts of Chief Captain Teancum, the Ghost Soldier himself. Thinking for a second he responded, "I personally serve under General

Moroni. I am one of Captain Teancum's soldiers."

She raised one eyebrow. "You are a Ghost Soldier?"

"Yes, ma'am, I am," he said, standing tall and straight like a good soldier. Teancum could not remember the last time he felt so much pride declaring he was a Ghost Soldier.

A single tear fell from the old woman's eye, and the bottom of her lip started to quiver. "You know Captain Teancum?"

A half smile broke across Teancum's face. "Yes, ma'am," he spoke in a low whisper, stepping closer to her. "I know him better than most others. When I say I will do all I can to free you, I say it with the honor and the reputation of the Ghost Soldiers as my collateral."

The look on her face when Teancum said those words suggested the weight of the world was lifted off her shoulders. The light came back in her eyes, and she gasped as she reached to hug him. Teancum grabbed her hands before she could get them around him, gently pushing her back. "I'm supposed to be a Lamanite," he reminded her, while pointing at his mud-covered body. "Hugging me might make someone question who I am."

"Well," she quipped, while wiping more tears from her eyes. "Any friend of General Moroni, or the Ghost Soldier Captain Teancum, is a friend of mine. How can I help you accomplish your mission, my boy?"

Teancum thought for a minute, trying to figure out if enlisting the help of the old woman would be a help or a hindrance. Then it came to him. "You said you do the officers' laundry?" She nodded in affirmation, pointing to a different section of the kitchen area where a large pot of steamy water was sitting over a fire with several items of clothing hanging to dry. Teancum walked over to the laundry area and looked over the clothing. Sifting through the stacks of soiled garments, he found one piece of clothing in particular. He picked it up, then looked down at her with a giant grin on his face. It was a large red sash worn only by the royal Lamanite guards. The men were handpicked by the king himself to be his personal escorts and bodyguards. She saw the garment in his hand, nodded and smiled back; only now there was vengeance burning in her eyes.

"Over your left shoulder," the old woman advised, as Teancum tried to wrap the long sash around his body like a royal guard. She helped him re adjust it, then tied the ends in a knot on his right hip. " There… Good enough." She took two steps back, inspecting her handiwork. "Stay in the

CHAPTER NINE

dark and shadows; don't make eye contact with anyone, and look like you belong there. No one will give you a second look with that on. You will easily pass as one of the king's guards."

Teancum smiled; he was thinking the same thing. *She is more tactically sound than most of the new recruits I see. She knows what she is doing*, he thought as he made a slight adjustment to his belt. It reaffirmed to Teancum he must come back to save her and the others after completing his primary mission.

"Well, let's get a good look at you," the old woman spoke, as she took two steps back from the shadows of the night, putting her hands down at her sides. Teancum walked slowly into the fire's light, standing in front of the woman. He slowly checked his surroundings, to see if they had drawn any attention to themselves. "You will pass, as long as no one takes a second look." She moved the sash a bit higher on his shoulder. "Now," she said as she put her hands on her hips, "we need a reason for you to be up and moving this early near the king's tent."

Teancum wrinkled his brow out of surprise to her statement. *She is good*, he thought. *I was planning to make this up as I went along, but she is strategizing this entire operation.* He smiled at her as he watched her slowly turn around as she thought of a reason for an off-duty royal guard to be walking around so early in the morning. *Now I know I must save her*, Teancum thought to himself.

"I have it!" she quietly exclaimed. "Come with me."

They walked over to the large baking table. She grabbed a wide platter, then loaded it with fresh biscuits and turned to Teancum. "Are you ready?" She asked. He nodded, not quite understanding what she was doing. "Follow my lead, young soldier." With platter in hand, she turned and started to walk toward the large tent in the distance. She showed no fear.

"Wait," Teancum spouted. "Ma'am, what is your name?" He desperately wanted to know her name. She had the soul of a true warrior and he needed to know who she was.

She turned her head and smiled at him, "Rachael. And yours, my young friend?"

Teancum almost gasped out loud when she gave the same name as his murdered mother. Instantly, he flashed back to the dreadful day when he found his family butchered by the Sons of Nehor. In his mind's eye, he could see himself in anguish, turning over the bodies of his mutilated loved ones. Then, when he found his mother's body, he saw the face of this woman in front of him, not his mother's.

"And your name?" She asked again.

Teancum was snapped back into reality by her question. The emotional effects of his vision were taking hold of him. He was sweating and shaking. "I… I am called—" he half choked and whispered as he fought against the wave of feelings crashing against him, along with the need to still be careful with his identity. *What did that mean?* he asked himself, as he cleared his throat, fighting hard against the tears. *Why her face and not my mother's?* He looked down at her and saw her questioning face. She was still waiting for an answer to her question. "Ghost Soldier." came out before he even had a chance to think of a response. He was almost embarrassed by his lack of mental control. Without showing any emotion, she looked at him for several seconds, then with a half-smile, she turned back around and continued to walk toward the king's tent.

Teancum swallowed hard, tightening his grip on his spear. Taking a deep breath, he followed her into the dark of the camp. In a surreal moment, he paused trying to clear his mind. He could not shake the feelings welling up inside of him. *Why her face and not my mother's? Was there deeper meaning? Was it symbolic of some greater message?* Shaking his head to clear his mind, Teancum subconsciously barked at himself, *You're deep in the enemy camp, dressed like a Lamanite officer and blindly following some stranger toward your possible doom. Focus on the mission!* The old woman stopped, turning back to see what was keeping Teancum. He made eye contact with her, and nodded his head to silently tell her he was coming.

They continued to move in and out of the shadows of several large sleeping tents and around wagons and stacks of supplies. Trying to be careful not to be seen and at the same time looking completely natural was a difficult job for Teancum. He was growing more concerned the closer they got to the main command tent. His eyes danced in all directions as he tried to avoid stepping on a sleeping soldier or tripping on something. One misstep, one word, one call-out in alarm and he would have hundreds of angry Lamanites swarming him from all directions. All around were tents, tarps and coverings packed full of exhausted Lamanite soldiers. Most of them had sleeping mats or cots to help make them comfortable. But some of the poorest or youngest were stuck sleeping on the ground, exposed to the night air and the elements.

CHAPTER NINE

As he moved he noticed there were no roving patrols and no one on fire watch, only thousands of exhausted Lamanite soldiers snoring and trying to sleep off the excitement of the day. In complete contrast, the old lady gracefully glided past the sleeping men like she was floating on air. Teancum saw a quiet confidence in her which he envied.

As they stepped around one large tent close to the king's location she froze in place and stood completely still. Teancum saw her stop and he slowly shrank back into the darkness of the tent covering next to him, his spear at the ready. As he stepped into the shadow two royal guards walked in front of Rachael. She bowed her head as they went past and Teancum lost sight of them as they walked around the back of the big tent. Rachael stood motionless for a few seconds then turned around and winked at Teancum. Readjusting her load, she checked to her left, then her right, and she was off again like nothing was wrong.

She has ice water in her veins, Teancum thought as he watched this unassuming little lady walk right up to the main entrance of the King's tent and speak to the guards standing outside. She offered them some food from the large tray in her hands and they eagerly took it. Then Teancum realized she was doing something very clever and very subtle. Slowly, while speaking kindly to the guards, she took a few steps to her left and turned her body so the guards needed to move away from the main entrance and turn their backs to Teancum so they could eat from the tray. With no one controlling access to the king's tent, Teancum knew he had a clear, unobstructed path leading to the front door. But he would need to move quickly and carefully.

Now! Go now! The voice in Teancum's head was almost shouting at him to exploit this one opportunity to enter the king's tent unnoticed.

Very carefully he moved out from the shadows and tried with all of his might not to make a sound as he approached the tent. Crouched and with his spear point at the ready, Teancum worked his way very quickly to the front of the tent. As he got closer, he could hear the conversation she was having with the guards. To hold their attention, she was almost flirting with them and making sure they had plenty to eat. It was working and Teancum reached the tent opening and moved inside. As he was entering the tent, Teancum stealthily passed behind the two guards and he and Rachael made eye contact for a split second as he looked at her in the gap of space between the two royal guards. A thousand unspoken words were exchanged in their glance. Mostly, Teancum was saying thank you for the assistance and Rachael was begging him not to forget her.

Teancum passed through the opening and was now inside the great tent of the Lamanite, King Amalikiah. He instinctively moved to the far corner and the darkest shadows. There he realized he was only in the ante-room and not the main chamber. This room was darker than the outside and he paused to allow his eyes to adjust. He could still hear the conversation between the two royal guards and Rachael going on outside. She commented to the guards that she must be on her way soon to deliver what remained of the food to other guards. Teancum knew he did not have much time and needed to move quickly into the next room or risk being discovered.

He could see light coming from the tiny gap between the two curtains leading to the great room where the king slept. Moving closer Teancum spied into the next room through the gap. He could see the king asleep on a large wooden bed covered in cushions in the middle of the room. He was taken back for a second as he saw the light skin of the sleeping leader spread out on the bed dressed only in sleeping trunks. He had almost forgotten Amalickiah was not a Lamanite, but a Nephite traitor. Teancum knew he needed to get into the main room as quietly as possible and he felt the spear in his hand would slow him down. He laid it on the ground and pulled out his large knife. Outside, the guards were moving around the door and Teancum held his breath as he froze in place trying not to make any noise. He stood there for several seconds, but no one came in. He was finally able to relax and turned back to the curtains to peek through.

"Cursed Zoramite scum." He whispered quietly as he looked at Amalickiah. The Zoramites were a clan from the Nephite nation that could trace their blood line all the way back to father Zoram. He was with Nephi in Jerusalem when father Nephi killed Laban and obtained the sacred records. False Zoramite tradations were later taught that Zoram was taken as a slave and did not go with Nephi of his own fee will. Because of that tradition, his posterity had always claimed to be victims and were in rebellion against the government and God's laws.

Unable to see anyone else in the room, Teancum gently slipped through the seam in the curtains and was now standing alone in the sleeping chamber with the king. The room was lit by only one small candle burning on a desk by the far wall. Teancum noticed there were carpets on the ground, large open chests of gold coins and stolen jewelry

CHAPTER NINE

stacked near the desk and a map hanging on one of the walls. Standing still in the dimly lit room, his heart was racing and he was starting to sweat. Teancum experienced a surreal moment of clarity as he stood there alone, looking at Amalickiah, the sworn enemy of justice and freedom.

This is the moment, the voice in his head rang out.

Teancum moved closer to Amalickiah and stood over the top of him. Then he noticed the leopard-skin cloak and spiked golden crown Amalickiah would wear as a symbol of his rank hanging from one of the posts of the bed. Amalickiah was sleeping on his back, face up. He was breathing deeply and snoring as he took in air. Teancum could see Amalickiah was in the deepest part of his sleep cycle, which made moving around the room much easier. If he had recently gone to sleep or was close to waking up, then any sounds or movement might arouse him. But at this moment Teancum felt assured he would not wake Amalickiah. Teancum readied his large knife to plunge it into the chest of Amalickiah but stopped as he thought about what he was about to do.

He is asleep and defenseless. Is this right? Can I kill someone in their sleep? Above all else, Teancum believed he was a moral and just man. He thought he would be able to do this. But now, standing over Amalickiah as he snored, he questioned his abilities and motive.

This man is personally responsible for the death of tens of thousands of your Nephite and Lamanite brothers and sisters. The faceless voice in his head rationally and calmly reminded him.

How can I kill a defenseless man? Is he not my enemy, because of this very same thing? If I kill him while he sleeps, how am I any different? Teancum questioned the guidance he was getting from beyond. Up to this point Teancum had been so obsessed with trying to figure out how to kill Amalickiah he never stopped to question if he could actually go through with it. Facing an armed and determined enemy fighter in the heat of battle or ambushing them as they tried to gain an advantage over him or his fellow Nephite soldiers was different. Those soldiers had put themselves in that position knowing they faced death because of their actions. Amalickiah was no angel— in fact he was the worst kind of human, a murder, a pillager, a traitor. But he was also defenseless. *Where is the honor in this?*

Remember the story of Father Nephi and the drunkard Laban in old Jerusalem. Remember what is written in the holy records, the guiding voice continued. *It is better that one man die than an entire nation fall. God has prepared you for this task and placed this man into your hands. You are the Ghost Soldier, you are God's justice— you must stop these works of darkness.*

Looking around the room, he understood it now, it all made sense. The pain, the suffering, the hard training and sacrifice. It all was a prelude to this moment in time. He and he alone now held the key to ending this conflict with the hated Lamanites. He had honed his body and his mind to a razor's edge and now the opportunity had presented itself and he was prepared. This was not luck nor chance. This was divine providence and he was to be the instrument of God's judgment.

Teancum refocused and adjusted the knife in his hand. Moving around the bed he looked down at Amalickiah from different angles trying to figure out how to best strike to guarantee a fatal blow. He needed to be completely sure of his attack. If he used the knife there was a chance Amalickiah would wake during the attack. It needed to not only be instant but deadly and completely silent or the guards outside would be alerted. While he moved around the bed, Teancum spied a rack of exotic weapons near the far wall of the tent. They were the spoils of war for the king's personal collection. On the rack he saw a long javelin made of fine steel and polished to a high shine. For some reason this weapon caught and held his attention.

Looking back at the body on the bed, Teancum's mind reverted back to his training as a physician. The flashing images of the bone structure, the nervous system and the internal organs ran back and forth through his mind until everything settled and Teancum had the perfect solution.

The javelin… To the heart.

He slipped the long knife back into its sheath and moved as quietly as the night itself over to the weapons rack. Pulling the javelin from its resting place, Teancum took a second to admire the craftsmanship it took to forge and create such a weapon.

I wonder if the master weapons maker who made this would ever know that his creation would help end a war? Like dropping a pebble in the water and watching the ripples spread out. Or killing a king in the name of peace. The irony made him smile but it did not last. He knew it was time to do his duty and finish this. Focused, Teancum moved over to the bed. As he stood at the side of the bed he realized the angle was all wrong. *I can't stab at the heart from the side, the javelin might deflect off one of his ribs. I can't take that chance.* Teancum worked out the problem in his mind. *I need to stand over the top of him to ensure I hit the heart.*

CHAPTER NINE

"My king...?" A voice called out from the other side of the curtains. It was one of the royal guards coming to wake his leader so they can make ready for the day.

Teancum focused. He was so close now but armed men were going to be coming into the room. Should he kill the king, or prepare to defend himself against the royal guards? Fighting one on one or even a few at a time, he was more than a match for any Lamanite, but with one signal he would be facing the entire camp. Then Amalickiah stirred.

Teancum knew, in this moment, his life was not as important as the task he had been given. *If the guards come in, then they will find their king dead!* Teancum took two steps back from the bed and readied himself. Moving forward with power he put his foot on the bed frame and pushed his body up in the air. With the javelin in both of his hands, Teancum came down hard and expertly rammed the weapon into Amalickiah's chest. With one mighty blow he pushed the javelin into Amalickiah's heart and through his body, killing him instantly. Teancum landed in a crouch beside the bed.

"My king?" The guard called out again. He pushed his hand through the curtains and started to part them open.

Teancum rolled over and came to his feet with his knife out at the ready. Moving like a cat, Teancum was at the side of the curtain as the guard entered. He was crouching low to stay out of the guard's peripheral vison.

The guard entered the room and saw the polished javelin protruding up and out of the chest of his lifeless leader. Gasping, he reached for his sword and started to back out of the room no knowing Teancum had moved in behind him. Before he could cry out and sound the alarm, Teancum covered the guard's mouth with his left hand and sliced open the Lamanite's neck with the sharp blade of his knife. The guard tried to fight Teancum off of his back but Teancum was ready for the counter moves. As the guard struggled to stop the bleeding from his neck and fight to get Teancum's hand off his mouth, Teancum kicked the back of his knee and pushed the Lamanite forward and to the ground. Landing hard on top of him. Teancum continued to hold fast to the guard's mouth to keep him from calling out to his comrades still outside. The struggle was short but very intense, and suddenly the guard stopped moving. Gasping for air, Teancum rolled off the body of the guard and checked the room to ensure no other Lamanites had entered. After several

CHAPTER NINE

seconds of stillness Teancum realized his actions had gone unnoticed.

Now... How to get out of here? He questioned. *I need to get past the guards around this tent, then I can blend in and walk out of the camp.* He looked around the room and found a large dark blanket resting on a chair. He remembered something he learned from the Nehor, and he had an idea. First, he dragged the body of the fallen guard to the opposite side of the tent from the exit. Then, as almost an afterthought, he grabbed the leopard-skin and crown off the bed post and tucked them under his arm. Moving to the far dark corner of the tent closest to the curtains, he stood with his back to the tent wall and covered his body with the dark colored blanket.

"Guards!" He shouted, "Come quickly!"

The two large royal guards standing at the front of the tent came rushing in and saw their king dead and the other guard lying on the ground with the gaping wound to his neck. They were so engrossed in what was before them neither of them realized Teancum was hiding in the shadows behind them and slowly moving to the gap between the curtains. With the dark blanket hiding him from view, Teancum made it to the gap. As the guards tried to help those men Teancum had already killed, he gently slipped through the opening. He dropped the blanket on the ground and exited the main entrance of the tent without a noise.

Teancum was still dressed like a Lamanite, but most of the mud covering his light colored skin had rubbed off. He was not concerned about his skin camouflage at this point. He was focused on moving as quickly out of the camp and putting some distance between himself and all of those Lamanites who would be searching for him as soon as the cry went up an assassin had infiltrated the camp.

Teancum saw the early morning sky starting to change from a midnight black to a gray, a telling sign the sun was not far behind. Judging the distance to cover both land and water, he knew he would never make it back to the boat in time.

Turning his attention to the thick woods he whispered. "Overland it is."

Behind him, the metallic clanking of an alarm and a shout went up from the center of the camp near the dead king's tent. A Lamanite was banging on a large iron gong and trying to arouse the Lamanites.

"To arms! To arms!" Someone with a deep voice started shouting from behind him. " The king has been assassinated! Search the camp, find the killer!" Teancum knew he needed to move fast.

Almost instantly the camp came alive as hundreds of weary Lamanites climbed out of small tents or from under blankets trying to get up and respond to the alarm.

Teancum kept his head down as he moved towards the edge of camp. Several young Lamanites stopped him for questioning, assuming he was an officer with the royal guard. Without looking up, Teancum pointed and in his best Lamanite accent told the sleepy soldiers to search the area at the far end of camp. It was still too dark for any of them to really notice he was not a Lamanite or see the king's cloak and crown bundled under his arm as he spoke. The group of Lamanites took their orders and quickly moved away from Teancum.

People see what they want to see. The words from the Nehor he trained with in the gathering grove years ago came back to him again. Teancum hated the bandits for what they did to his family but respected them for their skills. Moving quickly he continued zig-zagging through the camp around sleeping tents, running soldiers, and equipment until he reached the edge of the camp. He crouched behind a tent and checked his surroundings then started to move towards the wood line. He quickly crossed the open ground into the thick brush. Now he was running full out through the trees, trying to put as much distance between himelf and the Lamanites. He had moved several hundred yards when a shout to 'halt' rang out. Teancum froze in place as he scanned in front of him for the source of the command.

Gid was sitting in the bottom of the boat and dozing in and out of sleep. The lack of rest and the gentle rocking motion of the waves was almost overpowering, and he struggled to remain alert. He scooped some seawater into his hand and splashed his face to help him stay awake. Looking out towards the beach, Gid could barely make out the tents of the Lamanite army and see the lone fire still burning in the sand. Gid then turned around and looked at the eastern sky. He could see dawn was fast approaching and he was growing concerned.

"Where are you?" He thought out loud, questioning Teancum's whereabouts. The fact that he was frustrated, tired, hungry and sitting alone in the small boat did not help. Like his captain, Gid was a man of action, and waiting for something to happen was not in his nature.

CHAPTER NINE

Gid started to doze off again when he heard the metal gong ringing out from the Lamanite camp and shouting coming from the shoreline. Startled, he was now fully awake. Acting on instinct, he pulled out his weapon and readied himself for battle but sheepishly realized he was far from the danger. He put his sword down and scanned the water between him and the beach for any signs Captain Teancum was swimming out to meet him. He was desperate to know his friend and captain was safe but he saw nothing. It was starting to get light, and Gid could see the camp better. There were soldiers running in every direction and chaos reigned.

"Well." Gid smiled as he spoke to himself. " That is a very good sign. Disorganization means no leadership… No leadership means the king is dead." He scanned the water again hoping for any indication of Teancum's escape. "Come on boss… Where are you?"

"Sir, we captured one!" A Nephite voice shouted out from the brush. Teancum stood with his hands high in the air.

"I am Teancum!" He shouted to the unseen voice in the shadows.

"My captain…?" A tall and muscular Nephite cloaked in the Ghost Soldier colors and well-armed emerged from the woods coming right up to Teancum. He looked his commander over from head to toe skeptically. *The uniform, the mud… Why was he coming from the Lamanite camp?* The Ghost Soldier asked himself. Teancum instantly recognized him as one of his officers and saw the concern in his eyes.

"No time to explain to you what is happening, lieutenant. We must get back to camp and wake the others. Do you have horses?"

"No sir, we walked in from our camp."

"Who is your fastest runner?" Teancum questioned as he looked back at the awakened camp in the distance. He took the man by the arm and moved deeper into the tree line.

The young officer pointed to one of his men. He was a lean, maybe twenty years old, with the look of an endurance athlete.

Teancum addressed the runner, "Leave your things for your friends to carry. Run back to camp and wake everyone. Tell them I am coming and to make ready for battle."

Without question, the soldier dropped his pack and heavy gear on the ground at the feet of the soldiers standing next to him. "Yes sir!" He snapped and was gone in a flash.

"Lieutenant, rally your men. We are leaving, now!" Teancum took one last look at the camp and gave a prayerful thought for the safety of Rachael and her sisters still in captivity. He then looked out at the dark water and smiled thinking about Gid still stuck in the boat. He knew Gid had a tendency to worry and would be going crazy right now out there in the water all alone. He wouldn't know what had happened to his captain and would be watching every Lamanite in camp waking up.

Gid was beside himself with worry. He could see the camp was fully awake now. People were running everywhere, shouting commands, clanging metal alarms and blowing horns. He moved around in the tiny boat unable to settle down. Looking out towards the eastern horizon he could see the edge of darkness near the bottom of the sky was slowly changing to a thin ribbon of gray. "Still a few more minutes before dawn… Do I stay and wait, or do I go?" Then the words of his commander echoed in his mind.

Remember, if I am not back by the time the sun breaks over the eastern mountains, set sail and head right for Moroni's camp. Don't look for me or wait. That's an order, do you understand…?

Gid knew what he had to do, but he did not want to abandon his friend and captain. Reaching for the anchor rope, Gid started to slowly pull it up. "I am going to leave like you ordered…" He spoke out loud as he scanned the water between him and the camp. "But you did not say how fast I needed to set sail." Gid continued to slowly pull up on the small anchor until it was clear of the water and back on board the boat. With the anchor out of the water, the boat started to drift with the early morning tides towards shore. Gid recognized what was happening and moved to set the single sail against the wind.

In short order he had the sail up and everything in place to pilot the boat back to the fishing village. Looking back behind him at the orange colored sky, Gid could tell it was time to go. "Come on boss…" He whispered as he searched the water for any sign of Teancum swimming back towards him. There was nothing and Gid could see several Lamanites gathering on the shore. *Looks like a search party is being formed*, he thought to himself. *That is a good sign. If they are searching for you, then they have not found you.* He smiled and pulled on a rope to swing the sail around and catch the wind. Tying off the rope Gid moved the rudder

CHAPTER NINE

and pointed the bow of the small vessel back toward its home. He was trying to remain positive about the safety of his captain and friend, but something kept nagging at him in the back of his mind. He looked over his shoulder again at the camp and said a quick prayer for Teancum's safety.

Rachael quickly moved back to the large, open-air kitchen. The rest of the Nephite women being held as slaves were awake and gathered in one group by the back of the cooking tent. The concern they felt could be seen on their faces and in their body language as armed Lamanites ran past them and alarms rang out. "Rachael, where have you been?" One of the other ladies cried out as Rachael joined back with her friends.

"Things are going to happen quickly. We need to be ready to escape when the time is right." Rachael whispered to the other women. "Gather your personal effects." She looked around to make sure no one else could hear what she was going to say next. "A Ghost Soldier from Captain Teancum's army was in camp. He snuck into the king's tent… I think he killed Amalickiah."

The gathered women all gasped and recoiled as she spoke. "How do you know these things?" One of the women questioned.

"Because I helped him sneak in to the tent." Rachael was getting upset. "He said he would return and help us escape. We need to be ready."

"You fool, you have killed us all! If the Lamanites find out you helped him kill their king they will show us no mercy." The concerned woman spat her words out.

"Keep your mouth closed and they will never find out." Rachael commanded in a firm but motherly tone as she pointed directly at the younger woman who was questioning her actions; her eyes were ablaze. She could see her news was having a very negative effect on all of the women. They all looked even more concerned and nervous. They had all been through so much already. Now with the entire camp on high alert and armed Lamanites shouting and running in every direction, panic was setting in. "It will be okay." She comforted the others as she continued to give direction. "Now go and get your things, quietly and slowly."

The body of Amalickiah lay undisturbed with the exotic javelin protruding from his lifeless chest. Several older and high-ranking members of the Lamanite army stood in silence around the bed looking at their murdered king. There was a feeling of confusion and wonder as they all tried to come to grips with the fact someone had assassinated their leader and more than likely escaped unnoticed. As they stood motionless, the heavy cloth partition separating the king's bedroom from the rest of the large tent parted. The air stirred, causing the lit candles in the room to flicker as a dark-cloaked Lamanite entered. He was massive, with broad shoulders and thick leg muscles. He was the commander of the night watch and a captain in the royal guard. He was the man personally responsible for the security of the camp, and one of Amalickiah's best and most trusted fighters.

"Commander," One of the lesser ranking Lamanites acknowledged him as he entered the room and walked up next to the bed. The other men in the room backed away from the bed and made room for him out of respect for his fighting abilities and sheer size.

"Has the body been disturbed?" He questioned without emotion. He was looking intensely at every inch of the bed for some clue or sign to help him identify the mysterious killer.

"Not that we know of," A second Lamanite answered back. They all stood in an awkward silence. The big Lamanite continued to scan the bed and walked around the room. He reached out and felt the exposed skin of his dead king and touched the blood oozing out of the fatal wound.

"He is still warm and the blood has not dried, this is a fresh wound. The assassin is close, he has not escaped yet." He spoke as he rubbed the blood between his fingers. Then the night watch commander saw the empty bed post. "Where is the king's crown and cloak?" He asked with a clenched jaw. He already knew the answer but wanted the rest of the men to hear him say it. They all had been in this tent several times and they all knew Amalickiah kept those items on his bed post. As if on cue the men in the room all turned and looked at the post.

"Stolen!" One of the men gasped.

"Guard!" The man in the black cloak shouted. Two royal guards entered the bed chamber. " The assassin is close…" There was strength in his voice now. "And he is in possession of the king's crown and leopard-skin. I want him captured, alive. Send one battalion into the forest. I want them to break up into squads and search everywhere." He paused and pointed right at the two guards. "I want the royal guard to search

CHAPTER NINE

the camp. Have them go tent by tent. Find who did this and bring them to me. The assassin will be in possession of the king's crown and animal skin cloak." he paused and looked at the body of the slain guard still lying in the corner of the tent. " The other guard who was on duty when this happened… Find him and have him report to me at once." The commander then walked over to the dead guard's body and squatted down next to it. He quickly examined the second body and came to a conclusion. "Attacked from behind and wrestled to the ground." He spoke to himself out loud. Then he spotted something on the ground next to the dead man's body. "Bring me a candle!" He ordered. Most of the men in the room outranked him, but none dared to counter his demand. Someone moved and handed him a small burning candle in a brass holder. He held the light close to the ground and looked closer.

"What do you see?" He was questioned by the oldest man in the room.

The commander quickly looked at the feet of the dead guard and inspected the bottoms of his sandals. He then lightly traced the impression of several foot prints in the soft dirt next to the man's body. " There are several prints in the ground here by the body." He spoke. " The assassin, he is a tall man, maybe my height. He is wearing soft leather boots with no distinctive markings on the bottom." He looked back at the dead guard. "Judging by the size of the guard and the nature of injury… The assassin is very strong and skilled."

As he continued to look over the foot prints, the curtain opened again and one of the royal guards entered. 'Commander, the guard who was on duty is here.

"Bring him in." The big Lamanite commanded as he stood and brushed his hands off.

The royal guard signaled and in walked a Lamanite who clearly was upset. His face was flushed and he had been crying. "You wish to speak to me, commander?" He spoke in a voice full of dread. He thought for sure he was going to be executed for allowing the king to be killed on his watch.

"Do you understand what has happened here?" The commander asked like he was the sheriff and conducting a criminal investigation.

"Ye.. yes, sir." The poor man stuttered his answer.

"Speak the truth and tell me what took place prior to you learning the king had been killed."

The crying guard looked down at the lifeless body of his friend and then at Amalickiah who was still in his bed. "Sir, my partner and I." He pointed down to his deceased comrade in arms. "We were standing watch at the front entrance of the command tent. One of the Nephite women we took as kitchen slaves brought us some food and we talked to her for a few minutes." He pointed again at his friend. "After she left he went in to awaken the king and I heard a shout from inside. I came in and found them both dead and raised the alarm… I swear this to be the truth."

The commander raised up one eye brow. "You saw no one enter or leave this tent?"

"No sir, I swear!" It sounded like the Lamanite guard was going to cry again. He had every right to be scared. He was on watch at the front of the royal tent and he was personally responsible for the welfare of the king. Not to mention the brutal reputation of the night watch commander was well-earned.

"A Nephite woman you say… Where can I find this slave?" The commander quizzed the guard.

Rachael was busy moving a small bundle of clothing when she heard a scream coming from the other side of the kitchen. She dropped her load on the ground and ran to see what the matter was. As she came out of the kitchen tent she saw several royal guards pushing the other women into a group. She knew they had not seen her yet and she carefully crept back into the tent to try to hide. As she was backing up she ran into the large frame of the night watch commander. She turned around and looked up at his imposing figure and tried to smile. She had been caught trying to escape but she tried to play it cool. "Good morning, sir." She spoke in a sweet tone. "Ready for some breakfast?" Without warning the large man crashed the back of his hand across her face and she was knocked hard to the ground.

"Put her with the others." He ordered his men as he stepped over her and moved towards the other slaves. Rachael was dragged by her arms and dropped in the middle of the group. They were now surrounded by men with spears pointed at them. Most were crying, while others stood in quiet acceptance; a few even tried to pray.

"Point her out to me." The commander barked to the guard who was his only witness.

After a few moments of looking over the women he pointed at

CHAPTER NINE

Rachael who was still sitting on the ground. "That's her, my commander. The older one on the ground with the silver hair. She is the one." He knew his identification of the old woman was a sure death sentence for her. He almost felt bad condemning her to death.

"Bring her." The big Lamanite responded and turned to walk back towards the command tent.

"Sir, what about the others?" One of the guards asked.

He stopped walking and without even turning around he answered. "Kill them… Kill them all."

Rachael cried out as she was pulled by her hair towards the command tent. The rest of the women all screamed and begged for their lives. All Rachael could remember before she passed out was the lamentations of her Nephite sisters as the royal guards closed in to finish the job.

The first splash of cold water jolted Rachael from her unconsciousness. She jerked and spat as she gasped for air. She was being hung upside down on a wagon wheel by ropes, and the excess water was running down into her nose and mouth. Her arms and legs were tied to the wheel in four different directions and the top of her head was touching the ground. Just as she managed to gasp and spit the last of the water from her mouth, a second bucket of water hit her in the face and she cried out in anguish.

"Who killed the king?" The dark cloaked Lamanite demanded quietly but forcefully. "Tell me and you will be shown mercy."

Gagging and spitting she tried to speak. "I don't know what you are talking about." She shouted. She knew more than enough; she also knew she was not going to live through this, regardless of what she said.

The wagon wheel she was tied to had been detached from a large wagon and leaning upright against the wagon frame. The Lamanite commander gave a nod towards two Lamanites standing next to the wheel. They, in turn, rolled the wheel until Rachael was upright again and facing towards the camp. Rachael's hands were tied to the outer spoke of the wheel and as the wagon turned, it rolled over her fingers, crushing them between the ground and the wheel itself with her weight. She cried out in pain as she felt some of her fingers crack and break under the pressure.

"Let's not play games, shall we?" The night watch commander

sounded almost insulted. He stood and walked towards a fire full of hot coals nearby. He picked up a long iron rod and poked and prodded the fire, causing sparks to fly up in the air as the burning logs continued to give off intense heat.

With tears in her eyes from the pain of her broken fingers, Rachael took a quick look around. She could see the entire camp was awake and engulfed in chaos. There were men everywhere. Some men were standing around while others drank wine, and still others were rummaging through large wooden containers or personal bags. Some of the sleeping tents were being taken down as large groups of armed Lamanites ran in all directions.

She could tell the camp was in disarray. "Kind of hard to fight a war and keep control of the clans when the leader is dead." She smiled a painful smile as she spoke. Her wet hair fell into her face and her lips were split from the back hand strike he gave her.

"You think that's funny...?" He questioned as he removed the iron rod from the fire and held the glowing hot tip of the rod out in front of him as he walked towards her.

CHAPTER TEN

THE KING IS DEAD

There was a strong morning wind blowing inland. Gid made it back to the small fishing village and docked the boat as an old fisherman and his grandson were walking towards the rickety old dock. With their nets in hand, they stopped and stared as a lone Nephite warrior climbed out of their boat and tied the mooring line to the dock.

"Good morning." Gid greeted the two fishermen as he walked down the dock with his belongings and away from the shore like nothing had happened. The two villagers stood in confused silence, wondering what was happening as Gid walked by.

Gid reached the edge of the trees and bundled the items in his hands the best he could. After he loaded everything in his pack he started to run through the trees and large bushes towards the ghost soldier camp. The ground was littered with thick vegetation, and Gid had to jump over down logs, swerve around moss covered boulders and dodge large tree branches as he moved. He was running at a quick pace for about five minutes when he ran into several of his comrades, in full gear, coming through the trees from the direction of their own camp towards him.

"Gid!" A voice called out to him. Gid was startled to see his fellow Ghost Soldier Teomner coming out from behind a tree.

" Teomner? What are you doing out here? And ready for battle?" He questioned.

"Captain Teancum," Teomner was breathless from running and pointing behind him. "He did it." He shook his head as if to say he

CHAPTER TEN

could not believe the next words coming out of his mouth. "He killed the Lamanite king! He has the Lamanite crown and royal leopard-skin." Teomner patted Gid on the shoulder. "We are moving towards the enemy camp to stage for an attack before they can regroup and counter."

"Teancum, here? Where is he?" Gid questioned Teomner.

"He is with the main force right behind us. We are the vanguard." Teomner responded as he waved his hand around at his fellow warriors.

Gid looked around at the few soldiers with Teomner. Even though they were all covered in their trademark Ghost Soldier cloaks and their faces were painted to blend with the environment, he knew each one by name. Brisling with an array of weapons, they were all good men, physically chiseled by hard training and rough living, with eyes like predators.

"What are you doing out here?" Teomner questioned as he regained his breath and stood up straight.

"I was assisting Captain Teancum with conducting a scout of the enemy camp." Gid paused as he thought for a second. He did not know what Teancum had told the others about how he was able to kill the Lamanite king, so he chose his next words carefully. "When we got separated. I waited until dawn and was trying to make my way back to the camp when you found me."

Teomner smiled and winked at Gid. "He told us the whole story. Glad you made it back to shore, sailor." Teomner was being a bit sarcastic with Gid. Gid laughed and shook it off. "Teancum is with the main body not far behind us. They are traveling the same general direction. So if you wait, you will run right into them."

"Thank you." Gid spoke as he reached out his hand to shake with his fellow Nephite. "Do you have any water?" Gid's supply had run out last night while he was waiting for Teancum to return to the boat. Waiting alone and in the dark had made him thirsty.

"Of course." Teomner handed his personal water skin to his friend Gid. Gid took a long pull from the skin and handed it back to Teomner. "We need to keep moving. Our orders are to scout ahead and set up a secure area for the rest of the force on the other side of that rise." He pointed off in the direction of the Lamanite camp to the same rise Gid and Teancum were on when Teancum hatched his plans to assassinate Amalickiah.

Gid understood and took a small step back from Teomner. He reached out his hand again and the two performed the traditional warrior

The King is Dead

handshake. Instead of shaking hands to say goodbye, they both grabbed the forearm of the other man, near the elbow, and held tight. They made eye contact and both chanted 'courage' as they shook their arms.

Teomner signaled his own men and they were off again, moving towards the rise and the Lamanite army camp beyond.

Gid did not need to wait long to make contact with the bulk of the ghost soldier force. No matter how hard they tried, they could not completely mask the sound of hundreds of well-armed men moving through the forest. Gid could hear them before he could see them and before long the lead squad of Nephites were coming out of the undergrowth and the shadows of the trees. The men were moving slowly, spears at the ready and scanning every inch of forest. Gid stood up and moved out from behind a rock. Not wanting to make a sound, he held his hands up in the air so the other men could see him. He made eye contact with two of the soldiers and waited to move until he knew they recognized him and relaxed their posture.

"Lieutenant Gid." One of the men who walked up spoke in a loud whisper. "Captain Teancum told us to keep an eye out for you. He is with the command group right behind us."

" Thank you." Gid said as he looked past the few Ghost Solders walking around him and saw his commander in the distance walking and looking at a map at the same time. The two made eye contact and Gid waved and raised up his eye brows to quietly say, *I'm glad you made it back alive, boss.*

"All units are in place and awaiting your command sir." A sergeant spoke to Teancum.

"Very good. Return to your post and ready your men, Sergeant."

"Sir, yes sir." The man moved quickly through the trees, considering his size, and was with his own men in a few moments.

"Sorry Captain, I missed the briefing. What are your plans?" Gid asked as he was adjusting his weapons belt and making himself ready to join the coming fight.

"You remember the story of Gideon from the Old World, and how he conquered the enemy with only a few men by making noise and breaking jars?"

"Yes…?" Gid drew out his response.

"We are going to try something like that, but with a slight modification." Teancum knelt down and drew a circle in the ground

CHAPTER TEN

with a stick. Gid and those around them all bent over to pay attention to what Teancum was doing. "This is the Lamanite camp. Here is the sea and cliff face." He made marks in the dirt. "And here is where I have positioned our forces." He then made three 'X' marks next to the camp. "On my signal we are going to blow trumpets, waive lit torches and bang our metal shields to make it sound like there are three much larger forces advancing towards them." Teancum looked back up at Gid and the others standing around listening. "We will give them a small opening to escape, here." He pointed to a section on the dirt map by the cliff where it meets the forest. "I have no problem facing them in open combat, and it might come to it. But we need to conserve our forces and start retaking the captured cities and freeing the Nephite prisoners. So we will start reclaiming the Nephite lands by evicting those Lamanite dogs from this patch of ground, questions?" Teancum looked at Gid and the rest of the gathered men. Most had heard the briefing before, but for Gid, it was his first time hearing it. He did have a question.

"My captain, what will the signal be?"

Teancum stood up and held out his hand towards a younger Nephite boy who was carrying the gold Lamanite crown and leopard-skin. The young lad handed the items to his captain and stepped back.

"I am going out into the clearing and telling the Lamanites who I am and what I have done. When I hold these items high in the air, light the torches, blow on the horns and bang the shields." Teancum smiled at Gid and stepped towards the Lamanite camp in the distant clearing.

"Now...?" Gid gasped excitedly as he reached for his two short swords and stumbled to move behind his commander. Teancum's boldness in the face of the enemy was legendary, and he should have seen it coming, but his sudden move towards the Lamanites still caught Gid off guard.

"Ready your men!" He whispered loudly to the subcommanders who were standing around them as Teancum was explaining his tactical plans to Gid.

Gid moved up next to Teancum as he continued to walk through the forest towards the noise and camp fires in the distance.

"What are you doing?" Teancum asked with a gleam in his eye.

"You left me on the boat all night while you had your fun. No offence my captain, but if you think I am sitting this one out... You're crazy."

Teancum smiled and continued walking.

As they reached the edge of the trees they were met by Teomner. "Sir,

The King is Dead

all of the ghost soldiers are in place and awaiting your signal."

"Excellent work, Lieutenant Teomner. Care to join Lieutenant Gid and I for a brisk walk into the clearing?"

"Don't mind if I do." Teomner smiled as he pulled out his massive broadsword.

"What did you discover from the Nephite woman?" One of the older, high-ranking Lamanites asked the night watch commander as he entered the command tent and took his place next to the ranking leaders of the disorganized army.

"She either had nothing useful to say... Or she died with her secrets." He snorted as he poured himself a goblet of wine and grabbed a hunk of bread from off the table they were all standing around. "So, now what?" he asked with his mouth full of half-chewed bread.

"We will need to appoint an interim commander until this matter can be settled. The clans will not hold together without a strong leader to guide and direct this army." One of the ranking Lamanites counseled. Some in the tent agreed with him.

"And who should the interim leader be, I wonder… You?" A second Lamanite questioned harshly. It was clear these two men did not like each other. "No" The interrupting Lamanite continued. "We must march this army back to the city of Mulek where Ammoron, Amalickiah's brother, is waiting with the reinforcements. According to our laws, he is the rightful leader and king now."

"You would choose to have Ammoron, one of those Zoramite dogs, as king, over one of your own?" The first Lamanite barked back as he stepped closer to the table in a sign of dominance. "He is a pale-faced son of a liar!"

The night watch commander could see this was going to be a long day as the men in the tent began to bicker back and forth between themselves on the best course of action to take next. He signaled for one of his personal guards to come to his side. "Have the royal guards prepare the king's body for travel, and strike our tents. We are leaving regardless of what these fools decide." He whispered in his soldier's ear as the in-fighting continued to escalate in the tent.

The verbal argument continued for several more seconds until one man pushed another and then weapons were drawn. The Lamanite people

CHAPTER TEN

were not one cohesive nation living under the banner of one leader. Yes, there was a king, but only because the local lords allowed him to claim the title. The Lamanite lands were all broken up into smaller clans, and they had been fighting amongst themselves since the days of Laman and Lemuel. Stolen sheep, insults, broken hearts, events which might have taken place hundreds of years ago still caused them to quarrel with each other. Only when there was a dominant voice from a strong-willed leader and the chance for plunder and slaves did the clans unite and attack the Nephites. Now with their strong-willed leader dead, the coalition was dissolving.

If Teancum had known what was happening inside the Lamanite command tent at that very moment, he would have stopped what he was about to do and allowed the Lamanites to destroy themselves. Instead he stepped out from the thick forest with his arms out to his sides holding the crown in one hand, and the leopard-skin cloak of power in the other. Gid and Teomner were at his side with their weapons out, ready to defend their captain.

Although the rest of his clansmen were scattered and disorganized, one lone Lamanite remained at his post and was acting as a watchman for the camp. He was sitting on a log near a large, smoldering fire pit and tossing bits of grass and twigs into the fire. His spear was resting on the ground next to him and he was clad in a loincloth and sandals. He was not old enough or important enough to have any real clothing or proper weapons yet. Now, with the Zoramite king dead in his tent, who knew what the future held for this young man. But he knew if he remained faithful and did his duty, then someday he would be rewarded by his clan chieftain. As he sat hunched over and baking in the sunlight, some movement caught his eye. He squinted as he looked across the wide open meadow and saw something near the tree line. At first the lone guard could not quite make out what he was seeing. The heat from the morning sun was playing tricks on his mind. But as he stood up and put his hand over his eyes to shield them from the sun's glare he could see Teancum and his lieutenants emerge from the shadows of the trees and move towards the center of the field. Then he noticed that whoever was walking out from the woods was holding the king's cloak and crown.

"How close do you want to get?" Teomner questioned as the three continued to move closer to the disorganized Lamanite camp. He was trying to sound confident, but there was concern in his voice.

"Are you afraid?" Gid teased back. Gid was showing signs of worry himself. The two lieutenants made eye contact and silently wondered between them if they had made a bad decision by coming out here in the open with Teancum. Only Teancum remained stoic and steady as a rock as they walked towards the camp full of thousands of enemy fighters.

The Lamanite sentry did not know what to do. He could not call for help; most of the other camp occupants were thinking of themselves and running around, rather than preparing for war. He could not leave his post to deliver the warning to his commanding officer that three Nephites were approaching, and one of them might be the same person who killed the king. Panicked, he desperately looked around for anything that could help him do his duty. He spied a small bugle sitting on top of a table not far from where he was posted and quickly picked it up. "Fortune has favored me this day!" He exclaimed as he moved towards the horn. In his mind he knew he was going to be the one who warned the entire camp of the coming Nephites. He saw them before anyone else and he would be rewarded for his diligence. He picked up the small horn and quickly blew into it three short blasts of air. He did this over and over again several times until he had the attention of those around him.

"Okay, now we stop." Teancum said as he suddenly stopped walking forward. "I wondered how close we could get before someone sounded the alarm."

Gid and Teomner were not wondering at all. They were wondering how they were going to survive if the Lamanites charged at them en masse. Looking around and behind them, they calculated how far they were from the trees and how quickly they could run back to hide in the thick brush if the Lamanites did charge at them. They knew the Ghost Soldier archers hiding in the trees could cover them, but would arrows alone be enough if they had to make an escape? All the while, Teancum stood motionless and without expression with the stolen Lamanite items held out to his sides.

The night watch commander was sitting at the far end of the large table with his head in his hands listening to the Lamanite army leaders argue and threaten each other over what should be done next. He knew most of them were tribal leaders and not real military officers, so the arguments were more about personal feelings and tribal honor instead of useful tactical options. He was starting to get an immense headache and was rubbing his temples for relief when he heard the first of the many

CHAPTER TEN

horn blows signaling the alarm. He was on his feet and moving before he realized what had happened. Stepping outside of the big tent he held still as he listened for additional horn sounds. The distant horn sounded again and several Lamanites started running towards the alarming sounds of danger.

The dark-cloaked commander was no exception, he was off like a rabbit running with the crowd towards the alarm at the far end of the camp. When he reached the edge of the camp he saw the young sentry still holding the horn and pointing out into the field. The giant Lamanite looked out and saw Teancum and his lieutenants standing alone, in the open and with the king's personal items.

"Form ranks!" He shouted to the gathered Lamanite soldiers around him. Kicking and pushing, he tried to get the soldiers to stand and prepare for an attack.

"Sir, I don't have a weapon." One Lamanite exclaimed as he resisted the commander's attempts to organize the defense of the camp.

"What…?!" The big Lamanite gasped. He gazed around and saw most of the Lamanites standing around him were unarmed. "Why are you not armed?" He was insulted he needed to ask this question of the Lamanite soldiers.

"Sir, no one told us to get our spears and swords."

The night watch commander knew most of these Lamanites were nothing but fodder for the battle, but this was a new low. "How could you not think to arm yourselves?" He lamented as he looked around at the sad state of the army. He was beginning to realize how much chaos the death of Amalickiah was causing when he looking out into the meadow. He could barely make out Teancum's face, the man holding the king's crown. "Assassin." He whispered with contempt in his voice. He turned to summon his archers when a voice came booming across the open plain. The Lamanites all stood still to listen, including the night watch commander.

"My name is Chief Captain Teancum. I am the leader of the Ghost Soldiers!" Even the mention of the Ghost Soldiers made the gathered Lamanites all recoil out of fear. It was as if they were facing Death himself. "You tried to fight me and my men on the road yesterday." He paused to allow those Lamanites who could hear his voice reflect on the beating they took at the hands of the Ghost Soldiers. "Last night I walked into your well-guarded camp and killed your king." He held up

The King is Dead

the items in his hand even higher for all to see. "Now, I have brought General Moroni and the entire Nephite army to your camp!" At this cue, hundreds of torches were lit in the dark recesses of the thick woods. The sun was not yet high enough to burn away the dark shadows inside the trees. Combined with the morning fog still lingering in the thick woods, the sight of all of the burning torches struck a chord of great fear in the hearts of the Lamanites. From their vantage point, it looked like the forest itself had exploded in fire. But from inside the trees, Ghost Soldiers were in position holding three or four torches and moving around to confuse the enemy. "When I give the order," Teancum continued; he could sense he was affecting the morale of the Lamanites with his words and theatrics, " Tens of thousands of armored Nephites will descend upon you and deliver justice upon your heads." This was the signal for all the trumpets to sound, for the drums to bang and for all the men of Teancum's elite unit to clank their metal shields together and shout as one. The war cries and noise of war echoed through the camp and across the open water.

"He brought every Nephite within a thousand miles!" An unseen Lamanite shouted out in a panic-filled voice. The Lamanites listening to Teancum knew they wanted no part of this fight. Not after what happened to us on the road yesterday. The thought of fighting the Ghost Soldiers, and what now appeared to be the entire Nephite army, was insane. And to fight without the leadership of a king to hold the different clans together and direct the entire force was even more disheartening. As if on a silent cue, every Lamanite within the sound of Teancum's voice came to the same conclusion. They instantly scattered in every direction; except one direction— towards the Ghost Soldier and his men.

"Stand your ground!" The Lamanite commander bellowed as he tried to grab hold of the fleeing Lamanites; but it was useless. He swiftly moved among the ranks to encourage the Lamanites to stand and fight, but it was futile. The effect of so many running in the opposite direction and all the noise and commotion coming from the trees gave the rest of the camp the impression an overwhelming force was descending upon them. And their only chance for survival was to run for their lives.

This was a catastrophic defeat for the Lamanites as the camp was emptied of soldiers in only a matter of minutes. Precisely as Teancum had predicted, the bulk of the fleeing army ran towards the small gap he left open for them where the tree line met the cliff. Teancum ordered all the

CHAPTER TEN

Nephite cavalry he had at his disposal to chase the retreating Lamanites and ensure they kept running and did not regroup. Then he turned his attention to the camp itself. Not only did he want to ensure he cleared the camp of any enemy soldiers, but he wanted to find Rachael and her friends. He signaled for his Ghost Soldiers to advance into the camp.

With his two lieutenant's by his side, Teancum put the Lamanite trophies back in his satchel and moved towards the center of the deserted camp with his spear in hand. The bulk of the army had fled but as with any engagement with the Lamanites there were some true believers who stayed to fight to the death. Teancum and his men quickly and efficiently granted these fools their final wish. There were some stragglers who surrendered to the ghost soldiers as well as the wounded left behind. Several non-military camp assistants, who supported the Lamanites, were also taken as prisoner.

Teancum worked his way around the abandoned tents and wagons fighting and scrambling as he went. He reached the command tent and orientated himself towards the kitchen area where he hoped he would find Rachael and the other Nephite prisoners. "There are several Nephite women who have been taken as slaves!" He shouted at his men as he breathed hard from the fighting. "Spread out and find them. Start with the cooking tents over there." He pointed with the bloody tip of his spear towards the Lamanite kitchen area.

"Yes sir!" Several of his men barked back as they moved in the general direction and continued to engage the few remaining loyal Lamanites who were defending their camp.

"Gid!" Teancum called out to his trusted lieutenant. Gid came jogging over with Teomner close behind. They both had been by his side for most of the lopsided battle, and bore the bloody signs of having engaged the enemy in hand-to-hand combat.

"Sir?" Gid responded as he approached Teancum.

" Take a group of men and secure this tent. It's their command center, and I know they did not have time to clear it out. Check for intelligence and lock up anything of value you find. Then continue clearing the camp of any combatants who are left. Teomner?" Teomner moved up next to Teancum as Gid left to carry out his orders. "Secure the prisoners and the wounded. Have them moved to the edge of the clearing where they can be grouped together according to rank and place them under guard. Then round up all the working wagons you can find." Teancum kicked

The King is Dead

a simple but sturdy looking Lamanite spear left on the ground by its fleeing owner. " There are plenty of weapons and lots of equipment and supplies they have abandoned. Gather up what we can use and burn the rest."

"Yes, sir." Teomner replied as he put his broadsword back into its sheath.

In no time, the rest of the camp was cleared of enemy fighters and a surreal calm rested over the area. The Ghost Soldiers were all professionals and experts at their craft. There were no loud boisterous celebrations of victory, no degrading of the defeated enemy, no plundering of the wealth left behind— only honorable men who instantly switched from warriors to peacekeepers. A strong guard was established at the far end of the camp to deter any Lamanites from trying to counterattack. The rest of the Ghost Soldiers went about gathering up any useful items the Nephite army might need and providing care for the wounded Lamanites. No Ghost Soldiers were killed in the engagement, but a few were wounded and received priority care. As Teancum was directing the aftermath of the battle one of his warriors came running up to him.

"Sir… My captain." He exclaimed breathlessly. It was clear he had been running.

"Catch your breath. What is it?" Teancum questioned after he gave him a moment to breath.

"Sir, we found the Nephite prisoners." The messenger pointed away from the king's tent. "But there is a problem… You should come and see for yourself."

Teancum walked slowly among the bodies of the dead Nephite women. They were all in a heap where the Lamanite royal guard had killed them and left their bodies to rot in the sun. He carefully turned a few over so he could see the faces of the deceased. He had seen a few of them when he was in the camp last night, but he was looking for Rachael. "Not here." He spoke in a loud whisper.

"Sir?" Gid questioned. He was too far away from Teancum to hear what was said.

"She is not here… The old lady who helped me kill the king." Teancum stood up and spoke in a clear tone but inside his heart was breaking. He was supposed to help them, yet here they were, jumbled together in a pitiful mass. He had failed, again. The old fire began to grow inside of

CHAPTER TEN

him. "They left in such a hurry, I doubt they took her with them." He was speaking out loud but to himself now as he scanned the camp. His eyes went cold and dark like a great cat on the hunt. "Check the camp again!" He pointed to a group of his men standing not far off. "Check with the wounded and camp attendants we took prisoner. We need to find her."

"Sir, I think I found her." Teomner said softly as he walked up to Teancum and the others. You could see the sadness in his eyes. He did not want to be the one to tell his captain the news. "Over behind the command tent." He exhaled and pointed in the direction he wanted Teancum to follow.

Teancum was a master of many things, and one of them was the ability to read body language. He could see and understand the nonverbal clues Teomner was expressing and Teancum knew this was bad. With urgent concern in his eyes he took off running towards the massive tent set up in the middle of the Lamanite camp, his soldiers following close behind.

There was a circle of men standing around the smoldering remains. One of them saw Teancum approaching and made way so he could see what they were all looking at. There, still tied to the wagon wheel, was the burned body of Rachael. She had been tortured for whatever information she might have had. When the Lamanite commander realized he could not get her to break, he had viciously murdered her. Teancum could smell the burnt flesh and it made him gag. His soul grew white hot with rage.

"Look at the burn marks on her hands and feet." Teomner pointed. "It looks almost like something hot touched her flesh."

Teancum knew instantly what had happened. His body was tense and his hands were clinched while he choked back the tears. "She was tortured." He almost spat the words out. He was so far beyond rage that breathing was proving to be difficult. "She knew about my plans and what I looked like. They tortured her for the information, but she did not break." Large tears came running down his cheeks as he spoke, his arms were shaking now. He had not felt this way since the cliff and that tragic, rainy night so long ago.

"How can you know she did not give your secret away?" Gid questioned. Teancum did not answer. He was in no condition to answer.

"Because we surprised them and they ran like dogs." Teomner answered after a few moments of tense silence. Everyone was looking at Teancum, but he was motionless and staring down into the empty eyes of

Rachael's corpse.

"Have our horsemen returned from following the retreating Lamanites?" Teancum finally spoke. He sounded almost inhuman.

"Yes, sir." Gid responded. " They reported that they chased the Lamanites to the small river just north of the camp and watched them as they crossed to the other side." The next thought in Teancum's mind came from a dark place inside of him. He wanted to cross the river and hunt and kill as many Lamanites as he could, until they killed him or he got tired of it— whichever came first.

"Good. Teancum continued. "I want every Ghost Soldier accounted for, every item of value you can take packed in wagons and with the prisoners, ready to move at dusk. Everything you can't take will be stacked in the middle of the camp and burned… Along with all the bodies. Except for her and the other Nephite ladies." Teancum pointed down at Rachael's body. "I want those Lamanites who surrendered to dig graves for each of the women they killed. Not one mass grave, they each get their own. And we will have a service before you leave to honor them." He looked at the others still standing next to him. "Dismissed."

They had all seen that look in his eyes before. Without a question the men of the Ghost Soldiers moved to fulfill their duties. All except one— Gid remained. He stood at his captain's side as the two of them looked down again at the lifeless and mutilated body.

"What?" Teancum asked in a short tone.

"Sir, you spoke as if you will not be joining us on the trip back home at dusk."

"I have some unfinished business with the Lamanites." Teancum responded as he gestured towards Rachael's lifeless body.

Gid knew he had to say something or his captain was going to get himself killed. "Yes sir, we all do. But going off by yourself again… It looks like fury, not calculated aggression." Gid turned so he could face his friend. "Teancum! You taught us to harness our intellect as well as our physical abilities, and not to react out of blind aggression." Gid stepped in closer so he could lower his voice and still speak with conviction. "Going off on a killing spree without support or a plan is reckless. And the boys will know it." He nodded towards the bulk of the ghost soldiers who were working in the camp. "You are not that person anymore. You are the leader of the ghost soldiers now, not a lone hunter." Teancum looked over his shoulder and sighed. He knew Gid was right but the anger inside of him would not let go. Gid saw this and continued. "You showed us, and the world, once again what a well-disciplined and well-trained group of warriors can accomplish. You snuck into the enemy camp and killed the king, then you routed the entire Lamanite army with a few hundred men." Gid put his hand on Teancum's shoulder. "Sir, you have done enough for one day."

Teancum knew Gid was right. He had pushed his luck with the daring, one-man raid on the Lamanite camp. He was starving and had not slept in two days. Chasing after them now, alone, would be foolish at best. He had stretched his men to the breaking point on this campaign and moved far past his own supply lines. He needed to think strategically now. "You are right. We will pull back and join with Moroni." Teancum looked over the progress his men where making on gathering up the equipment and supplies left by the Lamanites. "Let's hurry this along before they realize we are not chasing after them and they counterattack." The Ghost Soldiers gathered as much of the swag as they could in the few available wagons. The rest was set ablaze and Teancum and his men moved quickly towards the safety of their own camp.

"Say that again…?" Moroni's voice was booming. Teancum had returned early the next morning and by noon Moroni had called a counsel of his captains. He heard what Teancum said but the very idea of what he had done was not quite registering with the general. The other Nephite military leaders who stood around Moroni were also whispering to each other and pointing. No one could believe what they were hearing.

"My general," Teancum spoke with joy in his tone. "Here is the gold crown and the leopard-skin cloak of the Lamanite king." Teancum still had the spoils of his adventure and he held them out for all to see. "I took them from the king's bed chamber immediately after I killed him in his sleep." Teancum turned so all the men in the command tent could see what he was holding. "My Ghost Soldiers have routed the entire Lamanite army, and they have retreated back toward the captured city of Mulek." The gasps of astonishment swept through the command tent. Moroni stood motionless with his mouth half open.

"You killed the king in his own tent… And your men routed the entire Lamanite invasion force… *And* you forced them back to Mulek?" Amiha tried to sound in control as he asked this rhetorical question. But his voice gave away his child-like wonder at the possibility of Teancum's words.

"Yes, Chief Captain Amiha. That is exactly what I am saying." There was a slight grin on Teancum's face. He was so proud of his men and what they had accomplished.

"Never in the history of our people have I heard of such bravery and devotion to one's duty." Moroni spoke like a proud father as he came around from behind the large map table and took Teancum by the shoulders. "Let the official record of this army reflect the great courage shown by Chief Captain Teancum and his Ghost Soldiers!" Moroni bellowed. "Remind me to always stay on your good side my friend." Moroni winked and whispered so only Teancum could hear. "Keep your treasures." Moroni gestured with his head towards the crown and leopard-skin cloak. "You have earned them."

Teancum nodded in a silent thank you. Tradition held that the commanding general would get first rights to any captured items of value. He knew Moroni had never and would never take as much as one thin silver coin from any of his men. It was all about the symbolism of Moroni relinquishing his authority over the precious items Teancum had earned, and allowing Teancum to retain the reward for his labors.

"I left a small scouting party behind to follow and report on the Lamanites' movements." Teancum advised Moroni but spoke loud enough for the other gathered leaders to hear. "My last report from them was last night. My scouts tell me the Lamanites are trying to fortify the city of Mulek. Looks like they mean to stay put for a while." Teancum finished and looked Moroni in the eyes. "We know where they are. The army can be there in under a week if we move quickly, sir."

Moroni smiled and nodded his head. "Agreed." Moroni moved away from Teancum and spoke to those gathered. "Send word to your spies to keep a careful watch on the city. Tell them to report any changes and to intercept any messengers coming or going from the city. They have just lost their king. We want to keep them scared, isolated and uninformed as much as possible." Moroni turned to the sergeant major and continued speaking while looking right at him. "Let's get this camp rolled up and ready to march."

"Yes sir." The old soldier responded emotionless. He had fought more battles than anyone in the tent. To the sergeant major, it was just another day.

CHAPTER TEN

"The rest of you will return to your units and make them ready to move out. I want reports on your progress by lunch... Questions?" There were none so Moroni dismissed them. "Except you, Captain Teancum. You and your two lieutenants need to stay for just a moment longer."

Teancum, Gid and Teomner all looked at each other with puzzled faces. Curious as to what Moroni would want from them they all turned and moved back to where Moroni was standing.

"Sir?" Teancum questioned.

Moroni waited until the tent was empty and then he removed a scrap of parchment from his vest. "I received a letter from the prophet Helaman this morning." He held out the parchment to show the three men the letter. They were all taken back by the fact that Moroni was getting letters from the prophet; not just anyone gets a personal handwritten letter from God's messenger. But they supposed that with the rank of commanding general comes certain privileges. "He speaks of forming a small army of two thousand young men from the people of Ammon."

"The people of Ammon? Sir, aren't they the ones who buried their weapons of war and took an oath to never spill blood again?" Teomner questioned. Gid and Teancum nodded their heads in agreement. Everyone knew the sad story of the sacrifice the Ammonite men made at the gates of their city after their conversion to Christ's teachings. And how they were ultimately saved by the Nephites, and made a covenant to never kill again.

"Yes. I am not sure what has transpired; the letter explained that it is the sons of the Ammonites who wish to fight." Moroni paused as he was lost in thought for a moment. "Helaman himself is among them now, so they are being guided by the hand of providence." Moroni continued as he put the letter back in his pocket and walked towards the large map hanging at the back of the tent. "The letter said they are doing this to help relieve the pressure Chief Captain Antipus is under. Antipus is doing his best to hold our flank along the frontier but he is in critical need of support." Moroni pointed to the opposite side of the Nephite country where a battle against other tribes of Lamanites was taking place. "Helaman has no formal military training but these boys have asked him to be their leader." Moroni turned back to face Teancum. "The prophet of God is asking for advisors to assist him in forming and training this army."

The King is Dead

Teancum instantly knew what Moroni was getting at. "You want some Ghost Soldiers to go to Helaman and advise him on the ways of war." It was not a question, but a statement of comprehension.

"Yes, Captain Teancum. We owe it to Helaman and Antipus. They have been holding the line and facing their threats alone, while we contend with the Lamanites here." Moroni looked past Teancum and at his two lieutenants. "I am asking you to send Helaman not just any Ghost Soldier, but your two best and brightest officers to train and equip this new army. I am asking them to fight alongside these brave boys and show Helaman how to manage and lead troops."

Gid and Teomner both looked at each other when Moroni spoke those words. They both knew that Moroni was speaking about them. Babysitting a holy man and a bunch of boys was not their idea of an adventure.

"Sir, may I—" Gid tried to protest but Teancum held up his hand to cut him off before he could finish.

"When do they need to leave?" Teancum responded.

" Today." Moroni answered after he took a breath of relief. He was asking a lot of Teancum and was not sure how he would respond to being told to let his two sub-commanders go. Not wanting to lose the momentum Moroni continued to speak. "Amiha will have the details for your travel ready for you by the noon meal. Thank you gentlemen for volunteering." Moroni grabbed his helmet and moved towards the tent opening. "You have my leave, gentlemen. Captain Teancum, take your time with your men. I will see you all at lunch." Moroni put on his helmet and quickly exited the tent leaving the three Ghost Soldiers alone to digest what had just happened.

"I am not a nursemaid!" Teomner protested. "Captain, why us?"

Gid joined the conversation. "You are planning the assault on Mulek, and you want us to go and teach some gentle farm boys how to march and stand at attention?"

Teancum grew hot with anger as he heard these words. "I did not ask you to do anything." He almost sounded insulted. "Your commanding general asked for my best officers, and I gave him what he wanted." Teancum turned to look at his lieutenants. " The siege of Mulek will happen with or without you two. Your duty now is to go and assist Helaman to raise up an army and prepare them for combat." Teancum got a fierce look in his eyes and his voice tightened. "You are Ghost

CHAPTER TEN

Soldiers. Regardless of what you are asked to do, you will do it better and faster and with more enthusiasm than any other soldier... Is that clear?" He was the unrelenting task master again and Gid and Teomner were his students.

"Yes sir!" They both snapped to attention like young cadets.

Teancum softened and continued. "Imagine what the two of you could accomplish with two thousand fresh and eager minds! What kind of unit you could create with your vast knowledge and skill?" He looked them in their eyes. "There are Nehor in those lands; bandits that have not been hunted like the ones we have dealt with here." He pointed to the map. "There are Lamanites in those lands, and our brothers are fighting them as we speak. They only have stories of the Ghost Soldiers and what we can do. Go and give them a dose of reality."

Both Gid and Teomner liked where this conversation was going. All they needed was a different perspective on the situation. Now that they understood Teancum's point of view, this mission sounded like a grand adventure indeed.

Moroni's officers met again at lunch time and reported on the preparations made to march the army towards Mulek. Gid and Teomner gathered and packed their belongs all morning. After saying goodbye to their friends and fellow Ghost Soldiers, they met with Teancum, Moroni and the rest of the core group of leaders to say their farewells. These two men would be sorely missed in the battles and adventures to come, but they had an important duty to fulfill. Not knowing what the future had in store for them, the two Ghost Soldiers made their way out of camp with their pack animals in tow and towards the unknown.

Teancum was sad to see his comrades leave, but he knew there was still much to do. By evening, General Moroni had the army on the move. The Ghost Soldiers were leading the way, scouting and covering the flanks while the main body of the infantry and cavalry moved down the middle of the wide merchant road leading to the city of Mulek.

After Teancum and Moroni freed the city of Mulek, they continued, for many months, to engage the Lamanite in open war. Some of the battles were fought in pitched engagements with both sides amassing and rushing at each other, hacking and slaying, killing untold numbers of men on both sides of the conflict. Other battles were won without a drop of blood spilt. Moroni gained courage from Teancum's example of

The King is Dead

unconventional warfare and used strategy and trickery to gain the upper hand on the Lamanites. Because of the great evil in the hearts of the leaders of the Lamanites and their traditions of hatred of the Nephites, the Lamanites continued fighting, and the war was prolonged.

There was great loss and sadness in the land. The men under Moroni's command suffered greatly. The lack of food, medical supplies and support from the Nephite government caused sorrow on an epic scale. In this time of need, Moroni reminded the people to turn their hearts towards their God. Because of Moroni, the people remembered who they were and what they were fighting for. With renewed faith in the God of their fathers, the armies of the Nephites began to overpower the Lamanites and drive them from captured city to captured city, freeing the inhabitants from bondage along the way. Moroni would receive reports from Helaman on the battles fought by his brave stripling warriors' and he was astounded at their courage and abilities. But it was Teancum and his brave Ghost Soldiers who were bearing the brunt of the fight. They were always out front, leading the charge or attacking from the sides or even from behind the enemy. They were the ones who breached the defenses of cities and forced the Lamanites from their armored forts and strongholds.

After many more months of battle, Moroni and his men had the entire Lamanite army, or what was left of it, on the run. The Lamanites knew they were beaten and had resorted to fighting a tactical retreat as they tried to salvage what remained of their once mighty army and moved back to the Lamanites lands with whatever plunder they could gather along the way. The Lamanites would loot and pillage towns and village as they retreated, killing the local population at will. They set fire to buildings, destroyed the livestock and burned entire fields of crops in an attempt to punish the Nephites and slow their advance. It was the innocent civilians who suffered most from the Lamanite aggression and anger. As the Nephites advanced, the Lamanites pulled their forces out of the towns and cities, leaving behind a wake of indescribable destruction. Teancum and his men were always at the tip of the advance and they were first to witness the carnage and destruction left by the Lamanites. Moroni received word from Lehi and his men that they were suffering the same in their campaign. Lehi was also driving the Lamanites before him, and they too were scorching the earth as they fled back towards the Lamanite lands.

CHAPTER TEN

Moroni was examining a map on one particular day when he realized he had a tremendous opportunity before him. "Lehi is here and pushing the enemy in this direction, yes?"

"Yes sir." Amiha responded. Amiha was dirty and covered with muck and blood. He and Moroni had been on the front line for three days and in almost constant contact with the Lamanites.

"You and Teancum have pushed our foes into this mountain pass… Here?"

"Yes sir." Amiha again responded. Moroni could tell he was almost drunk with exhaustion.

"Look here…" Moroni pointed toward a spot on the map for Amiha to see. He silently prayed that his friend would feel what he was feeling "If we can get Lehi to wheel his advance to the right and move the enemy's line of retreat in this direction, then the two Lamanite forces will merge here." He pointed to a second spot on the map and continued to speak. "We can catch them in the middle of our armies and pinch them between us." Moroni nodded his head and focused his tired eyes on the map. "We can attack them from two different angles and finish this madness, once and for all."

"A double envelopment…yes sir." Amiha was on autopilot now. He was beyond tired, past the point of feeling, and totally missing the fact that Moroni had come up with a possible end to the war. "My report from the front is the same as it has been for the last few weeks." He took a sad, deep breath and continued his report. "We found a small farming community which had been raided and burned by the retreating Lamanites. They killed every man over the age of 15 and took the women. The children they all tied together and put them in the river, hoping to drown them all at once. But some of the older boys and girls were able to save the younger ones and get them out of the water." He stopped talking and rubbed his head out of frustration. "Now we have 78 more orphans who must be cared for." Amiha stopped talking, his mind had locked up and he could not even process the thought of caring for more wounded civilians and orphaned children. They had been on the move and in constant contact with the enemy and couldn't feed or care for their own men. He stood in painful silence hoping he could wake up from this prolonged nightmare.

Moroni was equally exhausted, both physically and emotionally He too fought to comprehend the level of hate the Lamanite felt for their brethren the Nephites. After a moment Moroni asked. "Did you see the enemy?"

Amiha came back to the moment and continued his report. "Yes sir." He cleared his throat. "We got to the village and the river ferry launched as the last of the Lamanites were crossing the river… Right here." He pointed to a location on the map in Moroni's hands. "We barraged them with arrows and killed several. They damaged the ferry, but Teancum and his men have forded the river and are still in pursuit."

"I can't get that man to stop to even eat supper." Moroni whispered under his breath. "Well done." Moroni spoke out loud. "We will use the river as a natural defensive barrier. Call a halt to the chase and pitch our tents on this side." Moroni commanded. "Send out scouts and a foraging party. See if there are any fish left in the river to feed the men."

"Yes sir." Amiha slowly moved back towards his horse. He was in a dazed from exhaustion, but trudged along without complaint like a good soldier.

"Forward men!" Moroni shouted as he rolled up the map in his hands and gestured for the soldiers around him to keep moving. "We will stop at the river!" Moroni put the map back in its metal tube and called for the sergeant major.

"You called, my general?" The trusted soldier responded.

"Sergeant major, I need a messenger— the fastest one we have. Captain Lehi is over those hills." Moroni pointed towards a set of hills in the distance. "I must get a message to him right away."

"Yes sir." It was just another day in the field for the old soldier.

A dispatch was sent to Lehi to adjust his method of attack and to drive the retreating Lamanites towards Moroni's location. Lehi quickly consulted his own maps and could see the genius behind Moroni's new orders. "I see your thoughts Moroni…" He whispered as he examined his maps. Lehi was having the same experiences with the retreating Lamanites that Moroni and his men were having. He and his army were also reaching the breaking point both mentally and physically. Lehi knew if this war did not end soon, all would be lost.

CHAPTER ELEVEN

The Last Great War Council

It was very late in the afternoon when Moroni was finally able to conduct his grand war council. "Gentlemen!" He bellowed over the noise of the other officers and soldiers under the large tarp. The men around him were exhausted, dirty and battered from war. Some were talking softly, or chewing scarce portions of food. Others were looking over reports and making small talk and a few were even asleep with their head on the table or leaning back in their chairs. Prompted by instinct, the men in attendance all stopped what they were doing, stood up and turned to face the general. "Thank you gentlemen for answering my call to attend this war council. Please be seated." Slowly the men before Moroni sat down. Some of them were still blinking rapidly, shaking and trying to clear their heads from the mental cobwebs. Moroni continued as he gestured behind him for someone to come forward. "I would like to take this opportunity to welcome Pahoran, the Grand Chief Judge of the Nephite government, to this council of war." Moroni gestured to Pahoran to sit at the far end of a table opposite of where Moroni was standing. Out of respect, the men again all stood up as Pahoran walked into view. Several of the soldiers banged theie mugs or knocked their fists on the table in a spirited token of their acknowledgement of the Grand Chief Judge's presence. Everyone knew of the usurping king-men and how they tried to overthrow the elected government and how Moroni personally rode to Pahoran's rescue and put down the rebellion. Pahoran acknowledged the reception he was given and motioned for those around him to be seated. Pahoran wanted to personally support the army and witness the end of the

CHAPTER ELEVEN

war himself.

"Men," Moroni raised up both of his hands to quiet his council. The room's attention was back on the general. " This has been a long and hard-fought campaign. Now that peace and justice have been restored to the capital we can expect much more support from our elected officials in the way of provisions and fresh troops." He nodded to Pahoran who in turn bowed his head acknowledging Moroni's words.

Pahoran, and the rest of the elected government, understood perfectly that Moroni would never allow this army, or the people he had sworn to defend and protect, to again suffer as they had at the hands of the wicked and traitorous king-men, the Lamanites or a corrupt government. "We have marched for more weeks than I can easily count with little sleep or food, fighting and driving the Lamanites from city to city. And now we are joined by my most trusted chief captains, Lehi and Teancum." Moroni waved his hand across the table and towards his old friends. Lehi was sitting on one side of Pahoran and slouching a bit in his chair. He was dressed in his full armor with his mighty axe resting on the table. His lieutenants and staff sergeants were all around him.

Like the rest of the Nephite soldiers in the counsel, Lehi was exhausted; mentally, physically and emotionally. The dark circles under his eyes, his gaunt face and the damage to his armor told the unspoken tale that Lehi had been in the thick of battle for too long and he was reaching his breaking point. Even a gallant warrior like Chief Captain Lehi could only take so much. This war had cost him dearly. Responding to Moroni, Lehi made a fist with his left hand and raised it up bending his elbow and shaking it back and forth to show everyone he was still in this fight. He may have been tired and hungry, but Lehi was not going to quit. Everyone was certain that victory or death were the only things that could possibly stop Captain Lehi. Very soon, one of those outcomes would manifest itself.

In stark contrast, Teancum, who was seated a few chairs down from Lehi, was awake and fully alert. The only thing Teancum had in common with the other soldiers in the war council was he was also dirty and unkempt. But his body language and emotions told a completely different story from the others. It looked like Teancum was almost excited about the prospect of facing the enemy in another fight. His head was up and his eyes were full of intensity and light. He was alert, engaged and ready to move forward with the war council. Teancum was wearing a loose-fitting tunic revealing his chiseled chest and arm muscles. Even after all he had endured, Teancum still looked like he could get up and run ten miles without breaking a sweat.

After Moroni recognized his two most experienced chief captains, the gathered men clapped, knocked on the table, pounded their fists and raised their drinking mugs to celebrate the joining of forces, once again.

"Men." Moroni raised up one hand again to quiet the crowd. "With the blessings of providence we have finally turned the tide of this war. Together, we have fought and defeated the enemies of freedom, justice and liberty. We have engaged these godless invaders from all points of the compass." Moroni waved his arm in a wide arc across the table gesturing to include all sitting before him in his comment. "And we, as brothers, have routed the Lamanites and relentlessly chased them like wounded rabbits running for the protection of their hole, across the land to this city." Moroni grabbed a large map of the city, unrolled it and spun it around on the table for all to see. He pointed to the image on the map representing the city. "Brothers, we have trapped the balance of what remains of the Lamanite army inside the walls of the city. They are now holed up behind the high stone walls."

Moroni stood up straight and looked over the gathered leaders of the Nephite army. "Gentlemen, given the narrative of our situation, I am asking for your counsel and advice on the next step. What are our assets and liabilities?" There was a few seconds of silence as those in the meeting tried to think how to answer Moroni's question.

A good leader will always look for opportunities to teach and train those he wishes to serve. Moroni was the ultimate leader and even during his own war councils he pushed his officers to learn and grow. Some of those men with him had been in constant contact with the Lamanite army for weeks. They had been fighting and moving and had not slept more than a few hours over several days. Moroni looked at Teancum and gave him a wink. Teancum was the only one in the meeting who was still alert enough to clearly, and without hesitation, answer Moroni's question. Moroni knew Teancum was aware and fully ready to give his opinion on the situation. But Moroni wanted his other sub-commanders to experience the challenge of battle planning when they were near complete exhaustion. Mental fatigue can cause mistakes and misjudgments as severe as physical fatigue can. He knew that when it came to training soldiers, there was no greater teacher then adversity.

CHAPTER ELEVEN

Teancum instantly understood Moroni's wishes and he remained quiet while the remaining command and staff mulled over the question.

"Sir, as you said we have the balance of the entire Lamanite army surrounded and trapped in one location." An officer standing in the back was the first to speak. " That is a geat advantage." Moroni nodded in agreement.

"General?" A young officer raised up his hand and stepped forward to address the gathered. " They did not have time to lay up stores or gather the flocks from the fields. So the only food and clean water they have is what was already inside when they took the city."

"Correct, another assist." Moroni acknowledged the second officer.

Captain Lehi raised up his war ax to announce his intention to speak. "Chief Captain Lehi, you have something to contribute to this council?" Moroni acknowledged his old friend.

"My general," Lehi spoke as he slowly rose from his seat, using his intimidating weapon as a crutch. He was so exhausted that the act of standing was almost impossible. His armor, clothing, and unkempt appearance bore the testimony of the weeks of constant moving and fighting. He was dirty, rusted, broken, blood-stained and torn. But there was a majesty and simple dignity to his presence as Lehi stood tall and solid as he addressed his general and those gathered. "Sir," Lehi tried to speak louder but just breathing was laborious. He coughed and cleared his throat; dust and dehydration had taken its toll. "My forces are disorganized and exhausted from pursuing and fighting the Lamanite army. Reports are still coming in but as of this moment, there are scores of wounded men behind us spread out for miles along the trail. Not just from my units but from all elements of this grand army. I have instructed the medics to take wagons and retrace the path we followed while chasing the enemy and gather up those left behind." He paused and slowly took two breaths. "Because of the lack of fresh water and unsanitary conditions, a fever is starting to affect many of those under my command. I alone cannot account for ten of my senior officers and scores of my mighty men." There was a pause as Lehi suddenly stopped speaking and it looked like he was lost in thought. His eyes went down, his shoulders slouched and his head was slightly bowed. His posture and body language was suddenly so contrary to the great Chief Captain Lehi everyone was accustomed to. He looked almost timid and frail. "I do not say this lightly, my general." He continued with sadness in his tone. There

The Last Great War Council

was a heavy cloud of despair and anguish hovering over him now.

If Captain Lehi, the mighty people's champion, was suffering, then how could the rest of them possibly manage to continue the fight without rest? Lehi continued as his body was frozen in place. The only thing moving in the room were his quivering lips and his chest as he struggled to get air into his lungs and say the next sentence. "It is my sad responsibility to report that at this moment… My army is combat ineffective." The blood ran cold in everyone's veins as Lehi said those words. "If my men are too exhausted to continue, then my assumption is that the rest of the Nephite forces are beyond the abilities to continue the assault on a fortified city." Some mouths gaped open while others quickly scanned the room with their eyes looking for someone or something to help make sense of what they just heard.

Did they really just hear Captain Lehi say he and his mighty men were unable to continue the fight? Did they just hear him say to General Moroni that the entire army is broken and unable to fight? The only two people not affected in some way by what Lehi had just said were Teancum and Moroni. Teancum was sitting up straight in his chair, looking forward and stone faced, with his arms resting on the table top and his fingers interlaced. Moroni was still standing at the head of the table and looking at Lehi, waiting for the next few words to come out of his mouth.

I knew it was bad, I knew the army was in bad shape, but I had no idea, Moroni thought to himself. *Hold fast and do not give your emotions away in front of the men.* He whispered in his mind, giving himself encouragement and instructions.

Lehi waited a few more seconds before he raised up his head and made eye contact with Moroni. He could only look at his general for a few moments and then he had to look away. The shame of admitting he and his men were unable to continue fighting was almost too much for him to bear. "My general," Lehi knew he could not take back what he had just said so he spoke from his heart now, "we must stop and reorganize. We need to gather what forces still remain and care for the wounded. Give me a week… Four days if I must, to rest and refit my men. Then we will take the city and finish this once and for all." Not knowing what else to do or say, Lehi fell back in his chair, a broken man.

Lehi was on the verge of a complete collapse and Moroni could not afford to lose his best field commander at this critical moment. He had

CHAPTER ELEVEN

to say something and say it fast before Lehi's own defeated opinion of himself affected the remaining command. Looking around at his commanders he saw the same utter exhaustion in their eyes; except for Teancum, who still remained alert and stone faced.

Teancum turned his head to look at Moroni. Their eyes locked and Moroni could see the fire in Teancum's eyes and his jaw locked tight. The veins in his forehead were bulging and the muscles in his neck were flexed. Moroni could almost read Teancum's thoughts. In just a glancing moment, Moroni knew Teancum was furious. He knew Teancum felt that stopping the attack now would be a deadly mistake. He knew that Teancum wanted to continue the strategy meeting and find a way to take the city back. Moroni nodded to Teancum who nodded back. Without any show of emotion, Teancum then turned his head back and faced forward. Moroni knew that was not the end of it with Teancum, but he must move on.

"Chief Captain Lehi!" Moroni bellowed out. Everyone turned to look at Moroni, not knowing what he would say next. "Lehi, you are one of the greatest heroes this army and the Nephite people have ever seen. Your abilities as a fighting man and military leader are not now, nor have they ever been in question by myself or anyone under my command. And now with your bold and honest admonitions of the conditions of your men, you have shown all of us the true depth of your honor and character." Moroni paused to give Lehi a chance to mentally digest his words. Slowly, Lehi raised his head back up and looked Moroni in the eyes. "If you say the army is ineffective in its present state, then so be it. No one is more capable to judge that fact then you." A silent tear of emotional release broke free from Lehi's eyes and traced along his dominant cheek bones, leaving a single track in the dirt and soot.

As a man of honor, Lehi spoke the truth knowing it could cost him dearly. Now, even more than before, he knew his general was a true warrior and leader. Lehi gave a slight nod in response to Moroni's compliment. "Gentlemen!" Moroni shouted as he looked around the table. "Is this the general consensus of my war council?" Moroni paused as he scanned the gathered faces. "Is there someone with a differing opinion on how to conduct the next phase of the war?" No one moved except Teancum. Teancum looked around the room and then lowered his head. He had the look of someone who felt like he had just been betrayed. "No…?" Moroni barked. "Then my command is this. No more

The Last Great War Council

strategy and planning, this army will stand down until further notice. See to your men, but do not let them slack in discipline and their duties, I still want sentries posted and patrols conducted. Deploy your hunting and scavenging parties. Amiha...?" Moroni turned to find his aid de camp. "You and Captain Teancum will establish the camp in the standard defensive posture. I want pickets up and a watch set on the city. We don't need any Lamanite surprises. See to it."

"Yes sir." Amiha responded. Teancum just nodded and remained stoic. His response did not go unnoticed by Moroni.

"Gentlemen we will reconvene this council tomorrow at sundown. I want a full report of the condition of your respective units. No fluff or sugar coating, give it to me straight. Questions?" He looked around the room for a response but there was none. Everyone just wanted to go and find a place to lie down but there was still so much work to do. "Very well... Thank you gentlemen, you are all dismissed." The leaders of the Nephite army quickly excused themselves and returned to their respective units to try to salvage what remained of their individual commands.

Everyone moved except Teancum. He remained, sitting still as the bustle of men trying to leave died down around him. Amiha took several steps before realizing Teancum was not with him. He turned and walked back under the tarp and stood inside the covering. Moroni saw that Teancum had stayed behind and he assumed the remainder of the conversation that started with the look Teancum gave him earlier was going to take place. As Moroni was gathering up his maps and notes, the sergeant major walked up next to him with a tray of food and a large cup of water.

"Sir...?" The old warrior spoke as he set the plate down in front of Moroni. Moroni took one look at the food and then nodded towards Teancum.

"Give it to Captain Teancum." Moroni said in a short tone.

The sergeant major and Teancum made eye contact and he walked around the table and placed the tray of bread, boiled squash and a meager slice of meat down in front of the Ghost Soldier.

"Thank you, sergeant major." These were the first words Teancum had spoken since he sat down for the meeting.

Teancum reached out and picked up the small hunk of cooked meat and popped the entire portion in his mouth. Chewing slowly, he closed his eyes and took in a large breath through his nose and let the air out in one long blast. Teancum was starving. At this point the boiled sole of a worn out boot would have been okay with him. But a piece of red meat seasoned with a pinch of salt and cooked over a flame provided a moment of heaven for the hungry man.

"Was there something you wish to add to this evening's discussion, Captain Teancum?"

"Moroni…" Teancum swallowed hard and spoke respectfully. "Sir, I would never disagree with you in public once you have made your mind up, but…" Teancum tapped his finger on the top of the table. "We must attack and do it now. Attack the city now while they are disorganized and unable to mount a proper defense. Yes, we will lose more men, but we could save countless more lives by striking hard and ending this war, tonight!" Teancum adjusted in his seat and continued. "My general, they are just as tired and weak as we are, if not more so. Those stone walls they hide behind are a great advantage to them now. Can you imagine how much more of a help those walls will be when they have a reactive guard force in place and are prepared to repel us?" Teancum was getting excited now. "If we just—"

Moroni held up his hand to ask for silence, and then walked around the table and put his hand on Teancum's shoulder as he sat down next to his captain. "My friend, your loyalty to this army and your devotion to the cause of freedom has never been in question. You have suffered more loss at the hands of the enemy than anyone else I know. But understand, this army is exhausted." Moroni looked for understanding in Teancum's eyes. "Lehi is right. We need to wait and press our advantage when we have reorganized and equipped our soldiers for a siege."

"But, sir!?"

"I'm sorry old friend," Moroni spoke with a trace of sympathy in his tone. "I must think of the welfare of the entire army as well as the republic. If we press the fight now and try to take the city without the proper siege equipment or without resupply, we could break what remains of this army on those high walls. We have Ammoron trapped inside those walls. He and all that remains of his godless army are not going anywhere, and no one is coming to their rescue."

Teancum turned to face the sergeant major who was standing behind Moroni. "You have seen more war then all of us… What is your opinion on the matter?"

The old soldier turned and looked at his supreme commander. Moroni nodded back giving the sergeant major permission to speak freely and state his position. "Sir, I must agree with Chief Captain Teancum. In a fight, you never give your adversary a chance to breathe or adjust to your tactics. We need to get over those walls and we need to do it now, before they have a chance to regroup."

Teancum and the wise old soldier made eye contact and Teancum continued where the sergeant major left off. "Sir… Moroni, there are Nephites trapped behind those walls."

This was the part of military leadership Moroni hated more than anything else. No matter what choice he made, men would die. There was no clean way to end the war. He also knew both sides of the argument had valid points. Captain Lehi was right, the army had been pushed to the very breaking point. No one had been spared from the exhaustion of constant pursuit and combat with the Lamanites over the past few weeks. They were overwhelmed with casualties and if they didn't stop and reorganize, many more will die. Teancum and the sergeant major were also right. A good general should never give the enemy a chance to regroup and establish a strong defense. The longer they wait, the harder it will be to root them out from behind those stone walls and many more will die.

"I pray every day that the Lord God will bless and protect us in this endeavor." Moroni loudly whispered. "Captain Teancum, I thank you for your advice and counsel, but my orders remain. We will stand down and prepare for a siege."

Teancum stood up and curtly spoke. "Yes sir, will that be all?"

Moroni looked up from his sitting position at Teancum and blinked several times. He knew Teancum was displeased but Moroni had an entire army to look after and the freedom of an entire nation to answer for. "Yes captain, that will be all."

Teancum quickly gave a hand salute and not waiting for Moroni to salute back, stormed off into the night. Moroni made eye contact with Amiha and spoke, "Go with him." Amiha turned and followed after Teancum.

The sergeant major stood in his stoic manner as Moroni was alone with his thoughts. A full minute passed before the old soldier spoke. "Sir, I'm sure they have your tent up and waiting for you. Shall we go?"

Moroni snorted and let out a frustrated half laugh. "Good idea sergeant major, let's put the general to bed before he can cause any

CHAPTER ELEVEN

more damage." Moroni grabbed the hunk of bread left on the plate by Teancum and held it up. "Did you eat?" He asked his old mentor and friend.

"I will sir, as soon as I know you are squared away."

Moroni nodded his head and took a large bite of the bread. It was a bit dry but the thick grain taste was a welcomed relief. His mouth still half-full, Moroni popped the remaining bit of bread into his mouth and smiled as he chewed. Grabbing the large cup of cool water, Moroni washed it all down in one giant gulp. "Okay old friend," Moroni spoke while swallowing the remains of his snack as he slowly stood up. "Let's get this fool of a general to bed."

"Put that swag down and get some men to the tops of the walls!" King Ammoron shouted to a group of Lamanites standing near the main gate. He was furious. The looting of the homes and buildings and robbing of its citizens inside the city was taking precedence over the preparations needed to defend against the Nephite attack which was sure to come. Turning to an older Lamanite standing next to him, Ammoron angrily continued shouting orders. " Tell your men to stop killing the Nephites; we might need hostages. And tell them to gather what food and water they can and bring it to the town center." Ammoron was burning with anger. "The mighty Lamanites were too tired or scared to put up a proper defense against the Nephite army, but now..." He dramatically waved his arms in the air. "Now that they are locked inside the city with helpless civilians, they are full of vigor?"

The Lamanites had swept away what remained of the local guard force and now had free run of the entire city. Small pockets of resistance remained where strong Nephite men were defending their families to the death, but there was no longer any hope of an organized counterattack from within the walls. The Lamanites were stealing, burning and murdering at will. Ammoron did not have a problem with this. His problem was the entire Nephite army outside the gates, and they were going to want their city back.

Ammoron turned as a Nephite woman screamed and clutched her chest as she was running across the street. She fell face-first into the mud with a Lamanite arrow sticking out of her back. From the opposite side of the street two Lamanite archers appeared from the darkness and

The Last Great War Council

were laughing at their handiwork. "Fools!" Ammoron shouted at the two archers. "We need live prisoners! Stop killing the women and children!" Ammoron turned to what remained of his command staff that were following him through the city. Everywhere, he saw Lamanites running around carrying stolen property or setting fires and causing more damage. "This is outrageous!" He shouted. "Get control of your soldiers, or I will have you all flogged!"

One of the sub-commanders turned to Ammaron. "But my king, the men… They have nothing to show for the war. All of their personal possessions and spoils of war were abandoned when their camps were overrun and we fled from the Nephites. They cannot claim victory and go home empty-handed. It would be a great dishonor."

"No one is going anywhere if Moroni attacks and we are not prepared to defend ourselves!" Ammoron barked in response. He spied a lone Lamanite running past him with a jug of fresh wine. Ammoron grabbed the soldier by the arm and ripped the jug from his grasp. Ammoron brutally kicked him and pulled the cork from the jug. Taking a very long drink he half choked. "Why don't you dogs understand?" There was genuine fear in his voice; he could feel the control of the army slipping away as the chaos of soldiers plundering, burning and killing swirled around them. "There will be no negotiation for surrender. He will execute every last one of you for allowing this to happen, and then enslave your children to his false god if we are not ready to fight."

Ammoron then saw a young Lamanite soldier trying to run past him while clutching a brass goblet and candle sticks. Ammoron, still holding the jug of liquor, body-checked the smaller soldier and knocked him to the ground. He then walked over to the soldier and took the candlesticks out of his hands. The young soldier was not sure what to do and looked at Ammoron with a mixture of surprise and contempt. Ammoron was so disgusted that he yelled at and kicked the lad until he was back on his feet and running away. Holding the candle sticks out in front of him he continued. "The treasures of this city are not going anywhere!" He shook the stolen item in their faces and then forcibly threw the candlestick on the ground. "Get your men under control and prepare this army for a siege. Then, when we are ready for Moroni, we will confiscate all the riches and every man in this army will get an equal share." He took a second long drink of wine and started to push those sub-commanders away from him. "Go!" He waved them away with his free hand. The

CHAPTER ELEVEN

Lamanite leaders all split off and started to give orders, trying to gain some control over the lawlessness.

Standing beside two of his brother Zoramites, Ammoron pulled them close to his body. The wine was already affecting his breath and thought process. "This is a lost cause." He spoke in a loud whisper. "These fools are doomed. We are trapped like rats and surrounded. It is only a matter of time before Moroni comes through the main gate and kills every last one of us." He looked his companions in the eyes. "Rally what brother Zoramites are left. Tell them to gather whatever treasure and slaves they can and meet me in the throne room at dawn… We are leaving."

Teancum was visibly upset. He knew the enemy was so close to a total defeat; they only needed one more strong push to fall off the edge and this war would be over. Teancum walked back towards his own camp and men with his head down. He was so full of rage and frustration that he was walking with his hands clenched and grinding his teeth. He felt useless and defeated; a feeling he hated. As he was walking through the woods towards his camp he heard the distant and muffled sounds of a woman screaming. *It came from the direction of the city!* Teancum turned to face in the direction of the scream and could see the silhouettes of the walls of the city and the fires burning behind them through the trees. Not knowing exactly where the scream came from he pulled out his sword and moved towards the edge of the tree line. There was a second scream but it was from a different voice and a different location inside the city. Teancum reached the edge of the trees and was preparing to go out into the wide open ground between the walls and the trees.

"Teancum!" Amiha shouted from behind. He was trying to keep up with Teancum and was several paces behind him. He too had heard the screams and was coming to investigate. Teancum stopped and turned to face Amiha.

"Teancum, it might be a trap! They could have archers on the walls waiting for you to come out into the open."

Teancum blinked several times. He was mad at himself. He was the tactical-minded man who always thought of things like that. How could he be so careless?

"You're right." Teancum admitted. He stepped backwards farther into the trees and relaxed his posture. More and more screams were now coming from inside the city walls. Both men and women were crying out in pain, and begging anyone who would listen for help.

"What do you think is happening inside there?" Amiha asked as he put his own sword back in its sheath.

"You know exactly what is happening." Teancum was mad and it showed on his face and his tone. Even in the darkness of the forest Amiha could see his expression. "Nephites are being murdered and ravaged." Teancum shook his head and continued. "We are the shield for God's people, we are their sworn protectors… And here we sit and do nothing!"

"What would you have Moroni do?" Amiha asked. "We cannot attack. We have no siege equipment and the army is in a sorry state. We would lose too many lives in a fruitless attempt to—"

Teancum cut him off. "All of this talk from Moroni and the rest of you about trusting in God and doing the right thing." Teancum was vocally upset. "My family trusted in God and look what happened! The old woman who helped me kill Amalickiah, she trusted in God. That boy who died in my arms bringing us news of Ammoron's location inside that city," Teancum pointed towards the stone walls in the distance. "He trusted in God!" He was almost in tears now. "Those screams coming from inside the city. Those helpless people are calling out right now to God and to this army to save them!" He lowered his voice and continued. "Right now, I don't see either doing anything to save those people who trusted them."

Amiha was beside himself. He had never heard Teancum speak this way. He knew Teancum was a man of faith and honor but the person speaking now was someone else. Someone he should be careful with. "Teancum, I agree with you. You know I do." Amiha put his hand on Teancum's shoulder. He was trying to calm him down and help him understand. "But you also know, we can't make a move without Moroni's approval. We are chief captains, honor and duty will not allow us to wage our own private war when we don't agree with the boss and his orders."

"But we also cannot sit by and watch as more innocent Nephites are slaughtered!" Teancum was shouting now.

"What would you have me do?" Amiha questioned in a soft tone. Upsetting the single most dangerous fighter in the entire Nephite army was not Amiha's desire.

Teancum looked like he had just been slapped. Like the wind going

CHAPTER ELEVEN

out of a ship's sail and stopping the momentum of a great vessel, the spirit in Teancum's voice and the fire in his eyes went out. "If I am the only one in this entire camp who understands true honor and duty, then so be it." Teancum looked back at the city in the distance and sighed. "Do you know what this war has taught me?" he questioned Amiha. Amiha shook his head saying no and looked at Teancum with deep sympathy in his eyes. "It has taught me what I can really trust in this world." Teancum pulled out his long dagger and held it out for Amiha to see. " This is what I trust, sharp steel in my hands!" He lowered his weapon and drew close to Amiha. Amiha gulped hard and braced for action. The intensity was building again in Teancum's eyes. As he continued to talk his jaw was clenched tight. "I am going over that wall, tonight. I will find the king and I am going to plunge this dagger into the heart of Ammoron and end this madness once and for all!" Teancum held the dagger out for several seconds. "Are you with me?" He asked Amiha.

"You know I can't go against Moroni's orders." As he spoke every nerve in Amiha's body was tingling with the idea of joining Teancum on a two man assault. But he knew cooler heads must prevail right now.

Dropping the weapon down to his side Teancum lowered his head and stood completely still for a moment. "You asked what I would have you do." Teancum spoke with his head lowered and in monotone to Amiha's response.

"Yes, I did." There was hope in Amiha's voice that he had convinced Teancum to wait for Moroni's instructions.

"You can be a silent witness to my actions here tonight, Amiha. You can testify that in their most desperate hour, not everyone broke faith with the Nephite people trapped with the Lamanites." Teancum looked up at Amiha. "You can tell the world that one man stood against many and refused to rest until the world was rid of the monsters hiding behind those walls."

"I'm not going to try to stop you, Teancum." Amiha spoke at just above a whisper. "I know you are angry, but be reasonable and consider the situation. You have not slept more then two hours or had a hot meal in two days. Are you thinking clearly?" Amiha was very concerned for his friend's well-being. "We need you here with us, leading the Ghost Soldiers and inspiring the army." He paused as he looked Teancum in the eyes and saw his intensity and resolve. He knew he was not going to convince Teancum to stay. He also knew he was not going to try to stop him either. "What would you have me say if Moroni asked where you are? I'm not going to lie to the General."

Teancum smiled and walked past Amiha towards his Ghost Soldier encampment. "Tell him whatever you want."

"Where are you going?" Amiha asked. He almost wished he had not, but it was too late. A fresh set of screams came from the walls of the city.

Teancum stopped and without turning around to address his comrade he answered Amiha. "I am going to do what I do best… I am going to kill an evil man."

Teancum moved quickly through the trees and was back at the ghost soldier encampment. Inside his tent, he rummaged through his storage trunks and large backpack for the items he would need on this next mission. He counted off to himself as he found an item and laid it on the bed. "Small pack, rope and climbing hook, blowgun darts and poison, grease paint, camouflage cover, climbing gear, dagger, and garrote." He kept looking around his small tent for additional items but he knew this was a race against time. Amiha could not keep this from Moroni and the sun would be up in a few hours. Packing quickly, Teancum loaded the items into the small pack or strapped them to his weapons belt.

Taking a step back Teancum took a quick assessment of his physical condition. He was exhausted, and he needed food and water in the worst way. Teancum could do nothing about the fatigue, but the issue with water and food was quickly remedied. He drank the remaining contents from a half-empty waterskin and then took a handful of his favorite snack, the dried fruit and nuts mixture he discovered on the cliff those many years ago when he first met the Nehor. Ever since he found that pouch full of the snack mixture, among the belongings of the bandits who killed his family, he always made sure he had plenty of it with him whereever he went. Chewing with his mouth open Teancum grabbed another full waterskin and draped it over his shoulder. He swallowed hard and filled his mouth up with a second helping. *That should keep me going for quite a while*, Teancum thought to himself as he carefully made his way out of his tent and back into the woods.

Amiha was walking along the edge of the tree line back towards the main camp when he was stopped and challenged by a Nephite sentry.

"Who goes there?" The voice called out from behind a large tree.

CHAPTER ELEVEN

Amiha could see him peeking out from around the trunk, his spear at the ready.

"It is Chief Captain Amiha. I am walking the perimeter and checking on our forces." Amiha said with his hands out to show he was not carrying a weapon.

"Rock." The sentry called out the challenge. It was the duty of the sentry to guard that section of the wood line. If the person who the sentry was trying to identify did not know the password, or said the wrong one, then the sentry would hold them at spear point and call for the sergeant of the guard. The challenge and password changed daily to confuse the enemy and keep them from getting past the first line of defense.

"Wagon wheel." Amiha responded. It was the correct password for the day and the sentry relaxed. Then he responded, "Sir, no one told me there was going to be a meeting of the chief captains at my location."

"What do you mean, soldier?" Amiha asked.

"General Moroni and the sergeant major arrived just moments ago. They are over there." He pointed to a large fallen tree just inside the tree line. Amiha saw two dark figures standing next to the tree, their outlines revealed by the flickering torchlights coming from the walls of the city. Amiha was surprised to see them here at this hour. The last he knew, Moroni was headed back to his command tent to try to get some sleep. Amiha walked over to the two men and stood next to Moroni.

"Sir?"

Moroni did not move, he stood staring at the city now controlled by the Lamanites. He had a large blanket covering his shoulders and draping down his back. It was not that cold out. It looked as if Moroni needed the comfort as he stood still.

"We watched as they pushed two people from the walls, I think they were both women." The old soldier spoke matter-of-fact. "When the screaming started the general wanted to see for himself what was happening."

Amiha looked at Moroni and he could see the conflict raging in his mind.

"Where is Chief Captain Teancum?" Moroni asked without turning to face Amiha.

"Sir, he went to scout the enemies' position." Amiha said in a flat tone. There was a pause and Amiha continued. "Sir…?" Moroni turned to face

Amiha as he continued to speak. "I'm worried about Captain Teancum."

Moroni looked puzzled. "Explain."

"The section of the Lamanite army that he and his men were pursuing these last few weeks were especially cruel to their Nephite hostages. He has been picking up dead and mutilated civilians and noncombatants along the wake of the Lamanite retreat for weeks… Now this." Amiha pointed in the direction of the sounds of people screaming.

Moroni took a deep breath and shook his head and looked away. He, better than most, understood the true price of open war with the Lamanites. He knew this reality was the price the Nephite people must pay for their lack of devotion to the principles of a true Christian society, and for not promoting and supporting freedom, justice and the rule of law. Moroni knew in his heart that when dealing with true evil one must strike hard, fast and true, or the evil will grow like a cancer and infect every aspect of the people's lives. Now, because of the Lamanite's blind hatred, the king men's treachery, and the hardhearted apathy of many in power, the innocent were suffering like no other time in Nephite history.

"It was Ammoron who was the author of so much death and destruction, wasn't it? He was with the group of Lamanites that Teancum was tracking?" Moroni asked, but he already knew the answer. He read the reports, he had walked through the infirmaries. He turned back to look Amiha in the eyes as Amiha responded, "Yes sir."

"And our intelligence is sure he is in the city?" Amiha and Moroni turned to look at the walled city in Lamanite control.

Amiha took a second to respond. He knew Moroni well enough to know where this conversation was going. A second chill of excited energy shook his spine as he answered. "With complete certainty. The intelligence had been confirmed by three independent sources. One of our spies even had eyes on Ammoron as he entered the main gates this morning. He managed to get the message out before they closed the gates and sealed what remained of the Lamanite army inside."

" Teancum knew of this intelligence?" Moroni asked.

"Yes sir… It was one of his Ghost Soldiers who volunteered to go ahead of the retreating Lamanites and try to warn the people of the city. He was the source of the visual confirmation. He died getting the message out."

Moroni looked up at the stars and tried to breathe through his nose to calm himself. " That was one of his own men?" Moroni took a deep

CHAPTER ELEVEN

breath. "I did not know that." It was all very clear to him now. Amiha was the last person to see Teancum and he was the one who started the conversation about Teancum's well-being. "He's not going on a scouting mission, is he?" He turned again to look at Amiha.

"No sir." Amiha replied. His head was down. He could not lie to his closest friend and general. "I'm sorry for not saying something sooner, but Captain Teancum asked me to keep his secret. He knew you would try to stop him." Moroni remained motionless and without expression looking at Amiha as Amiha continued "He is going to try to kill Ammoron, just like he killed his brother in his sleep." Amiha broke eye contact with Moroni and looked at the city on the distance. "Though this is different, I fear." He pointed to the giant walls surrounding the city. "That is a walled city, not a camp full of tents out in the open. They will be expecting an attack. And I don't think they will be guarding their king as carelessly as they were last time." Amiha looked back at his general. "Do you think he can succeed?"

Moroni turned and also looked in the distance at the great walls of the city. "Yes… Yes, I do." After a moment Moroni lowered his head in shame. " Teancum was right." Moroni conceded. " This needs to end here and now." A fresh round of tortured screams came bellowing out from deep inside the city. They all looked and watched as another woman was pushed off the walls and plunged to her death. The drunken Lamanites cheered as she fell. Moroni said a quick prayer for the safety of those Nephites still trapped inside and for his friend Teancum. The irony struck Moroni as amusing. He was asking God in heaven, the source of all happiness, the most loving and forgiving, the bringer of joy and creator of all life, to help Teancum kill another man. Yes, an evil man, but it still caught him as odd.

Moroni stood motionless looking at the city. In a sudden and most unexpected emotional moment, his eyes started to water, and his bottom lip was quivering. He could not comprehend the horror those poor civilians were going through. The countless faces and images of dead and wounded flashed before him. For just a moment Moroni wanted to stop fighting, to stop killing men. He wanted to stop ordering boys to their doom, and he wanted to see the end of the suffering of the victims of this war. He wanted to be a man of peace and turn his back on this whole cursed world.

Then he remembered he carried the Sword of Laban, and was anointed

The Last Great War Council

by the prophet of God to serve his flock as their high-protector. He put his left hand on the hilt of his great sword and felt the influence of past generations of strong leaders on his soul. The old, calm and reassuring voice which had seen him through so many trials before spoke to him again.

See this through. Don't let the sacrifice of so many brave souls go to waste. Finish this once and for all!

"Sir, your orders?" The sergeant major spoke. His voice was like an anchor for Moroni in a strong storm of emotion. The old and faithful soldier had agreed with Teancum at the counsel and he knew what must be done. They had the bulk of the Lamanite army and their king trapped, but he needed Moroni to speak the words. The sergeant major spoke his piece but he knew his place. It was the general's responsibility to lead, not his.

Moroni turned to face his friends, once again a true leader. "We will honor Teancum's selflessness. My orders have changed, get the men ready." He commanded with fresh hope. "We attack at dawn."

"Yes sir!" Amiha and the sergeant major spoke in unison. They saluted and turned to leave.

He turned away from his commanders to look at the city and the approach his army would need to take to assault the main gates. An idea suddenly came to him. "Amiha?" Moroni called out.

Amiha turned back to face Moroni. "Yes sir?" Amiha spoke as he walked back to Moroni.

"Amiha… Summon what remains of the Ghost Soldiers. Have them assemble in their camp. I need to speak to them. I have a task specifically for them."

Amiha had a curious look on his face. He took two more steps towards Moroni as he spoke softly so no one else could hear what he had to say. "There are not very many among the Ghost Soldiers who are able to fight. The last few weeks have been very difficult on them. And they are now without Teancum to lead them."

"I understand." Moroni put his hand on Amiha's shoulder. "But the cause of liberty has need of them…" Moroni turned to glance in the far distance at the main gates of the city. "Hopefully for one last mission."

The sergeant major spoke next. He was still standing a short distance away from Moroni. "Sir, would you like me to send a search party out for Captain Teancum?"

CHAPTER ELEVEN

Moroni looked his father's oldest friend in the eyes. "No…" He smiled as he continued. "I think Teancum has earned the right to disobey my orders this one time. Besides, his rogue actions might be the spark we need to set this plan in motion."

CHAPTER TWELVE

THE PREDATOR FINDS HIS PREY

Moroni was not surprised by what he saw when he arrived at the Ghost Soldiers camp. On the contrary, it was exactly what he had expected and hoped he would find. "God bless these men." He whispered under his breath to Amiha as he dismounted from his horse and handed him the reins. Amiha quickly scanned the scene before him and nodded his head in agreement. While the rest of the Nephite army was still trying to reorganize and set up camp, the Ghost Soldiers had their tents up and their section of the large Nephite military camp was in complete order. Moroni started to walk towards the center of the ghost soldier camp as the sergeant major called the camp to formation. Instantly the camp came alive as men in varied stages of dress came out of tents and ran to fetch their armor and weapons. Torches were lit and a fire was stoked to add light to the ground where Moroni, the sergeant major, Amiha and Chief Judge Pahoran were now standing.

All the warriors who could still hold a weapon and continue the fight were quickly armed and standing in inspection formation. The more seriously wounded and those too sick and weak to continue the fight also responded to the call to assemble and stood to the sides of the main formation. The medics and some of the less injured had even carried those wounded men who were bedridden out from the field hospital to be a part of the assembly for the general.

As they gathered, Moroni assessed the condition of the men before him. The Ghost Soldiers all looked more like scarecrows than fighting

CHAPTER TWELVE

men; unwashed, unshaved and bloodied, their armor dirty and damaged. Most were still wearing their tattered and stained uniforms. Many in the formation had bandages wrapped around a wound or holding an arm in a sling. From a distance someone might think because of the general physical condition of the men in the formation, this was a defeated unit that had lost the will to go on.

But the look in their eyes spoke the truth. Moroni could see there was still fight left in them. They may be hungry and dirty, but these men were still the Ghost Soldiers. They all had the look of someone who had been to hell and back and survived; a lean, hungry, and dangerous look only the brave possess. Teancum had trained and conditioned these men to the very breaking point of physical, mental, emotional and spiritual endurance, far beyond anything any other Nephite army had ever experienced. And the end result was standing at attention before Moroni. These men, these legendary Ghost Soldiers, were still in this fight. The reason for the hard training was plainly evident in the fact this elite unit of fighting men, after all they had endured, still stood up straight like good soldiers and readied themselves for the next battle. These men knew there is no second place in war and failure was not an option for a Ghost Soldier. Victory or death was the battle cry. When their general called for them, they answered like men, like true heroes— like warriors.

The formation was broken into two companies, with Gid and Teomner standing in front of each company. They had finished their mission with Healman and the young stripling warriors and made it back just in time to be a part of the final assault. The battle standard of Chief Captain Teancum was carried by a lone soldier and he held a position of honor in front of and between the two companies. But there was also a second standard held high next to the first. It was the Title of Liberty, the warrior ethos of the Ghost Soldiers. These men exemplified the core values of their holy creed— honor, strength, courage and discipline.

As Moroni approached the assembled men with Pahoran, Amiha and the sergeant major following behind, Gid called the two formations to attention. In one unified motion both companies snapped in response and stood solid and straight as oak trees. The wounded did the best they could to show their respect, and Moroni quickly saluted back and told them all to be, "At ease." Moroni had a sudden flashback to a time not so long ago when a young soldier was driving the wagon full of wounded at the battle of Jershon on the day he fought alongside his father for the last time. He remembered the pain in the soldier's eyes as he tried to stand and salute Moroni. Moroni saw the same pain in the eyes of those wounded Ghost Soldiers now standing before him. It broke his heart, and added to his resolve to end this senseless bloodshed.

"Gentlemen." Moroni began. "Gather around me." The men of Teancum's elite fighting unit moved in closer to their general. Moroni, who was bigger and taller than anyone else, had no problem, projecting his voice over the tops of the soldiers before him. "Your country owes you a debt of gratitude that it can never truly repay." He quickly looked over the gathered standing in a close semi-circle around him. "As long as I have something to say about it, the legend of the Ghost Soldiers and the tales of your heroic deeds during this war will follow you for the remainder of your days." It was obvious the tired warriors liked the sound of that. "Gentlemen, I know you have been in almost constant contact with the enemy for weeks. You have been moving, fighting, and tracking the enemy all while bearing your wounded along the way. You are starving, exhausted and we have all lost so many of our friends, families and brothers in arms to this madness. I can't possibly ask any more of you than what you have already given to the cause of freedom."

There was a pause. "But it is not me that is asking… It is freedom itself that is asking the Ghost Soldiers for one more day." He stopped to let that sink in. "Freedom needs one more day from you men and so does Teancum, your captain." A questioning look spread across the faces of the men. "I have just received word that your captain is, as we speak, making a lone assault on the walls of the city." The men gathered around Moroni all suddenly became very animated and there was a sense of urgency in the air. Moroni continued. "Men, your captain is going to find and kill the Lamanite king, and he needs our help."

Excitement rose up among the troops, war cries went up and several of the soldiers shook their weapons in the air to acknowledge the bravery of their leader Teancum. They all knew if anyone could penetrate the high walls and the defenses of the city, then find and assassinate the evil Lamanite king, it was Teancum. The leopard-skin wrap and crown that belonged to Amalickiah was still hanging outside of Teancum's tent. He did it once already, he could do it again. They all knew it and they all wanted to be a part of history.

Moroni moved his head in silent acknowledgement of what everyone else was thinking. "I have full confidence Captain Teancum will succeed,

CHAPTER TWELVE

and with their leader dead, the Lamanites inside the city will be in chaos." Several of the Ghost Soldiers agreed with Moroni. "Men, we have a chance to end this war once and for all. The balance of the Lamanite army and the majority of its ranking leaders are all trapped in one location behind those stone walls." Moroni waved his hand towards the city in the distance. "I am going to order the full might of the Nephite army to attack the city at first light." There were more shouts and war cries among the ranks. Moroni raised up his hand to tell them to quiet down at the same time the sergeant major shouted, "At ease men!" It became instantly quiet. No one wanted to cross the sergeant major.

"Yes, thank you, sergeant major," Moroni smiled. It still amazed him how much blind respect and obedience others gave that old soldier. Moroni continued, "But there are some obstacles with this plan. Which is why I am here, you are vital to the effort." Moroni tried to make eye contact with as many Ghost Soldiers as possible. He needed to make a personal connection with the men. Moroni knew what he was going to say next would change everything. "It would be senseless to attack and not get inside the walls of the city as soon as possible. If we don't breach the defenses then we will crash into those stone walls like ocean waves against the rocks and accomplish nothing but getting many more Nephites killed."

Moroni paused and moved back and forth in front of the men. "Teancum is going to kill the king, of that I am sure. If we are going to exploit the opportunity Captain Teancum will provide us with, then I don't have time to build towers or make ladders and strong ropes to get my soldiers up and over the walls." Moroni continued in a more sober tone as he moved around to see into the faces of the men standing before him. "We, as an army, are not equipped or prepared for a prolonged siege. This war has driven our people to the brink of ruin and it needs to end, now! We have neither the resources, nor the fortitude to sit and wait them out any longer." Moroni stopped and looked straight ahead. "Gentlemen," He pause for a deep breath. "When I give the order to assault the city, I need those front gates open." The warriors before Moroni looked at each other. Some had already figured out what he was asking, the others were about to find out. "And Captain Teancum will need a distraction so he can accomplish his mission and escape in one piece."

There was another pause. "Men, I need the Ghost Soldiers to attack before dawn— I need you to take and hold the main gate and tower above it and keep the gate open long enough for the army to get inside." Not even the air moved after Moroni said those words. "Take the tower and hold the gate open until relieved… Those are my orders to the Ghost Soldiers."

There was complete silence as the soldiers around Moroni grasped the enormity of the task they had been asked to perform. Moroni's voice had an edge of determination now. "When the sun rises in the morning we have a chance to finally end this war. With the help of God's divine intervention, by the time the sun sets, their king will be dead, the city retaken, the helpless Nephites being held hostage inside will be free and the Lamanite army will be destroyed once and for all. By the time the sun sets tomorrow we will have justice and be at peace. Freedom is asking you for one more day… What say you?"

There was no movement or sounds among the troops, each man was alone with his thoughts. There was no misunderstanding Moroni's request was tantamount to a suicide mission. They were all professionals and every soldier in formation understood the enormity of the moment and the risk involved. No one knew what to do or what to say. Everyone was so hungry and tired and after hearing Moroni's orders they were wrestling with their inner emotions. They were all asking questions in their minds, *Can I fight one more day? Do I have the strength or the will to go on? Haven't I given enough?* And the most important question— *Is this last mission worth my life?*

"Men." Moroni continued, he could read their hearts and feel their apprehension. "You are not the summer soldiers who are brave only in good conditions, fair weather and with a full belly. The Ghost Soldiers have never backed down from a worthy fight. You have been preparing for this moment from the time you were born. Everything you have done, from how you lived your life as a child, to the military training you have endured, to the countless battles you have fought has led you to this place and this holy ground. What freedom is asking of you is almost incomprehensible, I know and understand this." He could barely say the words out loud.

Moroni held his right hand to his chest. "But that is exactly who you are and what you have accomplished—the incomprehensible. When the story of this war is told to future generations, this night and the coming dawn will be the last chapter written. What will they say about you? Will they say that you rested while others fought and gave the last full measure of devotion for their God, their religion, their freedom, their peace and their families? Will they say that Teancum, the Ghost Soldier himself single-handedly assaulted the enemy held city while his men left him to die alone and dishonored his sacrifice?" Moroni was growing louder and more animated with his words. As he continued to speak several of the men raised their chins up and stood a little taller. "Or will they say that even the gates of hell could not keep the great Captain Teancum and his fearless Ghost Solders from conquering evil? Even when all seemed hopeless and lost, the Ghost Soldiers were seen leading the final attack! They charged directly into the teeth of the monster and showed the rest of the world what honor and true valor looks like!"

Moroni and the sergeant major could sense the indecision and hesitation among the troops was fading. This was a good sign, but more was needed. If the most elite of the Nephite army were questioning their abilities and loyalty to Moroni and the cause of liberty, what would the rest of the regular Nephite army do when the order came to attack those high, well-defended walls? The sergeant major had been in enough battles to know low morale can defeat an army long before the enemy has a chance to. He knew he needed to act and act fast to capitalize on the changing hearts of the men. These men needed to be inspired and guided by a strong leader to rally and guide them forward towards victory. But he did not have time to explain this to Moroni, the old soldier knew he needed to move, and move quickly. He made eye contact with Moroni and his body language told Moroni all he needed to know. Moroni could sense his mentor and friend had an answer to this and he nodded, giving him permission to act.

"All right." The sergeant major shouted as he turned his spear upside down and drove the sharp metal tip into the ground. Everyone turned to look at him. "Enough of this sniveling. Do you want to live forever?!" The old soldier walked past Moroni and nodded as he went by. "Sir." The eye contact they made spoke volumes. Moroni trusted his seasoned friend enough to allow him the latitude to take control. The sergeant major continued towards the gathered Ghost Soldiers and shouted, "Make a hole!" while gesturing for those in front of him to move.

Instinctively the men jumped out of the way and a large path was opened for the sergeant major as he walked past all of the soldiers and stopped several feet past the back of the formation. He snapped to attention and stood motionless for several seconds with his back to the crowd of soldiers watching him. Then, looking over his left shoulder he shouted. "Ghost Soldiers! Every *man* who can still hold a weapon and fight, fall in!" This was all that was needed to motivate the men to action.

The old warrior had been swinging a sword long before most of these Ghost Soldiers had been born. Everyone knew, respected and feared him. He had been in the thick of war with the cursed Lamanites from even before the attack on the City of Manti. He was exhausted, wounded, starving, and still he mustered the courage to stand and fight one more day. If someone like the sergeant major could find the inner courage to carry on, then these younger, well-trained, conditioned and motivated soldiers could carry on as well. These men would never follow a hollow or weak leader, nor would they follow someone they did not trust and respect. The sergeant major had both trust and respect to spare. He was, not only in the eyes of the Ghost Soldiers, but with the entire Nephite army, a true hero.

So when he spoke, they responded. Clamoring to find their place, Teancum's elite force quickly fell back into their two formations. Even some of the wounded who were standing on the sides were ignoring their injuries and trying to find a place with the others. It only took moments for the Ghost Soldiers to reform their formation lines; standing tall and proud again. There was almost a hint of a smile on the Sergeant Major's face as he turned around and saluted Moroni. "The Ghost Soldiers are formed up and awaiting your instructions, sir." He announced with military pride. Moroni saluted back and stepped forward.

"Thank you sergeant major, that will be all."

"Yes sir." He dropped his salute and made an abrupt left face, and moved out of the way. His job was done. They were a fighting unit again.

Before Moroni could continue his address to the Ghost Soldiers, the sounds of clanking pots and squeaking wheels could be heard coming from the darkness behind him. Moroni smiled and said, "Perfect timing."

From the shadows, a covered wagon being pulled by two oxen emerged and came to a stop several yards away. Moroni turned back to face the men before him and shouted. "Lieutenant Gid, Lieutenant Teomner—front and center!"

The two soldiers left their respective positions in front of the formations and moved quickly to Moroni. Standing at attention they both saluted and said in unison, "Reporting as ordered, sir!"

CHAPTER TWELVE

"Gentlemen," Moroni spoke quietly. "In the wagon behind me is a hot meal waiting for your men." Gid and Teomner both shot a surprised and happy look at each other. More than even sleep and medical attention, the Ghost Soldiers all needed food, this was a godsend. "Feed them and then prepare to assault the main gate. With Teancum gone, you two are now the leaders of the Ghost Soldiers. It is not my place to instruct you on how to employ your own special tactics." He paused and looked down at both of them with a serious look. "I need the main gate open at dawn when I charge with the infantry from the wood line, and it needs to stay open until the rest of the army is inside. I don't care how you do it, just get it open and hold until relieved. Do you understand?"

"Sir, yes sir." They both responded with concern in their eyes.

"Very well… Gentlemen, I will return in one hour and we will conduct a leader's reconnaissance of the main gate." He tilted his head as he continued. "You have until then to create a workable assault plan and get the Ghost Soldiers ready to move." Moroni turned to face Pahoran who was standing a few paces behind Moroni. "Chief Judge Pahoran, do you have anything you wish to say to the men?"

Pahoran took two steps forward and spoke in a loud voice. This was the first time most of these men had ever been this close to the Grand Chief Judge of the Nephite people. Throughout time, a common thread among soldiers of any age was an inherent distrust of politicians. They were considered pampered men who would talk tough and call for war on another nation, but not be willing to fight in those wars themselves. To men of action like the Ghost Soldiers, words were empty. Actions defined you among them, not empty words and threats.

This moment was no exception. Although they all knew of the letters Moroni sent and the civil war that Pahoran had fought, there was still a feeling of suspicion among the troops. But they were professionals and did not let their feelings show in their actions towards Pahoran. If General Moroni trusted Pahoran to stand by his side at the eve of the last desperate battle of this war, then the ghost soldiers would do the same. "Men," Pahoran called out. "The citizens of the Nephite nation cannot express enough the gratitude they have for the extreme sacrifice you have made for them. The stories of your deeds in battle have spread from one end of the land to the other. Even the Lamanites know and fear you. You are all heroes in the eyes of your government and the people we both serve. It is both a privilege and my honor to stand before you."

Like good soldiers, the men stood quiet and respectful as Pahoran spoke. Pahoran was caught off guard by the lack of response from the formations of warriors. He was accustomed to interaction and applause from his audience. He did not feel disrespected, it was just different speaking to a gathering of soldiers than speaking to civilians.

Catching himself, he continued. "As a token of my personal respect, for you and your Captain, I have personally arraigned for a meal of hot potato soup and warm bread for you to have before the coming battle tomorrow." Pahoran waved to the teamster driving the covered wagon and the tarp was removed revealing a massive cauldron of thick, hot soup and several dozen loaves of bread in the back. There were also two cooks standing in the back waiting to serve up the meal to the men. This was more food in one place then they had all seen in weeks. That fact was not lost on the men who all suddenly lost their military bearing and became very excited about the prospects of a hot meal. Pahoran held up both hands to gesture for the men in the ranks to quiet down. "May you find your strength and courage, and feel of the love and respect every peace-loving Nephite has for Captain Teancum and his Ghost Soldiers. Thank you gentlemen for your dedication to the cause of liberty." Finished speaking, Pahoran nodded back to Moroni.

"Thank you, Chief Judge Pahoran." Moroni responded. He quickly turned back to face Gid and Teomner. "Dawn, gentlemen." He pointed at both of them to emphasize his words. "Open and hold the gate until you are relieved."

"Sir, yes sir." They both saluted.

"For liberty, gentlemen." Moroni nodded. "Carry on." He finished and turned to leave.

Teomner turned to look at Gid. "Food!?" He whispered to his close friend and fellow Ghost Soldier.

"Hot soup!" Gid responded with a big smile on his dirty face.

Teomner turned to face the men in the two formations. "Those soldiers who will be participating in the assault, eat first. Form a single line and eat. We still have much to do." Teomner paused and raised up his hands. He could see the men starting to move towards the wagon and there was still more instructions to give out. "Thirty minutes, and then I want all officers and platoon sergeants to meet by the firepit for instructions."

Teomner looked to Gid and gestured with his face asking if he had anything he wanted to say before the men were released to eat.

CHAPTER TWELVE

At that moment the thought of eating a meal caused Gid's stomach to growl loudly, and they both chuckled at the sounds coming from Gid's belly.

"I guess that answers that question." Teomner said laughing.

"Yup, it sure does. Let's eat!"

Teomner looked up at the men standing before him. "Dismissed!"

A shout went up and the starving Ghost Soldiers all ran to the wagon to try to be the first for the food. A line quickly and very efficiently formed and the men were all handed large bowels of thick potato soup and giant hunks of grain bread. The cooks were handing out bowls and bread as fast as they could, and in no time all the soldiers were eating, smiling and laughing with hunks of half-chewed food in their mouths. With help from the teamster and a few medics, the cooks then fed the wounded and those too sick to get their own food. After everyone had been fed, the lead cook saw there was still lots of soup left, but not enough bread for everyone to get a second helping. Looking around he spotted a small pot of hot water set over a fire not far from the wagon. "See if that is clean water." He told the younger cook. The boy jumped down from the wagon and walked over to the boiling pot to inspect it.

"It's okay." He looked back and gave the older cook the thumbs up.

"Bring it here."

The young cook carried the hot water to the wagon and put it up in the bed. "Pour it in the soup." The older cook ordered as he took the last few hunks of bread and broke them into smaller pieces and dropped them into the soup. Understanding what his boss was doing, the younger cook poured the hot water into the soup and then grabbed the large ladle and mixed in the bread with the soup.

The older cook finished with the bread and grabbed a metal spice can he had next to him on the floor boards of the wagon. Opening the can he pinched out several doses of salt and sprinkled it over the soup. Grabbing a small bowl, the lead cook scooped out a helping and quickly tasted the new concoction. "Not bad." He spoke out loud and smacked his lips. Putting the bowl down he turned to face the soldiers who were all sitting around eating. "There is plenty more if anyone wants seconds!" He shouted. No one needed to be told twice, and in no time the remaining soup infused with the bread was quickly finished off.

The Predator Finds His Prey

Teancum worked his way through the dark woods and around to the backside of the city walls. The blended colors of his cloak made him almost impossible to see in the shadows. It took him longer than he had hoped but finally, under one of the dimly lit watch towers, he found what he was looking for— a darkened section of the wall overshadowed by the outcropping of the watchtower. "Perfect." He said to himself and smiled.

Moving back further into the trees, Teancum found a small ravine and quietly lowered himself into it. Removing the hood of the wooden coloered cloak off his head, he became completely still for several minutes. He listened for any sounds of Lamanite patrols or anything that might give away his unguarded position. Hearing nothing but the night calls of the insects, he slowly and carefully emptied the contents of his ruck sack on the ground. *Going to need this*, he thought as he carefully took off the cloak cover and set it aside. Next he found his climbing hooks and shoe spikes and set them next to the cover. Off in the distance the snap of a branch echoed through the trees. Teancum froze in place and dared not even breathe.

The sound came from off his right shoulder and he very slowly turned to see if he could discover the source of the noise. There was movement among the trees and it looked and sounded like whatever or whomever it was, was coming towards him. The darkened shadows carried from tree to tree as the unknown presence moved closer. Teancum carefully moved his hand down to the handle of his knife. The darkness of the woods was thick and the moonlight was covered by the clouds. Teancum knew that at night, movement and sound would give his position away quicker than anything else. So he remained still and quiet as a tomb as the shadows closed in. *If it's a Lamanite patrol I hope they don't see me and walk right on past*, he thought to himself. *It would make sense they would have foot patrols in this part of the woods. This section of the forest is much thicker and is growing closer to the walls of the city.*

That section of the defensive wall was poorly lit, so having soldiers acting as an early warning positioned in the trees was sound tactics. Teancum was not worried about being discovered. With the element of surprise on his side he was more than capable of killing all the guards in the patrol. It was the time wasted fighting and dealing with hiding the bodies he was concerned with. *About twenty feet now*. He calculated in his mind as the shadows moved through the trees and brush coming even closer to him. He could hear the quiet sounds of leaves being crushed

CHAPTER TWELVE

under the weight of the unknown intruders. *Whoever is coming this way is very good at moving quietly*, he thought to himself as he watched and waited for his chance to spring and strike.

Tightening the grip on his knife, Teancum slowly took in a breath and readied himself for close combat. Teancum could now see more than one shadow moving towards him and he slowly started to draw out his knife. As the first shadow rounded a large tree, Teancum tensed for the attack, but instead came face to face with a large male deer. The two were no more than ten feet apart and they both just stared at each other. Relived he was not in mortal danger, Teancum slid the knife back into its sheath and whispered, "Good evening my brother." The deer flicked its ear and continued to look at Teancum. Then a female deer and two young fawns came into view. The male deer looked back at his family and then back at Teancum. "There are two hungry armies in these woods. I would be quietly moving my family too if I were you." He smiled and nodded at the deer. Teancum was no threat to the deer and the deer knew it. The big buck let out a snort and the family continued towards its unseen destination. For a moment, watching the family of deer move away from him, Teancum's heart ached for his wife and children. He realized that he had been so consumed with fighting this cursed war that he could not remember the last time he'd thought about them. That feeling stung his soul and he vowed to never go another day without reflecting on the memories of his dear departed wife and young daughters.

Shaking off the emotions, Teancum focused on the task at hand and continued to ready himself for the daring assault on the fortified enemy city. Opening up a small wooden container of black grease paint he had in his satchel, he took a generous helping and rubbed it all over his face and hands. When he was done, Teancum put the camouflaged cover over his body and tied the loose ends around his arms and legs. He then took a length of strong rope and a grappling hook and stuck it in a small bag along with the climbing hooks, shoe spikes and other assorted dangerous tools of his craft.

Once the items were secured in the bag, Teancum attached a long, thin strip of leather to the handle. Checking to ensure he still had his knife, throwing spikes, blow darts and garotte safely secured on his equipment belt, Teancum pulled the hood of the camouflage cover up and over his head. He almost instantly blended in with the foliage around him. He was not going to need his trusty spear, bow or his sword for this mission.

Just like before, he knew there would be plenty of weapons inside the city for him to use and right now those large objects would only slow him down.

His backpack was quickly stuffed with the items Teancum did not need and the pack was shoved into the exposed and tangled roots of a very large tree. Making a mental note of its location, Teancum took one last deep breath before starting the movement to the wall of the city. Walking slowly and hunched over, acting more like a predator than a man, Teancum moved around the trees and ferns until he was near the edge of the tree line. Stopping just before exposing himself, Teancum knelt down behind a tree and tied the long, thin unattached end of the leather strap, fastened to the smaller bag, to his right ankle. Looking up, Teancum could see Lamanite sentries with torches walking along the top of the wall. He also saw Lamanites in the watch tower, they were looking out into the forest trying to see if General Moroni was moving to attack. He watched for several minutes hoping to spot a pattern in the sentries' movement on top of the wall. The only consistent thing he observed from the Lamanites movement was a lack of discipline— no set patrolling or stationary guards. Teancum would see a lone guard with no torch and then several all carrying torches, walking back and forth across this section of the wall.

As he observed more closely, he realized something. *They are too busy or preoccupied with what they are doing to look out from behind the ramparts and survey the wood line.* He looked at the long dark shadow that was cast over the section of wall in front of him by the outcropping of the watchtower, and judged the distance to his location from the base of the shadow-covered section of the wall to be about one hundred yards. He then looked at the ground between him and the wall.

Flat and grass-covered... Great. He was hoping for a small natural depression to hide his silhouette or some bushes and rocks to break up his outline as he crawled towards the wall. "What?" He smiled and whispered to himself. "You did not think it was going to be easy, did you?" Orienting himself in the direction he wanted to crawl, he slowly lowered himself down to the ground and flat on his belly. *Here we go,* he thought as he slowly and quietly dragged his left knee up until it was parallel with his hip. Reaching out with his right arm past his head to its full extension, he pushed and pulled his body along the ground so slowly and as quietly as a mouse creeping across the field.

CHAPTER TWELVE

As he continued to move along, the bag tied to his ankle was pulled along with the leather strap. This technique allowed Teancum to carry extra equipment while keeping his hands free and the equipment from interfering with his low crawling methods. In the quiet darkness, and with his expertly-designed camouflage cover hiding his body outline from the Lamanite guards in the watch tower, the Lamanites were completely unaware that directly below them, the Ghost Soldier himself was closing in on their section of the wall.

Teancum figured it took him about thirty minutes to crawl the distance from the tree line to the base of the shadow-covered section of the city wall. Once he was up against the wall and deep in shadow he knew he was out of sight from the guards. Teancum carefully removed the camouflage cover and pulled the bag attached to his ankle to him. He was sweating profusely, and some of the black grease paint had come off. Teancum was not worried about reapplying a second layer until he was over the wall and inside the city. He quickly opened the bag and removed the rope and climbing equipment. He removed his sandals and put on the shoe spikes.

These were hard leather shoes with a metal plate shaped like a foot running the length of the shoe. Where the sole of the shoe would have been, a four inch sharp spike protruded out from under his toes. The metal plate had eyelets along both sides, and thick leather straps ran crisscrossed over and under the foot and through the eyelets. There was a thick leather hide that came over the top of the bare foot to keep the tops of the feet from being cut by the leather straps, and allowing Teancum's foot to be tightly secured to the metal plate. The climbing hooks were a simple farming tool ranchers developed to pick up bales of hay. It was a "J" shaped piece of metal with a handhold on one end and a sharp tip on the other. As a boy, Teancum learned to use these hooks to pick up the bales of hay and toss them high onto the stack for the winter stores. He found a much more deadly use for them now as climbing hooks to ascend rock and wooded walls.

It was too risky to try to use the grappling hook and rope to climb the side of the wall. Although the guards at the top were sloppy, there were still too many walking around and Teancum had no way of distracting them away from this section of the wall. He slowly stood up and inspected the large stones. They were evenly shaped and uniform in size. Teancum smiled as he realized that this city's walls were built exactly like so many other Nephite city's walls. "You guys are consistent," he whispered as he thought about his friend Moroni and the defenses he had ordered around the major population centers in the Nephite lands. This made Teancum's attempt to ascend to the top of the wall so much easier now that he knew the stones would be uniform and spaced the same. He and his men had practiced several times climbing walls exactly like this one. *Not easy... But not impossible*, he reassured himself.

Checking one last time that he had all of his needed equipment secured in his satchel and his weapons were firmly attached to his equipment belt, Teancum pulled the hood of his cloak back over his head. Taking a deep breath, he took one of the hooks in his hand and set the spiked end into the gap where the corners of four of the massive stones meet. When he was sure of that hold he drove the spike on the opposite foot into the crease between two other stones and pushed up. Repeating this with the other limbs, Teancum was able to quickly scale up the side of the wall in only a matter of minutes. He could have made it up very quickly, but he was moving slowly to ensure he was as quiet as possible. The only real sounds he made while climbing were slight ringing sounds when the metal of his spikes hit the stone walls as they were digging for a grip. Those sounds went completely unnoticed by the preoccupied Lamanite guards on the tops of the wall and in the guard towers.

Teancum reached the top and readied himself to climb over the side and onto the catwalk. This was the most dangerous part of the climb. He would be exposed and helpless for a moment as he angled his legs and arms up and over the side. From his extensive training and experience, Teancum knew he was defenseless until he was completely over and had both feet on the catwalk, so he had to hurry, but still not draw attention to himself.

With intensely honed body control, athleticism and strength, Teancum pulled himself the rest of the way up and over the top of the wall and came down in a crouching position on the wooden planks of the catwalk without a sound. He was facing the guard tower, ready to attack at the first sign of trouble. Pausing for a moment, he realized his presence had gone unnoticed and slowly, he turned his head to scan his surroundings. He was at the opposite end of the city from the main gate. This end of the city was relatively quiet compared to the fires and noise coming from the center. There were several large buildings not far from his position and he knew he needed to move off the catwalk, down the scaffolding

CHAPTER TWELVE

and into the cover of the shadows below. He concluded that climbing down the large wooden planks and poles holding the catwalk in place would be the safest route for him to reach the city street below.

He set himself to move when three Lamanites stepped out from the guard tower and onto the catwalk. They were moving his way, but none of them were paying attention to where they were going. They were all looking inside a small box of jewels one of the Lamanites had stolen. The first man had the box in his hand, while the second held a lit torch close to the box so they could see the contents. The light from the torch blinded the men from the danger right in front of them, and Teancum quickly covered his head and moved his body as close as he could to the wall in hopes the men would walk right past him without noticing him. He held his breath as he tried to remain as flat as he could and hoped his cloak would camouflage him well enough so the enemy soldiers would walk on by.

The men would have safely gone past Teancum if one of them had not been greedy and grabbed for one of the rings inside of the box. His actions caused the man holding the box to drop the contents on the wooden planks, and all three Lamanites stopped walking and turned to try to gather up the treasure. The closest Lamanite was on his knees laughing as he gathered up the fallen jewelry when he saw a strange shape in front of him. Looking up, he made eye contact with Teancum who was now standing and ready to deal with these three undisciplined Lamanites. The man on his knees was shocked to see the Ghost Soldier with grease paint on his face and his cloak flapping in the breeze.

Gasping, he was unable to call out a warning before Teancum grabbed his head and spun it around breaking the man's neck and killing him instantly. The sound of the Lamanite's body hitting the planks caused the other two men to turn around, but Teancum was too quick and too well-trained for them. The second man grasped at his throat as Teancum passed right by him and drew the ultra-sharp blade of his knife across his neck, severing his jugular artery and the man's ability to cry out. The third Lamanite was still holding the burning torch, and Teancum quickly grabbed his hand and pushed the torch into the Lamanite's face, burning his eyes and skin. The Lamanite dropped the torch and reached for his damaged face with both hands. Before the burned man could cry out, Teancum spun behind the injured Lamanite and put him in a rear choke hold. The man desperately grasped at Teancum's powerful arms as they

The Predator Finds His Prey

quickly squeezed the life out of him. Teancum felt the man pass out and go limp in his arms. Then with a slight jerk, Teancum was able to break the third Lamanite's neck and the lifeless body dropped to the catwalk with a slight thud. Teancum knew he had no time to waste as he was exposed out in the open. Quickly, he removed his climbing spikes, put his soft books back on and made his way over the side of the catwalk and shimmied down the scaffolding to the ground.

Teancum still had on his camouflaged covering and was carefully moving in the shadows away from the wall and towards the inner park of the large walled city. Bounding between the darkened recesses of the buildings, he moved like a cat, quiet and unseen; hunting some unsuspecting prey. Moving through the streets was proving easier than he had anticipated. With several large buildings burning in the distance, he could see the Lamanites trying to prepare for Moroni's attack and looting the wealth of the city, no one was giving a second thought to a passing shadow. But something was nagging at Teancum as he adjusted to the new environment and moved past the Laminate occupiers with the skill of an assassin. *I should have pushed those bodies over the side of the wall.* The trademark of a Ghost Solder is they don't leave any traces of their presence. Teancum drilled this concept into his men night and day. But now there were three dead bodies on the catwalk lying in the open. That was a pretty convincing sign someone had been there. *No time to go back,* he thought to himself. He was hoping the Lamanites would be too consumed with Moroni and his army just outside the gates to wonder what had happened to the sentries he killed.

As Teancum continued to move around the city, the streets were getting more and more congested with Lamanites. *If I stay on the streets, then it's only a matter of time before I'm discovered. I need to find some high ground and get my bearings,* he thought to himself and scanned the tall roof tops looking for the best vantage point. Down the main cobbled street, Teancum spied what he was looking for— a large structure with several outcroppings, balconies, and awnings all along the outside. "Perfect," he smiled and whispered. Staying low and moving without making a sound, Teancum worked his way from his location to the edge of the building. *Nice, easy climb to the top,* he thought as he looked up the side of the building at his ascending point.

Adjusting his pack and checking to ensure his equipment and weapons were secure, Teancum bent over and grabbed a handful of dirt from the

CHAPTER TWELVE

ground. Rubbing the grit on his palms he took a deep breath and reached up high on the outer wall of the building for the first handhold. Grasping firmly, he jammed the toes of his right foot into a crack in the mortar and pushed up. Reaching higher with his free hand Teancum grabbed the base of the first set of balconies dotting the outside of the building he was climbing. With both hands now grasping the bottom ledge of the balcony floor, Teancum swung his body up and onto the railing. "That was the easy part." He whispered as he scanned the upward path before him. Teancum continued his climb up the side of the building using his body's natural abilities and the convenient hand and footholds along the way.

"Sir, come quick, we found something." A breathless Lamanite begged as he entered the city's armory. Every big city had a room like it; a large room with stacks of weapons and armor waiting to be issued to the city's guard force or militia in times of emergency. A very large Lamanite with a black cloak, brass gauntlets and the red sash of the Lamanite royal guards across his chest was standing in the center of the room next to a table and looking over some scrolls. The black cloak and arm gauntlets were the symbol of his high position and rank as the night watch commander.

"What is it?" He barked. Time was not on his side. As the captain of the night watch, his job was to secure the walls and gates of the city and make what forces are available ready to repel the inevitable Nephite attack.

"Sir," The messenger gulped hard and tried to catch his breath. "We found three dead sentries on the catwalk along the western wall."

"Was it another fight between clans?" Clan and family infighting was always a problem within the Lamanite army. It was not uncommon for two men from different clans to settle clan business with a knife fight. Now, with tensions flaring over the king's order to stop looting the city and the coming Nephite attack, it was not beyond the realm of possibility that it was just a turf fight between rivals.

"No sir, I know those men, they are from the same clan. There is something else…"

"What?"

"They did not have their swords out. Whoever killed them did it before they could react to defend themselves."

The captain of the watch quickly came to a possible conclusion. "So the killer was someone they all knew and trusted to be close to them," He paused as the next phrase almost slipped out of his mouth. "Or they were ambushed."

The tall Lamanite held quiet for several seconds and contemplated this sudden news. Putting the parchment down he started to bark out orders. "You!" He pointed to a soldier standing next to him. "Go tell the king's guards to be on alert for a possible intruder and an attempt on the king's life." He pointed to a second Lamanite standing near the back of the room. "You, finish accounting for all the weapons in this armory." He pushed the stack of papers and scrolls towards the second Lamanite. "You!" He pointed to the messenger. "Show me!" The Lamanite proceeded to lead The commander to the location of the three dead Lamanites.

"Here sir, here are the bodies."

"Did anyone touch or move them?" The watch commander asked.

"We did, sir… When we were checking for a sign of life." A second Lamanite responded. There was a bit of hesitation in his voice. He was unsure if checking on his comrades was a good thing in the eyes of the night watch commander or if he had made a mistake.

"Understood." The commander acknowledged the need for the friends of the dead men to want to see if they were alive. "But they were found in this area, yes? You did not carry them from someplace else?" The tall Lamanite questioned as he looked around and inspected the scene.

"No sir, we only turned them over to see if they were still breathing." The first Lamanite spoke up.

The commander was inspecting the area around the dead men. He looked focused and intense. The others around him got out of his way as he moved about checking for signs or an indication of what happened. He made his way over to the side of the wall and looked out at the far tree line. Off to his left he could see the distant fires of Moroni's camp. "This is a very dark and quiet section of the wall." The commander remarked. "If I was going to climb the wall and assault the city, this is where I would have done it." Taking a step back the watch commander made a visual sweep to see if there were any other marks or signs of an intruder.

Finding none, he turned to leave, that's when he saw it. It was very faint and hard to see. He had passed by it already, and no one else had

CHAPTER TWELVE

realized it was there. He dropped to one knee and called for a torch. He was handed a lit torch and brought it down close to the wooden planks of the catwalk. There, etched every so lightly in the fine dust, was a single footprint. But this was no Lamanite footprint. He looked at it closer and saw it was bigger than a normal Lamanite foot, and there were no sandal markings or bare foot imprints, just the basic form of a right foot. The tall Lamanite quickly scanned the feet of those standing around him just in case he missed something, but no— those around him all had on sandals.

"Sir? What is it?" The first Lamanite asked.

"A footprint... But there are no identifying markings." He pointed to the shape in the dust. See how it is shaped like a foot but there are no imprints for the toes, or a clear outline and tread from the sole of a sandal or boot?"

Every Lamanite standing around him leaned in closer to see what the night watch commander was looking at.

The commander looked up in the direction the print indicated the person who left it was traveling. "The person who made this print is wearing a shoe that is sturdy, light and does not leave a trace." He was lost in thought for a moment as his eyes were locked on the shadows of the buildings in the distance. "I have seen prints like this before." The tension was building inside of him and his jaw line flexed as he spoke.

"Where?" One of the gathered Lamanites asked.

"Inside the tent of King Amalickiah. Right after we found him murdered in his sleep by the Ghost Soldier."

"Teancum... Teancum is here, in the city?" The second Lamanite gasped. Every man standing around the commander took one step back, tightened their grips on their spears and started looking around like a herd of deer who just picked up the scent of a lion.

The commander was the only person who was not negatively affected by the thought of the Ghost Solder loose in the city. He remained still as stone looking out into the city from the high wall. The only thing moving on his body was his big chest as he took in air and a slight grin formed on his face. "Finally..." He whispered. "We meet." His eyes were gleaming with intensity.

Turning to his men the commander barked out instructions. "Now you know what to look for, scan the ground and pick up his trail. Go!" Those men who accompanied the commander took off in a flash. Every one of them wanted to be the one who found the trail on the ground left by the

The Predator Finds His Prey

Ghost Soldier. He then turned to the friends of the slain soldiers. "Have your captain get some replacements up here and double the watch." Looking at the dead Lamanites he nodded and continued. "See to your fallen friends." Then without a word, he was up and walking past the others towards the stairs leading down from the catwalk. His black cloak flowing in the night air. The commander was two steps from the bottom when one of his men called out.

"Here! Commander, I have found a print!"

Looking around the commander quickly made an assumption. "So… You are in the city, and moving in the shadows." He looked at the soldier who found the single print in the sand near the corner of a merchant hut. "What direction does the print indicate he is moving?"

The soldier already knew the answer but he looked back down anyway. "East… Towards the center of the city!" He pointed as he answered.

"Well done, now go and assemble twenty strong men. We have a snake to hunt."

Teancum was on top of one of the higher buildings near the center of city when he heard the clanking of the metal and the panic-driven shouts coming from below him. Crouching low and staying in the shadows, he peeked over the side of the roof. He watched as small groups of heavily-armed Lamanites ran in every direction. Someone was directly below Teancum on the street shouting orders and directing the Lamanite soldiers where to deploy. Teancum adjusted his position to get a better look at the person in charge and giving commands. Crouching along the roof top, he moved over to a banner pole hanging off the front of the building and used it as a balance as he could carefully lean over the edge to get a better view down below.

"That's no ordinary Lamanite," he whispered as he looked down on a large and dangerous looking warrior who was waving his big sword and shouting at the Lamanites running by him. Teancum watched for several more seconds and was about to move back when the big man grabbed a smaller-sized Lamanite and pulled him out of the street. This smaller Lamanite was dressed differently than the rest of the soldiers running along the street. He had on a bright green tunic and seemed a bit awkward trying to run while holding a spear.

"You! Where is King Ammoron?" The massive warrior asked the

CHAPTER TWELVE

smaller man. He was screaming at the smaller Lamanite while flailing his muscular arms. Teancum got the impression they knew each other, but it was not a friendly relationship.

"He is still with the harlots in the great hall," was the response. It was clear the Lamanite did not like the Zoramite king and cowered away from the big man.

"Does he know yet about the Nephite assassin moving freely in the city?"

"I don't know my lord when I last saw him he had been drinking too much wine," the smaller Lamanite answered.

"Go, find your king and advise him of the intruder!" The night watch commander ordered while pointing his sword at the small Lamanite's chest.

This was a much better prospect for the young Lamanite than hunting and fighting the Nephite killer. He had been with the Lamanite army during the last retreat. He wanted no part of fighting Moroni, Lehi, or Teancum and his Ghost Soldiers. "Yes, my lord!" He shouted and smiled as he dropped his heavy spear and ran back in the direction he came from.

Teancum almost jumped when he saw the young Lamanite run away. *Got to follow him.* He quickly and carefully moved along the roof line trying to keep the messenger in sight. Teancum could spend days in vain searching for the king and waiting for the exact moment to strike. But, if he could keep the young Lamanite in sight, then he would lead Teancum to the exact location of the evil king. And Teancum overheard the king had been drinking. If he was not passed out drunk, then his reflexes would be slow, making him an easy target for Teancum's vengeance and God's justice.

Teancum watched as the young boy ran past the far edge of the building he was atop. Looking ahead Teancum saw several buildings all in a row lining the street in the direction the boy was running. The buildings were all different shapes and sizes and separated by alleys. *I could drop down to ground level and try to follow him on foot*, Teancum thought. He looked down to the street below to find a good place to quickly climb down and follow the messenger. As he looked over the edge, he saw several more Lamanite soldiers running towards the sound of the alarm.

Backing away from the edge to avoid detection, Teancum spoke

CHAPTER TWELVE

out loud. "Not that way, too dangerous." Looking back up the street he saw he was going to lose sight of the young Lamanite if he did not act quickly. Teancum looked over at the rooftops in the direction the messenger was headed. Smiling to himself Teancum got up and backed up to the farthest point on the roof from the edge. "Okay." He said with determination in his voice. He was out of options and had to move. "Why not?" he spoke and sprinted towards the edge of the building. As he reached the roof line he took a mighty leap and flung his body into the night air.

Arcing high over the alley, Teancum jumped with all his might and came down hard on the next roof. When he landed Teancum did a complete forward roll to absorb the shock of impact and came up to his feet at a dead run. Mentally shaking off the pain of the impact, Teancum continued to sprint towards the building's edge. As he approached the next jumping off point Teancum saw the next roof line was not flat but pitched and covered with tiles. *Go for the roof peak*, a voice in his head barked out a command as Teancum took his next mighty leap. Flailing with his arms, Teancum tried to adjust his angle and speed mid-flight, but to no avail. He came down hard again and slightly off his target. Hitting the side of the pitched roof Teancum broke several tiles and he fell onto his side, striking his ribs on the roof's peak.

A blinding pain shot through his body and he was sure he just cracked some of his ribs. Gasping for air, Teancum jumped to his feet and forced his body to keep moving. Teancum looked ahead of him and saw there was only one more roof to go before he came to a crossstreet. *One more roof to go, I can see the runner better from that roof*, he thought to himself as he winced from the pain in his ribcage. Holding his left side, Teancum ran along the top of the pitched roof and with all the strength he possessed and lept onto the flat roof of the last building. Not as graceful as the first tumble, Teancum landed, rolled up and jumped to his feet. Gasping through the pain for air, Teancum looked down and saw the messenger turn down a side street.

No choice now, he thought as he quickly scanned the area below him to find the quickest way down to street level and continue the foot pursuit. He saw near the front of the roof he was on there was a trellis with a pulley and rope system attached to it. Moving quickly, Teancum went to the trellis and looked over. It was of sturdy construction and designed to move heavy items to the roof. He looked around and saw construction items up on the roof with him. Teancum instantly assumed that the owners of the building must be adding a new floor to the building. Looking back down below he saw a large bucket attached to the rope and pulley. The bucket was full of rocks. *Should be enough to slow me down*, he thought as he grabbed the rope with both hands. Stepping to the edge, he looked in the direction of the messenger and caught just a glimpse of him as he disappeared around a corner. Taking a deep breath, and holding fast to the rope, Teancum stepped off the edge.

Just as Teancum was stepping off the edge, two Lamanite soldiers came around the corner and were standing right where he was going to land. As the bucket full of rocks came off the ground and shot upwards past them, the two startled Lamanites looked up to see where the bucket was going. The pulley did its job very well, and Teancum was quickly on the ground in a matter of seconds. But as he landed, he was now standing face-to-face with two startled and confused Lamanites.

"Hello, there." Teancum said in a friendly voice and let go of the rope. The old large metal pulley screeched as the free-falling weight of the large bucket of rocks strained it almost to the breaking point. Both Lamanites looked up at the sound of the pulley but it was too late for the one on the left. He was crushed by the large bucket, killing him instantly. The second Lamanite was in a state of confusion and shock; his buddy had just been crushed to death by a falling bucket full of rocks, and suddenly there was a Nephite standing in front of him who had appeared out of thin air. The stunned soldier looked back at Teancum in confusion. Teancum, in one fluid motion, ran past the second Lamanite and at the same time passed the sharp blade of his long knife across the exposed neck of the Lamanite. The second Lamanite dropped his spear and grasped at the fatal wound to his neck. Falling to his knees and then collapsing to the ground, he was dead before Teancum reached the corner to follow the messenger.

Teancum rounded the corner of the narrow street and could see in the distance the bright-green colored tunic of the messenger moving towards an open courtyard. At the far end of the court yard, Teancum saw the messenger run up to a large house with white pillars and two large Lamanite royal guards standing as security by the main doors. There were several torches burning brightly and illuminating the scene before him. Teancum watched as the messenger said something to the guards, who let him pass.

CHAPTER TWELVE

He must be inside that building, Teancum thought. As he looked closer, Teancum saw several more well-armed Lamanites start to assemble in the courtyard in front of the house and line up into formations. "Not that way," he whispered.

Looking for another way in, Teancum saw there were people quickly walking around on the top of the house. *A roof top garden?* Teancum wondered. He looked again. *No guards… Just servants.* Teancum scanned the buildings next to the house and saw one of the buildings was much taller than the house. *I can see much better from up there.* Moving back into the shadows, Teancum worked his way around to the back of the buildings, and past several more Lamanites running in the street as he tried to find a way up to the rooftop. Teancum was moving through the alleyway behind the tall building when he heard Lamanites coming his way. He thought he was trapped, but found an unlocked door at the rear of the taller building and quickly stepped inside.

When he closed the door he discovered he was standing in the kitchen of a Nephite family's home, and he was not alone. Sitting around a small table in the dim light of one candle was a mother and some small children. They were doing their best to survive the Lamanite occupation, and not knowing what to think about a strange cloaked man in their home, they all had fear in their eyes. "Shhh," Teancum put his finger to his lips to tell them to stay quiet. He listened as the Lamanites walked past the door. Waiting for several seconds he turned to the mother and spoke. "I am one of the Ghost Soldiers, I serve General Moroni and I am here to help free you from the Lamanites." Frozen in fear, the mother did not move. He continued. "I have a task to perform, and I need to get to the top of the building." He pointed up as he spoke. The mother sat motionless while looking at Teancum. Then she slowly turned to face her oldest son who was maybe ten years old. They made eye contact and she nodded at him. The boy got up and grabbed Teancum by the hand. "Come with me." He said quietly.

Teancum was led out of the kitchen and to the heavy cloth covering the inner doorway of their simple home. The boy pushed the tarp aside and motioned for Teancum to follow him. Teancum followed him out and found he was standing in an open courtyard in the middle of the building. This was a large living complex with an open area in the middle. The boy pointed to a set of wooden switchback stairs leading to the rooftop. Teancum rubbed the boys head and said, "Well done." The boy smiled and ran back inside to be with his mother. All the residents of the city could hear the clanking of the alarm and the Lamanite soldiers running around. They knew something was happening outside, and every noncombatant was hiding out of fear. And rightly so, they knew that not all Lamanites were evil or a vengeful people. But the Lamanite leaders were and would stop at nothing to find an assassin, including harming women and children.

Teancum could see the faces of several frightened Nephite men peeking out from behind their cloth door coverings. When he looked in their direction, they all cowered back inside and closed the covering behind them. He shook his head when he thought about how many civilians there were inside the city. *Why do you not fight for your own freedom? What a help it would be for Moroni if the men still in the city would fight back!*

"If there are any warriors among you, now is the time to rise up." Teancum challenged them angrily. So many brave men had already died for their freedom and still they cowered and let others die for them.

Teancum did not have time to rally the civilians and form a militia. Although no one in all of the Nephite army was better equipped to do so, he needed to accomplish his objective first. The death of the evil king would do far greater damage to the Lamanite army. Adjusting his backpack, Teancum moved to the stairs and carefully started to ascend up the few levels to the rooftop. When he was about halfway up he noticed the clanking of the alarm had stopped. He paused and wondered why it had stopped. "That could be either good or bad news." He thought to himself and continued to climb.

Teancum reached the top of the stairs and stepped onto the roof. The moon was in its fullness and peeking out from behind fluffy clouds. Up here, he could feel the night breeze and smell the fresh air; he took a moment to be still and take in the air. He could hear the sounds of many more Lamanites running through the streets. His left side was starting to cause him serious pain and it was hard for him to breathe deeply or raise up his left arm. "Blasted ribs." He lamented rubbing his side and moving towards the edge of the roof. He got down on his belly and gently crawled the last few feet, slowly easing his head up and over the tip of the roof to get a better look at the garden top of the house below him. It looked like it was clear of people, but he could hear voices shouting from inside the house. He could hear the words 'king' and 'Nephites' over the

CHAPTER TWELVE

rest of the clatter but that was all.

"This has to be the place." Teancum said to himself. "Now, how am I going to get over there?" He still had his strong rope diagonally wrapped around his chest and his climbing hook in his pack. Judging the distance, Teancum felt he had enough rope to span the gap between the two buildings. He started to remove his pack when a voice called out from behind him.

"You! Don't move!"

Teancum slowly turned his head and looked behind him. There, standing not far away, were three Lamanites. It was one of the Lamanites who worked for the commander of the night watch, and two of his assistants. One was holding the small boy who showed Teancum the stairs. He had the boy by the arm and was holding a knife to his side. The boy had a swollen eye and blood running down his lip. The second assistant was a smaller Lamanite, but he had the boy's mother on her knees in front of him and was holding her by her long brown hair. She was crying and begging them to let her son go. "I'm sorry, they had my son." She cried out to Teancum.

"Shut your mouth!" The smaller Lamanite spoke and slapped the side of her face with his palm.

"You, Ghost Soldier." The leader pointed again at Teancum with his spear. "Drop the pack and your blades… Slowly rise to your feet."

Teancum held up his hands to make them think he meant no harm. Teancum knew the difference between a brave man and one who talked tough. This Lamanite was afraid of Teancum but was not going to show it. "Okay, fellas… Don't need to hurt the woman or the boy." Teancum rolled slowly to his back and sat up. He slipped off his pack and looked at the leader with his hands out and raised up his eyebrows. He now had his first good look at the three Lamanites before him.

"The blades… Nice and slow." The Lamanite leader commanded. Teancum could sense a hint of fear in the inflection of his voice. Looking closer into his eyes Teancum saw the answer he was looking for. *Not a real warrior.*

Teancum smiled. "Gentlemen, there must be some misunderstanding." Teancum stood up with his hand out in front of him and took three steps forward.

"Your blades!" The man with the spear shouted nervously and jabbed the air in front of Teancum. Teancum seized the moment and moving with the speed and expertise that one would come to expect from the Ghost Soldier, grabbed the wooden shaft of the spear just below the metal tip with his left hand and pulled hard. The Lamanite soldier was caught off balance and came forward with his spear. Teancum violently snap-kicked the soldier's right knee, bending it backwards ninety degrees, demolishing every ligament and tendon holding the top of the leg to the bottom. In agony, the leader of the soldiers let go of the spear and grasped for his shattered knee.

Spinning around to his right, Teancum took the stolen Lamanite spear and thrusted it into the man holding the boy, piercing his chest cavity and lodging the sharp metal tip into his heart. Teancum used his momentum and forced the man backwards with the spear shaft, causing him to let go of the boy. Teancum jerked back on the spear and it dislodged from the Lamanite soldier. He was dead on his feet and fell backwards when the spear came out. Teancum turned to face the little Lamanite who was holding the woman by her hair.

There was terrible fear in the man's eyes. When he saw what Teancum did, and how quickly and efficiently he killed his friends, he started to back up towards the stairwell, pulling the woman with him by her hair. Teancum took two steps forward then realized the leader was trying to get up on his one good leg and call for help. Teancum turned around and with a mighty push, drove the spear almost completely through the injured Lamanite. Letting go of the spear, Teancum drew out his long knife and turned back around to face the last enemy soldier. He had dragged the woman back to the stairs and was standing close to the rail separating the stairs from a long drop to the bottom. As Teancum approached him he saw the woman's expression had changed. She was no longer crying, but had a look of deadly determination on her face. Her eyes were fixed, her jaw was clinched and the expression on her face conveyed absolute hatred.

"Back, or she goes over the edge!" The small Lamanite shouted.

What the Lamanite did not realize was that the woman had repositioned herself and was now crouching like a tiger waiting to strike. Teancum saw it and paused for half a step. The woman made eye contact with Teancum and smiled a devilish smile. Then, with the force only a mother protecting her young could muster, she brought her left elbow up and struck her captor right under his chin. His head snapped back in an explosion of blood and skin. The sound of his jaw bone breaking could be

CHAPTER TWELVE

heard from ten feet away. With blinding pain shooting across his face, he let go of the hold he had on her hair and started to back away, grasping his damaged face and jaw. The woman knew Teancum would finish the job, and she rolled to her left to get out of his way. Teancum reacted and in four steps was at full speed. Jumping sideways into the air, Teancum hit the soldier square in his chest with both of his feet knocking him over the stair rail and plummeting to his death. Teancum was up on his feet in a flash checking his surroundings for any remaining soldiers he had not see. When he was satisfied hey were all safe he moved to help the woman to her feet.

"Are you okay?" He asked. She looked up at him as he extended his hand to help her. As he looked into her eyes, he was overcome by her natural beauty. He was uncharacteristically at a loss for words as he helped her to her feet and they stood face to face. Her long brown hair was gently moving in the evening breeze, and her deep blue eyes danced in his mind like the full moon's light on the oceans waves. She had the will and courage to fight back. Teancum was instantly smitten.

"I'm fine, thank you sir." She spoke at barely a whisper. Teancum was love-struck and focused on her full lips as she spoke. There was awkward silence.

"Mom!" The boy shouted. It broke Teancum out of his trance and he took a step back. He could tell the woman did not want him to move away. Her heart was still beating rapidly from the near-death encounter and this hero who saved her. The young child ran up and hugged his mother around her waist.

"I am fine, are you hurt?" She quickly inspected the injuries to her child's face. He shook his head and lowered his eyes.

"I'm sorry, sir." The boy meekly apologized. "They said if I did not help them find you they were going to hurt my mom and sisters."

"It's okay, lad." Teancum reassured the boy as he shook his head trying to snap out of his love spell. "Take your mother back inside and be on guard. General Moroni and his men are outside the gates and coming to rescue the city. Stay inside until its safe." He instructed as he escorted them to the stairs. "I have work to do." He finished as he gently let go of her arm.

She took two steps down the stairs and turned to look back up at Teancum. Brushing her hair out her face she spoke "My name is Diana." She smiled at him and his heart beat a song of love for the first time since his wife died.

"Diana." He mouthed the word with gentle care.

It was as if time had stood still as they looked at each other. Nothing else needed to be said. It was love and they both felt it. They understood the feelings flowing between them. They both wanted to stay in the moment, but the sounds of battle finally came crashing through. He had a job to do and she needed to care for and protect her children. She smiled again and turned to leave.

In this moment, Teancum wanted nothing more to do with fighting or this war. He only wanted to hold Diana in his arms and be a simple ordinary man again. He watched as Diana and her son quickly descended the stairs, careful not to make a sound. About halfway down she stopped and looked back up the stairwell and smiled at Teancum. His heart fluttered at the sight of her smile and bright eyes.

When she reached the bottom, Diana's maternal instincts kicked in and she clasped the boys head and pulled him close to her, she covered his eyes with her hand as they walked around the dead body of the Lamanite Teancum knocked over the railing. Teancum felt sympathy and warmth overwhelm him as he watched this simple act of motherly love and protection. The boy and his siblings had already been through so much. But still she tried to shield them from the horror and reality of war and what evil men can do.

The two reached the door way of their simple dwelling and she pulled the heavy tarp away from the opening and let the boy enter first. Diana started to enter after him but she paused in the door way. Teancum watched as she placed her right hand on the door frame. It looked like she was going to turn around again. Teancum held his breath waiting for her to look again in his direction. For him, it would be a visual acknowledgement of the feelings between them. But she did not move. Instead she stood still for several seconds facing into her home, her back to Teancum. Teancum could see her body rising and falling with every breath. He could almost feel the conflict playing in her mind. *Who is this man? Can I trust him? What will become of us after this war is over?* Teancum wanted to call out to her. He wanted to run down the stairs and take her into his strong arms. He wanted to hold her, brush her hair from her face, smell the flower sent on her skin, dry her tears and kiss her soft lips. He wanted to tell her as long as there was breath in his lungs, she and her children would be safe from all harm. He yearned to tell her he

CHAPTER TWELVE

was done with fighting and war. He was done with all of this madness. For her love, he was willing to stop being the Ghost Soldier and just be her companion.

The light of humanity in his eyes, which had been gone for so long, suddenly broke through like the sun bursting through dark storm clouds. Subconsciously he cried out and gripped the railing tight as he leaned over to try to get closer to her. There was a softness to his face and his shoulders relaxed. He felt emotions again which had long been forgotten and driven from his mind by pain and war. Emotions which he did not even dare consider might be a part of his life again. But as he stood there, looking down over the railing and hoping she would turn and look at him, he was forced to realize the ugly truth. He was the Ghost Soldier, and there was a war to be fought. He thought of the marks on the boy's face and the image of the smaller Lamanite holding her by the hair.

You are dangerous. Your presence here is a threat to her and the children, his dark thoughts reminded him. *What is the task you have accepted? What is the life you live now?* He was on a mission to find and kill the leader of the enemy army. He was an assassin. The hardness crept back into his heart. The storm clouds which had parted to let the healing light shine through were now reforming and calling up the rage within. The hope that was filling his eyes and his soul was receding. He was the Ghost Soldier, and he was the only one who could win this war with one mighty stroke. His face went taunt and the look of a hunter returned.

"She is not going to look back." He whispered to himself. "She knows who you are and what you do." He slowly pushed away from the railing. Taking two steps back he took a deep breath and wiped the tear from his eye. "It was not meant to be." He whispered. "Maybe when this is all over… I will come back." He felt so old, and so tired. The pain in his side returned. His heart was broken all over again and he struggled to push the ache back down, deep inside of him. Exchanging the sorrow in his heart for righteous indignation, Teancum refocused on the task at hand; finding a way to cross the span between the two buildings and assassinate the evil king. *This madness ends tonight.*

Diana did finally turn around and look back up the stairwell, but the man who saved her was gone.

Teancum worked his way back to the far edge of the building's roof and picked up his strong rope. Judging the distance between the building he was standing on and the one next to him, where he thought the king was staying, he determined he had more than enough rope to cover the span. The building across from him was not as tall as the one he was standing on and Teancum smiled. *Climbing down a rope is easier than climbing up.*

Checking to ensure there were no Lamanites standing in the alley between the two buildings and no Lamanites on the opposite roof, Teancum cast the rope, with the climbing hook attached, across the span towards the corner of the other roof line. Teancum aimed for the corner of a small retaining wall built around the garden area of the roof. The climbing hook landed exactly where Teancum aimed and two of its hooks grabbed into the wall, tightly securing it in place. Teancum then gave it a strong tug to drive the hooks deeper into the wall, much like a fisherman giving his fishing pole a quick jerk to secure the line. Satisfied the hook was secure, Teancum found a secure anchor point on the roof where he was standing and pulled the rope tight. Securing it with a trusted knot, Teancum tested the tautness of the line by plucking it like the string of an instrument. Satisfied the rope was secure, Teancum moved to the edge and eased himself out onto the rope. Hanging upside down and going head first out onto the rope, Teancum wrapped both of his knees over the top of the rope and propelled his movement across the rope by pulling hand over hand as his weight was supported by his legs.

About halfway across he started to feel the friction burn through his leather leggings, and the pain from his injured ribs was starting to effect his grip. Teancum paused to readjust his position on the rope and suddenly lost his grip on the rope with his left hand. The sudden and drastic change in his balance caused his legs to come off the rope. Teancum was now dangling precariously from his right hand high over the alley floor below desperately clinging to the rope. The pain from his injured ribs and the strain this put on his right arm was almost overpowering. Teancum struggled to regain a grasp of the rope with his left hand. A chill of sheer panic flashed through his mind as Teancum imagined himself falling to his death, and Diana and her children standing over his body crying. Refusing to succumb to the panic and thoughts of falling, Teancum summoned his inner strength and with one final effort, regained his two-handed grip and strained with his might as he pulled his legs back up and over the rope.

CHAPTER TWELVE

The night watch commander was standing over the body of the Lamanite Teancum pushed over the railing. He could see the blood from the fatal injury was still fresh. Reaching down he touched the dead man's chest. "He is still warm to the touch." He whispered out loud. " This just happened." He had been hot on Teancum's trail since the bodies were found on the catwalk. Between tracking the foot prints on the ground and following the path of dead Lamanites left in his wake, the massive Lamanite figured out where Teancum was going and now he was searching every building in the area of the great hall and the king's bed.

Looking up the switchback stairway leading to the roof, he stood and shouted as he pointed. "You two, question those people who live here. Find out how this happened. The rest of you with me!" Pulling out his curved sword, the large Lamanite commander moved to the stairs and started climing. He was moving much faster than his assistants and when he reached the roof top he was alone for a few seconds. With his sword out in front of him, the night watch commander quickly spun around checking every angle to see if the assassin he was hunting was still up there.

What he did find were the bodies of two more of his soldiers lying on the ground in pools of their own blood. The other Lamanites caught up and breathlessly moved up next to him. Pointing with his sword he barked, "Check them," as he gestured to the two fallen men before him. The other Lamanites moved around his hulking frame, and the commander walked in a semi-circle trying to make sense of what happened on the roof.

"They're both dead, sir," one of his men answered matter-of-factly.

The night watch commander stopped and was lost in thought as he stared at the two dead bodies when he heard the slight sound of a creaking rope coming from behind him. He furrowed his brow as he considered what might be making the noise. Turning around he started walking to the edge of the building. But before he reached the edge, he found a length of rope tied off and creaking under the weight of something. Following the rope with his eyes he saw it led out over the edge of the building. "I have you now." He muttered under his breath as he smiled and moved to the edge to see what was on the other end of the taunt rope. As he reached the edge and looked over, he saw Teancum reach the opposite building and pull himself up onto the ledge.

"Assassin!" The tall Lamanite yelled out as he raised his sword swiping at the rope, but it was too late. Teancum was off the rope and safely on the roof of the next building. The rope fell to the side of the building and Teancum, who was still on one knee, looked back over his shoulder at his pursuer on the far roof. They made eye contact in the moon's light and Teancum could see pure hatred in the Lamanite's eyes. Teancum gave him a quick smirk and a wave as if to say, 'Better luck next time.' Then he quickly dove for cover behind the retaining wall as two of the night watch commander's assistants came running up with their short bows and fired at him.

The arrows barely missed Teancum and glanced off the brick wall, falling down into the alley below. Teancum rolled three times on his side and popped back up on to his knees. Only his upper chest and head was exposed over the retaining wall, and in his hands he had his poison blow dart already loaded. He had spent years perfecting this move, and he had used it in the past with much success. Aiming for the closest archer, Teancum let the poison-tipped dart fly. It struck the hapless Lamanite archer in the left thigh and almost instantly the poison took effect. The Lamanite cried out in agony as the intense burning from the poison spread across his body. Shaking and jerking, the Lamanite dropped his bow and fell to the ground in agony. The other Lamanite standing next to the commander looked at his suffering comrade then back at Teancum.

Teancum did not have time to reload a second dart, but instead put the thin blowtube to his mouth and acted like he was sending a second dart towards them. Instinctively, every Lamanite including the mighty commander dove out of the way or dropped flat to the ground to avoid getting hit by Teancum's deadly dart. When Teancum saw every man panic and dive for cover he smiled. "Works every time," he whispered as he stowed his blowgun and moved low behind the wall, past the rooftop garden and to the door which hopefully would lead to the evil king.

After several seconds the big commander peered quickly over the edge to see if Teancum was still there. Realizing he had been duped, he cursed himself and those around him. "He is going for the king!" He shouted as he jumped up and made his way to the stairs, his dark cloak flapping as he ran. "With me, men!"

CHAPTER TWELVE

Diana was holding her children in her arms and huddling under the table. They heard the Lamanites questioning the others who lived in the building about the dead soldier at the bottom of the stairs, and knew it was only a matter of time before they were found out. She knew they were coming for her, but there was no escape. The alley was filling up with soldiers and the courtyard was guarded. The torches cast shadows, the heavy boots rang out and shouts of commands were heard as unknown persons passed back and forth across the dark tarp covering the entrance to their humble home. Diana closed her eyes and said a silent prayer for her family as she pulled them even closer to her. In the distance she heard a man screaming, and then several others coming down the stairs. More shouting for the men to follow someone then haunting silence. She held her breath, waiting for the moment to come when the Lamanites would burst in and seize her. Seconds past, then a minute, then several… Nothing, just silence.

Teancum made it to the door leading downstairs before the Lamanites on the far building could see where he moved to. He was checking the handle to see if the door was unlocked when he heard commotion coming from the other side of the door and the locks being undone. Then a voice rang out.

"Hurry men, to the roof!"

Teancum quickly stepped to one side of the door and pressed himself up against the wall under a shadow cast by the torch light. He was an expert at not being seen, and with his uniquely-colored cloak covering his face and body, Teancum became the shadow itself, his long knife at the ready. The door flung open and three royal guards in their red sashes and armor came bursting through the opening and stood with their weapons at the ready just feet from the door. They were too excited and preoccupied to notice Teancum standing right behind them against the wall.

"I heard shouting up here." One of them spoke as they all looked around.

"What is happening?" One of the guards asked the man who appeared to be in charge.

"That is not your concern, soldier. Your job is to guard the king." The leader gave the concerned soldier a stern look. "Now, you two sweep the roof top and check for intruders." He pointed with his sword in the direction he wanted the two Lamanites to look. The three of them stepped towards the center of the roof top garden checking around large pots and under tables as they went. Teancum held his breath and waited for one of them to turn around and see him, but it did not happen. By some stroke of luck they did not check behind them as they entered. When the three guards were far enough away from the door, Teancum moved very carefully and quietly towards the opening. To keep the guards from following after him, Teancum carefully and quietly shut the door and engaged the locks from the inside.

Knowing he did not have much time before the guards realized the door was shut and locked, he quickly made his way down the flight of stairs to the next level in the building. Reaching the bottom and moving through the shadows of the candle's light, he peeked around a corner and saw he was standing in the entrance of a large room. There were several Lamanites quickly packing large trunks and moving items downstairs. It looked like they were moving all the stolen items of value the army had looted from the people of the city down to several wagons waiting for them outside. It was chaos and everyone looked scared and was moving with a sense of purpose.

How am I going to get past all of them? Teancum thought as he scanned the area in front of him of some. *And where is the king?*

After several moments, the guards on the roof realized what had happened and were now banging on the roof door, trying to break it down. Teancum was now trapped between the guards in the great hall and those on the roof trying to come back down. He could hear the guards on the roof banging on the doors, and it was only a matter of time before the others realized where the banging noise was coming from.

From his hidden vantage point, Teancum looked again at those working in the hall packing and moving the boxes and trunks of stolen property downstairs. They all looked panicked and hyper-focused on the task at hand. Realizing his only way of surviving and finding the king was to get past these people, Teancum grabbed two small boxes next to the hallway where he was standing. Holding one box on each shoulder, Teancum hid his face between them and walked past the workers and soldiers and towards the exit like he was one of the workers and belonged there. So many people were coming and going from the large hall, laborers moving heavy items, soldiers running back and

CHAPTER TWELVE

forth, women crying, people yelling orders and pointing, others closing lids and building boxes by banging on nails with hammers that the disorganization around him was acting like a kind of camouflage.

Teancum calmly moved past all of them without one person giving him a second look. He was almost through the exit when the young Lamanite with the bright-colored coat came running past him and bumped against him shouting, "Out of my way!" To retain the illusion he was a humble worker, Teancum bowed and moved out of the doorway as two escort guards followed the Lamanite messenger into the great hall.

"The king, where is he?" The messenger asked an older looking Lamanite who was explaining to some workers which boxes to pack and which to leave behind.

"He is in there, and he is drunk again." The older man said in disgust and pointed to a closed door along the far wall. There were two royal guards standing on either side of the doorframe.

The messenger moved to the door and Teancum saw him speak to one of the guards. Teancum could not tell what was being said, but he did see the guard hold up his hand as if to tell the young Lamanite to wait there. The guard knocked on the door, waited several seconds then allowed the messenger to walk in to the room. Teancum felt a rush of emotion as he thought about the next few seconds of his life. Could he make it all the way across the room and past those two guards? He did the calculations in his mind as he stood still and waited. Would the king walk right past him on his way out the hall? How long would he be able to wait by the door, in his hasty disguise, before someone realized he was a well-armed Nephite there to assassinate their leader? As questions of doubt raced across his mind, he saw the three royal Lamanite guards who were trapped on the roof come bursting through the far entrance. They looked angry, well-armed and determined to find who ever locked them up on the roof.

"Not good." Teancum whispered as he lowered his head and tried to avoid eye contact and blend in the best he could with the other workers. He knew now the chance to kill the king had passed. With the two boxes still against his head hiding his identity, he was trying to get out the door and down to the courtyard with the other laborers.

"Halt!" A commanding voice shouted above the noise and confusion in the hall. Everyone stopped what they were doing and held perfectly still. Teancum knew his little ruse had failed and he was discovered. He closed his eyes and prayed quickly to the God of Heaven that he would live his last few moments well. Still holding the boxes on his shoulders, he slowly turned around to face his enemy and ready himself for a fight. But to his surprise, no one was looking at him. Everyone in the large room was looking at the door where the king was located. It was open now and two more guards had exited. An older Lamanite man followed the guards out with the young messenger close on his heels.

"Make way for the king!" The older man shouted as he waved his hands to signal for those in front of him to move out of the way. Several people moved and created a path through the great room for the king to walk unimpeded to the door where Teancum was standing. Teancum was stunned. The evil Lamanite king, the one person who controlled the fate of this war, the single soul Teancum was trying to send directly to hell itself was going to be walking right towards him.

Could this be a trap? Teancum thought. *No, they would have been on you long before this if they knew you were in the building.* Then he remembered there were people who knew he was in the building— the large, dark cloaked Lamanite from the opposite roof top and those three guards who he locked out on the garden. He looked across the way and saw the leader of the guards he locked out trying to make his way to the older Lamanite man who told everyone to make way. Teancum instantly knew what the guard was going to say to the old man. *He is going to tell that guy that there is an intruder loose in the building. They will double the guards around the king and start roving patrols.* Teancum had to act fast.

Everyone had their backs turned to Teancum and were facing the door waiting for the king to appear. Teancum slowly knelt down, out of eye shot from the rest of the people in the room, and loaded his blow gun with a fresh poison dart. He knew he had only one chance at this, and the timing needed to be perfect. There was a small break in the crowd of people and Teancum readied himself for the exact moment the warning guard would pass by it. Taking a deep breath Teancum held it until the Lamanite guard's leg came into view. Blowing hard and fast he sent the small dart sailing through the air. Passing through the natural opening created by the throng of Lamanites, the dart flew and struck the guard in his calf muscle. The guard felt the dart stick to his skin and he swiped at the dart thinking it might be a bug bite. In two more steps, the guard started to lose his balance and wobble while he walked. In two more steps, the guard fell to his knees and was dead when his head hit the

CHAPTER TWELVE

floor. His body twitched violently and foam came from his mouth.

There was a collective gasp as those around the guard moved back and out of the way. At the same moment the guard fell from the poison, King Ammoron appeared in the doorway from his private room. Everyone was so preoccupied with the large royal guard foaming and jerking on the floor, they did not see the king walk into the room. But Teancum did.

Ammoron, the Zoramite king, was too far away for Teancum to strike with his knife and he only had a few seconds before the rest of the Lamanites would realize he was there. Looking left and then right, Teancum saw what he needed leaning against the wall not far from the door he had tried to walk out of.

It was a lone spear. Not a fine and well-made steel weapon like the one he used to kill Ammoron's sleeping brother those many months ago; this one was a plain wooden spear with a thin strap of leather wrapped around it for a handhold. *Someone's personal weapon,* Teancum thought as he reached for it. Teancum took the long shaft in his hand and turned to look at his target. Teancum felt the weight of the spear in his hand as he moved to an open spot in the crowd. *The balance is good and the tip is sharp...*

"There you are." Teancum mouthed as he stepped around a gawking woman who had her hands up to her mouth and was gasping while looking at the dead royal guard on the ground before her. Ammoron was taken back by the fact no one acknowledged him as he stepped out into the open of the great room. He was still drunk and had one arm wrapped around a crying Nephite woman while the other held a large goblet containing wine. He was looking around the room and getting ready to shout his contempt when he saw Teancum step out from behind a group of Lamanites.

Ammoron was first and foremost a Zoramite warrior, so when he saw a Nephite holding a weapon he knew right away Teancum was there to assassinate him. But his motor skills were impaired and his decision-making abilities were severally impaired by his drunkenness. With the combination of alcohol and the sudden rush of adrenaline, Ammoron could not make the words come out to warn his loyal guards. All the false king could do was muddle some unrecognizable grunts and try to point at Teancum. At the same time he was spilling his wine and struggling to get his arm off the crying girl.

Just like he was taught as a boy by the finest combat instructors his

The Predator Finds His Prey

grandfather Pilio's money could buy, Teancum lifted his weapon in his right hand and held it parallel to the ground and level with his eye. After cocking back his right arm, he held out his left arm to aim the spear right at Ammoron's chest. Ammoron gasped and tried to move the young woman in front of him as a shield. She tripped over her own feet and fell forward as Teancum let fly the wooden shaft. Straight and true, the weapon flew across the room unnoticed by everyone but the king, cutting through the early morning air like a silent lightning bolt. It struck Ammoron just to the right of the center of his chest, missing his heart but puncturing his lung and severing a large vein. Dropping the goblet on the floor and stumbling backwards, Ammoron cried out in lethal pain. The sound of the spear striking Ammoron and his gasp of pain caused everyone in the room to turn and look at him.

This was the break Teancum needed and, as carefully as he could, he made his way to the exit trying desperately not to draw attention to himself. There were shouts and screams as the people in the room saw the deadly weapon protruding from Ammoron's chest and suddenly realized their king had been attacked. Ammoron was staggering and quickly losing the fight for his life. It was only a matter of moments before he died, and with his final desperate gesture, he pointed towards Teancum and cried out, "Assassin!"

Teancum had reached the threshold of the exit door when he heard that word. He instantly knew his fate had been sealed. He stopped, took a deep breath and turned to look behind him at the large gathering of soldiers and servants still in the great room. Some were standing around the fallen royal guard, and others had moved over to the king. But all of them were looking at Teancum now. They all saw his face and everyone knew what he had done. Teancum knew there was nothing else he could do now but run as fast as he could. With a bit of sarcasm he smiled and gave a nod and salute. "Well..." He said and winked. Then he turned and ran through the door with every armed Lamanite hot on his heels.

Down the hallway and to the stairs he fled, blowing past confused onlookers along the way. The gaggle of Lamanites made it to the doorway of the great hall and shouted warnings over each other as they ran after Teancum. Teancum made it to the marble stairs and started down, clearing several steps at a time. He made it to the first switch back landing and paused for one second as he reached for a small pouch tied to the back of his equipment belt.

CHAPTER TWELVE

He continued to move down the flights of stairs while he emptied the contents of the leather bag on the steps behind him. Inside the bag were dozens of very small multi-pointed metal spikes. As he spilled them behind him, they laid a painful trap for the pursuing Lamanites as they scattered across the hard marble surface. He had almost reached the bottom of the stairs when Teancum saw that all the noise and commotion had aroused the attention of the guards at the front door. Several of them had entered the reception area and were looking around for the cause of the shouting when he reached the bottom of the stairs. Teancum knew he did not want to stop and fight the guards and he needed a quick distraction.

At that moment the first of the Lamanites chasing him down the stairs reached the section of steps covered with the small spikes. Teancum heard at least three different men cry out in pain as they stepped down hard on the spikes, driving them deep into the flesh of the bottom of their feet. "Up there, they have an assassin cornered!" Teancum shouted at the unsuspecting guards near the front door while pointing towards the staircase. Reacting on pure instinct, the guards rushed past Teancum and up the stairs hoping to get a crack at the unseen assassin. Teancum stood still for a second and blinked several times with a bit of a smirk on his face. Even he was surprised at how easy that was. Several more Lamanites entered the great building and Teancum again pointed up the stairs. The soldiers saw the royal guards running up the stairs with their weapons drawn and they instinctively followed. *I guess they think I am a slave and I dont want any trouble.*

Smiling to himself, Teancum walked towards the front doors and exited onto the large porch. His survival instincts suddenly took control of his body and Teancum ducked and rolled onto his shoulder before he even realized there was a threat. The big sword belonging to the night watch commander passed merely a few inches over Teancum's head. The big Lamanite saw Teancum coming out of the building and attacked without warning. Fortunately for Teancum, his reflexes were honed to perfection and he rolled up to his feet away from the attack. Without looking back, he was at a dead run in only two steps and heading for the side of the building, with several more Lamanites in hot pursuit. Hurdling over the railing, Teancum landed hard on the cobbled street in front of the grand building and ran blindly in the direction of the main gate. The large Lamanite stopped at the railing from the elevated porch and watched as Teancum moved with the grace of a jungle cat killing two more Lamanite soldiers as he ran.

"That way! Bring him to me alive!" He shouted to his men as they all took off after Teancum in a grand foot chase. "Impressive." He whispered. He watched as Teancum rounded a corner and moved out of sight. "My horse!" He shouted. The night watch commander knew his minions would chase after him and keep Teancum in sight. All he needed to do was ride up behind and finish this once and for all. The Lamanite war captain mounted his horse and galloped off in the direction of his pursuing men.

CHAPTER THIRTEEN

The Hunter is Now Hunted

Teancum ran hard, and tried to change direction as often as he could to try to confuse the Lamanites who were chasing after him. He knew that if he caused enough chaos, he might be able to give them the slip. As he ran he would try to spill items in the streets or get animals to wander across their path. Around one corner he even grabbed a lit torch and tossed it into the bed of a wagon full of hay, starting a large fire and spooking the poor horse that was tied to the wagon. The horse reared up and pulled the burning pile of hay down the street causing several of the Lamanites to jump out of the way. But everything he tried did not seem to help. The farther he ran, the more Lamanites would join the chase.

There was a new enemy effecting Teancum's abilities now, fatigue. He hd not slept more then a few hours or had a decent meal in days. He could feel his body reacting to the stress he was putting it under. Breathing became harder, there were pains in his joints and the injury to his side was causing him to run with his arm close to his chest for support. He knew he needed to change his tactics or he was going to be captured. At that moment he remembered the times he trained with his father-in-law, the garrison commander, during the early morning runs around Zarahemla, and the training he put his Ghost Soldiers through. "Time to give these Lamanite boys a lesson in fitness." Teancum smiled through the pain as he headed for the nearest thatched roof cottage. Climbing up the side of the low hanging roof line, Teancum made his way to the top and ran along the spine of the roof. Reaching the edge of

CHAPTER THIRTEEN

the roof, he lept with all of his might and grabbed the railing of an iron gate wrapped around a balcony. In one fluid motion he pulled himself up and over the balcony and rushed inside the small apartment.

Several of the Lamanites were hot on his tail and tried to follow. The first Lamanite was running along the thatched roof and fell through. One moment he was there and the next, he was gone. The second man missed the railing completely and fell the ten feet to the hard ground with a thud. The third Lamanite made it across and was holding onto the balcony but he lacked the upper body strength to pull himself up. The chase went on like this as Teancum made his way out of the apartment and back down to the ground floor and out a side entrance. As Teancum stepped out onto the street and tried to run in a different direction, the massive Lamanite on his horse came around the corner and saw Teancum trying to escape. Shouting out a warning, the night watch commander spurred his horse around as Teancum bolted into the alleyway. The alley was very narrow and blocked off at the far end by a locked gate. Teancum knew what to do and ran until he was almost at the gate. Not stopping his momentum, Teancum pushed off and up the alley wall with his right foot and was able to leap up and grasp the top of the gate. He pulled himself up and over the locked gate and fell to the ground on the other side. Rolling over to his side, Teancum winced in great pain as the injury to his side was getting much worse. He could taste blood in his mouth now.

"You men!" The night watch commander shouted from on top of his horse to the men around him. "Go over the wall after him!" He then pointed to the Lamanites gathering behind his horse. "You men go around and cut him off, I have had enough of this. Chase him down and capture him!"

As he was speaking, one of the Lamanite soldiers had managed to climb to the top of the locked gate and was about to peer over the edge at the side where Teancum was last seen. As he poked his head over the side, he saw Teancum at the bottom with his blow gun up to his mouth. This was the last thing the Lamanite saw before Teancum planted one of his poison darts right between the man's eyes. The poor Lamanite's body shook and jerked and he fell backwards off the wall landing dead at the feet of the other Lamanites still trying to find a way over the top.

Teancum smiled and moved towards the other end of the alleyway. "That should keep them from coming over the top." He smiled and then winced in pain as he tried to run while holding his side. As Teancum exited the alleyway, he confronted two unaware Lamanite soldiers who came to the alley opening wondering what all the commotion was. Both of them were unprepared for a conflict and Teancum made quick work of them. A third Lamanite soldier saw what was happening and came rushing to their aid. He tried to thrust his spear at Teancum, but Teancum ducked under it and stabbed the third soldier several times in rapid succession.

Teancum was hurting badly and starting to run out of energy. He needed to escape and quick. Finding a place to hide was not a option now. He had just killed a second king and the entire Lamanite army would turn this city upside down looking for him. The only way he was going to survive the night was to get back over the wall and make his way to the Nephite camp. He moved again, trying to keep to the shadows and dark corners of the city, with his cloak helping him stay hidden from view. More alarms were sounding now. He knew the word was spreading that King Ammoron was now dead, and the Nephite assassin was loose in the city. The Lamanites would show no mercy to him or any other Nephite they suspected of helping to kill their king. Then a flash of the image of Diana and her children broke across Teancum's mind. "No!" He almost shouted. He could not let them suffer the same fate poor Rachael did in the Lamanite camp after he killed Amalickiah those many months ago. *You need to draw the Lamanites towards you and away from any possible attempt to involve her in what you have done.* He scolded himself for his continued carelessness. *You are the Ghost Soldier!* He cried out in his mind. *Act like it!*

Teancum looked back at the bodies of the three Lamanites he had killed and saw one of them had a short bow and a full quiver of arrows.

He then looked down the street and saw a group of Lamanites gathering and pointing in his direction. He knew they were making plans to move towards him and search.

"Let's give them something to think about." He said in an encouraging tone. Reaching down he gathered up the bow and arrows. He put the quiver on his back and pulled out the first arrow. Nocking the arrow, he stepped out into the street and began to rapid fire arrows in the direction of the group of Lamanites as he quickly walked from one side of the wide street to the other. The first arrow struck a Lamanite in the back of the leg, just below his back side. The second arrow hit a different man in the

CHAPTER THIRTEEN

upper chest. The rest of the Lamanites were all diving for cover when the third arrow struck a soldier in the bottom of his foot and popped out the top of his foot as he jumped over a crate to hide.

"I am the Ghost Soldier!" Teancum shouted as he continued to move to the opposite side. He fired all of his arrows and dropped the weapon on the ground. Kicking in the door of the building he was standing next to, Teancum gestured for the cowering Lamanites to follow him inside.

The large war captain rode up on his horse and saw the men hiding behind cover. "Well!?" He shouted. "Go after him!"

The men all had panicked looks in their eyes. They were wondering which was worse— the possibility of facing the Ghost Soldier or disobeying the night watch commander.

Teancum entered the dimly-lit room and realized he was in some sort of kitchen. In the far corner there was a large cooking stove and a pot of steaming hot water was simmering on the top of it. *The cook must have left it there*, he thought. He had an idea and Teancum grabbed the pot of hot water. He moved back to the partially opened door he had kicked open and closed it almost all the way. Moving a sturdy box next to the door he stood up on it and placed the pot of scalding hot water on the upper edge of the door and against the trim. "Bath time." He whispered as he finished setting the trap for the first Lamanite to walk through the door. He left the trap in place and moved deeper into the building.

"I will kill the lot of you for disobeying my orders! Now get up and follow after that man. He killed your king!" The night watch commander was shouting now and waving his big cimeter around in a threatening manner. The scared Lamanites had no choice but to follow his instructions. Holding their own weapons out in front of them, they made their way to the building and the door where Teancum was last seen. "He is only one man. Now go in and bring him to me!" The big Lamanite commanded.

The lead Lamanite turned to the others standing behind him. "We go in a rush and overpower him…yes?" He asked the others. They all agreed and the lead Lamanite moved to the front of the door. He took a big breath and hit the door with his shoulder pushing it open. The pot full of scalding water tipped over and the entire contents spilled down and over the head and shoulders of the lead Lamanite. Then the pot itself bounced off the top of his head. Screaming out in pain the Lamanite grabbed for his eyes in the miliseconds it took for the water to cover him. Then he

The Hunter is Now Hunted

dropped to the floor as he was knocked unconscious from the pot. The other Lamanites all took several steps back from their comrade and tried to make sense of what had happened.

"I am the Ghost Soldier!" came echoing from deep inside the darkened building.

The night watch commander came bursting to the front of the armed Lamanites standing outside the doorway. They were all still looking down at the motionless body of their friend who had been scalded by the water trap.

"Where is he?" He bellowed at the men around him.

One of the other Lamanite soldiers pointed into the blackness of the dark building towards the last sounds Teancum made. There was fear in the Lamanite's eyes as he gestured towards the Ghost Soldier's location. Everyone looked in that general direction as the night watch commander squinted to detect any movement.

The delicate sound of rushing wind broke the tense silence. It was almost like a small bird had flown past the Lamanite men undetected and unseen. A second later the pointing man started to shout in agonizing pain. He reached for his neck with both hands, but the damage had already been done. Falling to the ground and convulsing, the poor Lamanite was the next victim of Teancum's poison darts. The quilled end of the handmade dart could be seen protruding out of the side of the man's neck and a small trace of blood drained from the hole it made in his skin.

"Back!" The big Lamanite shouted as he dove for cover behind the door frame. The rest of the Lamanites moved quickly to avoid being the next victim. "Bring torches and surround the building!" He shouted as he rolled to his side and barked commands to the rest of the Lamanites. Several more enemy soldiers had arrived and in just a few seconds they had surrounded the large building on all sides. Torches were quickly handed out and a ring of fire was created around Teancum's last known location.

Teancum had moved deep into the center of the building. It was a tall building made of stone and wood. They could not see him, but Teancum could see and hear everything going on outside. Teancum anticipated the Lamanites next move before the big Lamanite gave the command. "They are going to try to burn me out of my hiding place." He whispered to himself. He had snuck into their camp and killed their king, again. They

CHAPTER THIRTEEN

would stop at nothing to finish off the Ghost Soldier himself. Teancum quickly made an account of his situation. "Not going out there." He said to himself as he tried to move to a window and jump out. There were several well-armed Lamanites waiting for him on the other side; with more arriving by the second. Looking up the wooden stairs leading to the next few levels Teancum mouthed the one direction that was his only remaining option. "Up!"

Teancum was almost smiling as he ascended the flights of stairs and headed for the roof of the building. He was completely focused on the task at hand and in his element. "A desperate battle with the enemy advancing from all directions… I love it!"

"Burn him out!" The night watch commander bellowed as he grabbed a torch and tossed it into the open door. Several more torches followed into the dark building and the first floor was instantly lit up in flames.

Teancum reached the fourth floor landing and realized it was as high up as he could go. He could smell the smoke and see the flickering lights of a burning fire coming from down below. Casting his eyes around, he saw a ladder against the wall nearest to him and an opening in the roof. Reaching for the ladder, Teancum climbed up to the opening and onto the roof itself. Like so many others in the city, it was the flat style roof made of wood beams covered with thatch and then a layer of mud that hardened in the sun to a rock-like finish. The smoke from the fire below was starting to billow out of the first floor windows and creep up to the next few stories and out the opening Teancum had just come from. Teancum moved to the edge of the building and carefully looked over the side. He could see several more Lamanites had arrived to aid in the hunt for the king slayer. He could also see that the next building was about the same height and the rooftop was almost the same shape and style as the one he was standing on. "I can make it across if I jump." He spoke to himself. "But I will need a distraction to get them looking someplace else."

Looking around Teancum found that some of the occupants of the building had moved some tables and chairs up onto the roof and set them up in a patio-like arrangement. "Perfect." He said with a smile on his face. Moving the wooden furniture to the opposite end of the building, Teancum stacked everything he could on top of the table and then he peeked over the edge again to see if there were any Lamanites standing directly below him. To his surprise, he saw three men who were right up against the building and looking into an open window watching the flames and for any sign of the Ghost Soldier. "Sorry, guys." He whispered and pushed the table and everything on top of it over the side. The falling furniture hit without warning and crushed the three men. One was killed outright, the other two cried out in agony as their bodies were demolished from the weight of the table and chairs. Teancum stood up and cringed as he listened to the cries of pain coming from below. He then moved to the other side of the roof and looked down. The lamentations coming from the wounded Lamanites had the effect Teancum was hoping for. Those Lamanites guarding that side of the burning building had moved around to see what happened to their comrades. *It's now or never...*

Teancum took several steps back and readied himself for the sprint and jump to the other roof. Just before he stepped off he rubbed his injured ribs and made a mental note to land and roll to the other side of his body and avoid hitting that side. In three steps, Teancum was at full speed and hit the edge of the roof with his right leg. Pushing off, he used all of his strength and the momentum of his run to propel himself the several feet across the span and onto the next roof, just like he had earlier in the night. But instead of a smooth landing combined with a combat roll to soften the blow and distribute the weight, this landing was awkward and off-balanced. Teancum heard the snapping sound before he felt the pain. The large muscle in the back of his left leg felt like someone had just stabbed it with a glowing hot knife, and Teancum's body crumpled as he hit the roof with all of his weight.

The night watch commander was on his horse circling the building looking for any sign of the Ghost Soldier inside the growing inferno. As he came around the corner he watched as three of his men were crushed by the falling table. Jumping from his horse, the dark-cloaked Lamanite went to their aid and pushed the table off one of his men. As the injured men cried out in pain several more Lamanites came running up. The night watch commander recognized some of the men as those who were supposed to be standing guard on the other side of the building. "What are you doing?" He shouted to the men. "Get back to your post and watch for the Nephite!" The men, realizing the mistake they had made quickly turned and moved back to the other side of the burning building. The big

CHAPTER THIRTEEN

Lamanite looked up to the top of the building and noticed there were no windows on that side of the building except on the first floor. Then he looked again at the broken and scattered furniture all around him.

Then it came to him. "He is on the roof. But why drop this stuff on this side?" Then he remembered that the guards had left their position on the opposite side of the building to come and see what had happened to their fellow soldiers. "A distraction…" He smiled. "You are good." The night watch commander pulled out his big sword and moved quickly to the opposite side of the building. The flames coming from the structure were licking at the open air outside the doors and windows, daring anyone to come closer. The heat forced the tall Lamanite to move away from the burning building and use his war cloak to shield his face from the heat. He moved in front of the next building and looked up at the roofline. "Same height… Not too far a distance, someone could make that jump if they tried." More and more Lamanite soldiers were arriving. Most came to see what was burning, while others knew of the hunt for the king's killer and wanted to help. One of the Lamanites walked up to the commander as he was looking up at the roofline.

"Your orders, sir?" He spoke in a matter-of-fact tone.

The night watch commander turned to look at the group of assembled armed Lamanites and spoke. "He is on the roof of this building. Go up there and bring him to me alive if you can!" He pointed to the roof with his big sword as he spoke. The Lamanites became very motivated and dashed for the main doors of the building. Here was their chance to prove to everyone else how brave and dangerous they were.

The night watch commander was no fool. He knew that the Nephite Ghost Soldier was a very dangerous foe and not to be trifled with. But now, he was trapped like an animal. The big Lamanite would follow those other men into the building allowing them to encounter the assassin first. He would let them spring any traps or attack the trapped Nephite in force, then be there to clean up the mess and get the glory for killing the king slayer.

Teancum rolled to his side and grabbed the back of his leg. Letting out a muffled gasp of agony, he rocked back and forth trying to work out the pain he was feeling coming from this fresh injury. "Outstanding!" He exclaimed breathless and in complete frustration. Getting out of the city

The Hunter is Now Hunted

alive now would take every ounce of skill and determination he possessed. As he tried to stand he could hear the sounds of Lamanites shouting and climbing the stairs to reach him. "Blast... They found me!" He could still use the leg, it just hurt every time he put pressure in it. Hobbling towards the roof access Teancum drew out his long knife and readied himself for a fight. Teancum was at the opening and looking down into the bowels of the building. It was designed and built just like the other one he lept from. "Some kind of housing center." He whispered. He could see the Lamanites advancing up the stairs but they were moving slow and only one of them had a torch so their vision was limited. "Better to fight them one at a time in the dark and in the confined spaces of the stairwell then try to deal with all of them up here at one once. And I need to get out." Teancum thought as he checked his surroundings and realized he was out of options. Grabbing the ladder leading down, Teancum shimmied down as quickly and as quietly as his damaged body would allow. He reached the dark landing at the top of the stairs and moved to the far corner to hide in the shadows as much as possible. He covered his head with his cloak, held his knife out in a ready position and waited for the first Lamanite to arrive.

By his count there were at least a dozen enemy fighters coming up the stairs in single file. The first two Lamanites out-distanced the rest of the pack and reached the top landing before the rest could catch up. They were so eager to get to the roof they completely bypassed Teancum standing in the darkened corner of the landing. He was motionless and covered in his special colored cloak.

Be still, Teancum commanded his body to remain motionless as he watched the two Lamanite soldiers argue for a few seconds over who got to go up first and kill the Nephite. A quick agreement was reached and they both moved up the ladder and were out of sight. *That's two less I will need to fight.* He smiled at this small but meaningful victory. Teancum refocused on the task at hand as the Lamanite with the lit torch was coming to the landing just below him. Teancum had an idea and he reached for his bola. Pulling the three weighted stones and attaching cords out from his equipment belt, Teancum stepped away from the back wall and gave himself enough room to spin the device over his head.

He had the bola going pretty well when one of the other Lamanites spotted him and shouted out a warning, but it was too late. Teancum launched the bola at the man holding the lone torch and let it fly. The

CHAPTER THIRTEEN

bola was sent sailing through the air and it struck the man holding the torch right in his forearm. The momentum and weight of the bola pulled the man's arm close to his face bringing the torch right against his head. The bola wrapped his head and arm together and the fire from the torch set his hair ablaze. Screaming, the panicked man holding the torch spun around and tried to free his hand. The fire instantly burst across his head and the other Lamanites, not knowing what to do backed away from their comrade as he twisted and turned in agonizing pain on the small stair landing.

The flames were getting bigger as the man stumbled and fell down the unprotected stairs landing motionless one flight down. Several of the Lamanites still on the stairs behind the burning man had to jump out of the way of his falling body. When his body hit the ground, the torch and the fire in his hair were knocked out and it was completely dark again in the building. The Lamanites on the stairs who were still hunting for Teancum were now at a terrible disadvantage— they had no night vision. It would take at least twenty minutes for their eyes to properly adjust from the glow of the lit torch to the dark environment. Teancum, on the other hand was ready for a fight.

He pulled the ladder away from opening, trapping the two solders on the roof and quickly moved his way towards the first Lamanite, stabbed him in both kidneys. The man's body tensed out of sheer pain and Teancum pushed him into the next Lamanite in line. The two Lamanites collapsed under the weight of the mortally wounded man and Teancum stepped over them while stabbing the second man in the eye, killing him instantly. A shout went out from the dark as Teancum continued to work his way down the stairs killing at will those who came to defeat him. Spinning and jumping, stabbing and pushing, Teancum worked his body and the weapon he held in his hand like a finely-tuned instrument. But there was a problem. Teancum was injured and getting weaker. He had not slept properly for several days. He was starving, even before he had made the fateful choice to climb those walls and hunt the Lamanite king. His ribs were injured and he could not breathe easily. He was fighting for his life while going down stairs with only one good leg. Even with all of this against him, Teancum was still outmatching anyone who dared to challenge him. But for how much longer could he last?

Teancum fought his way past the lifeless body of the man with the burnt hair and continued to engage the Lamanites as they appeared before him. The last few Lamanites panicked because they could hear and see the dark shapeless form killing their friends at will and descending down the stairs. They ran for the main doors and out into the relative safety of the open area. The night watch commander was standing outside the doors when the other Lamanites came rushing out; running past him screaming for their lives.

"What?" He demanded.

"The Ghost Soldier... He is killing everyone!" One of the scared Lamanites shouted as he ran past the night watch commander.

"What is it?" The tall Lamanite turned to face the open door leading back into the dark building and the killer Nephite lurking inside. The sounds of death were still echoing from deep within. "He is only one man!" He reassured himself. The dark-cloaked leader felt a chill run up his spine. Fear was something he was not accustomed to feeling.

Teancum reached the bottom floor leaving a pile of dead opponents in his wake. The stairs and landings were littered with the blood and bodies of those hapless soldiers who dared to challenge the Ghost Soldier. Gasping for air and wincing in pain, Teancum tried to gulp oxygen into his burning lungs but the injury to his side was preventing him from taking a deep breath. He was also trying to hold his balance but his leg was giving out on him. Leaning against the rail post, Teancum could see out into the street where a very large contingent of Lamanites had gathered. The flames and smoke from the adjacent building were driving those enemy soldiers back and away from Teancum's location but given his physical condition, and the number of fighters outside, Teancum knew that confronting them and fighting his way out of this was not going to succeed.

Looking around he spied an open window near the back of the building. Limping, Teancum moved to see if there were any Lamanites guarding that opening. He carefully peeked out and found that he was in luck. He was starting to bring his leg up and into the frame of the window when the first loud popping sounds came from the building next door. The fire had been burning out of control and the large wooden supports holding the entire structure in place were starting to give way. Someone standing outside shouted, "It's going to cave in!" And every Lamanite moved away from the flames. Teancum heard the shouts and

CHAPTER THIRTEEN

hustled to get clear of the window. He did not want to be anywhere near the burning building when it came down.

The big Lamanite commander was standing far away from the flames and watched as the roof of the burning building came crashing down the center of the building crushing every floor in its path. When the mass of burning timbers and support material hit the ground floor everything exploded in a ball of burning embers and thick smoke. The ground shook as people ran for cover or turned and shielded their eyes and faces from the heat and flying debris. Teancum, never one to pass up a good opportunity to disappear right under the noses of his enemy, took advantage of the chaos of the collapsing building and walked right past the very men trying to flush him out. With his head covered by his cloak and keeping his eyes down to avoid making contact, Teancum limped as he blended in with the crowd and moved to the next alleyway undetected; or so he thought.

The Lamanite with the dark cloak was looking around and taking account of the madness before him when something caught his eye. A man, covered in a cloak, was walking away from the flames. He was walking with a bit of a limp and was not in much of a hurry. The unknown man also did not seem to be that interested in the events happening around him. He kept walking with his head down, towards the darkened shadows of the next alley. The hulking Lamanite crinkled his brow and thought for a second. He then looked at the burning remains of the building, then at the bodies still lying outside the next building. Like a clap of lightning, it came to him. "The Ghost Soldier! He is trying to escape!" Pointing with his sword, he shouted, "Assassin!"

That was Teancum's cue to start running. With his injured leg he was not going to get very far but he had to try. Down the dark alley he went, hugging the sides to avoid exposing himself out in the open. The big Lamanite pushed several soldiers towards the alley and commanded them to give chase. The first two Lamanites came around the corner and stood in the entrance of the alley trying to see if they could locate the Nephite.

The night watch commander came and stood right behind them. "Go after him!" He bellowed to the two Lamanites. Just then one of Teancum's poison darts hit the Lamanite on the left in the chest. The poor soldier felt the stick of the dart and batted the dart off of his skin, but it was no use. The poison took an instant effect, and the Lamanite was howling and convulsing. The second Lamanite had not experienced

The Hunter is Now Hunted

Teancum's tactics and did not know what was happening to his friend. He was lost in the moment and looking at his friend when a second dart hit him in the neck. Before he could even get his hand up to check what had stung him, he was on the ground next to his friend dying in pain. The night watch commander knew what was happening and instantly brought up his cloak to protect his face and body from what he was sure was the next poison dart. As he was spinning around to get out of sight, a third dart poked through his cloak, just out of reach of his left eye. It was so close to the Lamanite commander's face he could see the poison dripping off the tip of the handmade bone dart. The tall Lamanite spun completely out of the alleyway and Teancum was up and moving again.

Got to keep moving… He urged his broken body to continue on. *Not much farther now.* He could see a section of the wall and he knew if he could get over it he would be in the clear. His chest injury was throbbing now and the taste of blood was in his mouth. Breathing was almost impossible and he gulped air as he moved. *Some great warrior…* He chuckled at his pain and predicament. *Can't even kill a king and escape a walled city without tripping over everything in your way.* He was trying to use humor to relieve the pressure, but he was also a physician. Teancum knew how badly he was injured, and how much more he would need to endure to escape. "Please Lord… give me the courage to carry on." He mouthed a silent prayer as he painfully moved out of the alley and behind some large woven baskets. That was when the first large rock struck him in the side of the head. Teancum was knocked over and his entire world began to spin. Blood was flowing from the rock's impact point below his right temple. He reached up with his right hand to determine the extent of the damage at the same time his warrior instincts were trying to get him back on his feet.

"Hit him again!" The night watch commander shouted to his soldier who was loading a second stone into his sling. The two of them were standing a distance away and could see Teancum's body outlined in the alley. The Lamanite with the sling sent a second rock racing towards Teancum, hitting him behind his ear. Teancum was knocked out cold and his body crashed down in the gutter outside the alley.

Carefully, the Lamanites moved towards the motionless body of the assassin. This man was a great threat and no one wanted to be his next victim. Finally, hidden behind a wall of shields, several Lamanites approached Teancum and one man poked at Teancum with his spear.

CHAPTER THIRTEEN

There was no reaction and the Lamanites knew this deadly Nephite was unconscious.

"Bind him with strong cords and bring him back to the great hall!" One of the ranking Lamanites barked. He was still standing behind the protection of the wall of shields.

"Wait!" The night watch commander contradicted the last order. "I have a better idea… Bring him to the top of the wall above the main gate."

CHAPTER FOURTEEN

No Greater Friend to Liberty

Gid and Teomner met General Moroni at the edge of the Ghost Soldier camp exactly one hour after they last spoke. They saluted each other and walked in silence for several minutes towards the edge of the tree line. There they could see the front of the walled city and the large, locked gate in the distance illuminated by the torches along the wall. They also saw something was burning inside the city, something big. There were Nephite sentries standing close by who had been keeping watch on the city. Moroni gestured for them to move away and give him and the two Ghost Soldiers some privacy.

"There, gentlemen is the prize." Moroni spoke in a low and emotionless tone, pointing at the gates. "Tell me of your plans."

"Well sir." Gid spoke first. "The plan is simple, we cross this open ground under the cover of night using our camouflage covers." Gid used his hands to gesture as he explained the rest of the plan. "We will assault the wall using long poles to hoist the men up and over. Then we will take the guard tower over the gate. Once the tower is secure and the bulk of the Ghost Soldiers are over the wall, we will move to the gate and open it to allow the rest of the army to enter."

"That simple?" Moroni questioned.

"Yes, sir." Teomner responded matter-of-fact. "We have been training with this new concept on getting men over the wall for months now and we have it down." Teomner looked at the distant walls and then back at Moroni. "I have full confidence the Ghost Soldiers will prevail, Sir.

CHAPTER FOURTEEN

We will have the gate open."

Moroni knew enough to know these men would open and hold the gate regardless of the odds. He shook his head in agreement and smiled at the two special soldiers before him. "So tell me." He asked. "Where will you start your crossing of the—"

His words were cut off by the sounds of a horse approaching from behind them. As the moon's light illuminated the face of the rider, Moroni was suprized to see Captain Lehi sitting atop the mount. He looked pale and had wrapped himself in a light blanket.

"Lehi…?" Moroni gasped. "What are you doing here?"

"Forgive me, my general." Lehi spoke. "I was told you were with the Ghost Soldiers planning an assault on the city." Lehi smiled. " There is no way I am going to let Teancum and his rabble take all the glory for this final victory." He chuckled and coughed hard into his hands. Gid and Teomner both knew he was joking. There had been a healthy rivalry between the Ghost Soldier and Lehi's mighty men for a long time and there appeared to be no end in sight. After sliding off his horse, Lehi looked unsteady on his feet when he landed on the ground. But he quickly gathered his strength and walked towards the three other men. "So… We attack at dawn?"

Moroni was about to speak when a lone horn blew from the city wall. All of the men turned to look in the direction the sound came from.

" There!" Teomner pointed to the top of the wall near the right side of the main watch tower. "Movement on the wall."

"I see it." Moroni responded as he squinted and tried to get a better view. He could see a very large Lamanite in a dark cloak was leading a group of other Lamanites. Some were holding torches, while others appeared to be dragging something along the catwalk. They all stopped when the large Lamanite met the soldier with the horn near the door to the watchtower.

"What now?" Lehi whispered. He instantly snapped back to his old self and barked at the Nephite soldiers who were acting as sentries when Moroni arrived. "You, soldier!" He pointed to the closest one. The soldier ran up to Lehi. "Fetch horses and have someone stand ready to deliver a message for the general."

"Yes, sir." The soldier spouted and ran off into the night.

Moroni looked at Lehi. "Just in case." Lehi spoke in jest, then winked back and smiled.

"Good to have you back my friend." Moroni smiled back.

"Sir, he is shouting something." Gid informed Moroni. They all turned to face the walls and held still to listen. It was faint but in the distance they could hear the words coming from the large Lamanite on the wall.

"Moroni…! Moroni!" He called out several times. The gathered all turned to look at the young General. He held his hands up to tell them to be still and wait to see what would happen next.

"You dare send your assassin again…?" The Lamanite bellowed. The sound of his voice echoed through the trees. Even the wind stopped blowing as everyone suddenly came to the same conclusion— the Lamanites had captured Teancum.

Teancum was fading in and out of consciousness. The last blow to his head had done heavy damage, and he could feel his hands and feet going numb. He could taste more blood in his mouth, and the injury to his ribs was hurting so badly he had trouble even breathing. The Lamanites who were dragging him dropped his body like a sack of potatoes on the hard wooden planks of the catwalk, right at the feet of the night watch commander. Teancum could hear the smug Lamanite shouting something, but it sounded like he was underwater.

Got to get to my feet. Teancum urged his body to move but none of his limbs were responding. He tried to roll over but when he moved he was kicked again by one of the other Lamanites standing close by.

"He killed the king!" The Lamanite who kicked him pointed and shouted to the guards in the watchtower. Those other guards left their post and came to stand next to the night watchman as he continued to shout and taunt the unseen Nephites and Moroni.

"Now you will see what the price is for your arrogance and cowardice Moroni!" The mighty Lamanite commander turned to the other guards next to him. "Stand him up." He ordered as he pointed to Teancum's broken body with his sword. Three of the guards reached down and grabbed Teancum by his arms and jerked him up to his feet. Teancum bellowed out in pain as he tried to find the strength to stand.

Moroni, Lehi and the two Ghost Soldiers all gasped as they saw their friend and leader hoisted up from behind the stone ramparts and forced to stand erect next to the Lamanite who was shouting the insults.

"They are going to kill him!" Lehi barked as he turned to move back

CHAPTER FOURTEEN

to his horse. Bounding up into the saddle like a man half his age Lehi looked down at one of the Nephite sentries standing a few steps away. "Your shield, now!" He commanded as he reached out with his left arm. The young soldier moved with blind obedience and took the few steps to close the distance between himself and Lehi while reaching up with his arms to hand his round metal shield to his Captain. At the same time the soldier who was assigned to fetch horses for the officers arrived back with several horses in tow, including General Moroni's personal mount.

"Lehi!" Moroni barked, "Wait!"

"Sir!" Gid shouted to get Moroni to look back at the wall.

Gid was the only one watching the wall while the others turned to see what Lehi was doing. The scene was difficult to make out in the distant torchlight. But it was clear that whoever the Lamanites were holding captive had given them a lot of trouble.

As the Lamanites tried to stand Teancum up, Teancum took advantage of the Lamanites perception that he was defeated and helpless and he lashed out at the two closest Lamanites. Teancum knew these were his last few moments alive. If he was going to go out, then he was going to take a few more of his sworn enemies with him. Moving with all the speed and strength he could muster, Teancum hit the closest Lamanite with a strong chop right to the neck, crushing the throat and fatally damaging the windpipe. The Lamanite helplessly grasped at his neck but the damage was done; he was a dead man walking.

Before anyone could react, Teancum grabbed the second closest Lamanite by the hair and slammed his head on the hard rock surface of the stone wall before him. There was an explosion of blood and teeth and the Lamanite went limp in Teancum's hands. Teancum pushed the Lamanite's body towards the others to make an obstacle between him and those still on the wall. As the body of the fatally wounded Lamanite fell to the floor, Teancum turned and tried to make a break for the stairs leading back down to the ground. He got four steps away when the night watchman grabbed a spear out of the hands of one of the guards and threw it at Teancum. The spear hit Teancum in the back of the right leg and pierced completely through his leg, with the metal point coming out the front side. Teancum cried out and tumbled to the wooden deck in agonizing pain.

The night watch commander viciously pushed the other Lamanites aside shouting, "Out of my way!" There had been too much loss at the hands of this Nephite and it was time to finish this once and for all. He moved towards the gravely wounded assassin as his heavy boot steps crackled on the wooden surface.

Grabbing Teancum by the shoulders, the dark leader jerked him to his feet and looked Teancum in the eyes. "I will give you this…" He snarled at Teancum as he spoke. "You do not disappoint." It was at this moment Teancum caught the sight of a Nehor assassin blade tucked into his weapons belt. He only saw it for a moment when the Lamanite was turning and the cloak was lifted revealing the hidden hilt of the Nehor blade. When he saw the blade of his most hated enemy, Teancum cried out in excruciating pain. With the last full measure of his strength, Teancum grabbed the arms of the cruel Lamanite and jerked his wounded leg up, trying to stab the night watchman in the gut with the spear point that was sticking out of his thigh.

"Woah!" The Lamanite almost laughed as Teancum tried to wound him. Teancum was so weak and moving so slow the Lamanite leader could tell what he was trying to do and he held Teancum out away from his own body to avoid the metal tip of the weapon. After three attempts to stab the Nehor, Teancum collapsed from exhaustion. "Let's get this over with." The night watch commander spoke in an evil tone as he turned Teancum around and pushed Teancum's body against the cold stones of the rampart wall. Holding Teancum against the rampart with one hand, the night watch commander grabbed the spear shaft sticking out of the back of Teancum's leg with the other. " This looks like it hurts." He sneared. "Let me help you with this." Grasping the wooden shaft firmly in his right hand the big Lamanite yanked with all of his might and pulled the spear out of Teancum's leg.

The shock and pain caused Teancum's body to go stiff, and it took the very breath out of his lungs. Teancum made a half turn and looked over his shoulder at the Lamanite. He was smirking at Teancum, and Teancum spit right into his eyes, covering the man's face with a splattering of blood and spittle. Shoving Teancum's body hard up against the cold stone wall with one hand the big Lamanite wiped the blood from his eyes and face with the other. The two enemies made eye contact, and Teancum laughed and smiled a defiant smile, exposing his broken teeth and mouth full of blood. The Lamanite laughed back and then grabbed Teancum by his equipment belt and the back of his tunic. Shouting, he picked up Teancum and held him over the edge of the wall,

CHAPTER FOURTEEN

dangling him helplessly over the side.

"Burn in hell… Nehor!" Teancum gasped.

"I serve the Sons of Nehor, Ghost Soldier." He whispered in Teancum's ear. "And tonight we shall have our revenge." Holding Teancum out farther past the wall he shouted into the darkness and towards the tree line. "Here, Moroni! Here is your great assassin!"

There was a collective gasp from the tree line as Moroni and his men watched helplessly as the great hero of the Nephite people was dropped head first from the high walls of the city.

"Nooo!" Lehi shouted as he spurred his horse forward into the open ground between the city and the protection of the trees.

"Lehi, don't!" Moroni shouted. But he knew it was useless to try to stop him. Turning to face Gid and the others. "Go! Give him cover!" He commanded.

Gid, Teomner, and some of the other soldiers quickly jumped on the other horses and galloped after Lehi.

"Commander, look!" One of the guards on the wall shouted as he pointed towards the far tree line. The night watch commander looked out across the open ground and saw Lehi charging at a full gallop with several other Nephites following close behind.

"Not enough for a full attack?" He questioned out loud trying to figure out the tactics. He quickly looked down at Teancum's lifeless body below and then back up at Lehi. "They are coming for the body of the assassin!" He hissed behind a smile. "Archers, to your posts!" He shouted as he moved back along the catwalk towards the watch tower over the main gate.

"Sir, should I sound the general alarm?" One of the commander's men questioned.

"No…" He replied as he looked back again at the charging Nephites. "There is only a handful coming, and we can easily repel them."

Three Lamanites with bows moved to the edge of the wall and started to fire arrows at Lehi and the other men. Lehi had his borrowed shield out in front of him and was moving with complete disregard for his safety as the first set of arrows came flying in over his head and all around him. He was determined to reach the body of his dear friend Teancum. If there was any chance someone could have survived that fall, it would be Teancum. A few more Lamanites moved to the wall and they were preparing to fire their arrows down on Lehi as he reached the wall and

Teancum's body, but the two Ghost Soldiers had different plans for the Lamanites.

Being a Ghost Soldier meant becoming a weapons expert, and Gid and Teomner showed the Lamanite archers what true marksmanship was. Firing from the gallop, the two shot rapid-fire volleys of arrows and killed four of the exposed Lamanites on the wall. Lehi reached Teancum and he jumped from his horse. With one continuous fluid motion Lehi demonstrated his amazing strength and agility. He scooped up Teancum's lifeless body in his arms and moved effortlessly back to his horse. As he was preparing to remount his steed, the remaining Nephites arrived and formed a loose shield wall around him for protection from the Lamanite arrows while Gid and Teomner kept most of the archer's heads down. Lehi put Teancum over his shoulder and with the dexterity and power of a mythical hero climbed up on his horse. The Lamanites were now trying to hurl large stones and spears down onto Lehi and the other men but because of the deadly accurate fire from the Ghost Soldiers they could not aim at their targets. They resorted to blindly tossing the stones over the side in the general direction of Lehi. A few of the stones bounced off the large shields of the other Nephites who had joined the rescue attempt but mostly they fell harmlessly to the ground.

Against all possible odds, Teancum was still alive and gasping for air. Lehi, amazed at the grit of his brother in arms barked words of encouragement to Teancum as he bounced off Lehi's shoulder. "Hold on!" Lehi urged. "We will get you all fixed up." Lehi knew better. He watched as Teancum was dropped from the height of the stone wall and now saw his injuries up close. How he even survived the fall alone was a testament to the toughness of the Ghost Soldier. Teancum tried to speak but with the extent of his injuries, it was impossible for him to form words.

"Yah!" Lehi shouted as he kicked his horse and urged him forward. The horse complained of the increased weight but moved under his master's command. While Gid and Teomner fired several more arrows back up at the Lamanites the Nephite soldiers with Lehi continued to provide cover with their large metal shields. Any Lamanite soldier who was unfortunate enough to expose his body long enough for the two Ghost Soldiers to mark them as targets were hit with their arrows.

Moroni could see the entire event unfold before him and his mind

CHAPTER FOURTEEN

raced into action. When he saw Lehi returning he turned to a sentry standing by him. "Run to the main medical tent and wake the chief surgeon. Tell him make ready his staff and be prepared for Chief Captain Teancum!"

"Yes, sir!" The soldier, who was barely old enough to be in the army, responded. Grabbing his spear the messenger took off at a dead run into the trees to deliver the General's orders.

"Watch the walls and the gate for any sign the Lamanites might try to follow Lehi back to the trees!" Moroni shouted to the growing number of soldiers who came to the edge of the tree line to see what was happening.

Moroni could see Lehi was galloping back but noticed he was heading away from Moroni's location. To help Lehi find his way back to the spot where the others were waiting, Moroni pulled out his great sword and stepped out into the clearing. He began waving it in the air and shouted "Here, come this way!" The metal on the massive sword of Laban gleamed in the moonlight and caught Lehi's attention as he rode back towards the Nephite lines. It also caught the attention of the night watch commander who was now looking over the stone parapets watching as the small rescue party galloped away with their prize.

"General Moroni…" he hissed as he squinted to see better in the moonlight. Even that far away Moroni's enormous frame and mighty sword clearly identified him as the general of the Nephite armies. "My bow!" He commanded as he held out his hand. One of his more demure servants moved quickly and handed him a large curved bow made of dark wood. The Nehor commander took the bow in one hand and reached back for a long, thick-shafted black arrow with a heavy iron point. Only the Nehor carried arrows such as these. The dark-cloaked commander stepped closer to the edge of the wall and nocked the big arrow. Pulling back on the taut string, the dark wood bow creaked in protest as the Lamanite brought the arrow as far back as his strength would allow. Aiming up and towards the figure of Moroni off in the distance, the Lamanite commander let fly his arrow. The string on the bow snapped forward with a hiss and the arrow was set flying on an arc towards the great Nephite leader.

In the black of night, Moroni had no idea the arrow was in flight and moving towards him. It was too dark to see clearly what was happening on top of the wall and his attention was on Lehi making it back safely to Nephite lines. The dark commander looked on with an evil smile as the thought of his lone arrow striking the Nephite boy general dead in the chest crossed his mind. Moroni took two steps to his right to try to get a look at Teancum as Lehi galloped past him and headed towards the main camp and the medical tent. As Moroni moved, the large Nehor arrow struck the ground exactly where he had been standing. Hearing the impact of the arrow into the soft ground next to him, Moroni looked back as the soldiers around him all moved away from the impact point of the lone Nehor arrow. Amazed at the power it took to send the arrow that far, and fearing there might be more on the way several of the soldiers around Moroni scattered and moved behind trees for cover. Moroni looked down at the arrow, then up and out towards the city wall. He could see the imposing figure of the cloaked commander standing tall on the top of the wall near the guardhouse.

He then looked behind him and, in a surreal moment, caught a fleeting glimpse of Teancum's wounded body as is hung over Lehi's shoulders. The indignation grew so hot inside Moroni he could barely contain himself. He moved quickly to his own horse, where his personal bow and quiver of stout arrows were kept. Unlatching his own big bow from its cradle on the saddle, he walked back to where the Lamanite arrow was still sticking out of the ground. Pulling the black arrow out of the ground, Moroni loaded his bow with the arrow and took careful aim at his Lamanite antagonist on the wall. The soldiers around Moroni came out from behind the trees to watch their leader defy the enemy and fire back with their own arrow. The bulging muscles in Moroni's arms shook and quivered as he pulled the string of his long bow back and held it still to ensure his aim was true. "For Teancum…" He whispered as he released and felt the air move as the arrow was sent flying back towards from whence it came.

The Lamanite commander was standing still and trying to see if his arrow did any damage and trying to figure out what Moroni was doing, when he felt a rush of fast moving air blow past his head just to the right of his shoulder. There was a loud thud, then shouts of panic from those around him. He turned his head and saw the small framed servant who was standing next to him lying on the catwalk with his own big black arrow sticking out of his chest. The burly Lamanite gasped and took two steps back and away from the dead servant. It took him several seconds to fully process what had just happened. Reliving the carnage left by the Ghost Soldier in his mind, and now seeing the archery abilities of

CHAPTER FOURTEEN

Moroni, the night watch commander felt again a very unfamiliar shiver of dread run the entire length of his spine. "If one man can do all of that…" He reasoned as he looked out and over the inner court yard of the city and the trail of dead Lamanites and the fires left in Teancum's wake. "And another man can do this…" He continued quietly to himself as he turned back and looked down at his dead servant with the large arrow protruding out of his still body. "What can the entire army do?"

Moroni walked quickly back to his horse and reattached his long bow. "Double the watch and bring word if there is change!" He shouted to no one in particular. Moroni lept up into the saddle of his horse and took off like a bolt in the direction Lehi had carried Teancum.

All of the commotion had awakened many Nephites and they were gathering around the main medical tent wondering what was happening when Moroni arrived. "Make a hole!" Moroni shouted as he jumped from his horse and stormed past the others. A pathway to the entrance effortlessly opened for him through the crowd and Moroni burst into the medical tent.

The medical staff had laid Teancum on the exam table, and two orderlies were trying to adjust the candles so the doctor could get a clear look at the wounds. Moroni could smell the blood and saw a large pool of it forming on the ground under the gaping wound in Teancum's leg. Looking closer, he could see Teancum's body was shaking and he was moaning and coming in and out of consciousness. "Hanni!" He shouted like a madman as he tried to get up and off the table. Moroni moved to Teancum's side and helped the attendants and nurses hold him down.

"Bind that wound!" The exhausted doctor shouted and pointed to the gushing leg wound as he tried to look into Teancum's eyes for some sign of hope. What he saw were the obvious signs of a terrible head injury. One pupil was wide open, and the other was a pinpoint. The whites of Teancum's eyes were now dark with blood and a clear liquid was coming out of his ears. Not many people had been working as hard and as long as the medical staff in the camp. The doctor's blood-stained clothing and hollow, sunken eyes gave testament of the extent of the doctor's efforts to try to save the lives of the wounded Nephites in his care. A young nurse tried to wrap the leg wound but Teancum was kicking and fighting against the attempts to hold him down.

"Hanni!" He cried out again but his face was swollen, broken and deformed from all the damage he sustained. Saliva mixed with blood was foaming up in his mouth and nose.

"Something for the pain?" Moroni questioned in a quiet tone to the doctor as he continued to assess the extent of Teancum's injuries.

"Not until I am done." The doctor replied back curtly. He was struggling to roll Teancum onto his side so he could examine his back and ribs. "Don't know what all the damage is, and the drug could mask something, or make his condition worse."

Moroni felt sheepish for asking but continued to help hold his friend and comrade. He knew enough about emergency first aid to know drugs could mask Teancum's symptoms, but he was caught up in the moment and wanted the pain his brother-in-arms was experiencing to end.

"Doctor, I can't get the bleeding to stop!" The nurse tending to the leg wound cried out.

The doctor stopped his assessment and moved around the table to see to the troubling wound. *Tourniquet…pressure dressing…elevation…direct pressure*, he recited to himself as he checked every step the others had taken to get the bleeding to stop. Looking closer at the location of the wound, and the amount of blood which had already been lost, he came to a finite conclusion. "It's the femoral…" He looked up at Moroni and gave his next order without breaking eye contact. "Three drops of poppy oil."

A different attendant moved closer to Teancum's head and pulled out a small vial of the milky substance that, coincidentally, Teancum helped to refine into the very potent mixture now used. Three drops were gently administered, and within seconds Teancum's body settled and relaxed. The broken man laying on the examination table was a living hero and legend to everyone in the tent. That fact was not lost on the staff as they watched Teancum slowly die right in front of them. The doctor grabbed Moroni by the arm and moved him out of earshot from the rest of the staff and those standing around.

"Massive head trauma, several broken bones, including his back… The pink foam coming out of his mouth is more than likely from a punctured lung, I'm sure he has a nicked femoral artery… And that is only what I can tell in the first few moments." He whispered to Moroni.

"Is it a death sentence you are pronouncing?" Moroni inquired back. The emotions of this reality were already clear on his face as he asked the question.

CHAPTER FOURTEEN

"I am sorry my general, but Captain Teancum is going to die. How long it takes will depend on his will to survive, and the strength of his body. But there is nothing I can do to stop it from happening now."

Moroni felt like he had to do something. He couldn't stand there and watch his friend and most gifted soldier give up the fight. "We are on the eve of this war's final battle... He is the Ghost Soldier, we need him!" Moroni pointed behind him at Teancum's body and struggled past his emotions for the right words. "This is not happening!" By now the sergeant major, Amiha and the other leaders of the army had arrived and were entering the tent. Lehi was in the corner sitting in a chair with his head in his hands, sobbing. His friend's blood was still fresh on his armor and cloak. Moroni turned back to face the rest of the medical staff and his commanders. "This is not happening!" He shouted as if his very words had the power to defy death itself. There was quiet and stillness as everyone looked back at Moroni waiting for his next command.

"Moroni." Teancum gasped and broke the moment. He held up his hand as if he was reaching out for help.

"My friend..." Moroni whispered as he moved up next to Teancum and grabbed his outstretched hand. "I am here."

"Strike now... the king." He choked and coughed as he spoke. The words were muddled from the damage to his face. "Their king is dead... In chaos." Teancum tried to rise up his head. "Strike the body... The head has been removed... Nephites inside are suffering... Attack!" He gasped to force more air out when he spoke to push the point but it caused him to collapse and his head dropped back onto the table. "The Nehor..." He whispered loudly. Moroni moved in closer to Teancum's face to try to hear what he was saying. "The Nehor..." Teancum grabbed Moroni's wrist and squeezed it tightly. "Kill the dark Lamanite... He is a Nehor."

Moroni flashed back to the moment when the great black arrow hit the ground next to him. In the moment it did not register, but now he remembered the Nehor used such arrows as a calling card. Then he reflected on the large, dark shape at the top of the wall who shot the arrow at him.

"Nehor." Moroni whispered. If anyone knew who members of the despised criminal band inside the city were, it would be Teancum. Moroni put his other hand on Teancum's wrist. "Do not worry my old friend, I will kill the Nehor for you." Moroni spoke softly to his dying captain. With those words Moroni felt the pressure release from the grip around his wrist and he saw Teancum's body relax on the table. Teancum took two more shallow breaths and then everything in his body stopped.

He was the only one who heard a sweet female voice call out to him. "Teancum, my love, are you ready?" His spirit body sat up on the table, and Teancum could see a shape forming inside a brightly-burning white light coming from the end of the room. As the light grew brighter and filled the room, there was a second human shape coming into view, and a third one much taller than the other two. Then three smaller shapes all moving and dancing around the first. His family had come to escort him home. Teancum never knew such joy as he reached out and once again took the hand of his beloved wife. It was over—the warrior was finally going home.

Teancum, the great Ghost Soldier was gone. Lehi was openly weeping, and several others were wiping away tears of sadness. Moroni took two steps back from the table and allowed the doctor space to make his final assessment.

"He has passed." The doctor looked up after checking Teancum one last time. He nodded to Moroni to come closer and pointed to Teancum's open eyes. Those cold and empty windows to his soul that were once full of light and knowledge were now motionless and void. Moroni reached up and gently closed Teancum's eyelids for the last time, showing his friend deep respect even in death.

Moroni stepped back again and gestured to the two attendants to cover Teancum's body with a clean blanket. Gid and Teomner were in the back of the tent standing beside Amiha. They were taking in the moment and being strong for one another.

"Is this really happening?" Teomner spoke under his breath. "Did Teancum just die?" Moroni heard Teomner speaking and he turned to face the two Ghost Soldier leaders.

"Gentlemen… Are your forces ready for the assault?" He was standing tall but everyone could tell his thoughts were someplace else. The tears on his dirty cheeks glistened in the candlelight.

"Sir…" Gid spoke up sniffing as he fought back his own emotions. "They are making final preparations as we speak. We will be ready."

"Good…" Moroni replied mournfully. "Men!" Everyone in the tent stopped what they were doing and turned to look at the giant of a man. "This man sealed his testimony of freedom with his blood. He gave his last full measure of devotion to the cause of liberty. No one fought harder

CHAPTER FOURTEEN

for the welfare of his people than Teancum." Moroni turned back and looked at the body of his friend. "He was the best of all of us…" Moroni made eye contact with Lehi who was still wailing in misery. It seemed to calm him down and Lehi sat up straight in his seat. "We will honor his memory and sacrifice…His last words were reporting his concern for the welfare of his fellow Nephites and that he had accomplished his mission. Their king is dead and they are in chaos…" Moroni paused for effect. Raising his hand and making a fist he continued. "We strike."

"Yes!" Lehi lept to his feet and growled like a hungry lion.

"We strike…!" Moroni was bolder with his words and slightly pumped his fist up and down in the air. Amiha and the others with him all took one step forward and responded in kind. "For freedom, we strike!" Moroni looked at the two Ghost Soldiers in the room. They both puffed out their chests and replied "Yes!" He pointed to Gid and Teomner. "Move your men into position and begin your assault." He then looked around the room and saw the fire in his soldiers' eyes. "The rest of you get this army up and ready for battle! This ends today… In God's name, and for Chief Captain Teancum, we attack at dawn."

CHAPTER FIFTEEN

The Last Full Measure

Moroni stood inside the darkened recesses of the tree line bordering the open grassy field and the wide path leading to the main gates of the city. He was scanning the ground in front of him looking for any sign of the Ghost Soldiers. "I know they are out there." Moroni thought to himself. Squinting at something moving in the grass he tried to focus but the fatigue from the long night and low-light conditions were playing havoc on his eyesight. Turning and looking towards the eastern horizon, Moroni could see the hint of change in the colors of the night sky as the earth crept ever closer to dawn. "Not much longer now," he whispered. Looking behind him he could see his battered and bloody army lined in one continuous formation reaching back into the woods as far as he could see. Moroni's plan was to advance the entire army, as one giant spear in one deadly thrust towards the open gate and get as many soldiers inside before the enemy could secure it.

"Report." Moroni spoke in a low whisper as Amiha rode up to him.

"As you ordered, the balance of the infantry is in position. The formations are ready to move on your command. The cavalry and support units are standing by as a reserve force to assist as needed. I also have them working on a crude battering ram if we need it."

"Excellent…" Moroni whispered, his voice was low and full of power. "Surprise is the key. I want complete silence among the ranks. If we are discovered then all is lost. Pass the word to the subcommanders to hold the men quiet. We will only get one chance at this… We cannot afford any mistakes." Amiha had not seen this level of intensity from Moroni in

CHAPTER FIFTEEN

some time. He was both shocked and excited to know the General was back in true form.

"Yes, sir. Consider it done." Amiha saluted and quickly left to pass the word. Moroni turned back to scan the ground before him but still saw no movement from the Ghost Soldiers. Under his metal helmet, the defined muscles in his jaw rippled as Moroni clenched down on his teeth as he looked again towards the east. He took a heavy breath to relax. The sounds of the air escaping from his lips echoed inside the armor covering his head. The anxiety of the coming attack was taking effect. The colors of the sunrise were becoming more defined. The order to charge was only moments away.

Turning back to face the walls of the city in the distance Moroni was alone with his thoughts and feelings. Only someone who has led men into battle and death would understand how the great General Moroni was feeling as he stood quiet and contemplated the near future. "God of our fathers…" Moroni pleaded in a whisper. Under the helmet no one could see his lips move, but his body posture gave away the fact the general was praying. His head was bowed and his great shoulders were hunched forward. Those who knew Moroni well instantly recognized he was pleading to the Father for guidance and mercy. "Grant us the strength to do what must be done." He continued. "I do not attack with this army for personal power or wealth Father, but to free the oppressed and stop those who would kill your children simply because they believe in you and rely on your grace. I beg for your mercy Father. Please soften the hearts of the Lamanites… But if it be your will that we redeem this land with blood then I pray for your hand to be with me and those brave men whom I command. Thy will be done, oh God. In your Son's name I pray to you… Amen."

Finishing his prayer, he took a deep breath and held it for a count of four. He slowly released the air and opened his eyes. He smiled as he remembered that it was Teancum who had taught him how to relax through breathing. Moroni was now ready in body, mind and soul for the coming sunrise and to give the command to attack.

Gid was about twenty yards away from the stone wall. He was sweating profusely under his camouflaged cover. Every joint and muscle in his body was crying out for rest. He knew that rest was the last thing he was going to enjoy at this moment, or for a while. If all went according to plan, this was only the beginning of a very long day. So he quieted the voices inside his head telling him to stop and found the kind of courage and determination to continue only a true warrior would understand.

    He and the rest of the Ghost Soldiers had slowly and quietly crawled on their bellies from the tree line several hundred yards away to this point. Now he was set and poised to signal for the Ghost Soldiers' assault. Gid knew that Teomner was off to his right and trusted that he was in position with his men to attack the opposite side of the watch tower overlooking the main gate. As slowly as he could, Gid raised up his head and looked to the east. The signal for Moroni to attack would be the first crack of sunlight over the mountains. The gray and purple colors of the coming dawn were crossing the horizon. Gid calculated in his mind that he had about twenty minutes before the sun itself came over the horizon.

    He knew it was time to give the signal and Gid slowly moved his head back down into the grass. Closing his eyes Gid spoke one last prayer in his mind. *Father, I only ask that you allow me to live the next few moments well. That you will help me find the strength to be a good soldier and do my duty.* Pulling his hand up to his face he clenched his fists, and tightly closed his eyes. "For freedom." He whispered. Then rising to his knees, Gid shrugged off his cover and gave the bird whistle to signal his men to move. Next to him, two archers rose up to their knees and pulled back their bows. At the same time several Ghost Soldiers behind Gid also rose up and grabbed a long stout tree trunk which had been cleared of all its limbs. It was more than fifty feet long and somehow they had managed to drag it with them across the open ground without being detected. Looking to his right Gid saw that Teomner had heard his signal and commanded his own men to do the same. On Gid's signal, several of the Ghost Soldiers grabbed hold of the tree as two of the men wrapped their arms around the very front of it. "Now." Gid commanded in a loud whisper and the men holding onto the front of the tree started to run towards the wall and the men holding the back of the tree pushed it forwards.

    "What was that?" One of the Lamanites sitting inside the guard shack on top of the watch tower asked.

    "What?" His sleeping companion asked drowsily.

    "Shhh, I heard something," the first Lamanite warned. As he got up from the cot and stepped into the doorway. "Hey!" He shouted to the

CHAPTER FIFTEEN

two guards on duty standing on the wall not far from the guard shack. They were leaning on their spears and trying not to fall asleep. They both turned to look at their fellow Lamanite. "Did you hear something?" He asked them both. They shook their heads and instinctively they both moved to the outer edge of the ramparts and looked over the outside of the wall.

Both Nephite arrows struck the Lamanite guards in their upper chest, knocking them backwards and onto the floor. The guard standing in the doorway watched as his two fellow guards were killed in front of him and was instantly in shock. Rather than cry out or sound the alarm, he did the last thing any rational person would do— he looked over the edge of the wall to see where the arrows were coming from.

What he saw stopped his blood from flowing. The two Ghost Soldiers who were holding the front of the long wooden pole reached the face of the wall and, on cue, they both jumped up and continued to run up the side of the wall as those men behind them pushed them up, using the long tree as a boost. The Lamanite looking over the wall was so stunned over what he was witnessing that he froze in fear. The two archers now standing by Gid took aim and both of their arrows struck the poor Lamanite, killing him before he hit the floor of the guard shack. The sound of the dead Lamanite hitting the ground caused the half-asleep soldier still in the guard shack to look up. Seeing his dead comrade lying in the doorway, he jumped up and grabbed his spear and tried to wake the other soldiers sleeping next to him.

Gid quickly looked to his right and saw Teomner was directing his men to do the same and push two soldiers at a time up and over the wall to attack the opposite side of the watchtower. The two soldiers with Gid reached the top and jumped over the edge of the wall. They landed back to back and pulled out their weapons. One Ghost Soldier moved towards the doorway while the other secured the catwalk. Gid saw the first of his men were on the wall and ordered his men to quickly lower the pole and send two more soldiers up. The next two men on the end of the pole both carried rope ladders, and they were quickly set and began to run up the side of the wall.

As the first Ghost Soldier entered the guard shack, he was met by five Lamanites all in varied states of readiness. The first Lamanite with the spear who was trying to wake his men gave a shout and thrusted his weapon at the Ghost Soldier. The Nephite spun to one side as the spear

CHAPTER FIFTEEN

passed harmlessly next to him. With a strong backhand swing, the Ghost Soldier ran the blade of his sword across the neck of the first Lamanite, cutting it deeply. The four remaining Lamanites were not prepared for this sudden level of violence and they cowered towards the back of the stone shack. Then a second Ghost Soldier entered from the right side door of the shack. He was one of the first of Teomner's men to come up the wall. The two Ghost Soldiers looked at the Lamanites cowering and trying to hold their weapons out in front of themselves. They looked at each other, nodded, then waded into the Lamanites with no mercy.

The second set of Ghost Soldiers reached the top of the wall and quickly went to work securing the rope ladders strapped to their backs. "Again!" Gid ordered as the long wooden pole was lowered and two more men were sent to ascend the wall. Gid looked again over to his right and made eye contact with Teomner. Teomner gave him a thumbs up and a quick smile and then went back to work directing his own men to move quicker.

A lone Lamanite was walking along the top of the wall and heading back to the watchtower when he saw a Nephite on the top of the wall trying to tie down a rope ladder. His instincts kicked in, and he shouted and charged at the Nephite with his spear. He almost got the Nephite, but at the last second a long throwing knife came slicing through the air and struck the charging Lamanite in his belly. Mortally wounded, the Lamanite dropped his spear and clutched at the knife sticking out of his body. The Ghost Soldier tying off the ladder looked at the wounded Lamanite then he looked behind him in the direction the knife came from.

Crouched on top of the rampart was another Ghost Soldier frozen in his follow-through swing, with several additional long throwing knifes hanging from his belt. He had just come up the wall on the pole and was climbing down on to the catwalk when he saw the attacking Lamanite. The two Nephites smiled at each other, then the soldier with the knives spied another Lamanite. He was unaware of the Nephite assault on the wall and lazily walking towards them along the catwalk. Grabbing a second throwing knife from his belt, he jumped down and started to run towards the unsuspecting Lamanite. The Lamanite looked up and suddenly realized what was happening. Screaming, he turned to run back towards the stairway leading to the main courtyard below. The blade of the Ghost Soldier's throwing knife struck him in the middle of his back severing his spine. Dropping his spear and shield, the Lamanite stumbled and tried to grasp the handrail leading to the stairs. With the loss of his legs and the blinding pain of the knife in his back, he lost all control and fell down the stairs screaming as he tumbled. His large metal shield and spear clanking down the steps behind him.

The noise of the wounded Lamanite falling down the stairs aroused the guards in the main courtyard, and they came out into the open area to see what was causing the ruckus. The dozen Ghost Soldiers who had made it to the top of the wall and the watchtower over the main gate all froze in place. With the clanking metal shield and cries from the wounded Lamanite, they all knew they had lost the element of surprise. Several of the Lamanites on the ground all ran to the injured soldier who had landed at the bottom of the stairs and was not moving. When they reached their fallen comrade and rolled him over, they saw the knife protruding from his back and knew it was not an accident. Looking up at the top of the stairs and along the wall the Lamanites could see the few Ghost Soldiers standing atop the wall looking back down at them. It was a surreal moment and both sides stood motionless.

Then suddenly one of the Nephite men drew out his sword and shouted, 'Follow me, get the gate open!' and charged for the stone stairway leading down. The Nephite who was fastening the rope ladders leaned over the outside of the ramparts and shouted down to Gid, 'Jericho!' then pushed the two rope ladder bundles over the side. They stretched out along the side of the wall almost to the bottom where Gid was standing. Gid grabbed the ends of the two ladders and instantly knew things were already turning for the worst. 'Jericho' was the Ghost Soldier's code word that a member of the unit was in desperate need of assistance. He was telling Gid that something had happened and to get the rest of the unit up and over the wall.

"Jericho!" Gid shouted back to his men. He handed the ends of the rope ladders to the two closest men and told them to climb. "The rest of you men," Gid ordered to the other Ghost Soldiers standing behind him, "Up… Get up there!" Looking at the men hoisting soldiers up with the long wooden pole Gid commanded, "Keep going, get them up there!" Gid then turned and shouted to his friend. "Teomner!"

There was no reason to be quiet now; with the distress call, the

CHAPTER FIFTEEN

Lamanites must know they are trying to assault the walls. Teomner was busy directing his own men when he heard his name called out. Confused at the reason Gid broke the silence, Teomner turned to face Gid. "Jericho… Jericho! Get them over the wall! Go, go, go!" Gid shouted and waved his hands. Without saying a word, Teomner knew what to do.

Moroni watched with quiet awe as the Ghost Solders made their attack on the wall next to the main gate. He was impressed with the method they were using to get men to the top of the wall. "Ingenious…" He whispered to the sergeant major as they watched men on both sides of the gate, two at a time, get pushed up the side of the wall and go over the top of the ramparts. Then, when the rope ladders came over the side he nodded his head in approval. "Smart… A well thought out plan." He muttered out loud. Moroni heard the word 'Jericho' and saw the demeanor of the men change as they started to climb the rope ladders. He saw the hurried way the soldiers were being pushed up the wall with the poles and knew something was wrong. Looking to the east for his cue to begin his charge, Moroni saw it was only moments away.

The Lamanites on the ground inside the walled city were not fully-armed or ready for a fight. Most of them had been drinking or were exhausted from spending the entire night dealing with the aftermath of the assassination of their king. When they saw the few Ghost Soldiers charging down the stairs, they retreated back to get their weapons and shields. One Lamanite started to bang on a large metal bar with a thick wooden stick and shouting, 'To arms!' over and over again.

"Shoot the man ringing the bell!" Gid ordered as an archer ran up to him. Gid had just come up and over the wall. He knew he could not direct the fight from the safety of the opposite side of the wall and took his turn getting hoisted up with the wooden pole. The archer took a quick aim and let his arrow fly. The arrow sailed low and hit the Lamanite in the thigh. The wounded Lamanite dropped the large stick he was using to bang on the metal bar and grabbed at the arrow in his leg. "To the gate, men!" Gid shouted as he pulled out his two short swords and made his way to the stairs.

The few Ghost Soldiers who had already reached the ground were heavily engaged with several Lamanites. It was no contest; the Ghost Soldiers were so much better at close combat than any Lamanite. The problem was there were only a few Ghost Soldiers on the ground and more and more Lamanites were arriving. For every one Lamanite killed, five more came running to fight. From his vantage point on top of the wall, Gid could see he had already lost three Ghost Soldiers and the rest were fighting for their lives.

Fighting by two's and in single combat the Ghost Soldiers were spinning, thrusting, kicking, and punching everywhere and nowhere at the same time. To the untrained eye, the scene looked more like a crowded dance floor then a battle scene as the brave Nephites fought towards the main gate. Gid reached the ground and was instantly set upon by several Lamanites. Using his two short swords as extensions of his own arms, Gid was able to slice, deflect and stab his way past the first set of enemy soldiers and move towards the gate. "Get to the gate!" He shouted. "Get it open!" Gid looked across the open courtyard and saw Teomner and his men fighting Lamanites and descending down the opposite set of stairs, running towards the battle. Gid took a quick glance up towards the heavens and saw the flashing colors of a red dawn streaking across the morning sky. "It's dawn," he whispered. Gid looked around and saw he was losing more men. "Fight, men! Hold your ground!" He commanded. He had to get the gate open— whatever the cost— or all was lost and the sacrifice of so many would be in vain. As more Ghost Soldiers arrived to assist, the battle became more intense and Gid continued to fight his way to the gate.

Moroni could hear the sounds of battle echoing from the walled city and inside the large wooden gate separating him from those brave soldiers. The veins in his body were pumping red hot blood and he gasped to control his breathing. The battle was upon him and the moment had arrived. Moroni looked one last time to the east and saw the first streaks of the yellow sun cresting over the far mountains. Pulling out the massive sword of Laban, Moroni turned to face the endless column of men behind him. Shouting and waving his sword in the air, Moroni let out his war cry. The entire Nephite army responded to their beloved leader and shouted in unison. Moroni looked back at the gates of the walled city and they were still closed.

Father... We are placing our trust in your providence, Moroni silently prayed. He then turned to face Amiha and Lehi. Amiha looked very concerned. "They will have it open!" Moroni reassured Amiha. Amiha nodded to acknowledge he trusted his friend and general. Still holding

CHAPTER FIFTEEN

the big sword in the air, Moroni took a deep breath and shouted "Charge!" Then he was off, followed by the Nephite army, and crossing the two hundred yards towards the secured gates.

The only Ghost Soldiers who remained outside the walls were those hoisting others up and over with the long poles. With the last of their brother soldiers on the wall, the strong men still on the ground dropped the poles and made their way to the rope ladders. Moroni had moved about fifty yards when he saw the last of the Ghost Soldiers climb up the wall on the rope ladders. He was moving at a jog while leading the army down the wide path and towards the gate. "Amiha!" He pointed with his sword. "Take some men and follow those soldiers up the ladder and help secure the gate!"

"Yes, sir!" Amiha responded. "Alpha Company follow me!" Amiha barked while sprinting his direction to move towards the ladders on the left side of the gate.

Moroni saw Amiha move away from the main force. Moroni looked back at the gate; it was still closed. "We trust in you, Lord." He affirmed and kept moving forward with his army.

Gid fought his way to the gate, killing two more Lamanites as he moved. His men were fighting an epic battle, but even the gallant Ghost Soldiers could not withstand the odds building up against them for much longer. They were vastly outnumbered and trapped with their backs against the locked gate and walls of the city. Now, Lamanite archers were arriving at the fight and firing at them from on top of the buildings across the courtyard. Teomner made his way to Gid's position and they gave each other a look admitting they were in trouble. Gid could see there were still Ghost Soldiers on top of the wall but they were busy fighting Lamanites who had gone up the stairs and were trying to retake the watchtower.

"Help me with the gate!" Teomner shouted as he strained to lift the heavy wooden brace beam out of its metal catches.

The night watch commander arrived at the courtyard and saw the madness before him. Through the fray he could see some Nephites trying to move the brace beam away from the gate. "If they get that open we are done for!" He shouted as he pointed with his curved sword. Several Lamanites were running away from the battle and the cloaked commander grabbed one by the neck. "Where are you going? Turn and fight!" He ordered.

"All is lost, where is the king?" The terrified Lamanite barked back. He broke free of the furious commander's grasp and kept running away. The Lamanites were at a disadvantage in this fight. Like every other engagement in this war, the Lamanites were forced from their homes by their leaders and were fighting for plunder and the bloodlust. While the Nephites were fighting only to defend their families and freedom.

"Your king…?" The massive fighter sarcastically responded as he looked around for any sign of additional ranking Lamanite leadership. He could see what the Nephite attackers were trying to do and he knew if they were successful in opening the gate this was going to end badly for the Lamanites. He knew they needed to organize a stout defense against the Nephites and they needed to do it right now.

"You!" He pointed to a large Lamanite standing next to him. "Try to rally the men and keep the Nephites pinned against the walls. Don't let them open the gates! Go!" Several more Lamanites followed as they ran to do battle with the Nephites. The commander looked up and saw more Nephites coming over the tops of the walls. He looked back at those Nephites fighting in the court yard. The skill and abilities of those few Nephites still fighting was impressive. Then he noticed their woodland-colored coverings and realized who they were. "Those are Ghost Soldiers!" He gasped. "The head of the snake has been cut away but the body keeps fighting. Not good… Not good at all."

Gid reached the inward side of the large city gate and tried with all of his might to lift the large wooden brace holding the gates secure out of its metal cradle. "Help me!" He shouted and three Ghost Soldiers came to assist. But even with all of their combined strength the brace was still too heavy to budge more than a few inches. The weight was too much for them and the brace came crashing back down into place.

Two Lamanites with spears broke through the melee swirling around the gate and charged at Gid and his assistants. The Lamanites assumed that because the Nephite attackers had dropped their weapons to try to lift the brace they were defenseless. On the contrary, these were Teancum's Ghost Soldiers. The two hapless Lamanites tried to thrust their spears at Gid and his men, but they were completely outmatched by

CHAPTER FIFTEEN

the hand-to-hand fighting skills of the Nephite warriors. They both were so quickly disarmed and killed that it almost seemed the way they were handled was rehearsed.

Gid took a moment after dealing with the two Lamanites to reassess. Looking around he saw the Lamanites were paying dearly but if the fight between his Ghost Soldiers and the enemy continued, the overwhelming number of Lamanite soldiers would eventually win the day. For every ten Lamanites killed, he was losing one man. But time and the math of combat was not in his favor. Gid turned and peeked through the crack between the two great wooden gates at the world outside the walls. Through the translucent waves of the mirage coming off the ground he could barely make out Moroni and the mass of Nephites coming out of the wood line towards the still locked gate. The tips of the Nephite spears and edges of their swords were gleaming in the first rays of a bright morning sun. Gid knew the entire outcome of this war rested on him getting this gate open. "Moroni is coming! We must open the gate!" He shouted to the few men still with him.

Although his close friend Gid preferred the elegance and mastery of fighting with two short swords, Teomner loved the feel of his big heavy two-handed sword. The power he could generate from combining his own raw strength with the weight of the sword's sharp polished steel was awe-inspiring. He was moving back to the fight to help hold off the Lamanites. He was cutting a wide path through the Lamanites with his mighty weapon at the bottom of the stairs which ran along the catwalk on the opposite side of the gate from Gid's position. "Don't worry about me! Fight to the gate!" He shouted and pointed to several of his men as they came to join him in fending off the charging Lamanites.

Their different and very distinctive fighting styles were reflections of their personalities. Gid was a thinker when he fought, efficient and precise. He liked to work out the problem and then find a creative way to resolve any issue. Spinning and jumping, moving and striking with the beauty and pageantry of a dancer, Gid employed every part of his body as a weapon. With knee strikes, elbows, and kicks, he lunged, dodged and lept across the battle space. Showing little emotion, Gid used the extensive training he received from Teancum to his great advantage. For Gid, fighting three men was as easy as fighting one.

Teomner, on the other hand, was a reactionary fighter. Teancum learned and understood that each man was different and each man needed to tailor his fighting style to maximize his own strength. Teomner's asset was the almost reckless abandon he showed when he fought the enemy, and this battle was no different. Kicking and punching wildly, slicing and stabbing with an animalistic aggression, Teomner was shouting, laughing and daring the Lamanites to fight him as he and his massive sword left a wake of destruction. He was making a mighty statement to the Lamanites, and they were getting the deadly message very quickly. The broken bodies of the enemy were all around him as Teomner struck out in all directions to engage the Lamanites.

The night watch commander was now at the edge of the battle raging in front of him when he saw Teomner swinging his mighty weapon, laughing and decimating all who dared challenge him. Spinning his own sword in his hand, the Nehor boss pushed and shoved his way past the other Lamanites in front of him and made his way towards Teomner.

Teomner kicked a Lamanite in the gut, causing the enemy fighter to double over from the pain, then swung his own sword down to strike the Lamanite. The hooded commander's curved sword caught Teomner's blade inches before he dealt the finishing blow, throwing him off balance. The commander then used his own body to check Teomner away from the injured Lamanite. Teomner stumbled for a few steps but quickly recovered and turned to face his newest opponent. Seeing an opportunity to attack, a second Lamanite charged at Teomner and tried to stab him with a spear. Teomner quickly side-stepped the thrust and cut a wide wound across the Lamanite's thigh. The wounded Lamanite stumbled back towards The commander. The big leader angrily pushed the wounded Lamanite out of the way and shouted and pointed to the other Lamanites who had encircled Teomner but were too afraid to challenge him. "Stay back… He's mine!"

Teomner was covered in the blood of his enemies and resting on his sword. He had already fought and killed over a dozen men and he gulped air into his lungs. Looking at the large cloaked Lamanite before him he laughed out loud while forcing air into his lungs and gestured sarcastically with his left hand for the big Lamanite fighter to come towards him. This new, fresh challenge would not go unchecked and Teomner was just getting warmed up.

The commander made the first move with a bold frontal attack. Charging directly at Teomner while shouting and swinging his sword over his head, he tried to finish the fight with one mighty death strike.

CHAPTER FIFTEEN

Teomner was no fool. He saw the angle and speed of the attack and waited until the last moment then, spinning away from the enemy blade, causing the hulking warrior to miss and the momentum of his swing carrying him past Teomner. The Lamanite recovered much faster than Teomner had calculated as Teomner slashed at his mid-section. The commander was able to move out of the way to avoid the tip of Teomner's blade. Now they were both close enough to each other to use their long blades and the dance of death began.

Striking and blocking, thrusting and parring, the sounds of hard steel clanking together echoed off the stone walls as these two great warriors moved and jockeyed for a position of advantage while trying to strike down each other. As he was stepping backwards and blocking several overhead chops from the commander, Teomner lost track of his surroundings and tripped over the leg of a dead Lamanite. Falling backwards he tried to control his fall and did a backwards roll, dropping his sword and coming to rest on his knees. The massive Lamanite was still moving forward and tried to thrust his sword at Teomner. Teomner grabbed a handful of dirt and flung it into the face of the large warrior as he stepped towards him, then Teomner rolled to the side and scooped up his own sword. The commander cried out and swung his sword wildly out in front of him with his right hand while he tried to get the dirt out of his eyes with the left.

Teomner knew this fight was taking too long. He could tell they were evenly matched and he could feel his strength failing and fatigue setting in. He was wasting time fighting this one man and not able to keep the Lamanites from retaking the gate and watchtower. He needed to get to the gate and help Gid and the rest of the Ghost Soldiers get it open. Seeing his opportunity, Teomner moved to get away from the new opponent but his path was blocked by several Lamanites with spears pointed at him.

"No!" The commander cried out as he shook his head and brushed more dirt from his face. "He is mine!" He ordered his men to stand down as he spat and waved the lamanites away from attacking Teomner.

Moroni could see the fighting on the walls between the Ghost Soldiers and the Lamanites trying to reclaim the watchtower and positons of advantage over the main gate. Clearly there were more Lamanites than

Nephites, and anyone could see it was a losing battle. But the Ghost Soldiers were making the Lamanites pay dearly for every inch they reclaimed. He was one hundred yards from the gate and moving fast but there was still no sign the soldiers on the other side had unlocked the gate. "They will have it opened!" Moroni shouted and kept moving with complete trust in God and his men.

Gid shouted, "Again…! We must get it opened!" And grabbed for the two Nephites closest to him. The circle of protection around the gate provided by the Ghost Soldiers was shrinking with every fallen warrior. Gid knew it was now or never. His men could not hold much longer and Moroni was only seconds away from reaching the gate. Closing his eyes Gid strained with the two other men next to him to get the massive cross beam out of its metallic cradles. He pushed with all of his might and whispered a prayer as he strained.

Suddenly the beam budged, then moved upwards; they were lifting it. It felt as if additional men had moved to the opposite end of the long wooden beam and were helping. Gid opened his eyes and looked to see which of his soldiers had left their posts to aid them. To his astonishment he saw one lone soldier standing on the other end of the beam lifting it out of its cradle all by himself. Gid was puzzled, *This is no Ghost Soldier*, he pondered. Gid knew every man in his command by first name. As this unknown soldier pushed up on his end, Gid could see that the lone fighter was exceptionally strong and much bigger than any other soldier under his command. "Even bigger than General Moroni." Gid whispered.

The large man's armor was made of a fine metal and polished to a mirror-like shine. His uniform was a flawless glowing white tunic, and the hilt of his large sword was expertly carved and adorned with gold. He had on a metal helmet of strange design that covered his entire head and face with a single T shape running across and down the front of his face. Gid could see the rippling muscles in his arms and the veins in his thick neck as he single-handedly lifted the end of the beam out of its resting place. *He is out-lifting the three of us by himself!* Gid thought as he strained under the weight of the beam. Gid gave one last desperate push and shouted, "Go lads!" Under the power of those brave Nephites, and the stranger, the beam was finally free from the cradle, but they did not want to drop it in front of the gate. "It will block the gate from opening!" Gid

CHAPTER FIFTEEN

shouted breathlessly as looked across the beam at the stranger helping them. The unknown warrior gestured with his head to bring the beam his way.

"This way, boys!" Gid commanded over the noise of battle and they grunted as they moved the beam out of the way. "Now!" Gid shouted as they dropped the beam to the ground several feet from the gate. Gid turned and quickly made his way back to the gate. Grabbing the large handle of the right gate he strained under the weight of the wood and iron but could not make it budge. "No!" He cried out as he looked back to find more help and saw the men who were helping him with the beam. One had fallen from several arrow strikes, and the other two were now fighting for their lives. *All is lost*, he thought.

Suddenly Gid felt a presence behind him and turned to find the giant, armored stranger standing behind him. "How did you get behind me?" Gid asked as he quickly scanned the location where the big man was last standing. The warrior grabbed the handle next to Gid's hand and started to pull. With Gid's help the gate budged and cracked. "Yes... We can do it... Pull!" With all his might Gid pulled and shouted. The iron hinges creaked and popped as metal ground against metal. "Almost!" Gid gasped. He felt the hand of the giant, armored stranger behind him on his shoulder.

Gid opened his eyes in time to see the last few remaining Ghost Soldiers who were trying to hold off the horde of Lamanites, succumb to the overwhelming onslaught of the enemy. The Lamanite soldiers were fighting to get past the few remaining Ghost Soldiers and close the gate. The scene painfully played out in slow motion as Gid watched, one at a time, his brave warriors give their last full measure of devotion to freedom. Each one of these mighty heroes stood their ground and refused to cower in the face of the enemy. They all knew this was a suicide mission, and still they came. Each man went down hard, fighting on until the life-force inside of them had been completely extinguished. There were so many dead Lamanites around the Ghost Soldiers that they were piling upon each other and could not be counted. A mighty price was paid for the life of each Ghost Soldier, but now Gid was alone.

With grief and determination welling up inside of him, Gid let go of the handle and reached for his two short swords. He knew he had failed to open the gate enough to let Moroni in. As he stood alone, his back to the gate and both of his swords in his hands, Gid readied himself

CHAPTER FIFTEEN

for his final battle on this earth. After they finished him off, Gid knew the mass of Lamanites would simply push the gate closed and reset the brace before Moroni could force it all the way open. But with his last ounce of strength and honor he was going to make the Lamanites pay dearly for his life. He was going to die with his men. He was going to ensure that his enemies would always remember this day. That they would remember the Ghost Soldier Chief Captain Teancum, the man who killed their king, and they would remember Lieutenant Gid and the rest of Teancum's men.

As Gid let out his final war cry and moved forward to waylay into the mass of Lamanites, he felt the big hand on his shoulder pull him back and push him behind the mountainous frame of the faceless man. The ground shook as the nameless armored soldier, bristling with hard, massive muscles, stepped past Gid and moved towards the remaining Lamanites.

For Gid, it was a surreal moment as he watched the nameless warrior draw out his own mighty sword and move towards the Lamanites. Gid looked at the markings on the back of the chest armor as the giant stranger stepped past. "It looks like wings." He thought to himself. When Gid saw the giant stranger's sword, he was sure he was hallucinating. The sword's blade looked like it was on fire. One thing Gid was certain of was the Lamanites were all backing away from the massive warrior with the flaming sword.

The gate, a small voice in Gid's head rang out.

This was the answer to his prayers. Not waiting to see the outcome of the Lamanites fighting with the giant and his fiery sword, Gid spun around and somehow wedged his body into the crack between the two gates. Bracing his back against the left gate, Gid brought up both his feet and pushed with all his might. As he pushed he looked over his left shoulder and saw, through the gap, Moroni charging towards him with the entire Nephite army close on his heels. Gid looked over his right shoulder and saw the giant armored man with the flaming sword standing as still as a stone and the Lamanites all staring at him; transfixed and afraid to advance.

Then it finally happened; Gid felt the gate shutter, then give a little. Crying out from the exhaustion in his legs and the pain in his back, he gave it one last push and the right gate moved free. Gid could no longer hold himself up and he collapsed to the ground. Rolling to his side, Gid looked up just in time to see General Moroni and the mass of Nephites only a few feet away from him. All he had time to do was roll away from the charging Nephites and curl up into a ball next to the gate itself to keep from being trampled.

"God be praised! Push the gate open all the way!" Moroni shouted as he ran through the opening with the Sword of Laban in his hand and his large metal shield out in front of him. Lehi and old sergeant major were close behind. As Moroni entered the courtyard on the inside side of the gate he was expecting to be instantly set upon by Lamanites from all sides. He found Lamanites alright, but they were waiting, hundreds of them, and not attacking. Instead they were several paces back and away from the gate. They were all standing transfixed and staring in horror at some unseen thing. It caused Moroni and the rest of his men to pause for a moment in confusion.

What Moroni did not know was the entire Lamanite force, trying to defend the gate, was mesmerized by the almost translucent form of the great warrior with the flaming sword who was slowly disappearing right before their eyes. When the image was finally gone it was replaced with the frame of General Moroni standing in its place. The Lamanites were all blinking and shaking their heads trying to make sense of what had just happened. Moroni saw he had the initiative and used this moment to press his advantage. He held up his mighty sword and shouted "For liberty!" while moving to engage the closest Lamanite.

Teomner and the big Lamanite were so focused on trying to kill each other they did not notice the other Lamanites had stopped watching and cheering them on and all turned to focus their attention on something happening near the main gate. Suddenly, and without warning, the Lamanites all started to flee in the opposite direction. Both Teomner and the commander were panting heavily and stood at a distance from each other leaning on their weapons as they watched the Lamanites move away from the gate in a panic. Teomner knew exactly what was happening and smiled at his foe. The commander was confused as he scanned the events before him.

"You lost the gate!" Teomner shouted at his opponent. The

CHAPTER FIFTEEN

commander looked back at Teomner with panic in his eyes. Teomner quickly looked in the direction of the gate and saw one person in particular fighting through the crowd of retreating Lamanites and moving towards him. "And may I introduce you to Chief Captain Lehi!" Teomner smirked and sarcastically gestured towards the gate like he was revealing a wonderful prize. The cloaked Lamanite had just enough time to look back in the direction Teomner was pointing to see Lehi come crashing through the faltering Lamanite defense.

Wild-eyed, like a man possessed, Captain Lehi was shouting and laughing as his big axe cut a swath through the Lamanites. Lehi looked up and made eye contact with the dark-cloaked Lamanite. "You!" He shouted and moved like a charging bull towards the cloaked watch commander. The moment Lehi saw the commander he knew he was the same Lamanite who dropped his friend from the high walls of the city. Lehi was going to kill that man and cut down anyone who got in his way.

Screaming in horror, the commander tried to get his own sword up to defend himself from Lehi but it was no use. Lehi was too strong, too fast and his axe was too mighty. Lehi brought his axe crashing down on the big Lamanite in one mighty overhand chop, breaking the fancy curved sword in half and cleaving the dark leader where he stood.

Moroni and his men were hewing down Lamanites like farmers in a wheat field with a scythe. Death was everywhere and the Nephites quickly cleared the main courtyard and guardhouse over the gate.

"Lehi!" Moroni shouted over the noise of battle. "Take the infantry! Go right at them!" He pointed with the sword of Laban towards the rest of the fleeing Lamanites who were falling back into the heart of the city. Lehi shook his big axe in the air and commanded those near him to follow his lead. Moroni turned and made eye contact with Amiha who had just cleared the top of the wall over the main gate of Lamanite soldiers and was now helping Gid up off the ground. "Amiha, lead the archers up to the city walls! Secure the high ground and fire down on the Lamanites!" Amiha signaled that he understood his commands and moved to obey.

Moroni tried moving toward Gid and saw that Teomner was also slowly moving through the rushing onslaught of Nephite soldiers trying to get into the city through the wide open gate. After a few more moments, the bulk of the Nephite forces were inside the walls and Moroni was able to take a full reckoning of the cost his army had paid to secure the gates to the city.

Everywhere he looked lay the bloody and broken bodies of the valiant Ghost Soldiers. He was still standing several yards from the gate as he slowly realized how the outline of dead Nephites had formed a semi-circle in front of the gate. "They died where they stood, holding a defensive line and giving their lives so Gid could unlock the gate."

Uncontrollable tears started to flow down his cheeks as Moroni thought about these brave men and their leader, Teancum. Moroni knew he still had a battle to manage and a city to save, but he wanted a few precious moments with the memories of these exceptional warriors. Moroni started to walk towards Gid but stopped when he saw Teomner had reached Gid first, and the two were mourning the loss of all of their dear friends. Moroni watched as the two surviving Ghost Soldiers slowly walked among the dead, looking for any signs of life.

The sorrow and agony on their faces as they continued to search in vain for any living soldier was more than Moroni could bear. As he was turning he gave one last glimpse over his shoulder. Both Gid and Teomner were standing absolutely motionless and looking right at him. After several seconds of awkward silence Moroni spoke, "I sent these men to their deaths." He felt his massive heart breaking. "They knew they were going to their doom… and still they answered the call of duty." He pondered for a moment. "Where do men like this come from…?"

"They went to their deaths because they believed in *you*, sir. And they believed in Teancum." Gid responded. He was covered in blood, dirt and the grime of battle. "You made a promise to them that if we held the gate long enough, you would free the city, rescue the Nephites trapped inside, and end this cursed war."

"I did." Moroni solemnly responded.

"We have kept our end of the bargain." Teomner joined in as he held out his hands towards his fallen brothers. "Here is the price we paid."

"See to your friends." Moroni spoke as he sheathed the big sword in his hands. Moroni knew that in his lifetime he would never again see such an elite group of fighting men like Teancum and his Ghost Soldiers. And now, all that remained were two officers and a handful of wounded men. "Your war has ended. You and all remaining Ghost Soldiers still alive have earned your discharge ten times over," he continued as he stood straight as an arrow. "I swear to you both that on my honor this city, and all who desire to be free people, will know true liberty and justice." He pointed to the dead at the feet of Gid and Teomner. "Let us show them and Captain Teancum the respect they have all earned. Let us gather this evening and light the sky with the flames of a great funeral pyre. Let us honor the dead as true warriors and send them to their rewards in heaven."

Gid was first to move, following closely by Teomner. They both stood up straight and held their chests and chins out like proud soldiers. Rendering a proper hand salute to their general, they held their position and waited for Moroni to acknowledge them. They were showing Moroni the military respect and courtesy soldiers give their commanding officers, and telling him they were grateful for his leadership and accepted his gesture of a grand sendoff for their brothers-in-arms.

There was nothing more for Moroni to say as he returned the hand salute. Moroni finished the salute and turned to face the growing number of messengers and subcommanders gathering behind him. There was still a massive battle raging inside the city and the army needed its leader. He gave directions and instructions to his men and they moved off with their assignments Suddenly, several cavalrymen came through the gate and rode up to Moroni.

"Report." Moroni barked, trying not to show the raw emotions he was feeling.

"Sir," A junior officer announced from atop his horse. "As you instructed, the woods have been swept clear of any Lamanite patrols and we also managed to capture a large supply caravan from the Lamanite homeland that was coming to their relief."

"Supplies…? What manner of supplies did we capture?" Moroni questioned.

"Mostly food, sir."

Moroni shook his head to clear out the sad images and fatigue that were present. "Excellent work, lieutenant. Bring the supplies within the walls and set up a food kitchen over there." Moroni pointed to an abandoned open air market. "Tell the camp cooks to start preparing the captured food for this army and the civilian survivors." Moroni paused and looked around him. "Also, have the medics move the field hospital and have them set it up outside the main gates." Moroni turned towards the sounds of battle coming from the interior of the large city. "Tell them to prep for many wounded men." Moroni looked up at the Nephite officer on his horse. "That is all, you are dismissed."

The Nephite saluted and turned his horse to move out of the gates. Several other mounted Nephites followed close behind.

Amiha suddenly appeared at Moroni's side. His tunic and armor were stained with the blood of the enemy, but he was in good spirits. "Sir, it's down to house-to-house fighting, but Captain Lehi is pushing them back. We could trap them against the back wall, but we need you at the front to guide the army, the men need to see you. They draw courage from your example."

Moroni heard the dark spirit in his mind speak to him. *You have given enough, let someone else do the fighting now. You are a general and should not be exposed to danger this close to the final victory. Who cares about the lives of a few more men at this point…victory is almost at hand!*

Moroni heard the promptings in his mind and looked around as he started to feel depression and fatigue. He saw the first stream of refugees who were trapped in the city by the Lamanites start to emerge from their hiding places and make their way towards the main gates and safety. Whatever possessions they still had were bundled in blankets or carried in their hands. He also saw the wounded men injured from the street fighting moving towards the gate and out to the medics still in the tree line. Everyone who walked past Moroni, looked at him and in their own way acknowledged Moroni. They all knew who he was. His imposing frame and the sword of power at his side were unmistakable. With a weak salute, a head nod or waive of a hand, they all knew he had freed them and brought the army this close to ultimate victory.

See how they worship and respect you… The voice continued. Moroni looked out at the people passing by and he could see them pointing and whispering and talking to each other as they went past. They were looking at him. *You are a great man, and it was your skill and leadership alone that brought this war to an end*, the voice in his head continued. *Let them honor you… Don't go back into the fight, stay here where the people can see you and you can revel in their gratitude. You have good officers to lead the men the rest of the way. Allow the Nephite people to seat you on the king's throne so you can ensure this madness will never return.*

Moroni's blood went ice cold when he heard the words 'the king's throne.'

"Never!" He shouted, startling those who were standing close by. He

CHAPTER FIFTEEN

turned to the officers standing next to him. "It was the God of our fathers and the God of freedom who brought us to this point." They all took a step back and with puzzled looks agreed with their mighty leader.

Pulling out his sword, Moroni started to move towards the sounds of battle. "All remaining Nephite soldiers, rally to me!" He shouted while holding his sword up high over his head. "Follow me!" Moroni exclaimed as he ran towards the interior of the great city and the sounds of battle.

The Lamanites continued to put up a stout resistance long into the afternoon. Even though they had lost their king, most of their leadership and the security of the high walls of the city, several pockets of Lamanite resistance continued to hold out. Barricaded behind heavy doors or holding the few top floors of a large building, small groups of enemy soldiers continued to fight on. Moroni began receiving reports of men under his command collapsing from sheer exhaustion as they continued to rid the city of the last Lamanite resistance. He ordered the fighting to continue even after he received word that Lehi had been carried from the battle field. Lehi had been wounded but he refused to stop leading the advance in his section of the city and fainted, falling from his horse. "What is it, doc?" Moroni asked as he entered the field hospital and came to the bedside of Lehi. Moroni had the grime of battle all over him and the doctor held out a hand to keep Moroni from coming any closer to his wounded patient.

"His wounds are not severe. He is suffering from a combination of heat, lack of water and overall fatigue." The tired doctor looked up at Moroni. "These men were exhausted before you ordered the assault on the city. Now they are moving forward on pure fury. Only the bloodlust is keeping your soldiers on their feet now."

The head surgeon was disgusted at the level of death all around him. He had no problem letting his emotions intermingle with his response to the commanding general. He finished binding Lehi's wounds and called for the orderlies to carry the big warrior away and bring him another wounded soldier. The moans and cries of the wounded and dying echoed through the make-shift hospital, as men and boys called out to their God or their mothers to come and ease the pain and help them transition into the next world.

"I am sure you are doing all you can to save these men, doctor. So am

I." Moroni spat a retort. He was on his last nerve and swaying back and forth from exhaustion himself. The words came out harsh and Moroni instantly regretted his tone. This poor doctor was not a soldier, but he and his fellow physicians willingly suffered alongside the men at war. Moroni took a deep breath and held out his hand as a form of an apology. He checked his tone and continued addressing the surgeon. "We are both doing everything we can to stop this madness. Once the city is secure I will search among the Nephites who are still in the city for anyone with medical training and will send you what help I can…."

The doctor knew Moroni was a good man and hated bloodshed as much as he did. He moved his head in agreement and acceptance of the apology.

A messenger came into the medical tent breathlessly searching for the General. "Sir… My general?" He called out from behind Moroni.

Moroni turned around. "Speak!" he commanded.

"Captain Amiha requests your presence at the city center. The last of the Lamanite holdouts— they have surrendered!" The older boy beamed as he gave the news to his idol and hero. He could not believe he was so lucky as to be the one to deliver the news of the end of the war to General Moroni himself. This was a moment of history and the young messenger was the one who carried the news. He would tell this story for the rest of his life.

The remaining Lamanites were forced to build the large wooden structure that would serve as the funeral pyre platform for Teancum and his Ghost Soldiers. The construction took longer than planned and it was well after dark before the bodies of the fallen men of Teancum's elite unit could be carried and placed in their positions of honor. The Lamanites were then pressed into service and charged with moving the dead bodies of Teancum's soldiers up and onto the wooden platform. If there was even a hint of disrespect shone towards the fallen heroes, then that hapless Lamanite was treated to the sergeant major's full fury.

Every fallen warrior was identified by Gid or Teomner. They knew each one of these men like their own brothers. They had their personal effects removed, accounted for and placed in a small bag. Then they were wrapped in a clean blanket by the Lamanites, who were under heavy guard.

CHAPTER FIFTEEN

There were several large fires already burning as well as torches to light the open ground of the courtyard inside the city gate. Moroni was standing near the gate and speaking with Pahoran and the city's surviving civilian leaders, when Amiha arrived at his side. The poor civilians had been through serious trauma with the Lamanites holding them against their will. They were all in tatters and covered in soot, but you could see the mantle of leadership was still upon them.

"Excuse me, my general." Amiha spoke up with military courtesy. Moroni stopped speaking and turned to face his dear friend. "Sir, the sergeant major reports that all the necessary arrangements have been made to honor the fallen. We await your next order."

"Very good, Captain Amiha. Sound a general formation. Have the men assemble in front of the platform." Moroni turned back and spoke to Pahoran and the other civilian leaders. "With your permission, Chief Judge Pahoran, I would like to honor Chief Captain Teancum and his men." Moroni did not wait for Pahoran to respond and started to move away from the gathered. He took a few steps and then turned back to face them. "You are all welcome to join me."

The Chief Judge and those with him did not hesitate to follow Moroni towards the large wooden platform holding the bodies of the Ghost Soldiers. Besides, Moroni's response did not suggest he was giving them the option to not join him. In his own subtle and understated way Moroni told the civilians, 'These men died for you. You will stand next to me and show them your grestest respect.'

"It would be our honor to stand with you tonight, General Moroni." Pahoran responded. "Come ladies and gentlemen." Pahoran gestured with his hands as the others moved with him towards the open ground near the platform.

"Is Lehi in position?" Moroni questioned the Sergeant Major as he arrived next to the steps leading up to the platform and the bodies of the fallen.

"He is, sir." The old soldier gestured with his head to a faraway section of the wall where a few Nephites were standing with lit torches. Lehi was among them, he was leaning on a stout wooden crutch and had a large bandage wrapped around his right bicep and his left thigh.

"Excellent." Moroni spoke as he put his hand on the shoulder of his father's most trusted friend and looked him in the eyes. These next few moments were going to be hard on them both. Moroni knew the sergeant major had a deep appreciation for Teancum and his elite band of warriors. The old soldier had been in more battles then could easily be counted and understood the sacrifice required by living the life of a warrior.

"They were all good men." He spoke as he allowed his emotions to surface for the first time. "Good men." The great fighter was tearing up and his lips quivered as he tried to keep his military bearing and looked back into his young leader's eyes.

Moroni gave his old sergeant a good squeeze on the shoulder with his hand and smiled back as he also tried to choke his own raw feelings down. "Form them up, sergeant major." He spoke. "Let's send these boys home to God the warrior's way."

"Yes, sir…" The gritty soldier turned away from his commander. He took a deep cleansing breath and wiped at the tears in his eyes. Filling his lungs to capacity he shouted, "Fall in!" The booming sound of his voice echoed off the stone walls and Nephite warriors moved from all points of the compass in response to the sergeant major's orders. Everyone knew his voice and everyone knew to move at double-time when he called. In no time a very large contingent of soldiers and several civilians had formed into ranks before the platform. Moroni wanted to address everyone gathered but he realized it would only be possible from the high platform.

Slowly, Moroni reached the top of the platform and turned to face the Nephites before him. Although he did not know all their names, the faces looking back at him were all familiar. Some of these men had been with him from before the audacious raid on the Lamanite king's camp during the great Jershon War. They were all bloody, dirty, starving and exhausted but they had answered the call to assemble. They had all endured untold hardships, watched their friends and families suffer and die, but they had never lost their faith in the God of their fathers and in their General. They followed Moroni into battle time and time again. Even this morning, when the odds were stacked against them getting inside the walled city, they followed. And now they all stood in silent reverence, waiting for their beloved leader and General to speak to them. Moroni could feel the spirit of the moment, he was unsure what to say to these brave men and he was unsure what words would be sufficient to honor the fallen who lay behind him.

Moroni scanned the crowd for some inspiration, for someone or something to give him the words to say, to enlighten him and prompt

CHAPTER FIFTEEN

him to speak. There was Lehi on the far wall. He was leaning on his crutch and holding a long bow in his hand. Then Moroni saw the chief surgeon standing outside of a medical tent. He was wiping his hands with a clean towel and looking up at Moroni waiting for his General to speak. Gid and Teomner were standing near the front of the formation. Both of them nodded back at Moroni when he looked in their direction. Down at the bottom of the stairs Amiha and the Sergeant Major stood facing the formation. Amiha looked up at Moroni after a few moments of quiet, with a concerned look on his face. He was just checking on his friend to make sure Moroni was okay. "Good men… Good soldiers." Moroni whispered as he turned his gaze back to the formation. Then it dawned on him what to say.

They are all good honorable men; they all did their duty. Tell them that. The enduring voice in his soul gave him counsel. Moroni smiled with relief and began to speak.

"At ease, gentlemen!" He projected his voice for all to hear. The entire formation shifted as the valiant men of the Nephite army relaxed their posture and stood in a more comfortable manner. "Many years ago, I was speaking to my father about the burdens of command and how some men acted different than others when given the opportunity and responsibility to lead me into combat. My father told me that some men were born for greatness and some men had greatness thrust upon them. Chief Captain Teancum was a man who had both. We all know the story of his life and we all know the tales of his deeds. And yes, the rumors are true. Teancum did make a lone assault into this city and he did find and kill the evil King Ammoron long before we attacked the gate."

There was a rumbling in the formation as every man gasped and processed that information. Gid and Teomner both beamed with pride as Moroni confirmed what they already knew. Moroni held up his hand to tell the formation to quiet down. "If anyone out there is keeping score…" He paused for effect. "That's the second king he killed while surrounded by the entire enemy army!" A burst of cheering erupted as the men of the Nephite army raised up their weapons and hands and celebrated the deeds of Captain Teancum. They all had earned the right to say they fought alongside the Ghost Soldier and his men. Moroni could sense the feelings in the hearts of his soldiers and he continued. "We who stand here this night to give thanks and say our final farewell to Captain Teancum and his company of heroic Ghost Soldiers. These men gave their full measure of devotion to bring this war to a victorious close."

A second cheer when up from the formation. "We honor them tonight!" Moroni raised up his hand and the formation cheered again. "We stand here together, with respect, to send them to their reward.... the old way, like true warriors!" Again the formation cheered. Secretly, every man was wishing that when they died, they too would be honored and sent on their journey to the next world like a true warrior. "We light the funeral pyre this night to say goodbye to our brothers-in-arms, but we will never forget them. I will never let this country or our people ever forget the great sacrifice Teancum and the other Ghost Soldiers made here in the name of freedom. The great sacrifice we all have made for our God, our religion, our freedom and peace and for our wives and our children!"

At hearing the words of the Title of Liberty, the gathered soldiers cheered louder than they had before. Moroni allowed the cheering and chanting to continue for a moment. He knew they all needed the emotional release. After a minute, Moroni held up his hand again calm down the soldiers. "My brothers… You are all truly my brothers. We have shared so many hardships together. We have bled and hungered together, we have cried and mourned our fallen together, we have celebrated victory and felt the sting of defeat together." Moroni paused again to let his words sink in. "Now we say goodbye to our own together." Moroni signaled to Lehi that it was time. Lehi pushed the wooden crutch to the side and brought the longbow in his hand up to his chest. A Nephite soldier standing next to Lehi handed him a stout arrow with a flaming tip. Lehi nocked the flaming arrow and drew back on the taut string. Moroni saw the loaded bow in Lehi's hands and took a few steps back down the wooden stairs to the ground. Lehi adjusted his aim up and said a quiet prayer as he held the bowstring back.

"For you, my brother. Go and find your peace." Lehi let fly the flaming arrow and it went soaring across the night sky leaving a trail of smoke behind it. The Nephites on the ground watched as the arrow left Lehi and crossed the expanse to land in the middle of the wrapped bodies of the Ghost Soldiers. The blankets wrapped over the bodies had all been covered in a flammable resin and they quickly burst into flames. The fire spread quickly across the entire wooden deck and engulfed the platform itself. The heat and flames were too much for those near the front and everyone needed to back away from the pyre. Moroni waited until the

CHAPTER FIFTEEN

bulk of the Ghost Soldiers bodies were completely enveloped in the cleansing flames and then moved back to the front of the formation. He turned to face his men and with the fire at his back he drew out the sword of power and held it high above his head.

"For Teancum… And for the Ghost Soldiers!" He shouted. "For liberty!"

Every soldier standing in the courtyard or on the walls all raised up their own personal weapons and shouted back. "For Teancum… For the Ghost Soldiers… For liberty!"

The massive fire raged on for the rest of the night. The smoke and sparks from the burning heap rising high into the sky were symbolic of carrying the spirits of the dead to meet the angelic guards at the gates of heaven. The heavenly gates opened wide and the Ghost Solders were met by their intrepid leader. Falling into formation, as good soldiers do, they marched past the gates and to their eternal reward.

It was very late the next day when a lone woman emerged from the shadows of the alleyway not far from the main courtyard. Her head was covered in a dark shawl to indicate she was in mourning. Her four small children were gathered all around her. Like a mother hen, she was trying to corral them with her arms back into the relative protection of the shadows.

The Nephite army had been fighting street-to-street with the Lamanites most of the night and the battle was long over. Several Nephites continued to sweep the streets and buildings for any pockets of resistance, but it was much safer to be moving around now. But not nearly as safe as it should be for a single mother and small children to be out. The woman nodded to her oldest son who moved quickly and unseen around several large items strewn about the courtyard.

The war was not clean or pretty, and the debris left in the streets was a testament to that fact. He reached the edge of the large smoldering pyre and looked around for several seconds for any sign of danger. Assuming the area was safe, he signaled to his mother to come over. The woman, her head still covered, took her little ones by their hands and guided them along the same path her oldest son took.

Moving around broken wagons, open crates and piles of rubble they carefully moved to reach the smoldering mass of wood and bone. Not far from the pyre, a steady train of wagons were coming in and going out through the main gates of the city. There were several Nephite guards inspecting the outgoing cargo to ensure Lamanites were not trying to smuggle themselves out of the city and escape justice. They were too busy to be bothered with the goings on of one lone woman and a handfull of children. Stopping short of the smoldering funeral pyre the woman had her children all sit down in the protective covering of an overturned wagon. Once she knew they were settled, she stood up and slowly walked to the edge of the burnt pile of ash and wood. She stood alone and very still for quite a while, her head down and tears dripping off her cheeks.

"I just wanted you to know you will never be forgotten." She whispered as she uncovered her head to expose her emotions to the open air. It was Diana and she had come to pay her final respects to the man she only knew for a few precious moments but somehow loved. She stood there all alone with her thoughts, crying and wondering how she was going to take care of her children. Life was hard enough for a single mother before the scourge of the Lamanites. Now that the battle was over and everything was in chaos things would only be more difficult. Standing there and pondering her fate she was suddenly brought back to the moment when her oldest boy walked up and grabbed her hand. He could see her crying from his vantage point under the wagon with his siblings. He knew his mother was sad and the only thing he could think to do was go and stand next to her.

As the two were standing alone near the sacred ground where all those brave Ghost Soldiers and their fearless leader were honored, they were spotted by Gid as he was walking in through the open city gates. His first impression was anger. He assumed they were scavengers trying to rummage through the charred remains of his comrades. As he moved quickly towards them to chase them off, he started to realize they were not thieves but mourners standing a silent vigil over the remains of Chief Captain Teancum and his men. He slowed his pace and walked up to Diana.

She saw the heavily armed man approaching and quickly re-covered her head, a tone of concern was on her lips. "I am sorry, my lord." She bowed and tried to back away pushing her boy behind her to protect him from harm. "We mean no disrespect…" She stammered as she looked over her shoulder for her other children.

"Please…" Gid calmly extended his hand to gesture to Diana to be at

CHAPTER FIFTEEN

peace and relax. He could see his presence had upset her. "Did you know these men?" He asked calmly.

Diana responded sheepishly. "I knew one of them." She wiped away her tears and brushed her hair from her weathered face. "I do not know his name. But he was the one who you sent to kill the Lamanite king."

Gid gulped hard and blinked several times to mask his emotions. "How did you come to know this brave man?"

"He saved our lives." Diana gestured to her children who were now hiding in the shadows of the wagon. The look on the children's faces told Gid that they had seen enough of war to know not to trust any man in armor and carrying a sword. Especially one who confronts their mother.

Gid smiled at the frightened little ones and then looked back at their mother. "That man was Chief Captain Teancum," Gid responded with a hint of pride in his voice. "He alone scaled the city walls and he alone killed the king."

The boy standing behind Diana got wide eyes and poked his head out from behind his mother's legs when he heard the news that the brave man who killed those Lamanites on the roof and saved him and his mother was the legendary Ghost Soldier himself. "I knew it!" He burst out and looked up at his mother with a smile on his face.

"Did you now…?" Diana quizzed him playfully. "That would explain his bravery." She continued as she looked back at Gid. "We did not mean to disturb. We only wanted to give our regards."

"No harm done, my lady." Gid bowed to show her respect. He looked back up and saw that she and her children were all dirty and appeared to be hungry. "How do you fare after all of this?" He questioned.

"We will manage." Diana responded as she rubbed her hands together. "Somehow." She put on a brave smile but Gid could see right through it.

Turning back towards the main gate Gid called out for one of the soldiers guarding the entrance to come to him. With spear in hand the young Nephite soldier dashed to his commander's side. "Yes, sir!" He barked as he arrived.

"Soldier, fetch this woman a sack of provisions and some extra blankets for the children."

The soldier looked at the children still under the wagon and did a quick count in his head of how many blankets and how much food he would need to get. "Yes, sir!" He responded with the equal amount of energy. Turning, he ran off towards the supply and relief wagons rolling into the city.

Gid turned back to Diana. "I am sorry for your troubles. If you knew my Captain then he would insist that you be well taken care of." Gid smiled again trying to calm her fears. There was an awkward pause and silence. Gid tried to make the best of it and looked back at the boy standing behind his mother.

The boy. Gid could almost hear his Captain's voice in his head. *Look after him.*

"You know…" A thought came to Gid after hearing the still small voice. "This morning I was appointed by General Moroni to be the military governor of this city until order and commerce can be restored and the will of the people to elect their own judges returns." He looked at Diana. "I will be in need of a squire to assist me in my daily tasks." He looked at the boy. "He will need to be brave, strong and truthful— but most of all, willing to live the life of a Ghost Soldier." Gid looked back at Diana. "The boy will be well-cared for and his family will be paid for his service to the army." He smiled as if he already knew the answer. "Do you know of such a young man?"

She smiled back and looked down at her cherished boy. "One name does comes to mind." She replied smiling down on him. She raised her eyebrows in an unspoken question, asking if he wanted to be squire for the commander of the city's forces. The boy looked at Gid then back up at his mother. With a bit of excitement he nodded his head in acceptance.

"Excellent!" Gid exclaimed. "Now… Before we go any farther, I will need to know your name, and who you want to become in this life."

The boy stepped forward trying to draw fresh courage as he faced his new mentor. "My name…?" He trailed off at the end.

"Speak up, boy! The personal squire of the governor general will need to be confident and proud." Gid explained.

Taking the challenge to heart the boy squared up his shoulders and held his chin up high. Filling his lungs with a courageous gulp of air he replied. "My name is Nicholas…" He looked up at his mother and then back at Gid. "And I want to be a Ghost Soldier."

THE END

INSPIRATIONAL ART

Invite true Christian heroes to serve as role models in your home with these full-color, fine art prints.

Each full-color print includes the heroe's key virtue,
a scripture reference, and their symbol. Across the top are the words
Honor • Strength • Courage • Discipline.

Print sizes:
5"x7" • 8"x10" • 18"x24"

Available at your local LDS bookstore or online at
TheWarChapters.com

Honor

Courage

STRENGTH

AUTHOR: JASON MOW

After serving a mission for the Church of Jesus Christ of Latter-day Saints, Jason joined the U.S. Army and served as a Paratrooper. He advanced through the ranks to the position of Team Sergeant for the Army's elite Special Reactions Team (SRT). He has experience and training in joint counter narcotics operations, protective services, counter terrorism, weapons and tactics training, and deployments to hostile areas.

After the Army, Jason began work as a civilian Police Officer. Jason has worked as patrol officer, gang detective, narcotics detective, street crimes detective, and spent several years on SWAT as an operator and instructor. He is a certified police instructor in firearms, defensive tactics, tactical driving, and patrol rifle operations. Jason has twice been awarded the Law Enforcement Metal of Honor for gallant bravery in the line of duty and was recognized as the Community Services Officer of the Year for his department.

In addition to the military and police training, he has a Bachelor's Degree in Education from Northern Arizona University and has graduated from the Arizona Law Enforcement Academy, the U.S. State Department International Narcotics and Law Enforcement program, and the United States Army Military Police Academy. He is also POST certified police instructor.

In 2006, Jason took time off from his Law Enforcement career and worked as a Civilian Contractor for the U.S. Government in Afghanistan. He worked at the National Police Academy in Herat as the lead Instructor. Jason also worked as the personal mentor for law enforcement operations to several regional Afghan government officials. He embedded with the US Army and traveled with small specialized teams of soldiers to remote locations throughout Afghanistan.

It was in Afghanistan that the first ideas for what would become the War Chapters series began to form. After a rocket attack on his base in Herat, he turned to the scriptures and found comfort in reading about the experiences of Captain Moroni. He wrote these scenes as they played out in his mind all throughout his time there.

Jason volunteers his time and skills doing humanitarian work, conducting personal recovery operations, medical aid, and security, in response to natural disasters around the world. He has deployed to assist during Hurricane Katrina and the earthquake in Haiti.

ILLUSTRATOR: GABE BONILLA

Gabe grew up in Southern California, and was one of those kids who was always doodling instead of studying. After serving a mission in Chile for the Church of Jesus Christ of Latter-day Saints, Gabe enrolled at Ricks College (now BYU-Idaho) and studied art and illustration.

Gabe transferred to BYU and continued his education there, eventually graduating from the BFA program in illustration. While at BYU he met his wife, Nicole Carson, also a Southern California native and graphic designer. They formed Bonilla Design & Advertising and have been working from a home studio for the last 16 years while raising their six children.

Since BYU Gabe has worked primarily as a graphic designer, but always enjoys a chance to get paint on his fingers. He recently switched to painting digitally on an electronic drawing pad. All the illustrations for The War Chapters Series were digitally illustrated.

In his free time, Gabe enjoys cycling, racquetball, and anything in the outdoors including sleeping under the stars, hiking a new trail, or shooting a few targets.